Lynda Page was born and brought up [...] of four daughters, she left home at seve[...] variety of office jobs. She now spends [...] helping her daughter and writing her [...] tranquillity of her daughter's holiday p[...] Epworth, North Lincolnshire.

 @LyndaPage9

 LyndaPageBooks

Don't miss her previous novels:

'All manner of page-turning twists and turns. Expect the unexpected'   *Choice* magazine

'When Lynda Page pulls the heart-strings, you won't fail to be moved'   *Northern Echo*

'Filled with lively characters and compelling action'   *Books*

'It's a story to grip you from the first page to the last'
                                                    Coventry Evening Telegraph

'A terrific author'   *Bookseller*

'Inspirational and heart-warming'   *Sun*

By Lynda Page and available from Headline

LYNDA PAGE
Let The Good Times Roll

headline

First published in 2015 by
HEADLINE PUBLISHING GROUP

First published in paperback in 2016 by
HEADLINE PUBLISHING GROUP

1

Cataloguing in Publication Data is available from the British Library

ISBN 978 1 4722 2925 0

Typeset in Stempel Garamond by
Palimpsest Book Production Limited, Falkirk, Stirlingshire

Printed and bound in Great Britain by
Clays Ltd, St Ives plc

HEADLINE PUBLISHING GROUP
An Hachette UK Company
Carmelite House
50 Victoria Embankment
London EC4Y 0DZ

www.headline.co.uk
www.hachette.co.uk

FOR MY DAUGHTER . . .

LYNSEY ANN PAGE

On the day that you were born I didn't believe I could love
you any more than I did then. But now, forty years later,
not only do I feel that same all-consuming love for you,
but I also feel a sense of admiration, respect and pride for the
wonderful woman you have become. No mother could be
prouder of their daughter than I am.

With all my love, your Mam xx

CHAPTER ONE

Arriving back from his daily inspection round, Harold Rose paused before the entrance to reception to take a last close look around the courtyard. He pushed metal-framed spectacles higher on his long thin nose, ran a hand over his fine mouse-coloured hair, then brushed an imaginary speck of dust off the lapel of his smart blue suit. He felt proud to see that everything here was exactly as it should be, just as he had while inspecting the rest of the holiday camp that morning. The whole area was heaving with excited-looking campers making their way to their chosen morning's activities.

Dressed in swimming costumes, rolled-up towels under their arms, some were making their way to the indoor and outdoor pools or else down to the beach; some were heading for the sports field and courts; others to the roller-skating rink, pedal-cart track or boating lake. Film-lovers flocked to the cinema for the morning matinee; the Paradise hosted Bingo sessions or there was a choices of pool, table tennis or darts to be had in the games rooms; for a glance at the morning newspapers the quiet lounge was the place to be. Across the courtyard the souvenir shop was filled with children spending their pennies on candyfloss, ice creams, sweets, or else buying a present to take home for their grannies and granddads, aunts and uncles. Queues were forming at the photographer's to hand over a few shillings for the snaps the camp photographer had taken of holidaymakers enjoying themselves during their stay, for them to reminisce over during the long winter months ahead. The hairdresser's

1

was full of women having their hair done, wanting to look their best for the afternoon's dance or the evening's entertainment in the Paradise ballroom. Mothers were handing young children over to the qualified nursery staff, looking forward to their few hours of childless freedom to do as they pleased. And behind the scenes as well as in front, the army of Jolly's staff beavered away to ensure that everyone had the best time possible during their stay.

For a whole week, or two for the more fortunate, Jolly's camp, like many others dotted along the coast the length and breadth of the United Kingdom, seemed to seal its patrons within an invisible bubble; the world beyond might not have existed. The main worries for the holidaymakers were whether or not the sun was going to shine on them that day and what was on the menu at mealtimes.

Heaving a sigh of relief, Harold thought, So far, so good. Admittedly, it was only just after ten o'clock on day two of the start of the season, but apart from a couple of glitches that had fortunately been rectified before they had escalated into anything serious, the camp was running smoothly. Harold vehemently hoped it stayed this way, to prove to the owner, Drina Jolly, that she hadn't made an error of judgement in putting him in charge while she was otherwise occupied overseeing the building of her new camp in Devon.

Managing a camp the size of Jolly's didn't allow for idle moments and Harold was about to go up to the office, hoping nothing serious had cropped up during his absence, when the actions of several nearby campers stopped him in his tracks, a frown furrowing his brow. The eager expressions on their faces were changing to looks of sheer disbelief then utter horror. They gathered their families to them protectively, shielding their children's eyes. Confused as to what could possibly be the cause of this sudden change in their behaviour, Harold turned his head to find the source of their concern. What he saw froze him in his tracks.

Weaving through the crowds as fast as if the devil himself were after him came a man, naked as the day he was born. He looked to be in his mid-thirties. His face was wreathed in terror, and both hands were clasped protectively around his crotch. Then Harold spotted the reason for the man's flight: a furious-looking woman was chasing after him. She was yelling at the man. What she was saying was lost to Harold over the noise of the crowd but he could tell it was far from words of endearment. She was waving a tennis racket aloft, the expression on her face indicating the damage she intended to cause with it when she caught her prey. She was at least dressed, unlike her quarry, in shorts and a flowery blouse.

So shocked was Harold by what he was witnessing that at first his brain refused to function. He stared like a village idiot at the pair of them as they dodged around the other campers and circled the ornate fountain dominating the middle of the courtyard, its four huge stone dolphins spewing water from their mouths. The couple began to run back the way they had come. More and more campers were looking after them horrified as they raced by, though there were equally as many who were obviously finding the situation extremely entertaining, judging by the looks of amusement on their faces.

It was an angry outburst from a nearby camper to the woman beside him that jolted Harold back into action.

'Good Lord! Just what kind of place have I brought my children to that allows such disgusting behaviour to go on? I'm going to speak to the manager and see what he's got to say about this state of affairs. And if it's not a satisfactory answer he gives me, we're going home, Joan, and we certainly won't be recommending this camp to anyone. Just the opposite in fact.'

There were murmurs of agreement from other like-minded campers within earshot. Harold felt panic flood through him as he saw a handful of men start to come together, worried that they would egg each other on to take their own form of retribution for the naked man's unacceptable behaviour. He gulped anxiously, beads of sweat forming on his brow and his heart beginning to thud painfully. Up until this time last year he would have jumped out of his skin should anyone have cried 'Boo' behind his back. He had been a virtual recluse, and would still have been that same friendless introvert had not young Jackie Sims, the then temporary office manager, made it her mission to show Harold his own worth and coax him out of his shell. Despite the monumental progress he had made since then, there was still the odd occasion that threatened to overturn his self-confidence. This was one of those times.

Harold was not comfortable with looking at his own undressed body in the mirror in the privacy of his bedroom, so the thought of confronting a naked stranger and presenting an authoritative front while he brought them to task for their outrageous antics did not appeal to him at all. And neither did facing an angry mob demanding answers as to how he intended to handle this situation, or worse still having to try to stop them dishing out their own form of punishment on the man should they so decide. Scuttling away to hide in his office, emerging when his underlings had dealt with the problem, felt like a more appealing option.

Harold flashed a furtive look around. The campers were concentrating on the naked man and his assailant so hopefully no one had spotted the presence of Harold himself. He made to sidle away inside reception when a sudden thought stopped him in his tracks. Reverting back to his old evasive ways was not a good sign. Did he really wish to return to being the old Harold Rose and live his former lonely existence? The thought made him shudder. No, he most certainly did not. He would not only be letting himself down then but those who had shown such faith in him, namely Jackie Sims and Drina Jolly. The thought of disappointing those two lovely women was far more repugnant to him than facing a misbehaving camper or possible lynch mob.

Kicking up his heels, Harold rushed off in the direction of the naked man and his pursuer.

Meanwhile the beach was just beginning to come to life. Two maintenance men were scouring for rubbish and bagging it up, another taking gaily striped deckchairs out of a hut secreted behind the dunes and placing them in rows on the sand. Any minute now Sam would be making his appearance with his ten donkeys ready for the onslaught of children that would soon descend, pestering him for rides and causing whatever torment they could to the mild-mannered, bearlike man.

Nestled by a dune, chin resting on her drawn-up knees, Patricia Mathers heaved a sigh of resignation. These precious few moments of solitude on the deserted beach, that she took each morning after breakfast, weather permitting, had a magical effect on her, helping to prepare her for the mayhem she knew would face her for the rest of that day. But the labours of the Stripeys nearby were telling her that it was time to make her way to her own place of work.

Patsy was an unremarkable-looking woman of twenty-four, her mousy-brown shoulder-length hair pulled up in a ponytail. She was tall for a woman at five foot ten, and considered fat by the standards of the day with her size sixteen figure. Despite having problems buying the trendy clothes she'd have liked to wear, which meant she confined herself to the likes of C & A or else resorted to making her own on her mother's old treadle machine when she returned home after the season, Patsy was comfortable in her own skin on the whole. In her opinion it took all sorts to make a world and people had no choice but to accept what they'd been born with and make the best of it.

With her adored and supportive parents' blessing, Patsy and her then best friend Sally had applied for a job with the entertainments team at the camp. It had seemed a glamorous alternative to their mundane junior office jobs, and the possibility of a rise to stardom on stage or television once their talents had been spotted by a London agent was an irresistible draw to both young girls. Without even taking the time to assess Patsy's talents for singing and dancing, or talk to her to discover her warm and engaging personality, sense of humour and conscientiousness towards any task she was given, as soon as she walked into the interview room, the then Head Stripey, working under the instructions of former owner Joe Jolly, bluntly told her that her physical appearance fell far short of their requirements for the team, and should she still want to work at Jolly's then she'd need to look for a position with one of the background departments. The talentless but pretty and shapely Sally was immediately snapped up, albeit her singing voice resembled that of a canary being strangled and she had no sense of rhythm whatsoever.

Patsy was thoroughly demoralised and humiliated by this tactless man's remarks and the way he unthinkingly prevented her from doing a job she knew she would be good at. She wanted no more than to return home to be amongst people who didn't judge her on her physical appearance but accepted her as she was. Sally, though, not wanting to be left in this new alien world on her own, begged her to stay. Out of loyalty to her friend, Patsy reluctantly accepted a job as a waitress in the restaurant. The work did nothing to task her intelligence but regardless she got stuck in and did it to the best of her abilities. Sally, though, soon abandoned her for new friends she made amongst the elite entertainments team and before the end of the season had fallen in love with another member of staff and gone off backpacking around Europe with him; Patsy had never heard from her since. It was the camaraderie of her own new workmates and the social life they brought her that made Patsy stay on and want to return the next season and all the others since. Over the years, being noticed by supervisors as hard-working and conscientious, well liked by her colleagues and not in the least a trouble maker, she had worked in most departments, liking some, others not so much, but always uncomplaining. For the last couple of seasons she had worked in the nursery with a team of forty others, under the supervision of a no-nonsense Norland-qualified nanny named Mavis Durham, looking after up to a three hundred babies and toddlers at a time in three-hour spells while their parents enjoyed a few brief hours of childless freedom.

Scrambling up, Patsy brushed sand off her unflattering blue uniform dress and cardigan then from her bare feet before slipping on her sensible flat-heeled work shoes. Giving a cheery wave and a shout of 'Good morning' to one of the maintenance crew working nearby, she hurried over the soft golden sand to the duckboards leading across the dunes, then on up a long winding path which skirted numerous activity areas, ending at the courtyard where the large nursery was situated amid the long single-storey block of retail outlets, opposite the entertainment centre and office buildings. Patsy had just trotted past the sports courts and arrived at a fork in the path that led off to the vast area of campers' chalets in one direction, the roller-skating rink and pedal-car track in the other, when she spotted a man racing towards her from the direction of the main courtyard, a woman chasing after him while brandishing a tennis racket. Patsy stopped short, doing a double take when it registered on her that the man was completely naked.

In contrast to Harold Rose, Patsy did not freeze in panic at this couple's display of unacceptable behaviour but instead she thought of how to stop them before damage was caused to the good name of Jolly's. She flashed a look around. It was ironic that considering there were thousands of campers holidaying here at the moment along with any amount of staff to look after them, there was not another soul within shouting distance for her to call upon now. It seemed it was down to her then.

The man was almost upon her. She slipped off her cardigan and took several deep gulps to prepare herself for what she was about to do. As he made to dash around her, praying that her timing was right, Patsy lunged at him in a sort of rugby tackle. She had marginally miscalculated the timing of her dive but thankfully her shoulder caught his leg mid-stride, knocking him off balance. As they both crashed to the grass, the man emitted a loud cry of shock at this unexpected attack and then pain as parts of his unprotected body contacted solid ground.

Despite suffering herself from her own impact with the unyielding earth, having quickly gathered her wits, Patsy had her cardigan covering up the man's abdomen and was standing stern-faced over him before he had realised what had hit him.

But before she could order the man to get himself back to the privacy of his chalet and put some clothes on, a breathless woman ran up to them and without further ado began to thrash at him with a tennis racket while bellowing furiously at him.

'You bastard! You rotten, stinking bastard . . .'

Doing his best to defend himself, he was yelling back. 'OW! Verna, that hurts . . . Stop, it Verna, STOP IT! I've told yer I'm sorry . . .'

With a murderous scowl on her face, Verna responded: 'SORRY! Is that all you have to say for yerself after what you've done? You pig . . . you cretin . . . you . . . I'll kill you, I will. I'll bloody kill you.'

Patsy leaped across to her and grabbed her arm, gripping it tightly and stating, 'Kill him if you must for whatever he's done, but do it off camp.'

The other woman wrenched free her arm and, before Patsy could stop her, hit her over her head with the racket, screaming, 'You keep out of this! It's none of your flipping business.'

It was Patsy's turn to cry out. 'Ow!'

With Verna's attention on Patsy, the naked man had seen a chance to make his get-away and was desperately trying to scramble upright, but the woman saw what he was attempting and resumed her thrashing of him, bawling, 'You stop where you are. I ain't finished with you yet. Not by a long chalk, I ain't.'

A panting Harold then arrived and told her, 'Oh, yes, you have. While you're here at the camp at any rate. Behaviour like this is totally uncalled for and won't be tolerated.'

Verna scowled darkly at him as if to say, Who the hell do you think you are, telling me what to do? She lifted her arm, intending to resume her lashing of the man on the ground. Seeing nothing else for it, Harold grabbed the arm and yanked her roughly out of her victim's reach, telling her in no uncertain terms, 'I said, that's an end to it.' His tone was enough to stop the woman in her tracks, her expression that of a naughty schoolgirl facing a reprimand from the headmaster for her childish behaviour. Now that, surprisingly to him, he had her attention, a stern-sounding Harold continued, 'This may be your idea of high jinks but the behaviour of both of you has upset a lot of other campers, not to mention the damage that could have been caused to the good name of Jolly's.'

He quickly turned his head to look back along the path he had just raced down, relieved not to see a mob of angry campers heading towards them. That didn't mean, though, that they had wisely decided against taking their own form of retribution on the naked man, and they could be en route right now. Harold went to address the man on the ground and was astonished to find him gone. He was just visible, haring off down the path towards the chalet area, clutching Patsy's cardigan over his manly parts, just his backside bare now, having seized his chance of escape while his attacker's attention was elsewhere.

Harold returned his attention to the woman and for the first time took a good look at her. She was slightly built and her age could have been anywhere between twenty-five and forty-five. It was impossible to tell due to the obviously hard life she had led telling heavily on her. It was clear to see though that in her youth she had been pretty. She was looking thoroughly ashamed of herself, very close to tears, and kindly Harold hadn't the heart to continue reprimanding her. Awkwardly he said, 'Look, I'm sure I can trust that neither you nor your husband . . . I take it that man is your husband . . . will be getting up to anything like this again? If not, I'm afraid I will have no choice but to ask you to leave. For now let's say no more about it. Both of you just concentrate on enjoying the rest of your holiday.'

Harold assumed Verna would be mortally relieved that she and her husband were not going to face any consequences over their antics and make a hurried departure in case he should change his mind, but to his consternation her shoulders sagged and she buried her face in her hands and began to sob miserably.

Patsy was very aware that she was late for work and would be in for a severe reprimand from Mavis Durham who did not accept any excuse for late arrival. 'Will you excuse me, Mr Rose? Only I need to get to work,' she said.

Preoccupied by the other woman's distress and not knowing quite how to handle it, Harold looked at Patsy blankly. 'Oh, er . . . yes, yes, you get off and . . . er . . . thank you, er . . .' He didn't know her name. Her badge was on the cardigan that she had used to cover the man's nakedness. Name badge or not, though, Drina would have known this young woman's name without having to look for it, like she knew the name of every one of her employees, in her endeavours to make them all feel they were not just a number but a valued part of the Jolly's team. Drina had a gift for such things, one that Harold didn't possess. 'Yes, thank you for your quick thinking today,' he continued, sorry he couldn't make the commendation more personal.

Although Drina Jolly would have known her name, Patsy didn't take offence that the new manager didn't. If he had any dealings with the nursery it was Mavis Durham he dealt with; Patsy couldn't expect him to remember her.

As she hurried off, Harold returned his attention to the sobbing woman. 'Look, er . . . Mrs . . . I really meant that this matter will not be taken any further. So just get on with enjoying your holiday with us and we'll forget all about it.'

She dropped her hands and lifted her head, showing Harold a face etched with utter misery. Then the next thing he knew she had thrown herself on him, burying her head in his shoulder and sobbing uncontrollably again. 'How can I enjoy my holiday?' she blubbered. 'He's ruined it, he has.'

Harold stood ramrod-straight, feeling extremely uncomfortable about this strange woman's closeness to him. He gave her shoulder a tentative pat. 'There, there,' he told her in embarrassment. 'There's . . . er . . . no need for this.' Then he ventured, 'I'm sure whatever it is your husband has done can be put right. Why don't you go to your chalet and sort this matter out with him?' Although judging by the woman's state it was no simple thing her husband had done.

She spat, 'I never want to see that man again. He can rot in hell for all I care. How can I enjoy myself, seeing my kids watching all the others enjoy their ice creams and sweeties, or buying a little gift for their granny and grandpa, when I know my kids can't have the same? I promised them they would be able to, but I can't keep my promise to them now 'cos of what that miserable excuse for a man did.'

Curiosity got the better of Harold and he asked, 'Er . . . just what did he do?'

She sniffed heavily before answering. 'Gambled our treat money away last night in a game of poker another camper set up in his chalet.' A fresh flood of tears rolled down her face then. 'We live in streets where most kids reach adulthood never having seen the sea, let alone have had a week's holiday there. This is the first time I've ever seen the sea meself. Over three years I've been saving for up for it. It ain't been easy either. Apart from my couple of quid housekeeping, which is grudgingly handed over by that self-centred sod I married, I'm lucky ever to see a penny more of his wage. The pub, bookies and his fags come before any extras for his family. If I didn't work, my kids'd never have shoes on their feet. Bless 'em, they never complain, though. Always grateful for whatever I can manage to give them treat-wise, which is not that much. But just this once I was determined to give 'em the best holiday I could, with enough pocket money to buy 'em a treat every day. At least if we never get a holiday again they'll have memories for ever of this one, I thought. I economised as much as I could and took on extra shifts at the bakery where I work whenever I could badger the old bugger in charge there to give me some. My two eldest . . . ten and eight they are . . . did odd jobs for the neighbours, and every penny they made they happily added to the holiday fund.'

Her face screwed up in anger then. 'I've forgotten how many times Les tried to get me to hand my savings over to him. Just a loan, he'd tell me, but I ain't daft and knew whatever I gave him, I'd never see again. It was laughable the times I caught him trying to find my hiding place only he weren't clever enough to realise I never kept it at home but in the post office. My mum, bless her heart, kept the book safe away from his thieving hands. No matter how many times he cursed me or threatened to lift his hand to me, he weren't having any of the holiday fund . . . over my dead body he wasn't. It was funny how he was as excited as the kids when it came time for us to pack and come here.'

She heaved a miserable sigh, adding regretfully, 'There's not many places for hiding anything in a chalet but I thought the place I did find was as safe a bet as any, under a stone beside the front door.' She swiped her eyes with the back of her hand before continuing. 'But the sly toe rag had obviously been watching me without me knowing. I should have realised what he was up to when he disappeared for half an hour last night, telling me he'd been stuck in a queue at the bar, when really he'd sneaked back to the chalet to steal the treat money. About ten I left him at the bar having a last pint while I went home to be with the kids. He told me he wouldn't be long, when all the time he was waiting for me to go so he could be off to a card game he'd wangled himself into behind me back! I was so tired I fell asleep so never knew what time he came in, and the first I knew about the missing holiday fund was when I went to get a couple of bob of it to buy the kids a candy floss or ice cream each this morning. I discovered it was all missing and knew immediately who'd had it.

'When I went back in the chalet, he'd just dragged himself out of bed and before I could tackle him he was having a right old go at me for not waking him up for his breakfast. I was so incensed that he had the nerve to be threatening me with a thumping for going off to breakfast without him. I mean, that was nothing compared to what *he* had done, stealing off his own family, so I just saw red. I grabbed the nearest thing to hand, which happened to be a tennis racket, and let rip.'

It must have struck her then that she was in an intimate situation, pouring out her woes, not only to a stranger but the manager of the camp. She hurriedly peeled herself off Harold and stuttered, 'I'm . . . sorry, I'm so sorry . . . I've wet your

12

jacket.' She gave the sodden area on his shoulder a cursory wipe with her hand.

Harold hurriedly assured her, 'Don't concern yourself. It will soon dry.'

She heaved a forlorn sigh. 'I'm sorry for behaving like a fishwife this morning. I was so beside meself that I didn't stop to consider the other campers. I just wanted to kill Les and in the most painful way possible. That's all I could think about.' A small smile then crossed her lips. 'It's him, though, that's got to live with the humiliation of half the camp seeing what he hides inside his underpants for the rest of the week, ain't it?' She sighed then. 'I s'pose I should be grateful the price of the holiday included all our food and entertainment.' She set her chin determinedly. 'I'll see my kids don't suffer over what their dad's done to 'em. I'll make sure their day is so full of doing fun things that they don't even have time to think of sweets and ice creams. I mean, let's face it, there's no shortage of fun things to do here at Jolly's, is there?' She forced a laugh. 'There's one consolation. Les has no money for beer or fags for the rest of the week and, believe me, without them he's going to suffer.' She flashed Harold a proper smile. 'Well, I'd best get back to me kids. Er . . . thanks for not asking us to leave. You won't hear another peep from us for the rest of the week, you have me promise.'

Harold thoughtfully watched her walked away. He felt mortally sorry for this woman who'd work so hard and gone without to give her children a week of freedom and fun away from the grimy streets they lived in, only for her selfish spouse to deprive her of being able to give them the extras that would have made their holiday really special. He found he couldn't let that happen, not when he had the money to replace what the father had gambled away.

When Verna heard Harold call after her she stopped and turned round to answer the summons, her face creased with worry that he'd changed his mind and was going to make them pay for their behaviour after all. Walking towards her, Harold

13

took a five-pound note out of his wallet. When he reached her, he pressed it into her hand. While she was looking at him dumbfounded, he said, 'Find a better hiding place than your last one, won't you?'

With that he hurried off up the path back to his office, leaving her staring after him, astounded.

There was no sign of a mob of disgruntled campers back in the forecourt. Harold could only conclude the men had wisely decided not to take matters into their own hands but to leave the camp's management to deal with the situation. Or more than likely it was their womenfolk who had put a stop to any would-be heroics by threatening them with retribution of their own if they continued.

The smooth running of one particular department hadn't crossed Harold's mind at all during his tour of inspection. As far as he was concerned the new staff running the general office – thirty-year-old Jill Clayton the office manager, who possessed impeccable credentials and experience at her job, along with her assistant, Yvonne Holt, herself fully skilled in office procedures and whose bubbly personality strongly reminded him of former employee Jackie Sims – were doing an exemplary job considering they had only been in the camp just over a week. He was firmly of the opinion he'd made the right choice with both of them over the numerous other applicants for the positions.

Matters in the general office were not, however, what they appeared to be and were about to change drastically.

Before he turned into reception, Harold took a last look around. It wasn't to check that all was well in the camp but because he was looking for one person in particular, who much to his disappointment he hadn't crossed paths with during his tour of inspection that morning. He was to remain disappointed as there was no sign of the individual he was seeking. It was still early in the day, though, he comforted himself.

CHAPTER TWO

'What other lies did you tell, Yvonne?'

The tone of voice the question was asked in was one of despair. It was spoken by Jill Clayton, an attractive young woman whose dark hair was neatly pinned into a French roll. Her hour-glass figure was dressed in a pink-and-green-patterned, short-sleeved shift dress, its hemline finishing demurely an inch or so above her knees,

The pretty, bubbly, eighteen-year-old girl whose shoulder Jill was currently leaning over in order to check on her work, turned her head to look at her in bewilderment. 'Lies?'

Jill straightened up and folded her arms under her shapely bosom, while ruefully shaking her head. 'The ones you told Harold Rose at your interview. That you could type, for one. Using one finger with a pause of a couple of minutes in between while you search the keyboard for the next letter you need, is not classed at typing, Yvonne.'

The girl looked sheepish and said awkwardly, 'Well . . . er . . . no, I s'pose not.'

'And the number of times you cut people off on the switchboard or put them through to the wrong extension tells me that neither have you much, if any, telephonist's experience as you claimed to Harold at your interview. As for your filing capabilities . . . well, judging by the number of things I've been looking for and found in the totally wrong file . . . Either you don't know the alphabet or you just can't be bothered to put whatever you're filing in its proper place. In fact, the only times you seem

15

eager to do a task I set you is when it involves going outside into the camp.' Jill eyed her closely. 'You obviously gave a sterling performance at your interview to persuade Harold to give you the job against all the other applicants, but it's very apparent to me you're not equipped to do the work required of you and I suspect you don't really like it either. So why did you make so much of an effort to land this job, Yvonne?'

With a grin on her face she shot back: 'Well, it's the ideal place to meet lads, isn't it? The camp is swarming with them. Spoiled for choice I am. Met a couple of cracking lads since I've been here, a lot more "with it" than those backward chumps in Mablethorpe and Skeggy, who are still wearing reefer jackets and granddad shirts that went out of fashion in 1964! I've been out with both lads a couple of times and had such a fab time too . . . but then I spotted Malc who works in the fish and chip kiosk and I'm seeing him later as it's his night off.' Yvonne's eyes glazed over dreamily. 'He's a sight for sore eyes. Dead ringer for Andy Fairweather-Lowe, the singer with Amen Corner. I think he could be the one, if I play me cards right.'

Jill hid a smile. She remembered herself at eighteen and then, just like Yvonne's, her head at the time had been filled with boys and the latest fashions. But unlike Yvonne, those two topics had taken a backseat while Jill had been at work. She'd concentrated there on improving her skills so as to obtain a better-paid job and be able to fund the latest fashions, which would attract the fellas. She was glad she had acquired the means to land herself a well-paid job when she had first met Dean, later to become her husband, and between them they were earning enough to save for a deposit to buy their first home, a pre-war, two-bedroomed semi in Mablethorpe, and to furnish it with the latest twin-tub washing machine, electric kettle and toaster.

She felt the need to have strong words with this young girl and point out that her work ethic could see her living a hand-to-mouth existence should she not meet Mr Right to provide a future for her. But from having constantly to correct or redo Yvonne's work, Jill was in danger of falling behind with her own, so couldn't spare the time. Considering she had only been in the job just over a week herself, she feared Harold Rose wouldn't be impressed with her performance and would see his decision to take her on to manage the general office as a mistake.

It wasn't Yvonne's fault that she had been given a job she wasn't equipped to do. Harold had been the one to interview and take her on, same as he had Jill herself. He had thoroughly checked Jill's own references and made sure she was as skilled as she claimed to be before confirming her position, but he obviously hadn't done such a thorough job with Yvonne. Jill really didn't like the thought of complaining about her assistant so early on in her own employment, and besides she liked Yvonne. What she lacked in office skills was compensated for by her appealing personality. But this state of affairs could not continue if Jill were to run the office as efficiently as she had assured Harold she would. She must speak to him about this matter on his return from the camp inspection.

Yvonne saved her that problem though. Giving a chuckle, she got up and began putting her personal belongings into her shoulder bag, saying proudly, 'Well, I lasted longer in the job than all my friends bet I would, so I won! My winnings should buy me a new lipstick from Woolie's for my date with Malc tonight.'

Yvonne might not have the right skills for her job in the office but Jill felt she would still prove an asset in another department. She ventured, 'Look, Yvonne, maybe there's another job here at Jolly's that would suit . . .'

Before Jill could finish, Yvonne was shaking her head, face wreathed in horror at the very thought. 'Chalet charring or waitressing ain't for me. I'd die sooner than tell a lad I did that kind of work for a living. I ain't got the experience for anything else, 'cept shop work, and the shops on the camp work funny hours and I ain't taking a job that interferes with my social life. Anyway, my old boss, Mr Moffett, has a soft spot for me and I know I can get my job back in his dry cleaner's so I'll be fine.'

A far cry from what Yvonne had told Harold Rose at her interview: that she was a receptionist for a solicitor, thought Jill.

By now Yvonne was jauntily heading for the door leading to the stairs, calling back, 'It's great finishing early so I have plenty of time to get ready for me date. I'll call in Friday to get me wages and cards. See yer then.'

Jill had just returned to her desk, not looking forward to telling Harold this state of affairs, worried he might see it as a failing on her part, when the man himself walked in, looking extremely confused. He said to Jill, 'Yvonne has just passed me at the bottom of the stairs in such a tearing hurry she didn't see me. She had her coat and bag with her so I take it you've sent her home. Has the poor girl been taken ill while I've been out?'

Jill shook her head. 'No, she's fine. She is going home though.' She then proceeded to explain what had happened.

When she had finished Harold was red-faced with embarrassment. Rubbing his finger between his neck and shirt collar, as though it were too tight and restricting his breathing, he said with difficulty, 'I'm entirely to blame for taking Yvonne on without thoroughly checking her credentials first. I was . . . well . . . just overtaken by the fact she reminded me of your predecessor, Jackie Sims. She was older than Yvonne, but Jackie was a joy to work with and we became good friends . . . still are. I stupidly assumed that as Yvonne was so similar to Jackie in personality, she would be in her abilities too. I should not have made that assumption. One thing Jackie would never, ever do was lie to get what she wanted as Yvonne did so blatantly.' He heaved a worried sigh. 'My error of judgement has left us short-staffed, it seems. Will you be able to cope until we get a replacement for Yvonne? Oh, but that's a stupid question. Yvonne was more of a hindrance than a help to you, I now realise. Er . . . I think, though, that it would be prudent of me to ask you to recruit your new assistant.'

Jill smiled. 'I'm sure that there's someone suitable amongst those who applied when you first advertised the job, but in the short term I'll contact the agency to send us a temp. Oh, there's a couple of messages on your desk that I took while you were out. One is from Chef Brown, who'd like to speak to you as soon as you have time, and the other is from a boys' home in Leicester wanting to confirm arrangements for their stay next week.'

Harold inwardly groaned. Not over Chef Brown; he and Eric had become friends over the last year since Jackie Sims had commandeered the huge man to be part of her plan to bring about Harold's rehabilitation. His despairing groan was at the thought of the dozen or so orphans who would be descending on the camp in a few days' time. If they were anything like the group that came last year from the same home, then the staff were in for a fraught time, trying to keep them entertained and under control.

Harold was just about to go into his office, Jill to resume her work, when the door leading to the stairs opened and the person whose non-appearance had caused disappointment to Harold during his camp inspection arrived.

No matter how expensive or stylish her clothes, how elaborate her hairstyle, how skilfully applied her makeup, forty-year-old Eileen Walters would never enter a room and have men swarming round her, vying for her attention. She would pass unnoticed as she crossed the floor to stand in a dark corner with all the other wallflowers not blessed with beautiful, or even pretty, faces. Hers was long and narrow, her skin pale, eyes deep-set and grey. For work she wore her fine dark hair scraped up in a tight bun on top of her head. She was five foot six and naturally thin, despite a healthy appetite. Due to her resemblance to the character from the film *The Wizard of Oz*, some unkind individuals nicknamed her The Wicked Witch of the West. The name was not at all justified. Eileen was a very considerate and understanding woman, always seeing the good in people. Her eyes twinkled with warmth and humour, and her style of management towards her army of chalet maids was firm but fair.

Her personality was what drew Harold to her and for him it made her the most beautiful woman he had ever encountered.

19

Secretly admiring her and fantasising over a relationship with her was as far as Harold had taken it, though. His self-esteem, thanks to Jackie, had grown considerably over the past year, but he still wasn't confident enough in himself to believe that a woman like Eileen would ever want to be with him. He contented himself with worshipping her from afar and his day was made when as now their paths crossed and he had an excuse to enjoy her company, even if it was only in a work-related capacity.

Harold would have been shocked to his core to know that Eileen did in fact very much reciprocate his feelings. She hadn't at first when she had had to deal with him instead of Drina, while Drina was away helping Rhonnie overcome her grief at the sudden loss of her husband Dan, who had turned out to be the illegitimate son of Drina's husband, Joe Jolly. Like others Eileen had initially found Harold to be very brusque and dismissive in his attitude. But as time passed, being the intelligent woman she was, it had dawned on her that Harold's behaviour was his way of covering for his own severe lack of self-confidence and self-worth. Then as his manner began to improve and he began to solve problems put his way instead of passing them on, it became apparent to Eileen he was working hard to overcome his difficulties and this allowed her to see the kind, thoughtful, intelligent man he had been all along. As more time passed and Harold allowed her to see more of his true self, the warmth she felt for him turned to liking, then attraction, and now, if she were honest with herself, she was in love with him. Whether he harboured any feelings for her she very much doubted as his manner with her whenever they came face to face was the same as she had witnessed him using with anyone else, polite and courteous. But she wasn't blind; had witnessed the way his eyes sparked behind his spectacles when he was addressing her, and knew she wasn't imagining the fact he purposely kept her talking whenever they crossed paths around the camp, or the way he would suddenly appear out of his office on some pretext when he heard her voice and then pretend to look surprised to see her, his eyes though betraying how pleased he in fact was.

She would so welcome the chance to get to know him better on a personal level as all her instincts told her they would both get on so well . . . and who knew where that would lead? All her years of believing she was destined to be a spinster might be proved wrong. Eileen herself had the courage to make the first advance and broad enough shoulders to accept she had been mistaken should Harold reject her, but she had grown up at a time when it wasn't the done thing for a woman to make the first move if they wanted the man in question to consider them respectable. All things considered, as far as Harold was concerned, it seemed she was destined to admire him from afar, imagine how life would be with him by her side, never actually experience it.

Jill might only have worked at Jolly's for just over a week but it hadn't escaped her notice that Harold and Eileen felt an extremely strong attraction towards one another; if pushed she would go so far as to say they were in love with each other. But from what she had observed it didn't appear that either of them was going to do anything about it.

Jill was a born romantic and felt it was a shame that these two people could be missing out on a very fulfilling and rewarding life together because neither of them would dare to take the first step. What she felt they needed was a push in the right direction and it would give her a lot of pleasure to be the one to do it. All she needed was a plan to bring them together in a social setting and then, hopefully, one of them would find the courage to take the lead. Leaving them together conversing about anything except what they both secretly wanted to, Jill picked up the telephone to call the agency and request a temp to replace Yvonne.

CHAPTER THREE

Marion Frear was doing her best not to throw herself at the young girl on the other side of the desk and throttle the life out of her. Marion was desperate for a job, any job, so as to earn some money, even if it was only for the few hours left today. She was long past the stage of being fussy about just what job it was or where, but this girl was standing in her way. Taking a deep breath to calm her inner frustration, Marion said evenly: 'Look, the company you were talking to just now seemed desperate for a temp to be sent as soon as possible. I'm available, so why won't you send me?'

Sixteen-year-old Sandra Watson gulped nervously. 'I've already explained to you, Mrs Frear, that I haven't the authority to send anyone out on a job. Miss Abbott gave me strict instructions before she left for her meeting with her prospective new client that if anybody telephoned in wanting a temp or someone permanent, I was just to take down the details and she would deal with it when she comes back. I've only been in this job for three weeks and my mam would kill me if I lost it for disobeying the boss's orders. Anyway, that job that's just come in is not suitable for you. It's just a junior position in a general office and you're a qualified personal assistant.'

Marion's anger inched higher and again she had to fight the urge to launch herself at the girl and punch her senseless. She was down to her last couple of pounds, hadn't time to wait for replies to interviews for jobs she had applied for via the local paper, then work a week in hand for her first pay packet. She needed money now, no matter how little, or life on the streets was looming for her and her mother.

When Marion had ventured into the agency three days ago, Miss Abbott, the owner, a rotund, forthright woman, wearing a tweed suit and sensible brogues, had seemed very impressed with her qualifications and experience. Thankfully she didn't question her testimonial from her last employer as it was falsified, Marion having had the foresight to steal several sheets of headed notepaper and hide them in her handbag before she was humiliatingly escorted off the premises for what had been deemed gross misconduct on her part. Assuring Marion that she would have no problem getting her work at the level of her skills, Miss Abbott had told her she was to telephone the agency at ten in the morning and four in the evening to check if a job had come in that was suitable for her to start the next day, or if it was for an immediate start that day then they would despatch a telegram to her address to inform her. Obviously she was expected to stay at home, ready and waiting for Miss Abbott's summons!

Apart from begrudging the money it cost, Marion had no problem telephoning in twice daily as there was a telephone box a short walk away from where she was presently residing, but she had no choice but to call in at the office regularly because if they sent a telegram to the address she had given, she wouldn't receive it. The address was fictitious. Should she have given her true address, Miss Abbott would certainly not have taken her on the books but immediately ushered her out of the office, classifying her as a low life with no fixed abode.

Eyes brimming with disdain, Marion leaned back in her chair and folded her arms. 'You look an intelligent girl to me, but obviously in your case looks can be deceiving,' she commented.

Sandra frowned, not sure whether she had just received a compliment or not. 'What do you mean?'

'Well, you don't want to stay a humble junior for the rest of your working life, do you?'

The girl shook her head vigorously. 'No, I don't.'

Marion unfolded her arms and leaned forward, fixing her eyes on Sandra's. 'Well, you will, unless you show Miss Abbott that you've got some initiative. You could end up running this place when she retires . . . owning it even. Well, she's no spring chicken any longer, not far off retirement judging by the look of her, and she's a Miss, so no children to pass her business on to. Wouldn't you like to be dressed to the nines, swanning about in a sports car dealing with clients, not left back in the office, taking messages?'

Sandra's eyes glazed over, seeing herself as Marion had described. She uttered, 'Yeah, I would. A red one. The boys would take notice of me then, wouldn't they?'

'You'd have them queuing up,' Marion told her as she furtively reached her hand over the desk, placing her fingers over the note with the details of the job that had just been called in and easing it back towards herself. Sandra still lost in her dream and the details of the job now safely in her handbag, having helped herself to a time sheet from a pile of blank ones on Sandra's desk, Marion left the agency, intending to present herself to the firm in need immediately as their new temp.

If Jill was surprised by the age and experience of the woman who arrived later that morning, introducing herself as the agency temp, then she didn't show it, was just pleased to have help while someone permanent for the position was sought.

And if Marion felt demeaned by being subordinate to a boss she was older and more experienced than, she didn't show it, too grateful to be earning some money at last. Besides, as far as she was concerned, this situation was only temporary until either the agency found her a job that befitted her skills or she managed to find one herself. Nor did she show her surprise on being introduced to the camp manager. She had been expecting a flamboyant individual, in the mould of a circus ringmaster, wearing a brash checked suit and tie, someone with a loud personality and a big belly laugh, the total opposite to the nondescript-looking, quietly spoken and modestly dressed man she was presented to. Most surprising to her of all was that he encouraged the use of Christian names for all senior staff including himself . . . except when dealing with the campers or when formality was called for. It was a complete contrast to the past jobs she had had where staff, and especially the hierarchy, were addressed by their titles at all times during work hours.

After having to monitor Yvonne closely, it was so liberating for Jill that the experienced Marion needed hardly any supervision after a short overview of what was expected of her, leaving Jill herself free to get on with the far more intricate managerial tasks. The time that had been taken up by Yvonne's inexperience and the correcting of her endless mistakes had inhibited Jill from getting to grips with all that was expected of her in her role as office manager and she still had much to learn. In truth she felt that until she had a firm grip of her own diverse duties, it was going to be nigh on impossible for her to take on the training of an office junior as well.

Miss Abbott telephoned just after lunch and apologised profusely for sending them a most unsuitable temp, saying she was doing her best to find them a suitable replacement who could hopefully start tomorrow and that she would confirm it before five o'clock tonight. With this in mind, at four o'clock Jill sought an audience with Harold in his office behind closed doors.

He sat patiently and listened while Jill explained her predicament. To her relief he readily agreed that it made sense to ask Marion to stay on in her temporary position until Jill was able to take on the training of a junior. Of course fair-minded Harold felt they ought not to expect the likes of Marion to work for a junior's rate of pay and said they would pay the agency the going rate for a more experienced temp.

As desperate as she was for money, Marion would have worked for a junior's rate sooner than risk earning nothing but kept this to herself and readily accepted the deal being put to her. She was mortally thankful that she'd happened to be in the agency when the Jolly's job came in, and that Miss Abbott had been out and her assistant easily manipulated.

CHAPTER FOUR

At just after six thirty that evening, Marion negotiated her way around the piles of junk lying rotting around the huddle of twenty or so dilapidated caravans situated on the expanse of muddy, weed-strewn waste ground at the back of a scrapyard and abandoned factory down beside the river, until she came to the most dilapidated caravan of all, supported by four piles of breeze blocks.

The late-April evening had turned decidedly chilly, but for Marion it was no relief to enter the caravan as it was colder inside than out due to the wind whipping between the gaps in the warped door and round the pieces of cardboard taped over a large hole in one of the two front windows. The owner of the caravan site was a mean-faced, chain-smoking, skinny man who looked like he'd not seen soap and water for years; nor did the shabby clothes he wore. All his caravans had been rescued from the scrap heap and repaired just enough to keep out the rain and most of the wind. He then charged desperate people extortionate weekly rents for the privilege of living in them. He resided in the best one himself with his long-suffering wife and five unruly children, using the rents to fund his drink and gambling habits while giving as little as possible to his wife to keep the family on. None of the caravans had running water or toilet facilities. All water was obtained from an old standpipe in the yard of the abandoned factory that had once been used for cleaning delivery vehicles. The toilet facilities for all the caravan dwellers consisted of a pit inside a ramshackle wooden hut with an ill-fitting door that had a habit of swinging open unexpectedly. The seat was just an old rough wooden box placed over the pit with a jagged hole cut in the middle of it, and users had to be careful when they sat on it to avoid splinters. The toilet hut was re-sited only when the stench became intolerable and the owner could be badgered by his tenants into doing so.

The caravan Marion resided in was rusting, damp and cramped, originally built as a four-berth towing holiday home two decades earlier. The caravan boasted one tiny bedroom at the rear and another bed was made up by rearranging the seating pads at the front of the caravan. The covering on the seating was threadbare and stained from age and lack of care, the once cream-coloured internal walls a dingy grey, the floral curtains faded and moth-eaten. There were two small windows to the front of the caravan and attached to the inside wall between these was a pull-down table. Light came courtesy of a paraffin lamp, heating from a paraffin stove, cooking and heating of water via a two-ring camping stove. There was a tiny kitchen area with two small wall cupboards and a sink where all washing was done.

The other caravans were hardly any better than Marion's, but those who resided in them considered them preferable to life in a homeless hostel or on the streets.

Marion had hardly got inside the door when an angry voice accused her: 'Oh, you've found your way back then? I was beginning to think you'd forgotten me.'

Marion put down the shopping she'd purchased on her way home, kicked the door shut behind her and snapped, 'I would have thought you'd have worked out that the reason I haven't been back before now was because I've been working, Mother.'

'Oh, that's something, I suppose. Shame you had to leave me here on my own all day, with no heating and nothing to eat. The work pays well, I hope?'

Marion was now slipping off her muddy shoes. 'It's only temporary. The pay isn't bad but it's not great either, so you'd best get used to the idea that this place is home, for the time being at least.'

There was a long silence before Ida Peters snarled, 'I wouldn't be having to get used to the idea of living in this Godforsaken hovel if you'd just been able to control yourself!'

Marion spun around to face her, eyes blazing with anger. 'Oh, for God's sake, Mother, when are you going to stop reminding me of my indiscretion . . .'

Ida snorted in derision. 'Indiscretion! An indiscretion is a moment's lack of self-control. You'd been fornicating with your boss for months, and still would be if you hadn't been caught doing what you were over the office desk! Pity you couldn't find what's in your husband's underpants as enticing, then we wouldn't be in this position. We had a lovely home with all mod cons, and with Lionel and you bringing in good money between you, no financial worries. Now because of you we've living in this miserable dump amongst people who'd sell their own mothers for the price of a packet of cigs or a pint of beer.'

Marion glared across at the older, solidly built woman who was wearing her winter coat, a thick scarf around her neck over a matronly navy dress, fur-lined winter boots on her feet, scarf tied tightly around her head. She was sitting on the threadbare seating under the front window, clutching her capacious handbag on her knee as if terrified someone was going to burst into the caravan and steal it from her, which was ironic because it held nothing of value except to its owner.

Ida was a woman who liked to get her own way and had a knack of making others feel extremely guilty when they dared to challenge her or decided not to do her bidding. Despite finding these traits in her character extremely testing, as had her long-suffering and now deceased husband, Marion never questioned or defied Ida, life being far easier that way. Recent events, and the resentment she felt towards her mother for the part she had played in them, had resulted in Marion's harbouring a deep resentment against Ida, which boiled to the surface now. She snapped back, 'Well, you'd better watch your step then, Mother, or I'll be selling you! But then they'd soon be bringing you back demanding a refund after I tried to offload Hitler's mother on them!'

Ida's face screwed up in indignation. 'How dare you associate me with that dreadful maniac?'

Marion looked at her stonily for a moment before grudgingly responding. 'Well, that was a bit harsh, I admit. But if you hadn't parked yourself on us when Dad died and acted like you owned the place, I believe Lionel would have forgiven me for what I did and given me another chance. Instead he saw it as his opportunity to get rid of you and become master in his own home again.'

Ida hadn't the grace to look ashamed for acting as she had. As far as she was concerned she knew best and it was her duty to point that out to people when they were going wrong. Besides she felt at liberty to rule the roost with Lionel as not only should he respect her as his wife's mother, she had believed he hadn't the gumption to stand up to her, just as her husband hadn't. She said, 'I had no choice but to . . . as you put it . . . park myself on you. Your father left me penniless, as you well know.'

'And whose fault was that, *Mother*? Dad was quite happy working for old man Smithers, getting his pay each week and pottering about on his allotment at weekends. But when Maisie Harris's husband started up his own car repair business and managed to buy them a house, you were green with envy so you nagged and badgered Dad into starting up the bicycle shop and had him working every hour God sent to pay the mortgage on the house you insisted he bought you. Dad was no businessman and the shame of going bankrupt cause his fatal heart attack, you know fine well it did.'

Her daughter's tirade of taunts was making Ida feel mortally uncomfortable because they were the truth and she could not find any excuses for the part she had played in her husband's untimely death. Arthur had been a good, kind man and had uncomplainingly put up with his wife's constant nagging to do better for her and their daughter, but now instead of feeling remorse for the miserable life she had given him, Ida was angry and bitter towards him for leaving her in her final years reliant on her daughter's benevolence for survival.

Desperate to get the conversation off this topic, she issued a scornful chuckle and said, 'Well, Lionel certainly showed he isn't quite the put up and shut up type you thought he was, by his reaction when he found out what you'd been up to behind his back.'

Marion heaved a sigh. Her mother was right. Lionel's response to the news she had been carrying on with her boss, which came to light when they had been caught having sex over his office desk, had shocked her to her core.

She had been seventeen when she had first met her husband, he then twenty, at a dance in the local church hall. Marion had thought she'd struck gold. Lionel was not only tall and boyishly good-looking but was a qualified draughtsman with a reputable company. He came from a good family, his father an office manager for a large firm, his mother a district nurse, and they owned their own home. Marion was beside herself with joy when he proposed. Good catches like him didn't grow on trees. Her mother was pleased with her choice, Lionel being just the sort of future son-in-law she could boast of to friends and neighbours. But the main reason Marion herself wanted to get married was because it would free her to live her own life the way she wanted, not the way her mother dictated she should.

They married when Marion was twenty-one. Easy-going, placid-natured Lionel provided very well for them both. They lived in an affluent area of Doncaster in a large, gabled, five-bedroomed dwelling in its own half acre of grounds with a tennis court and outdoor swimming pool. They holidayed twice a year; led a busy social life with other successful people. Marion's housekeeping allowance was generous enough for her to have a good amount left over each week to spend as she chose, and her mother lived with them and ran the house for her. Marion was more than happy about this since it left her more time for her social activities. She wanted for nothing, in fact. The only sadness in their lives was that children never came along. It was a fault on neither side, it just never happened.

At the age of thirty-eight, though, Marion was growing dissatisfied with her life. She felt it lacked excitement. Lionel was in his early forties and beginning show signs that he wanted to slow down, not socialise so much, instead spending his evenings relaxing on the sofa reading the newspaper or watching the television – that was when he was allowed to watch a programme of his choosing, on the odd occasions that Ida was out and not dominating their viewing. Their sex life began to decline too as Lionel's libido lessened with age whereas Marion's need for regular sex was as strong as it had ever been. And to make matters worse, her mother being the bossy, domineering woman she was, was becoming a source of great irritation to Marion now that her own age was making her less tolerant of others. She thought that her going back to work might help to relieve both her problems. Lionel was the sort of man who was happy if his wife was, so if that was what she wanted to do then he supported her.

She had qualified as a secretary at the local college on leaving school. Typing was like riding a bike: once learned, never forgotten. She had constantly used her shorthand skills over the years when taking notes at her women's group meetings . . . before she became Chairwoman . . . so brushing up wouldn't be difficult. Her last job before leaving to marry Lionel and become a woman of leisure had been as an assistant to the office manager so she was used to responsibility. When she informed her mother of her plans to return to work, for once Ida had no opinion to offer. This arrangement suited her fine. With her daughter out at work all day she would have unrestricted control of the house and what went on in it, instead of having to battle with her daughter to have things done her way.

After completing a refresher secretarial course Marion secured herself a job with a successful engineering company as supervisor of their general office, a staff of five girls under her. She enjoyed her job, got on well with her colleagues and enjoyed the odd night out with them.

She still felt her life lacked any excitement though. It was to come via Barry Goodman when he joined the firm to replace their retiring works manager. Barry was a forty-two-year-old married man with two teenage children, well aware that his good looks and charm were irresistible to women. Unknown to his wife, throughout their marriage he had enjoyed numerous illicit relationships with other females to whom he'd promised the earth, but as soon as the excitement waned for him he had no problem abruptly ending the liaison, leaving them bereft, their own marriages broken beyond repair. As soon as he was introduced to Marion he meant to make the attractive woman his next conquest. The arrival of Barry in her life was just what Marion had yearned for to bring her some fun and she was a willing conquest. Unlike the other women Barry had had affairs with, she had no interest in him leaving his wife for her as she loved her husband and knew the likes of Barry could not provide for her as well as Lionel did, or would ever put up with her mother living with them.

For a year the pair managed to keep their relationship a secret until the evening that was to prove their undoing. Their respective spouses believing them both to be working late in their respective jobs, they both believing they were the only ones left in the factory, they were so eager to enjoy each other's bodies that neither of them thought to lock Barry's office door. They were caught in the middle of the act when the owner of the firm walked in on them.

Marion had been immediately dismissed whereas Barry was merely given a severe reprimand. She felt it most unfair that she should pay such a hefty price for her affair and Barry get away with just a slap on the wrist, but there was nothing Marion could do about it. It was a man's world after all. To punish her further, as Marion cleared her desk Barry appeared and made it clear to her that their tryst was over and while he was telling her this he was acting and looking at her like she was something he would scrape off his shoe.

During her illicit relationship Marion had been of the opinion that should her easy-going husband find out, he would be upset, of course, but she was safe as he adored her and would soon be begging her not to leave him. She would promise not to do it again and all would be well. Lionel had never raised his voice to her before, not even when she had defied him and bought something frivolous and expensive that he hadn't agreed to, so to have him furiously spitting out his contempt for her, his disgust at her betrayal of their wedding vows all for the sake of a bit of excitement, had rendered her speechless. She'd stood by frozen in shock as he'd jumbled all her belongings together in a case then thrown her and it out of the front door, warning her never to darken his home again. Before she had had time to gather her wits, Ida was being pushed unceremoniously out too, along with her hastily packed belongings, with a cry from Lionel of, 'Good riddance.'

The two women had stood stupefied in the front garden for what seemed an age before Ida had gathered her wits and, seething in anger at Lionel's treatment of her when she had nothing to do with her daughter's infidelity, started insisting Marion do whatever it took to redeem this situation and get them back inside. If Marion didn't tackle Lionel, she would do it herself.

Marion tried all she could to get him to talk to her, but the only response she received to her hammerings on the door and protestations of how sorry she was and that it would never happen again, was the threat that if she and her mother did not remove themselves from his garden Lionel would call the police and have them both prosecuted for harassment and trespass.

Judging from her experience of her own marriage, how she had nagged her husband into doing her bidding, Ida was adamant Marion should persist in her hounding of Lionel until she wore him down. Marion, though, strongly felt that he was far too angry over her betrayal of him to listen to reason at the moment and that they should leave him alone for a few days, to simmer down and realise what his life would be like without her in it. Ida made it clear she wasn't at all impressed with Marion's decision, still positive her way was best, but she soon cheered up when Marion told her she would book them into a good hotel for the duration. She wasn't worried about money. She had a little over thirty pounds in her purse from her last wage and her housekeeping, that she had meant to use for new clothes. More than enough to last the week that she felt it would take Lionel to come to his senses.

Marion was confident of success when she went to see her husband a week later after he got home from work. She decided it best to leave an extremely miffed Ida back at the hotel, not wishing to remind Lionel of the annoyance he had endured with her in his house. She needn't have bothered, though, as whether or not Ida was there, a week apart had not changed Lionel's mind; in fact, he was far angrier than he had been when he'd first found out. Marion's hopes of a reconciliation soon faded when he told her that he was a man who could shrug off most matters that would have seen others commit murder, but his wife's infidelity was something he just couldn't dismiss. He told her he wanted to be free of her as soon as possible to get on with his own life, and had only allowed her into the house so as to sign the divorce papers he'd instructed his solicitor to draw up. If she did so without argument he would give her a thousand pounds, but that was all she would get out of him and a thousand pounds more than he felt she deserved.

He waved the wad of notes tantalisingly in front of her. Marion had no choice but to sign as he had made it clear there was no going back and the money would go a long way towards providing a new future for herself and her mother. But as soon as she did sign the documents, he was manhandling her roughly out of the door and locking and bolting it behind her, his shouts to her from the other side telling her that she was a fool if she had thought she was going to be rewarded for her betrayal of him. She could apply for a copy of the decree absolute from the local court.

Marion had never had to fend for herself before so it was a frightened, worried woman who returned to the hotel to tell her mother of the outcome, only to face a barrage of wrath from Ida. Her daughter's need for excitement had led to them both being rendered homeless. So what was Marion going to do about it?

Marion had no idea, but she did know that she couldn't stay in Doncaster, not at least until the sensation of what she had done had died down. The type of people whose circle Marion and Lionel had moved in were the middle-class, educated sort with influence in the city. They would be openly horrified by Marion's behaviour and bound to take Lionel's side. She'd be humiliated every time she crossed paths with any of them. Her pain at the ending of her marriage through her own stupidity was bad enough, but to bear on top public opprobrium from her former friends and associates was too much.

For once Ida agreed with her. She was dreading facing the cronies to whom she had bragged incessantly because she had moved up in the world now, living in a private house in its own grounds while they still resided in their rented two up, two down terraces. Now they'd be sniggering behind her back over her sudden change of circumstances due to her daughter's adultery.

Marion deeply regretted not having had the foresight to be careful with her money until she knew for sure what the outcome would be of her attempt to fix her relationship with Lionel. Their week's stay in the hotel and the meals they'd eaten had made a big hole in her thirty pounds and the cash in her purse was now down to less than half that. Staying another night in this hotel would be utterly foolhardy so they packed up and agreed to leave Doncaster for the time being. They headed for the train station, with not a clue where their final destination would be.

They arrived just after eight-thirty. A bitter wind whipped down the platform. There was no relief from it as the buffet was closed until the morning, the two-bar electric fire in the draughty, ice-cold waiting room broken. The only train waiting at the platform was the eight forty-five mail train to Skegness, stopping at several places en route to pick up mail and deliveries, arriving back in Doncaster in time for the cargo to be loaded on to the London mail train at one forty-five. There were no other trains due until six forty-nine the next morning.

The likes of Skegness was deemed by the circle Marion had moved in as a holiday destination for the lower working classes so she was comfortable in the knowledge she'd have no surprising encounters there. Ida's circle of friends couldn't afford a holiday so she was in no danger either.

They were never to reach Skegness that night. The train came to a grinding halt a mile short of Mablethorpe and the only explanation given to disgruntled passengers was that a steam-pressure valve had broken. This meant that the passengers had to walk the short distance to the next town, then arrange themselves other transportation on to Skegness. What was already a dreadful day for Marion and Ida was getting worse. It was well after ten by the time they reached Mablethorpe and her age was telling greatly on Ida, who'd grumbled continuously as she'd heaved her heavy body and case of belongings down the side of the railway track, Marion laden down with her own. She knew that her mother didn't have it in her to travel any further and so it seemed she had no alternative but to spend precious money on a bed and breakfast room and continue on to Skegness the next morning.

They were fortunate to find an establishment within a short walk of the station that was showing a vacancy sign in the bay window. The landlady, a sprightly elderly woman, would normally have locked up and gone to bed by this time of night but the station master had telephoned her to warn that customers could be descending on them due to a train breakdown. The kindly old dear welcomed the exhausted pair of women and quickly settled them into their room. The place was cheap, on the shabby side, but clean enough if you didn't look too closely. Marion fought back tears of self-pity. This was a far cry from the sort of establishment she was used to staying in when she and Lionel had gone away together. But she had no one to blame for her downfall but herself. Ida for once didn't make any complaint, just grateful to rest her aching body in one of the two single beds.

Marion opened her eyes the next morning and it took her brain a moment to register why the room was unfamiliar to her, until the journey here and the circumstances that had led to it were recalled and brought a wave of utter misery flooding over her. But then her misery was overshadowed by a rasping noise and automatically she looked over in the direction it was coming from to see her mother lying a couple of feet away, looking far from well.

Marion shot out of bed and went over to her, putting her hand on Ida's forehead. She was worried when it struck how hot the skin was.

At her touch, Ida opened her eyes and hoarsely croaked, 'I feel terrible. My whole body hurts. It's that walk down the track last night in the cold that's done it. It was too much for a woman of my age.'

She looked at Marion and spoke as if her daughter was personally responsible for the train breaking down. Marion was too worried about her to take umbrage though. She had extremely limited medical knowledge but knew that what her mother was suffering from was far worse than a common cold. 'I'll ask the landlady to call the doctor,' she said.

He arrived a short while later. It seemed Ida had bronchitis and she was ordered to stay in bed for the duration or risk pneumonia setting in.

The landlady had no problem with their prolonged stay, delighted with the business however it had come her way. For an extra fee she offered to do Marion an evening meal and whatever food Ida could stomach plus any washing that needed doing.

It was a week later before Ida was well enough to get out of bed and by this time Marion's resources were down to less than eight pounds. During the times she wasn't nursing her mother she had taken herself out to get away from Ida's constant moaning and had grown familiar with her surroundings. She decided Mablethorpe wasn't a bad town, plenty of shops, the people friendly enough. It was as good a place as Skegness, she supposed, to lie low in for a while. When she had scoured the local paper for a job there were plenty on offer but the jobs were menial and pay was low, nothing for a women with her skills or providing the kind of wage she could demand in a larger town; she expected that she would fare no better in Skegness. This meant, though, that she and her mother were going to have to live on much less money than Marion had reckoned on. She had noted there was an employment agency where hopefully she could secure temporary work until she got something permanent. She had also noted the rents on flats locally. Now she knew what wage she could expect to earn, Marion was worried to find that only accommodation offered in rundown areas would be affordable, and pokey places with one bedroom at that. Her mother wasn't going to like that one bit but she would have no choice but to accept it. Before Marion could even consider applying for a flat to rent, though, she would need to save up for the deposit and enough to buy them the basics they would need, such as bedding and kitchen utensils.

She had enough money to pay for another week's stay in the bed and breakfast so she would need to get temp work and quickly. But just as important, somewhere for them to live right now that was cheap and where a deposit would not be asked for.

With this seeming unanswerable problem weighing heavily on her mind, Marion had taken herself out in the hope that the fresh sea air would help her come up with an answer. A while later it was with a sense of shock that she saw her wanderings had led her into a part of town no one who valued their belongings or their life would venture into voluntarily. She found herself beside a disused factory, its walls crumbling, no glass remaining in any of the windows, weeds flourishing profusely in every crack and crevice, discarded litter piled up against walls and filling gutters where the wind had blown it. Facing her behind a high metal fence, accessed by two iron gates, was a scrapyard filled with precarious-looking piles of old rusting cars, mangles, tin baths, ovens, in fact all manner of broken metal objects, plus mounds of old tyres. There was a muddy path running between the abandoned factory and the perimeter fencing of the yard.

She could either return the way she had come or chance seeing where the muddy path led. It seemed pointless going back. Hopefully the muddy path might be a short cut to a main thoroughfare. By the time she was a few yards down it she was regretting her decision as her good leather shoes were caked in sludge, which had also splashed up the back of her legs, and she had suffered a couple of nettle stings from the abundance of thick clumps that hung over the path. She had been out for quite a while now, longer than she'd intended when she'd set off, and unless the kindly landlady had looked in on her mother, Ida would have been on her own for the duration and would not be happy at her daughter abandoning her for hours on end, so Marion's need to get back to her lodgings was urgent.

She reached a bend in the path, which also coincided with the back fence of the yard. As she rounded the bend she was surprised to find that the path edged down the side of an area of waste ground that was filled with a higgledy-piggledy jumble of old caravans. It looked as if they had all been thrown up in the air and left where they landed. Having just skirted by a scrapyard, she assumed this place was a dumping ground for unwanted holiday homes. It was a seaside town after all. But then as she continued her journey down the side of the waste ground, to her surprise she saw a young woman, a baby in one arm, a bucket in the other hand, come out of one of the caravans.

Marion stared over at her in shock, having trouble comprehending that people were actually living in such dire conditions. They must have fallen on terrible times to have resorted to such depths. The thought of ending up in such a place absolutely horrified her. She made to continue but then stopped short as it hit her like a thunderbolt that very shortly her circumstances would be as dire as these people's. However appalling the idea was to her, and the way Ida would react didn't bear thinking about, Marion felt she would be wise at least to enquire if any of the caravans were vacant and what the rent was. Whoever owned them could not be charging much considering the condition they were in and the state of the surrounding land.

She arrived back at the bed and breakfast a while later to find a very disgruntled Ida, who was annoyed at being left alone so long on her 'death bed' . . . albeit as Marion was to find out later the old landlady had sat gossiping with her for over two hours, so she hadn't been on her own for long at all. Ida soon perked up when Marion informed her she'd been so long as she had secured them somewhere to live and they would move in as soon as she was fit enough to get out of bed. When Ida wanted all the intricate details of their new home, Marion just told her to wait and see, and for once her mother's bullying tactics wouldn't budge her. Ida's reaction was going to be bad enough when she did discover just where they would be living, so the later she found out the better as far as Marion was concerned.

Three days later, down to their last two pounds and loose change, Marion and Ida moved into their new abode, with the rent on it paid for a week. Marion hadn't at all taken to the dirty, surly-tempered owner of the caravans and neither did she think he was charging fairly for the use of his dilapidated dwellings, but he knew he had the upper hand with folks seeking his kind of accommodation and it was either accept the price or not, he didn't care, there were plenty more where she came from. Thankfully his terms were just a week's rent up front but he did make it abundantly clear that he collected the money every Friday evening for the following week and, if it wasn't forthcoming then and there, eviction was immediate.

As soon as Ida clapped eyes on the site and realised this was the place where she'd be living for the time being, she had gawped in horror and flatly refused to go any further. Marion told her that this was all they could afford and either she moved in or she was on her own. Ida had no choice and she knew it.

Now she barked at Marion, 'Did you get some paraffin? I've been frozen to the marrow all day. And what's for dinner? I'm famished.'

Still wearing her coat, Marion picked up a can of paraffin she had put down by the door when she had arrived and answered one of her mother's questions by going over to the heater and emptying some of it into the tank. 'Chicken soup and bread,' she announced.

Ida looked appalled. 'That all! Hardly enough to keep a gnat alive.'

Marion screwed the top back on the can and lit the heater, which gave out a loud explosion as it burst into flames and sent up a nauseating stench, before straightening up and saying matter-of-factly, 'Well, if you can afford any better, Mother, I'll gladly save the soup for tomorrow.' Without waiting for an answer, she added, 'And you'd better get used to it as that's all we can afford for our evening meals until I get paid next Friday. The paraffin I bought today has to last until then as well.'

Ida pulled a face by way of letting her daughter know what she thought of that.

Ida didn't speak again until they were sitting at the broken table eating their soup from enamel bowls Marion had bought from a second-hand shop along with other basic necessities. Her mother's tone was brusque. 'I hope you gave some thought to how you plan to get us out of here while you were working away in your *warm office*?'

Marion ignored her jibe, ignored her question too. She had given lots of thought to improving their situation but until her job prospects improved, this was the best accommodation they would find.

41

CHAPTER FIVE

Harold smiled gratefully at Jill as she placed a cup of milky coffee and a plate with two digestive biscuits on his desk before him. He thanked her while pushing a thick ledger towards her. 'Well, all seems in order with the accounts. Could you return the ledgers to Mr Gifford and thank him on my behalf for a good job done? I'd do it myself but I've still the daily inspection round to see to before I need to get ready for the civic lunch in Louth.'

Jill looked at her boss knowingly. 'You're not really looking forward to the lunch, are you?'

Sighing heavily, Harold shook his head. 'Not really. I'm not even sure what it's in aid of, to be honest. I've got the invitation here somewhere,' he said, making an attempt to find it amongst the stack of paperwork in his in tray but giving up when his quick flick through didn't reveal it. 'In my opinion most of these dos are just an excuse for the local bigwigs to have a three-course lunch and all they want to drink at the expense of the local ratepayers. I don't enjoy having to mingle with all those bumptious types, boasting about how well their business is doing, and those listening pretending to be impressed and patting backs in praise, when really they're seething inside because they aren't doing so well . . . and more than likely neither is the one doing the boasting either. If it weren't for the fact that I'm representing Mrs Jolly in her absence, and she'll want to know all the gossip when she telephones me next, I'd make an excuse not to go.'

In an effort to give his morale a boost Jill said, 'Well, you might enjoy it this time, you never know.'

I doubt it, Harold thought. Still, the lunch was only for a couple of hours and not a whole evening like some of the civic dos were.

He asked Jill, 'How is everything out in the office?'

'Going well. I'm really getting to grips with how everything is done. I'm very lucky that my predecessors put some excellent systems in place, but if you don't mind my saying so I have come across a few ways in which improvements can be made. I wondered how you'd feel about that?'

'You're in charge of the general office and if you come across ways to make your life easier then I have no problem with whatever changes you make.'

He was just about to ask her how Marion was getting on when the telephone on his desk rang. He excused himself from Jill and picked it up. Marion was informing him that she'd had a call from reception asking him to come down as he was needed to deal with a matter they couldn't handle. It was a matter of extreme urgency, she stressed.

Replacing the receiver, he told Jill, 'I'm needed in reception. I expect it's just a camper with a complaint he feels only the camp boss can deal with.'

'Would you like me to go on your behalf?' Jill offered. 'I feel I know enough about how the camp runs now to deal with most things. If it turns out to be something I can't handle then I'll hand it over to you.'

'I'm sure you could deal with it, Jill, and I appreciate your offer, but I might as well see to it then head straight out on the inspection round.'

'Well, hopefully it won't be long now before I'm taking turns with you on the daily round.'

He pushed back his chair and got up. 'I doubt it will, judging by the progress you're making. You have settled in well, Jill, and I'm more than happy with your work.'

Harold entered reception a few minutes later and the totally unexpected sight that greeted him froze him rigid. It took several long seconds for him to accept that his brain wasn't playing tricks on him but what he was seeing was most certainly real.

The blinds on the windows and door had been pulled down so those outside could not see in. Three men and a young woman were in the public area of the reception room. The men were all tall and solidly built, dressed in working clothes of the sort farmers or labourers would wear. One man was middle-aged, the other two much younger. One of the younger men was standing guard by the outer door. A second was standing by the far end of the counter. The older man stood in the middle of the room. The young woman was sitting on a chair, one in a row of several over by the far wall, her head in her hands, obviously in great distress. All three on duty receptionists were all behind the counter, huddled together, shaking in terror.

Harold could fully appreciate their fear. He himself was absolutely terrified. The older man was brandishing a shotgun. On Harold's entry he lifted it up and pointed it at him. The look on his weather-beaten face told Harold that he wouldn't be afraid to use it if he had to.

Before Harold could begin to try and fathom what the three men could possible want here that they needed to be armed for, the older man was demanding, 'You the boss?'

Harold knew that the last thing he should do was let this man see his fear, that he needed to act calm so as not to alarm any of the men in any way and give them an excuse to inflict damage on their hostages. As petrified as he was, he prayed he could pull it off. He swallowed hard, then spoke as calmly as he could. 'My name is Harold Rose. What . . . er . . . can I do for you, Mr . . . er?'

The man roared ferociously at him, 'You can bring me the bastard who did this to my daughter, that's what you can do.' He turned momentarily to address the young woman slumped in the chair by the far wall. 'Stop yer blubbering, Thelma. Stand up and let the man see what's been done to yer while you was

44

at his camp. Come on, girl, do as I say. ' Head hung low, the girl slowly and awkwardly got up. It was plain to see that she was heavily pregnant. When she slumped down in the chair again, to re-bury her face in her hands, her father turned back to address Harold.

'My girl came here with her friends last September for a week. Me and her mam thought she was too young to go off for that length of time without us, but she convinced us they were coming to a family holiday camp, one with a good reputation and where the staff took good care of the campers, so we gave in.' His face screwed up in rage. 'Yeah, the staff look after yer all right, don't they!' he spat, momentarily pointing the barrel of the gun at his daughter's swollen stomach before aiming it back at Harold. 'One of your staff got Thelma drunk then took advantage of her, *that's* how well he took care of her. We had no idea she'd been got in the family way because she was terrified to tell us, hiding it by wearing tight corsets under baggy clothes. She knew how devastated we'd be. Me and her mother had high hopes of our only daughter. She was going to escape the hard life of farming to be a teacher. Her mother was dreaming of her big white wedding. Now none of that will happen. Our precious girl's life is ruined. She can't go to college with a baby under her arm and no decent man will marry her now she's been defiled. I want the bastard responsible fetched here to face the consequences of what he's done.'

Harold's eyes bulged and he stuttered, 'You've . . . you've come here to kill him!'

The older man looked at him as though he were stupid. 'What good would killing him do? He's going to marry my girl and give her baby a name, that's what he's going to do. But rest assured, if he refuses to make a respectable woman of her, then I *will* bloody kill him but that would be due to kindness on my part . . . to put him out of his misery after I've let Thelma's brother's loose on him first.'

Fraternising with guests on a personal level was against the rules of employment at Jolly's. It was a rule that was hard to enforce, though, on a camp of this size with its hundreds of employees so a huge amount of trust was placed in the staff by management. Regardless, if an employee was caught red-handed doing something they shouldn't, then they were severely dealt with. On the other hand, if a member of staff was being unjustly accused of something they weren't responsible for then they had the right to clear their name.

Harold told the angry father, 'Look, if this man . . .'

He erupted angrily. 'There's no *if* about it! My daughter's no liar.' He then cried, 'Fetch him, I said. Fetch him NOW.'

Harold froze as he saw the man's finger squeeze against the gun's trigger. He blustered, 'I'm sorry, I'm sorry. I didn't mean to imply she was. You have my word that one way or the other I'll do all I can to help resolve this situation. Look, er . . . why don't you put down your gun and we'll all go to my office . . .'

'And discuss this over a cup of tea? There's no way I'm going to risk that man getting wind of this and making a run for it. I want him fetched NOW, I said.' The man waved the gun menacingly by way of telling Harold to see to it immediately or else.

The burly youngster by the door spoke up then. 'You want me to show the boss man we mean business, Dad?'

'Do you?' the older man bellowed at Harold.

He automatically raised his hands in surrender and blurted out, 'No, no, there's no need for any violence. I promise you, I am taking this seriously. I'll . . . I'll need the man's name?'

'All Thelma knows was that he was called Terry.'

'That's a common name. I know of one Terry but I should imagine there are a few of them considering how many staff we have working for us here. And also there is the fact the Terry you're after might not be working for us any longer. Staff come and go as I'm sure you'll appreciate.'

'Well, if the one we're after no longer works here, then you'll have a home address for him and we'll pay him a visit there.'

'Is there anything else you can give me to go on to find this Terry you're after? Does your daughter . . . Thelma . . . have any idea what his job was here?'

'As I've already told yer he got her drunk and she don't remember much. She does remember him telling her that he was an important member of the management team, so important the place would fall apart if he left.' He shouted to Thelma, 'Describe what he looked like. Hopefully you can remember that at least?'

Before she had time to respond one of the receptionists nervously piped up, 'I know which Terry you're after.'

Harold spun to face her, a hopeful expression on his face. 'You do?'

Janet Wainwright vigorously nodded.

The older man snarled, 'Well, spit it out, girl.' He waved the gun at her.

Janet's mouth opened and closed fishlike, her terrified eyes darting between the man with the gun and Harold.

He might not be the bravest of men but Harold's anger rose at this man threatening a member of his staff, female at that, with physical harm if she didn't obey him. Before he realised what he was doing, he'd leaped forward and brought his hand down hard on the barrel of the gun. Caught off guard, the man dropped it, sending it clattering across the floor. A gasp of horror resounded from the receptionists as Harold and the irate father both dived to grab the gun, while both younger men came dashing to aid their father. Before they had reached him, though, the far bigger and stronger older man had already thrust Harold out of the way, re-taken the gun and was on his feet and aiming it at him, while warning, 'Don't try anything like that again or you won't live to regret it.'

Harold was still infuriated by the man's treatment of the receptionists. 'What kind of person are you to threaten women with harm if they don't do as you say?' Without giving the man chance to reply, he addressed Janet. 'Which Terry do you think it is?'

She gave a nervous gulp before telling him, 'Terry Jones, Mr Rose, I'm positive it is.' Then through fear and nerves she babbled, 'It's a well-known fact he makes out that the camp would fall into rack and ruin if he wasn't working here, and he always makes out he's part of the hierarchy and not just the Stripeys' supervisor so as to impress young girls. They wouldn't look at him twice otherwise. He's not what you'd call good-looking although he thinks he's God's gift! He tried it on with Jackie Sims last year, blackmailed her into going out with him. Jackie was too clever for him, though, and made him regret picking on her. She made him look like a right idiot and it took ages for him to live it down. Jackie described him as a creep who looked like a weasel. In my opinion she described him perfectly. Most of his staff hate having Terry as their boss 'cos he doesn't treat them very well, orders them about like they're his personal slaves, but they daren't say anything because he has the power to get them sacked on some trumped-up charge he's concocted.'

The other two receptionists were nodding and murmuring agreement with their colleague's analysis of Terry Jones.

Harold just hoped that these accusations against Terry weren't true as it was abhorrent for him to think that they had a member of staff, one in such an influential position, who could use his place here to gratify his sexual needs and treat those he was in charge of so shoddily.

He asked Janet, 'Would you please put a call out on the camp radio asking Terry Jones to report to reception as a matter of urgency? Put it out twice, please. If he doesn't hear the announcement himself, some of the Stripeys will and go find him and tell him he's wanted.'

No one made a sound or moved a muscle while they waited for Terry Jones to arrive and the atmosphere in the room was taut with tension. As the seconds ticked past and there was no sign of him, Harold grew increasingly anxious that the older man could begin to question whether they had somehow managed to warn Terry that he was a wanted man and he'd made a run for it. If the gunman lost his temper all of them in this room be on the receiving end.

Harold almost collapsed in relief when the door handle was

48

tried. The young man by the door immediately unlocked it and opened it up wide enough to grab hold of the person on the other side and haul them in. He then shut the door and re-locked it.

Terry Jones had believed that his summons to see the boss was to update him on how the new entertainments team recruits were settling in, so to be unexpectedly yanked through the door was a shock. It took him a moment to gather his faculties. When he did he saw several pairs of eyes staring at him accusingly. He asked Harold, 'What the hell's going on? And what's that thug by the door think he's doing, manhandling me like that?'

The thug in question took a step forward, snarling, 'Who are you calling a thug, you . . .'

His father cut in, 'Back where you were, Frank. I'll be the one to deal with this.'

As he spoke Terry flashed a glance over to the big man and that was when he spotted the gun. Eyes bulging in terror, he uttered, 'What the f . . .'

The older man snarled at him warningly, 'Don't you dare use bad language in front of my daughter and the other ladies present.' He then waved the gun at Terry. 'I want the truth from you.' He nodded over at his daughter, sitting hunched over on the chair by the wall, who when Terry arrived had dropped her hands and sat staring at him. 'You remember my daughter? Thelma, her name is.'

Terry looked at Harold quizzically. 'What's going on here?'

He replied evenly, 'Just answer the man's question, Terry.'

Terry looked across at the young woman for a moment before giving a nonchalant shrug. 'No, can't say as I do.'

Harold had been watching Terry closely and had seen a flicker of recognition spark in his eyes when he had first looked over at Thelma, before he had then given his denial. Harold knew he was lying. He did recognise the young woman. But whether that recognition was just as a camper he'd seen around during her stay last year or because he had been intimate with her and now astutely realised the reason why he was finding himself being interrogated, was what needed to be uncovered.

Thelma's father broke in, 'That is not what my daughter is saying. So just to be sure, take a closer look, son.'

Terry flashed another look across at Thelma, before giving another bemused shrug and saying cockily, 'Look, I meet lots of people, hundreds a week, and I'm a popular man . . . have girls throwing themselves at me all the time. I'm sure I would remember her if I had met her, she's a pretty girl, but I haven't.' It was then that Thelma's condition registered with him. He held up his hands in mock surrender, blurting, 'Hey, now, just a minute. You ain't going to pin that on me. Whoever the father of her kid is, it's not me.'

Terry then issued a small squeal of fright as the barrel of the gun was pushed into his chest and Thelma's father erupted. 'My daughter is no liar. She says *you* are the father.'

If Terry was intimidated by this man's threatening behaviour towards him in any way he did not show it, just answered the man's question as cockily as he had the one before. 'Well, it's her word against mine then. I don't remember her, because I haven't met her before. Now go and find some other poor sucker to take the blame for getting the stupid cow up the duff.'

Harold froze as he saw Thelma's two brothers' faces turn purple with rage at Terry's derogatory reference to their sister, fists clenched tightly, preparing to launch themselves on him and make him pay for his bad mouthing of her. Meanwhile it was apparent to Harold that Thelma's father was desperately fighting to control his own fury at Terry's disrespectful attitude towards his daughter as he was systematically tightening then loosening his finger against the gun's trigger.

Again Harold, having no idea where he was finding the courage from, found himself diving forward to shield Terry from the three men, shouting out, 'Is harming Terry worth you all going to prison? He says he's not the father of Thelma's baby and unless you can prove otherwise I can see no other option but to accept . . .'

50

'I can prove he is my baby's father.'

They all turned in the direction the small voice had emanated from, then watched in silence as Thelma awkwardly got up and made her way over. She walked around Harold, who was still shielding Terry behind his back, to look the young man in the eyes. Her own filled with tears, Thelma spoke sadly.

'You can't take all the blame for what went on that night. I might only be seventeen but I'm not stupid. I didn't have to drink all those drinks you bought me. I knew I wasn't used to it so had no clue how alcohol would affect me. I was just so overwhelmed that you had singled me out from all the others you bragged you could have had that night. I was stupid enough to be flattered by all your flannel.

'After about ten o'clock my memory isn't at all clear on what happened. I have vague memories of my friends trying to get me to go back with them to the chalet, but you promised them you'd look after me, saying you were just going to take me for a stroll down the beach. I don't remember us actually taking a stroll but I do recall us sitting in the dunes and you kissing me and trying to put your hands up my top. I remember trying to push you away. I'd never been with a boy like that before and I was scared. I'd promised my mam and dad I'd behave myself and I didn't want to let them down. You told me that there was nothing to be scared of and nothing awful would happen as you'd make sure it didn't. Then next I remember . . .'

She went silent for a moment before continuing. 'Afterwards I remember you saying we ought to go back as it was getting late and you had an early start in the morning and I had too because I was going home. I'm sure you promised we'd keep in touch and I'm positive I gave you my address.' She paused for a moment before she dropped her bombshell on Terry. 'But what I do remember clearly is that you have a long scar just below your belly button. I saw it when you stood to pull your trousers back up. I asked you how you got it. You told me you'd gone to the aid of an old man who was being mugged and that's what you got for your troubles. I remember thinking

51

what a brave man you were. It was only later when I was back home that I realised what the scar actually was. It wasn't from saving an old man from a mugger but from having your appendix out. I know that for a fact as my friend had to have hers out last February and her scar is in the same.' She paused momentarily again before she asked him: 'If you hadn't been with me in that situation, then how would I know about your scar in such a private place?'

Terry was staring wildly at her, obviously looking for a plausible reason to explain how she knew about his scar, other than the real one.

'Well, have you a scar where my daughter is saying you have?' Thelma's father was demanding.

Terry looked at Harold, eyes pleading with him as his boss to help him out of this dire situation.

Harold's response to him though was, 'Answer the question, Terry.'

Terry still declined.

Thelma shot him a look of contempt before she placed her hand on her father's arm and said to him, 'Dad, please, please don't make me marry him. What kind of man is he to deny he knows me, deny the child I'm carrying is his? I thought you were right to come and make him stand by me and the baby, but now I see him for the kind of man he is. I'd sooner be thought of as a slut and bring my baby up by myself than have to spend my life with the likes of him as my husband, knowing he is only with me as he was made to marry me. If he treats all women like he has done me, I can't imagine what sort of father he'd make.' She then implored, 'Please, Dad, please don't make me marry him?'

At his daughter's heart-wrenching pleas all the fight seemed to leave the older man. Heaving a sigh, he smiled tenderly at her. 'Be assured, love, if I hear anyone call you a slut, they'll have me and your brothers to deal with. You won't be raising this baby on your own. I'll be the best granddad I can, and I know once your mother comes round she'll be a doting grandmother.'

'And we'll be the best uncles we can,' both brothers joined in.

The older man said to Terry warningly, 'You may think you've been let off lightly, but one day you'll get what's due to you. People like you, who go through life not caring who they hurt to get what they want, always lose out in the end.'

At this turn of events Harold didn't know whether to laugh or cry in relief that this terrifying situation had been defused and none of them was any longer in danger of drawing their last breath.

With his arm protectively around her, Thelma's father said, 'Come on, love, let's get you home.'

They had arrived at the door when the man told the other three to go ahead. He turned round and walked back over to Harold. His face filled with remorse, he said, 'I'm sorry for the situation I put you all in. If it's any consolation, none of you was ever in any danger. The gun wasn't loaded.'

Harold thoughtfully watched the party leave. Not that he condoned the way the man had handled the situation, terrifying innocent people witless, but part of him fully appreciated that all he had done was only to try and do his best to protect his daughter and her child from a miserable future. Thank goodness Thelma had made him see that she would have suffered a miserable future had he insisted Terry did marry her.

Harold realised that Terry was talking to him in his usual cocksure manner. 'I'll get back to my Bingo calling then before we have a riot on our hands.'

Harold settled a cold stare on him and told him matter-of-factly, 'I'll get Jill to find someone to replace you. Go upstairs and wait for me in my office, I'd like a word.'

Terry answered knowingly, 'Oh, yeah, you'll be wanting an update on how the new recruits are doing.'

A while later, Harold gave a mystified shrug and said to Jill, who was sitting in the chair opposite his desk, 'I'm having trouble understanding the arrogance of the man. Terry felt I was being totally unfair sacking him for breaking Jolly's rules on staff conduct. He acted so insulted when I told him that after hearing what other staff felt about him, I was inclined to believe the young girl's story against his own. He realised then that he was going to be dismissed from his job and had the nerve to try to get me to change my mind by telling me I'd be hard pressed to find someone else who was as good as his job as he was! I'd had enough of him by that time and told him to be packed up and off the camp within the next hour and his dues and cards would be sent on to him. Can you believe his parting shot was to ask me for a reference?'

'I just can't believe that Marion and I were working away not a clue what was going on downstairs. Thelma is wise beyond her years. I admire her for choosing to face a life of stigma as a single mother rather than marry to the sort of man Terry showed himself to be. I hope the receptionists don't suffer any after-effects, though. It must have been a terrible ordeal for them. I don't know how I'd have coped, facing an angry man with a gun. What about yourself?' Jill asked in concern. 'I know you come across as fine, but you've just been through a terrifying time too. Hadn't you better be checked out by Nurse and have the rest of the day off, like you ordered the receptionists?'

Jill was right. He wished he could do as she suggested, and go home and have a couple of brandies to calm himself down, but he hadn't yet done the daily inspection round and was due to be at the civic lunch in an hour.

He responded, 'I'm fine.' Then grinned and added flippantly, 'All in a day's work. As I asked the receptionists, please keep this incident to yourself. We don't want what happened reaching the ears of the campers, for obvious reasons. Now I'd best get ready for the lunch.' He had his best suit and a fresh shirt hanging in his private washroom. He made to scrape back his chair and get up, Jill to return to her desk, when something occurred to him.

'Oh, goodness, I haven't given any thought to replacing Terry Jones. I can't leave the Stripeys without a supervisor.' He paused for a moment. 'I suppose the job should automatically go to Terry's own appointed second in command. It was Steve Taylor, but a week or so ago Terry told me he'd replaced him as he wasn't up to the job. Now I know what I do about Terry, I wonder if that was really the case. Perhaps Terry was wielding his authority against Steve to make a point to him and the other staff.' His face screwed up in thought. 'Terry did tell me who the replacement was, a young woman in his team he felt would be worth giving a try out.' He took off his spectacles and gave them a clean, screwing up his face in concentration. 'I just can't recall her name at the moment.' He put his glasses back on and replaced the handkerchief. 'One of the entertainments staff will know. A few of them will be in the Paradise right now supervising the morning's activities. Would you be good enough to pop over and ask one of the Stripeys to point out Terry's assistant to you? If she can come and see me straight away, I'll deal with the matter before I set off for that lunch.'

CHAPTER SIX

While Harold and the reception staff were suffering their ordeal, over the courtyard in the nursery Patsy's morning wasn't proving too enjoyable either. A few ill-mannered children were causing mayhem, running riot in the nursery. The staff were unable to bring them under control and their antics were upsetting the rest of the children. No shift passed for the nursery staff without some minor incident or other transpiring but none of them could ever remember their young charges causing quite so much such strife. Hopefully the next lot due in for their three hours of care would be well mannered, play nicely together and not torment each other. Or even better, sleep for the whole time they were there.

Patsy herself didn't care whether the next batch of children were well behaved or not as it was her half day off, and after the morning she'd had, to say she was looking forward to it was an understatement. As soon as her shift finished at twelve, she meant to rush back to her chalet, change out of her uniform, then head off for the stop just past the camp entrance gate to catch the four-minutes-past-one bus into Mablethorpe. Once she had done her shopping, she planned to sit on a bench on the sea front with a cup of tea bought from a kiosk and a bar of Cadbury's Milk chocolate and do some serious thinking about her future.

She'd had a letter yesterday from her mother. After her usual relaying of family news and then all the gossip regarding neighbours and friends, she had come around to expressing the real reason for writing this particular missive. An opportunity had arisen that she felt Patsy ought to consider seriously. A cousin to whom Patsy was very close had been to see her mum, to ask if she thought Patsy would be interested in coming in with her on a business venture. She was buying a post office and general store in a very busy thoroughfare in Patsy's home town. She would run the post office side and Patsy could manage the general store and have free licence to sell what she wanted. She'd earn a wage as well as a share of the profits from the store side.

The cousin had made it clear that Patsy was her much preferred choice to join her, but if she decided it wasn't for her then her cousin did have another couple of people in mind so she would like an answer quickly. Her mother had stressed what a great opportunity this was for Patsy, one which might not come along again, and when she was making her decision she should remember that she was twenty-four now and it was time she gave serious thought to her future. She knew Patsy enjoyed working at Jolly's but, after all, it was only a summer job when all was said and done. Patsy knew her mother well and realised that she was also seeing this opportunity as a way to get her daughter to settle back home, where she was more likely to meet someone steady to give her mum the grandchildren she so desperately wanted than while working at the likes of Jolly's. The majority of staff only came to work at a holiday camp for one season, maybe two, to have fun and sow some wild oats away from their parents' watchful eyes before returning home to settle down and get married or else make serious careers for themselves.

Patsy really liked working at the camp, meeting such a diverse group of people and enjoying the good social life that she led there. She wasn't quite sure whether she was ready to return home and settle in an eight-to-six job. And to leave Jolly's after all this time, a place she considered her home for seven months of the year, would be a terrible wrench. But then, as her mother had written, opportunities like she was being given were a once-in-a-lifetime occurrence. Ten years older than Patsy, her cousin Melanie was fair-minded and approachable, and although she would be the overall owner of the business would treat Patsy as her equal, there was no doubt about that. Her cousin was the sort who made a success of everything she did, so Patsy had no fear of this venture failing. Deep down she knew she'd be a fool to turn this opportunity down.

She certainly had a life-changing decision to make and was hoping the sea air and soothing sounds of waves on the shore would help her do that.

At a quarter to one, dressed in a pair of bell-bottomed jeans and a long blue and white striped shirt with pointed collar and cuffs, over which she had on a shorter knitted blue tank top, and carrying an anorak over her arm in case it grew chilly on the beach front, Patsy was approaching the ornate fountain dominating the middle of the camp courtyard, en route for the entrance gates, when she heard her name being called.

She stopped and turned around to see one of her nursery colleagues waving frantically at her. When the girl arrived to join her, she took a moment to catch her breath before asking: 'Do us a favour, Patsy. Old Starchy Britches –' this was the nursery nurses' nickname for their no-nonsense boss – 'has asked me to drop the monthly staff assessments into the general office, but if you would do it for me I can sneak behind the bins at the back of the shops and have a crafty fag. You know what Starchy is like. If I'm back a second later than she thinks it should have taken me, she'll give me a right rollicking and a black mark on my next assessment.'

Patsy looked at her apologetically. 'Oh, I would, Judy, but it'll make me late for the bus into Mablethorpe.'

'But it's not due for another fifteen minutes.'

'That's if it's on time. When have you ever known the buses to arrive on time? If it's Sid that's on our route this week then he drives like a maniac, so he'll be early. If it's Brian, then a snail moves faster, so he'll be late.'

Her colleague was desperate for her cigarette, though, and wasn't about to give up on not having it easily. 'Well, if it's late, what's your problem? And if it's early then you've still got time to pop up to the general office and hand in the sheets. Won't take you more than a minute. Oh, go on, Patsy,' she begged. 'While we've been standing here arguing the toss, you could have been up in the general office by now and on your way back down.'

Patsy issued a resigned sigh and took the sheets from her. 'You owe me one,' she shot at Judy and ran off in the direction of reception.

As soon as Patsy entered the general office, Jill called across to her, 'That was quick. We only put word out a few minutes ago that Mr Rose wanted to see you. He asked me to tell you to go straight into his office as soon as you arrived.'

Patsy was wondering what on earth the camp manager could possibly want with her, a mere nursery worker, that was so important they'd sent someone to find her. Her mind thrashing wildly over what the reason could be, she headed over to the boss's office, only pausing long enough as she passed Jill's desk to hand her the nursery staff's assessment forms.

With one foot on his chair, Harold was in the process of tying his shoelaces when Patsy politely tapped on his door and, because Jill had told her to, didn't wait for a summons from inside but opened the door and entered. Standing just over the threshold, she smiled a greeting at Harold. 'Your secretary told me you wanted to see me, Mr Rose?'

While he finished tying his laces he called to her, 'Yes, come in, come in. And those of supervisor level address me as Harold.'

She eyed him quizzically. 'But I'm not a supervisor, Mr Rose.'

To her astonishment he told her, 'You are now.' He finished tying his laces, took his foot off the chair, placed it back on the floor and turned fully to face her. Recognition struck him. 'Oh, you're the very quick-thinking young lady who was responsible for bringing down the naked runner a couple of weeks ago and putting a stop to his escapade. Thank you again, Miss . . . er . . .' Twice he'd met this young woman and twice he had embarrassed himself by not knowing her name.

She put him out of his misery. 'Patricia Mathers. Patsy for short.'

Harold suddenly remembered he should be making a move to set off for the lunch. He said rapidly, 'I do apologise, but I really should be on my way out right now to an appointment so I need to make this quick. For reasons I can't go into, Terry Jones is no longer working for us. This means that his role as Entertainments Team Manager has become vacant and his obvious successor is yourself, with immediate effect.' He smiled warmly at Patsy. 'I appreciate we are rather throwing you in at the deep end but, having seen how you conduct yourself in a crisis, I'm sure the team is safe in your hands. I note you aren't wearing your uniform so take it this must be your afternoon off, but you'll appreciate that will have to be postponed in the circumstances. I know I really should gather the team together and formally announce you as their new supervisor, and I will do that tomorrow morning. I'll come along to the briefing straight after breakfast at the back of the stage.' Harold handed her Terry's set of keys before grabbing up his raincoat from the back of his chair, where he'd put it earlier. 'Please excuse me, but I really must leave you to it now.'

Throughout Harold's announcement, Patsy had been staring at him dumbstruck. Any curiosity she had over the reason for Terry Jones's sudden departure was overridden by her utter confusion as to why the boss had chosen her as Terry's successor. Had Harold Rose really assessed her capabilities to head such an important team as the entertainments one based purely on her reaction to the naked runner? It seemed that he had, and who was she to question the judgement of a man in his position?

The proposal from her cousin faded into oblivion. It had long been Patsy's dream to be a member of the entertainments team, but to be in charge of it! She felt an enormous sense of elation, but that was followed by a wave of trepidation and worry that she wasn't up to the job. Then determination set in. How many people actually got the chance to fulfil a dream?

Well, Harold Rose was giving her hers and she meant to do her best to repay his faith in her.

She suddenly realised that Harold had left and she had a team to supervise and ought to get on with it. She thought of how her past supervisors would have handled this situation and came to the conclusion that the best place to make a start would be to go through the paperwork in Terry's office where he would have a rota showing what activities were planned for the coming week, what staff he'd assigned to oversee each one, and what plans he'd formulated for the forthcoming shows and such like. And she should go through all the entertainments team's monthly assessment records by way of getting a feel for each individual and their strengths and weaknesses. She had a lot of work facing her and the sooner she got started the better.

First things first, she needed to change into her Stripey uniform. Luckily she wouldn't need to pay a visit to the stores as she still had a set hanging on her clothes rail after wearing them during her spell in charge of the bicycle sheds before she had joined the nursery team. She then wondered what Mavis Durham's reaction had been to learning she had lost an experienced member of her staff so abruptly, leaving her with the chore of training up another. The nursery staff had already had a fraught morning and it seemed they were in for a bad afternoon . . . not caused by the children this time but by a very miffed supervisor.

A short while later Dixie Carter arrived in the general office. Her name was actually Daphne, which she hated as it was so old-fashioned so she had renamed herself Dixie when she had first come to Jolly's. She was a petite, slim, twenty-two-year-old girl, with natural blonde hair framing her impishly pretty face. She was selfish by nature and should she see something she wanted, didn't care how many people she used or what she herself had to do to get it. That's how she had got Terry to oust his last second in command and put her in his place. By sleeping with him . . . as much as it had privately disgusted her, her feelings towards Terry being the same as the rest of the staff's. Jill had just left the office to return the ledger books to the accountant as Harold had asked her to do earlier, so it was Marion who greeted Dixie.

'May I help you?' Marion's manner was always very formal when addressing visitors, employees or otherwise, as that was how she'd been trained at college. She was having difficulty adapting to the less informal approach Drina Jolly insisted she liked her staff to use.

Dixie told her, 'I understand Mr Rose wants to see me.'

Marion looked bemused. 'Mr Rose is out and won't be back until later this afternoon. Are you sure he wanted to see you?'

'Well, that's what Mary told me Katie had told her.' Dixie's pretty face then screwed itself into an annoyed scowl. 'If this is their idea of a joke then I don't find it funny. I'll make sure they both know in future not to mess . . .' She stopped herself mid flow. It wouldn't do for anyone connected with management to learn how she responded to people who crossed her and for that trait in her character be put on her staff records, to be noted when promotions were in the offing. She gave a forced chuckle and said instead, 'Oh, well, no harm done, I suppose. I'll be off to continue what I was doing when I was waylaid by Mary.' She then grumbled more to herself than to Marion, 'I'm looking for Terry Jones as we were supposed to be having a meeting at two to discuss me having more spots in the Friday night Stripey show . . . only I can't find him anywhere so where he's hiding himself is anyone's guess.'

Not that she had been personally told the details of Terry Jones's departure, but her desk being in such close proximity to the boss's office, and thanks to her own nosy nature, Marion had gathered that Terry Jones had been dismissed for unacceptable conduct. She was about to tell the young woman that she was wasting her time looking for Terry Jones as he was no longer employed by Jolly's but Dixie had already rushed off and was halfway down the stairs.

Still not having found Terry twenty minutes later and none of the other staff Dixie encountered having seen him either, she decided to try his office again. It was based in the foyer of the Paradise. As she approached she could see a light shining from under the door so assumed Terry had returned from wherever he had been hiding, giving no thought to leading her a merry dance. She forcefully pushed open the door, ready to give him a piece of her mind, but instead stood gawking open-mouthed in the doorway to see a woman sitting in his chair, engrossed in looking through what Dixie perceived as Terry's personal paperwork.

She burst out, 'Oi! What do you think you're doing? This is the entertainments manager's private office. Now get the hell out!'

At the unexpected interruption, Patsy's head spun around and she stared blankly at the newcomer for a moment before recognition hit. Smiling at the girl, she said, 'You're Dixie. I've seen you . . .'

A self-satisfied grin spreading over her face, Dixie interrupted her. 'Yeah, in the shows. And I'm good. Too good for Terry's amateur efforts. Once a talent scout or a theatrical agent spots my talents, I'll be high tailing it out of here. And one better hurry up and get here, I'm fed up with waiting.' She gave a superior flick of her head and said knowingly, 'I've always felt that I was made for the big time.'

Patsy had been going to say she had seen Dixie heading some of the campers' activities when she had been coming and going around the camp. But she had also seen Dixie in shows, and her singing, dancing and acting abilities, in Patsy's opinion, fell far short of the standard she'd seen on television or that she suspected talent scouts or agents would be looking for. She might be new to being a supervisor but regardless was well aware that to get the best out of people they needed encouragement, not discouragement, so decided not to express her opinions to Dixie but instead smiled and said: 'If I get wind a talent scout is in the audience, I'll tip you the wink.'

Dixie beamed. 'Oh, ta.' Then her eyes blazed. 'Who do you think you are anyway, tipping me any wink? You're just a lowly nursery nurse and I'm assistant Head Stripey. If there are any winks to be tipping, I'll be the one to be tipping 'em. Now I still don't know what you think you're doing here, going through Terry's paperwork, but I'd get your arse out of that chair and do a disappearing act before he arrives and reports you to the boss. You'll end up out on your ear for snooping where you shouldn't.' Curiosity got the better of Dixie then and she asked, 'Just what are you looking for anyway?'

Patsy put down the papers she was studying and swung around in the chair to face Dixie. 'I'm familiarising myself with Terry's duties and getting a feel for the staff. You see, Terry has left . . . I don't know the ins and outs of why. Maybe Mr Rose will tell us at the meeting tomorrow when he introduces me to all the staff as the new Head Stripey . . .'

Patsy was interrupted by Dixie angrily crying out: 'What! What do you mean, you're the new Head Stripey? I'm Terry's second in command so it should be me.'

Patsy looked thoughtfully at her. In theory that really should be the case, that the next in line was automatically promoted when the position above become vacant, but for reasons known only to Harold Rose himself he hadn't followed tradition in this instance. 'Well . . . er . . . all I can say is that Mr Rose gave the job to me so he must think I'm the right one for it, and if you have an issue with that I suggest you take it up with him.'

Dixie opened her mouth, about to tell Patsy that was just what she would do, but then clamped it shut. She thought, what did this lump of a nursery nurse with a face that would sink a thousand ships know about heading up the most prestigious team in the company? She obviously possessed no artistic talents or she'd already be a member of it. Dixie felt a strong urge to go and demand to see the boss, ask him if he'd lost his mind putting this woman in the job above her. But to challenge Harold Rose over a decision he had made would only result in him seeing her as challenging his authority, and that wouldn't do her promotion prospects any good. Then she thought of something better she could do. Her plan to oust Stephen from his job as Terry's second in command so that Terry would promote herself into the position had worked a treat. It had been easy, just a few arranged mishaps to make Stephen look incompetent had done the trick. Albeit she had had to promise Terry a night of passion with her that, when it came to honouring it, had made her feel physically sick. But there was no reason why the plan she had used against Stephen wouldn't work again. So that's what she would do. Make Harold Rose see his error of judgement by making Patsy look bad. And while she was planning the best way to make this happen, Patsy would think Dixie her greatest advocate.

She forced a smile on to her face and said, 'Look, you're right. Mr Rose promoted you to the position because he felt you were the best person for the job. Congratulations. I'm pleased for you, I really am. Anything I can do to help you get to grips on things, just ask.'

A surge of relief swept through Patsy. For a moment then she'd thought she had an enemy in the camp but thankfully it seemed she had an ally. 'If you've got a few minutes now, I'd be grateful.'

CHAPTER SEVEN

O ver in Skegness, standing at his office window, Reg Brady, a short, stocky, barrel-chested man, stared thoughtfully down into the large yard below. His stubby thumbs were hooked inside a pair of navy braces, holding up a pair of grey suit trousers; the cuffs of his white shirt sleeves rolled up to his elbows, revealing thick hairy arms.

All but a sizeable space in the middle of the yard and a wide path leading over to two large wooden doors at the entrance was filled with building materials and tools of his trade. At the moment two flat-backed lorries were occupying the space in the centre, each being loaded with items by two brawny middle-aged men and a skinny youth, ready to take to a job that started tomorrow.

Compared to some building firms Brady's was a small outfit employing ten men, subcontracting others in as and when needed. It had a good reputation for quality workmanship at fair prices. One of the lucky ones, having returned home from serving his country in the Great War, Reg's father nevertheless was unlucky in finding permanent work. Desperate to feed his family, he went from house to house touting for work, prepared to do anything. Gradually, through persistence and hard work at very reasonable rates, people were knocking at his door offering him work instead of him having to go out looking for it. Reg joined his father on leaving school at fourteen, his main job being to push a rickety handcart from yard to job then back to the yard every day, the cart being loaded with the collection of second-hand tools and materials required for each job.

Reg's father hadn't been an ambitious man, quite content that the work coming in was sufficient to provide for his family and allow him a couple of pints at the end of the week. It wasn't until he died after a short illness when Reg was twenty-five and he took over the business that changes took place. Unlike his father Reg was ambitious, wanted more for his family than his father had provided. Through dogged determination he had built up the firm to what it was today, no longer operating from the back yard of a terrace house but in a former livery yard; no longer undertaking odd jobs that paid a pittance but building and maintenance projects yielding reasonable profits that had enabled Reg to purchase a couple of flat-backed lorries and a transit van to replace the old cart. He'd bought his own house and car, and given his beloved wife the standard of living he had promised her he would on the day they had married twenty-eight years earlier.

All in all Reg should have been a contented man but he wasn't, far from it. Three years previously his adored eldest daughter, Sally, had died and until the man who had caused her untimely demise had been made to pay, Reg would never be able to come to terms with her loss and get on with his life. And worse still for him was the fact that neither would her mother or younger sister.

Unlike her slim, pretty younger sister, Sally had been a short, plump, homely-looking girl, shy and naive. She had worked in her father's office, learning the intricacies of the job from an old retainer and had been looking forward to taking over the running of it when the present office manager retired in a couple of years. Come Reg's retirement, it was planned that both his daughters would take over the running of the family firm. Sally had much preferred to stay at home of an evening and watch the television, read romantic novels or listen to her collection of middle of the road music in her bedroom, Val Doonican and The Seekers being her favourite performers, rather than go out to pubs and clubs. It was believed by her family that she had never had a boyfriend.

Her mother had found her in bed one morning, writhing in agony, and had later collapsed in shock when a doctor at the hospital had informed her that her daughter was suffering from septicaemia caused by a dirty instrument used to abort her baby and that there was nothing that could be done for her. Sally had died in agony four days later, her last coherent words being of deep sorrow for the shame she had brought on her family. During that four days the desolate family had kept a bedside vigil and during Sally's rare bouts of consciousness had managed to glean from her bits and pieces of information that explained how she had come to land up in the dire situation she had.

Roughly three months before, she had been on her way to post a letter to a pen friend she corresponded with in America when she had bumped into a group of her old school friends. It was one of the group's birthday and they were going to celebrate it with a trip to the funfair on the Skegness front. The high-spirited group persuaded Sally to join them. They were a nice bunch of girls and, although she wasn't fond of fairs in general, Sally agreed. Her friends had cajoled her into going on the dodgems and into the House of Fun but when it came to the Waltzers she had flatly refused, such rides frightening her, so while those of the group she was with at the time clambered into several cars, she had watched from the sidelines.

During the ride one of the two men operating it had come over to where she was standing, lit a cigarette, told her his name was Ray then started to flirt with her. Being unused to male attention in a romantic way, she lost all sense and reason, allowing herself to be swept off her feet by his patter and found herself agreeing to meet him for a drink when the fairground closed down for the night. She was both nervous and excited about her assignation, this being her very first with a man. He was waiting for her as promised at the entrance to the fair. Despite her friends' warnings to her not to go, she went off with him. He took her to an isolated spot by the dunes and for a while they talked and drank from cans of lager he had bought with him . . . Sally was not keen as she didn't usually drink but did so that night as she didn't wish to appear juvenile to him.

Then unexpectedly he'd leaned over and kissed her and the next thing she knew he was all over her, kissing and fondling her while continually repeating words of endearment. He had had his way with her before she really had time to realise what was happening. After it was over he told her he was just off around the back of the dune to relieve himself and wouldn't be a moment, then he would walk her back home and make arrangements to see her again. Half an hour later Sally realised he wasn't coming back. Feeling humiliated and defiled, she hurried back up the beach and off home, where she scrubbed herself clean and cried herself to sleep. To add to her mortification that she had allowed herself to be seduced so easily, she discovered the next morning that the man had emptied her purse of the couple of pounds and loose change she had in it without her even noticing.

When she had discovered she was pregnant nearly three months later Sally was out of her mind with worry and couldn't bring herself to relate her shame to her beloved family. Despite the thought terrifying her, she felt that there was no other option for her but to have an abortion.

Sally's story was far from unique and in truth, apart from the fact that the man had stolen from her purse, he had done nothing unlawful as she had given herself to him willingly. Regardless, fuelled by his overwhelming grief after her death, Reg was adamant that the man was somehow going to pay for callously taking advantage of his daughter's innocence, even if it meant Reg himself had to go to jail for murder. But his quest to avenge his daughter did not prove easy. Along with two of his burly workers, on the night of Sally's death Reg had gone to the fair to seek the man out. The owner of the Waltzers informed him that casual fairground workers came and went, some stayed only a day, some a few weeks, so he could hardly be expected to remember the names of all those who worked for him. And besides, many casual fairground workers were on the run from the police or from other villains so there was a distinct possibility that Ray wasn't his true name.

Having nothing to go on by way of identification, the search for his daughter's killer, as that was how Reg saw him and so did her mother and her sister, ground to a halt. They believed they had no other choice but to accept the fact that the man would never be brought to task for what he had been responsible for, and as best they could they must get on with their lives without Sally being present.

But all that was about to change.

There was a knock on his office door. Reg turned from the window to look over and see who his visitor was. He first smiled with recognition, then frowned in concern when he saw the look on their face.

'What is it?' he asked.

What the visitor told him froze him rigid. 'I know the identity of the man who was responsible for Sally's death.'

Reg then listened in stunned silence as it was explained to him just how his visitor had made the discovery. When they had finished he turned back to face the window staring blindly out of it for what seemed an age before he asked: 'How do you fancy a change of job for a while?'

CHAPTER EIGHT

Patsy was frowning with concern as she and Dixie discreetly watched a panel of four Stripeys judging the talents of a hundred or so excited young hopefuls who wanted to be among the thirty taking part in the twelve-to-fourteen years talent show scheduled for Friday afternoon in the Paradise ballroom.

Patsy had been in her new job for just over two weeks now and it had taken her all that time to decipher Terry's almost illegible scrawl on his numerous scribbled notes and planning sheets as she attempted to work out his procedures for running the department. As she had laboured it had become clear to her that Terry was lazy, didn't forward plan for any event, just seemed to think his job entailed him assigning staff haphazardly to cover each event for that day then let them get on with it.

It didn't appear he had brought anything new to the job since taking it on. His predecessor she knew had been excellent at his job but was sacked along with his accomplice for stealing from campers two seasons ago. It also seemed that Terry's idea of inducting a new member to the team who had never handled a particular task before was to throw them in at the deep end, expecting them to learn from their mistakes, instead of taking the time to impart his wealth of experience to them and putting them alongside an experienced member of staff until they were competent to handle a job on their own. Patsy was already aware of Terry's predatory reputation and it was glaringly obvious to her that when he assigned staff to manage events, Terry would award the best jobs to his favoured team members. It appeared though that where an event involved young pretty teenagers, then Terry always put himself in charge. It was her guess, judging by his past history, that he would try and bribe the prettiest with a promise that he would ensure she won, in exchange for certain favours.

Patsy was most surprised that Terry's total unsuitability to head up such a crucial team of people, whose contribution towards the campers' enjoyment of their stay was paramount, hadn't been obvious to the management. She could only conclude that it was the loyalty to Jolly's and the experience of many of the Stripeys under his charge that had masked Terry's shortcomings.

It was hard enough to take over the job of another with no handover whatsoever, but to take over from the likes of Terry was proving frustrating to say the least. As it was the beginning of the season the full complement of Stripeys wasn't on board yet. Thankfully most of those here at the moment had been with Jolly's for a more than a couple of seasons and been trained by Terry's predecessor so were very competent at their jobs. But there were those amongst them who had started their jobs with Terry as boss and the difference in their attitude was marked. She had repeatedly observed the same faces hiding behind the back of the shops smoking; in groups idly chatting together; looking disinterested and disengaged during events. Terry's one good point, if indeed he had had one, was that he was always clean and smart but some of the Stripeys' uniforms fell far short of the expected standard as did their personal hygiene. Their bloodshot eyes and general air of tiredness made it obvious their after-hours enjoyment was more important to them than their work was, and left them hardly any time for sleep.

Terry's idea of running a department was far removed from Patsy's and she meant to have it back operating as efficiently as it had in the past under more conscientious leaders and then make it even better by implementing her own ideas, not only for the benefit of the campers in making their holiday live up to all their expectations but for the sake of the staff themselves.

She wanted to be the kind of leader who actually led and made the staff fulfilled and happy in their jobs. She knew a daunting task faced her but was determined to succeed if only to repay a debt of gratitude to Harold Rose for giving her the job and a chance to prove she had what it took.

Patsy was still totally unaware of the fact that she was given it only because Harold had mistaken her for Dixie; he was made aware of this when Mavis Durham came charging into the general office the morning after Patsy was promoted, demanding to see him, extremely miffed that a member of her staff had been moved to another job without any warning and she'd learned of this state of affairs via another nursery nurse who shared a chalet with Patsy. Harold had stared at her dumbstruck for an age, trying to work out how this had happened, until he had to conclude that in his rush to leave for the function he had obviously thought Patsy was Terry's assistant when she had come to the office on another matter.

The right thing for him to have done was own up to his error, return Patsy to her previous position and install Terry's real assistant as Head Stripey. But not only had he already introduced Patsy as their new boss at a Stripey gathering, but when he had talked to her afterwards in the Head Stripey's office she had thanked him so profusely for giving her this opportunity, been so adamant she would give it her all, that he hadn't the heart to disappoint her and decided it was only fair Patsy be at least given a fair trial in order to prove her worth or not. And considering the Stripey who had been Terry's assistant hadn't come forward to challenge Patsy's appointment, he assumed they must be in agreement with it. He would give Patsy a month and assess the situation then while he kept a discreet eye on her progress, he decided. Mavis Durham had gone back to the nursery after Harold had told her he agreed that this matter could have been handled better, regardless of the need to appoint a replacement for Terry, and that a new nursery nurse would be recruited as a matter of urgency.

Patsy said to Dixie now, 'Would you mind going to join the

judging panel and taking charge as discreetly as you can? I fear if they carry on upsetting the youngsters in the way they are, we're going to have an army of angry parents out for our blood.' Before Dixie went off, Patsy caught her arm and told her, 'I just want to thank you for all the help you're giving me to get to grips with my job. I really do appreciate it.'

Dixie shot her a look as if to say, There's no need to thank me, it's my pleasure. As she turned and headed off to join the panel of Stripeys judging the contestants for the talent show, she thought to herself: You wouldn't appreciate me so much if you knew how much I was going to help you out of your job and get it for myself.

At just after twelve that night, Dixie thrust open the door to her chalet, barged through, kicked the door shut behind her then threw herself on her bed. Her chalet mate, Valerie Pringle, a fellow Stripey who'd started the same time as Dixie, had arrived back just ahead of her and was sitting on her bed, wiping off her makeup with cotton wool and cleansing lotion.

She asked Dixie, 'How's the plan shaping up?

Dixie shot back, 'Give me time. I'm still planning my strategy . . .'

Before she could get any further Val erupted into laughter. '*Strategy!* That's a big word for a girl dragged up on a council estate to know. And you're not Churchill planning a war.'

Dixie eyes blazed at her. 'Just because your parents owned their own house and my parents rented theirs from the council, doesn't make you any better than me. I didn't have to have my baths in a tin tub in front of the fire, with water heated up by a boiler in the outhouse, like you and your family did. We had a proper bathroom with hot and cold running water. And we had a garden to play in, not a tiny paved yard. And the school I went to on our estate was modern with new facilities, not like the old one you told me you went to.'

Not finding fitting words to respond, Val changed the subject back to what she had originally asked. 'So what *strategy* are you going to use to get Patsy sacked and Harold Rose to appoint you instead? It's been over two weeks you've been planning how to tackle this. If it had been me I'd have done loads by now to make her look an idiot and show Harold Rose what a mistake he made in giving her the job. Instead of helping her settle in you could have been unhelpful, pointed her in the wrong direction not the right one, if you get my drift.'

Dixie sneered at her. 'You brainless cow. Remind me not to ask you for your ideas if I want help with a plan in future. Not that I would need any help from anyone as I'm capable of planning things for myself. If I did what you said it wouldn't take Fat Ugly Pat long to work out who her enemy in the camp was, and what I was up to, and even if she didn't report me to Harold Rose for my backstabbing and get me sacked, she could easily replace me with someone else as her assistant and then I'd never get her job, would I? My mother always told me to keep my enemies close. I have to be careful what I plan, to make sure nothing can come back on me.'

Val looked impressed. 'Yeah, I see your point.' She paused for a moment before adding, 'I don't think that was nice what you called her, Dixie. She a big girl but not fat and she's not what I'd call pretty but she's certainly not ugly either. I have to say, I quite like Patsy. It was nice what she told us when she got us all together the first day she started: that she appreciated us all bearing with her while she settled into the job and came up with ideas for changes to make our jobs better for us. And if we had any ideas for improvements, to feel free to tell her. Unlike Terry, who was only interested in using the job for his own ends and virtually leaving us to it. You couldn't call him a boss in any sense of the word, but I have to say I feel Patsy would make a good one, given the chance.'

Dixie raged at her, 'Hey, whose side are you on, Val? I thought you were my friend. You'd best not say anything like that to the others. I want them turned against her, not rooting for her.' She wagged a warning finger at her chalet mate. 'When you get the opportunity you're to subtly tell the others that it's me that's really running the show, that Patsy is using my ideas . . . only the good ones she comes up with, mind, not those that fall flat . . . making out that they're her own, and then they'll start to look to me to lead them, leaving her out in the cold. Once I've made her look a fool a few times, Harold Rose will have no choice but to toss her out on her ear and promote me. You got that?' She smirked at Val. 'I might not have put any of my plan in action yet but meanwhile I've been sucking up to her and making her think I'm the best thing since sliced bread, so she'll listen to me. When I tell her how useless you are at your job, it'll be you that'll be packing your bags!'

Val looked aghast. 'You wouldn't do that! I love my job here.'

Dixie's smirk broadened. 'Well then, if you don't want to go home with your tail between your legs, you'd better do as I say.'

Tight-lipped, Val returned to cleaning her face. Whether she liked it or not, Dixie had the upper hand as she was in a position to make trouble for any member of the entertainments team as Patsy's assistant. Val had had the devil's own job persuading her mother to allow her to work away from home in the first place, and had only gained agreement by begging and promising to behave herself. So if she returned in disgrace on the trumped up charge she knew the devious Dixie would concoct, her mother would be furious and make her go to work alongside her in the hosiery factory where she could keep an eye on her. The thought terrified Val and so she had no choice but to do Dixie's bidding. What Val hadn't told her was that the reason none of the other Stripeys had protested about an outsider being given the job was that it was preferable to having Dixie as their boss.

Having put Val straight on what she expected of her, Dixie stretched out on her bed, folded her arms behind her head and leaned back against the wall, deep in thought. If she were more honest she would admit to Val that, to her own annoyance, as she had grown to know Patsy while working alongside her, Dixie had found herself liking her too. Patsy had a personality that drew you to her and enveloped you with her genuine warmth, thoughtfulness for others and great sense of humour. And she was far more intelligent than Dixie had given her credit for. Anyone who could make a morsel of sense of Terry's methods of operating from his scribbled notes and haphazard staff schedules, which had all proved gobbledegook to Dixie herself, had to be bordering on a genius. Even just two weeks into the job she was proving herself a far better boss to work for than Terry had been. Patsy actually thanked you for anything you did for her; never disappeared for lengths of time to pursue her own interests when she should have been doing her duties as supervisor; didn't treat Dixie or any of the team like they were village idiots when they made mistakes. Dixie was secretly impressed by the ideas Patsy had shared with her for how she planned to improve the department. Unwillingly, she found herself excited by the prospect of helping Patsy to implement them. In all the time she had been part of the entertainments team she had never known Terry come up with any new ideas. In truth Patsy did not deserve what she had coming to her. But Dixie had never let sentiment cloud her vision for the future she wanted for herself. Patsy was blocking her way, but not for much longer if Dixie got her way.

She leaned down and fished with her hand under her bed until she found what she was after. She withdrew her hand clutching a notepad with a biro clipped to it. She then leaned down again, pulled up her handbag and took out a folded piece of paper. Unfolding the paper, she laid it across the notepad. After studying what was written on it for a moment, with eyes flicking back and forth between the writing on the piece of paper and the blank sheet in her notebook, she began to write.

All this time Val had been watching her. Now curiosity as to what she doing got the better of her. 'What you up to, Dixie?

The other girl lifted her head from her task and shot her a sly grin. 'Just practising copying Patsy's handwriting and signature in case I need it later on. Woman of many talents I am, Val. I became a dab hand at forging my mother's writing to excuse my absences from school when I was playing truant. Even she didn't know my forgeries from the real thing . . . and neither will Patsy if I ever have to forge her writing . . .'

In a chalet a couple of rows behind Dixie's and Val's, Patsy too lay stretched out on her bed, arms folded behind her head, deep in thought.

Her chalet mate Jan, a nursery nurse of twenty-two, turned over in the bed adjacent to Patsy's and grumbled, 'I can't sleep, knowing you're lying wide awake. Look, if this new job is causing you sleepless nights then maybe it's too much for you and you should come back to the nursery. There's no shame in admitting you've bitten off more than you can chew. I miss you at the nursery, Patsy. It was fun when you were there. It's still fun but not half so much. And no one else has the knack of shutting up screaming kids up like you do.'

In the darkness Patsy smiled and said in all seriousness, 'I just threaten them with the bogeyman and it usually works.'

Jan exclaimed, aghast, 'You scared them into shutting up?'

Patsy chuckled. 'Don't be daft. Of course I didn't. Most are only missing their mums. A cuddle and a few soothing words usually did the trick.'

'Well, that's just what I do, but I don't seem to have the success that you did.' Jan chuckled herself then. 'I might try the bogeyman next time and see if that works.' She paused for a moment before adding, 'So can't you sleep because the job is too much for you?'

'There were times I thought it was, when I first started. But now I've given up trying to work out how Terry operated . . . well, to be honest, I don't think he had any structured system. I'm just going to implement my own. I've learned a lot over the years I've been with Jolly's about how other supervisors run their teams and I'm going to operate using a mixture of their methods and some new ideas of my own.' She heaved a worried sigh. 'I just have to hope now that my plan works and I don't end up with the team in chaos and me out on my ear.'

No matter how much Jan would like that to happen for her own selfish reasons she told her friend, 'I know you, Patsy, and you're going to make the best Head Stripey Jolly's has ever had. Now for God's sake, settle down and go to sleep so I can. I have hundreds of lively kids to deal with in the morning, and if old Starchy Knickers find me asleep in one of the cots tomorrow because I didn't get any sleep tonight, I will hold you personally responsible for getting me the sack.'

Patsy chuckled as she switched off the light and snuggled down under the covers.

CHAPTER NINE

Head chef Eric Brown was shaking his head in frustration; nursery supervisor Mavis Durham had her lips pursed in disapproval; Eileen Waters, cleaning supervisor, was looking everywhere but where she wanted to and that was at the love of her life who had no idea he was at the centre of her affections; retail supervisor Donna Salter was tapping her notepad with the end of her biro, eyes fixed on Harold Rose in anticipation; Sid Harper, head of maintenance, was looking impatiently at his wrist watch and wishing he could find an excuse to leave as he'd said all he had to and was thoroughly bored now; Head Stripey Patsy Mathers desperately wanted to put forward a suggestion but still hadn't been in her new role long enough to speak out of turn; Bill Johns, bar manager and secret drinker, bordering on alcoholic, was desperate for alcohol and praying for something to happen to break up the gathering; Jason Potts, camp photographer, was wishing he'd his camera with him so he could take a photograph of all the varying expressions on the faces of the gathering, from indifference to annoyance, so he could make up a collage and enter it into a national competition as he felt sure it would win; fairground manager, the fearsome-looking Jim Davis, was shifting restlessly in his seat, fighting sleep as he detested meetings of any sort and this one was going on far too long for his liking; Jill Clayton was looking impassive, pencil poised ready to continue taking down the minutes of the meeting as soon as someone spoke; Harold Rose was feeling slight discomfiture as he didn't like being the centre of attention, which he was now as the meeting's chairman.

It was the fortnightly heads of department meeting and those present were all packed around Harold's desk, empty cups of tea and coffee before them, only a couple of custard creams left on a plate that had been full when the meeting first began over an hour ago. The minutes of the last meeting had been read, actions taken on outstanding issues relayed, and each head of department had had their say on current issues and problems pertinent to their department and been satisfied with plans for rectification by management. Staffing issues had been addressed. Thinking business was concluded, Harold was just about to draw things to a close when Eric chose that moment to bring up a problem that in its way affected all the heads of department, who had got together beforehand and elected him their spokesperson.

He said now, 'We've never had trouble on this scale before, Harold. We all appreciate that coming here must be like being let loose in paradise to them, but you'd think in the circumstances they'd be grateful to be given a holiday and on their best behaviour. Admittedly it's not all of them, just a handful, with a ringleader who's a right little tearaway. Tommy Biddle his name is. I didn't know kids knew swear words like the ones that came out of his mouth when I gave him short shift for coming into my kitchen like he was Lord Duck Muck, when he knows very well it's out of bounds to the campers. He and his band of minions have been stealing from the shop, but managed to scarper and get rid of their spoils before they were caught so no proof could be produced. They've caused mayhem, running around the restaurant, dodging in and out of the other tables while people are still eating, knocking into the waitresses and causing some to drop what they were carrying. None of the gang would come off the boating lake when their time was up and didn't until an hour later.

'I could go on, Harold, but in a nutshell they are causing mayhem around the camp and us managers one big headache.

It's obvious Tommy Biddle and the gang are intent on causing as much trouble as they can before they go home. We should do what my dad did to me and my brother when we messed about. Give them a good hiding then lock them in the coal shed and only feed them bread and water. That might teach them a lesson.'

Several of the gathering looked appalled at the idea of doing that to the boys, whereas other expressed agreement.

Harold had been aware of the misbehaving children but out of respect for the managers had left it to them to deal with, only getting involved when they requested him to. He had secretly hoped to be spared having to confront the children's carers and question their ability to control some of their charges. But whatever action they took, Eric's suggestion was not the way to deal with the matter. Harold reminded the big man: 'This is a holiday camp, Eric, not a Borstal. We have to feel some pity for these boys. No parents of their own to love or guide them . . . being raised by a succession of strangers who come and go at the orphanage.'

Eric gave a shrug of his massive shoulders. 'There were lots of kids around the streets where I grew up who lost parents in the war one way or another, some both of them even, and they didn't act like hooligans. In the past, the staff sent to shepherd the orphans have been the sort even I wouldn't have dared said "Boo" to for all my size, but the staff sent this time, from what I've seen, haven't it in them to organise a piss up in a brewery, let alone thirty delinquent kids.' He then realised his language had strayed and apologised to the women for his use of it in their presence, before adding, 'For the sake of the other campers and our sanity, I don't see that we have any other alternative but to send them home. In this business we often have to deal in one way or another with unruly kids but I know I speak for us all when I say I don't think I can stand another four days of the level of disruption this handful of boys are causing.'

The expressions around the table showed everyone agreed with Eric.

Harold heavily sighed and said with concern, 'It seems a shame that the rest of the orphans should suffer because of the bad behaviour of a few. Doing something for these poor kids to bring a bit of fun into their pitiful lives, even if it's just for a few days, is something very close to Mrs Jolly's heart. I know if she were here now she wouldn't send them back to the orphanage without at least giving them another chance. I shall have the troublemakers rounded up and give them a warning that if they don't stop their shenanigans then they will be sent home in disgrace, leaving the rest of their party here, and will have to face whatever punishment awaits them from the governor of the orphanage.'

Eric wasn't the only one to look at him as though he were mad. 'Well, you're the boss,' was all he said.

'Mmm,' murmured Harold. There were times when he wished he weren't, and he hoped he didn't come to regret his decision over the young ruffians.

The meeting was then brought to a close and they all took their leave. Before she departed Harold took Patsy aside and asked her how she was continuing to get on in her new role. He felt a certain amount of guilt for mistaking Patsy for someone else and heaping the responsibilities of a job on her that she didn't have the experience to tackle. To his gratification, though, she enthused to him about how much she was enjoying her new position and expressed nothing but gratitude to him for giving her the opportunity to better herself. She was determined not to let him down.

In the general office Marion couldn't fail to notice the wide grin on Jill's face as she fed paper into her typewriter in order to type up the minutes of the meeting.

Marion couldn't resist asking what the cause of her boss's amusement was and hoped the switchboard didn't buzz for her attention before she'd heard the answer. She certainly had nothing in her own life to make her smile and a bit of a cheer up at the expense of someone else would be most welcome. 'Did something funny happen in the meeting?'

Jill looked over at her, bemused.

'Well, you've got a grin on your face to rival the Cheshire Cat's and I'm just being nosy about the cause?'

Jill looked surprised. 'Have I? I didn't realise. Oh, well, yes, I did find something about the meeting very amusing, but then to the people concerned it's not really a laughing matter.'

Curiosity sparked in Marion's eyes. 'Just what is the so-called *matter*?'

Jill looked thoughtfully at Marion for a moment. It was against her nature to gossip about anyone, and certainly not her boss to whom she knew she owed her loyalty. It was a bonus of this job that she actually liked her superior and had grown very fond of him over the weeks she had worked for him. But she wouldn't mind another woman's opinion on the plan she had in mind and some ideas on how she could carry it out, which as yet had failed to present themselves There was no danger of Harold overhearing as he had followed the managers out to do the morning camp inspection.

Jill's eyes sparkled with excitement. 'Well, you see, it's obvious that Harold and Eileen are in love with each other, but neither of them is willing to be the first to do anything about it.'

Marion had too many of her own problems to take much more than a passing interest in any other member of staff, but was aware of course of Harold and knew Eileen by sight. 'Well, I expect between them they haven't had that much experience with the opposite sex. Neither of them has that much going for them. Harold's certainly no Rock Hudson. I mean, he's nice enough but he's very correct in his manner, a bit stiff really, I can't imagine he'd ever say a swear word, even in anger. I expect spending a night in his company would be about as exciting as a game of draughts. As for Eileen, well, she's not exactly Elizabeth Taylor, is she? More the type that's never had a boyfriend, let alone sex.'

Jill's eyes widened in shock. She had not expected such a response from Marion. She responded sharply: 'Well, they might not be the sort to turn heads but looks aren't everything,

Marion. In their individual way they each have a lot to offer one another. Eileen is a lovely person and so kind, she's a brilliant dressmaker and very knowledgeable about all sorts of things because she reads such a lot. As for Harold, well, he's not only kind and considerate and intelligent too, a qualified accountant, he has his own house and I can't imagine he's short of a bob or two. And he's got to be completely trustworthy for the owner of Jolly's to have left him in sole charge. I haven't met Mrs Jolly yet but from what I have gathered this camp means everything to her so she's not going to hand over the reins to anyone lightly.'

Marion mentally scolded herself. She had spoken her thoughts out loud without any thought to the wise. Her position here at Jolly's was dependent on Jill's say so, and it was apparent she was the type always to show loyalty to a superior. If she felt Marion didn't share the same loyalty, she might decide to replace her with someone who showed more respect towards their boss. As there were no other jobs open to Marion yet she couldn't risk jeopardising her position here. She put a contrite expression on her face and said apologetically, 'I am sorry, Jill. I should never have spoken about Mr Rose and Miss Walters like that. I didn't mean it. It's that time of the month and you know what that does to us women. You're right, they would make a lovely couple.'

She felt the need to veer away from the subject of her own bad behaviour. Smiling at Jill, she asked: 'So what did you find so funny about them in the meeting?'

Thankfully for Marion it seemed her hastily thought up excuse satisfied Jill as the sparkle returned to her eyes and she responded. 'Oh, just that it was so obvious they were doing their best not to look at each other in case they happened to give their feelings away and make fools of themselves.'

Marion privately thought that if Harold didn't possess enough gumption to ask a woman out, he deserved to be on his own. Being careful though she responded, 'It is such a shame that they're both too shy to speak up, isn't it?'

Jill nodded. 'Yes, it is, and that's why I intend to play Cupid.'

'Oh, how?'

Well, I've decided that they both need a nudge in the right direction or they'll never get together but I've been wracking my brains and not been able to come up with something yet that's not so childish or obvious they'll guess it's a put-up job. But now I've trusted you with this, I'm roping you in to help me come up with something. So, any ideas?'

Marion pulled a face. 'Not off the top of my head but I'll give it some thought.'

Jill looked excited. 'Well, between us, I'm sure we'll come up with something.'

CHAPTER TEN

At a quarter to three that afternoon Harold sat perched on a high stool at one of the stainless-steel work benches in the big camp kitchen along with Eric Brown, drinking tea, while butter from a freshly baked scone dribbled down his chin.

The men were as different as chalk from cheese despite both being forty years old. Where Harold was slight and ordinary-looking, with thinning brown hair and metal-framed spectacles, Eric on the other hand was almost as wide as he was tall, which was nearly six foot, with a mass of unruly greying hair sprouting from the top of his head as if he'd stuck his finger in an electric socket. He had brown eyes that twinkled merrily though they were almost lost inside his round chubby face. He had a smile for everybody except for the odd occasion when something or someone managed to upset his normal good humour. Stained chef's whites strained across his wide girth and black-and-white-checked chef's trousers covered legs like tree trunks

This odd couple had become good friends ever since last summer when Eric had agreed to aid Jackie Sims in her quest to improve Harold's solitary life. When time allowed, Harold would visit the kitchen for a chat with Eric mid-afternoon when he knew that the chef would have finished catching up on paperwork and be taking a break before the kitchen staff returned to start making preparations for the evening meal.

They both sat in silence as they ate. Eventually Harold sighed contentedly and said, 'No one could ever accuse you of not being an able cook, Eric.'

The grin that split his huge face told Harold how pleased his friend was with this compliment. 'I can't claim to be in the likes of Fanny Cradock's league but what I make is edible. Though I'd like to see *her* cope with feeding thousands of empty bellies three times a day! To be fair, though, I couldn't do it without my army of under chefs and kitchen assistants. Got a good bunch with me at the moment, I'm glad to say, and I hope they all remain until the end of the season. Oh, all except one, that is. I meant to tell you about him in the meeting this morning but it slipped my mind with the rest of the managers badgering me into being spokesman about those little tearaways.'

Harold drained his mug of tea before he told Eric, 'Well, on that subject, after the meeting I had the boys in question rounded up. Captured is more like it! Half a dozen strapping Stripeys went after the boys as they were running riot around the tennis court, pinching the balls and throwing them at the campers who were trying to play a tournament at the time. Anyway, I gave them a severe talking to, told them what would happen to them if they didn't start behaving themselves, so hopefully we'll have no more trouble with them.'

Eric hid a smile. Knowing this mild-mannered man as well as he did, he felt Harold hadn't it in him to frighten anyone into submission. Oh, no doubt the lads would have looked suitably shame-faced after the reprimand, but it was his guess that as soon as Harold had left, they'd have been laughing mercilessly behind his back and it wouldn't be long before they were causing mayhem again.

Harold was looking at Eric. 'I get the feeling you're not hopeful of them behaving themselves for the rest of their stay?'

Eric shot him a knowing look. 'Well, let's put it this way: if I were a betting man I'd sooner take odds on them misbehaving than not. Another scone?' he asked, pushing a plate piled with them in Harold's direction.

Harold pulled back his shirt cuff and glanced at his wrist watch. 'I really ought to be getting back to the office.' His eyes then fell on the scones and the temptation to have another was too much. 'Yes, go on then.' Cutting the scone in half, he spread each piece with a thick layer of butter, picked up one half and took a bite, then spluttered out a blast of crumbs when Eric asked him, 'So, my friend, just when are you going to pluck up the courage to ask Eileen Walters on a date?'

Harold's face turned red with embarrassment and he blustered, 'I . . . I . . . I . . . What on earth made you asked me that? '

Eric leaned over and slapped a meaty hand against Harold's back. A friendly gesture on his part though it nearly toppled Harold off his stool. 'Oh, come on, man, it's as plain as a pike-staff to me that you fancy the pants off the woman.'

Harold was about to deny it but liar he wasn't, and especially not to a friend. His face contorted into an expression resembling that of a silly schoolboy admitting he had a crush on a teacher. 'I do rather like her, Eric.'

'She's a nice woman, is Eileen. A dab hand with a needle, too, which is handy when you haven't a woman of your own. She patched a tear in a pair of trousers so well for me you can't see it. What's holding you back then?'

A film of sweat appeared on Harold's brow and he ran a finger around his collar. 'Well . . . er . . .'

Eric cut in. 'Oh, I see. Your old problem rearing its ugly head, is it? Listen, mate, all us blokes are feared of looking a fool when it comes to approaching a lady we have our eye on, in case she rejects us, so you aren't anything special in that respect. You either take the bull by the horns or you let her get away, it's that simple.'

Harold didn't at all like the thought of another man capturing Eileen's affections, but overriding that was his fear of rejection. 'But what if . . .'

'Just forget the *what if's*, Harold. If every man stopped to consider all the pitfalls, the human race would have died out aeons ago. Just have a go, man.'

Harold heaved a deep sigh, shifting uncomfortably on his stool. 'But . . . well, you see . . . I've . . . er . . . never asked a woman out before and I don't know how to go about it.'

Eric thought: I should have known that, since I'm quite aware of how emotionally crippled Harold was before Jackie made it her mission to do something about that.

'You might not be talking to the right man,' he said slowly. 'I'm no expert as I've not asked that many out myself.'

Harold eyed him in surprise. 'Haven't you? I'd have thought a good-looking man like you would have had lots of lady friends in your past.'

Eric grinned. 'You're too kind, sir. I've had a few dalliances over the years but can't claim to have had lots. I can't actually remember when I last had a girlfriend. A good while ago now it must be. My brother was the one for the women. He had a way with them that I didn't share. I never knew a woman to turn him down once he decided he liked the look of her.'

'You've never mentioned you have a brother, Eric.'

A fleeting look of sadness crossed his face. 'I haven't seen him for years, eighteen at least. It hurts to talk about him so that's why I don't. We were close at one time, but the day he got married everything changed.' Eric's eyes glazed over and it was apparent to Harold that his friend's mind had travelled back to the past as he continued speaking.

'We looked very much alike when we were younger, some even took us for twins, but he's a year older than me. Still, if I say it myself, we were both good-looking lads. In all other ways we were as different as bread from butter, though. I was the quiet one, the plodder, got a job as a labourer on a building site and stuck that until I joined the army when I was eighteen, in the catering corps. Jeremy, though, was a Jack the Lad, flitted from job to job. He only had to look at a woman with his big brown eyes and you could practically see their legs turn to jelly. He never stayed with anyone for more than a couple of weeks at a time . . . he was a free spirit was Jerry and settling down and having a family was the last thing on his mind. We were both tall and slim in those days. I don't know if Jerry still is, but I'm certainly not, am I?' said Eric, patting his huge stomach. 'I blame the job for my size. Well, you have to sample what you cook, to know whether it's sweet enough or needs more seasoning. Despite the differences between us, my brother was a good sort and I idolised him Then Jerry met Alison and his Jack the Lad days were over.

'He met her at a dance and at first he fancied her rotten. But after a few dances he realised that she was the clingy sort and didn't want to get involved with her. Getting rid of her wasn't that easy. Everywhere he went after that, she would be there, making cow eyes at him. One night he'd had too much to drink and ended up making love to her, but afterwards made it clear that he wasn't interested in having a relationship. He thought she'd accepted that as he never saw her out and about afterwards. But a couple of months later her father caught up with Jerry when he was out with his mates one evening.

'Alison's dad owned a very prosperous business making Sheffield plate cutlery, was quite a wealthy man, with a big house, flashy car, friends in high places. He told Jerry that Alison was pregnant with his baby and if he didn't do the decent thing and marry her then not only would he never see his child, but her dad would make sure that Jerry, me and our father all lost our jobs in the factory where we worked, as Alison's old man was good friends with the owner. Furthermore he'd make sure we never found work in the town again. Jerry was also warned that once he and Alison were married, he was to cut all ties with us. We were scum from a back street as far as her father was concerned, and not good enough to be part of their family. Jerry was to work for his father-in-law from then on. He was having no common factory worker marrying his daughter.

'Jerry never told us any of this until after the marriage had taken place as he said he knew that I and our mum and dad would sooner be on the streets than live with the knowledge that he'd been forced to marry a woman he'd only been with for one night, didn't love or particularly like in fact, just for our sakes. But he loved and cared for us deeply enough to make that sacrifice. We never saw Jerry again. It broke my parents' hearts, and mine too, to know that we never would.

We never stopped worrying about what kind of life he was living under the watchful eye of his tyrant father-in-law and needy, clingy wife, and we never stopped missing him. We only learned my parents were grandparents and I was an uncle through the announcements in the local paper on the births of both their children. We occasionally saw photographs of Jerry and Alison together at some posh do or other and he looked happy enough so that was our only consolation, that somehow he'd learned to love his wife and was living happily with her and their children.'

Eric stopped talking then, seeming to give himself a mental shake. 'Sorry, Harold, I got carried away. I didn't mean to bore you. But anyway, it's a shame things went the way they did with my brother or you'd have been able to telephone him and he would have told you exactly what to do to get yourself a date with Eileen.'

Eric's story had touched Harold and he felt sorry for his friend for having a brother he wasn't allowed to have anything to do with, thanks to a single mistake made years ago. He asked the big man, 'Any reason why you never married, Eric?'

He gave a shrug. 'Just never met anyone I thought enough of to want to spend the rest of my life with, and of course when you're in the forces not many girls like the thought of having to move around and keep starting afresh with every new posting. I've got used to being on my own now and rather like my life the way it is: being able to do what I please, spend my money as I like, and have no woman ordering me about and nagging me for leaving the toilet seat up! If I ever do meet a woman in the future, she'll have to be very special for me to give up what I've got.'

Eileen was a special enough woman for Harold to give up his bachelor life and settle down with her. But that would never be on the agenda if he didn't summon the courage up to ask her out on a first date.

'You said you'd had a few dalliances in your youth, Eric, so in that case you must have initially asked the lady in question to go out with you. So how did you approach it?' he asked, hoping for step-by-step instructions.

Eric looked thoughtful for a moment and then confessed, 'While shaking with nerves and hoping the girl I had my eye on liked the chat-up lines I'd picked up from my brother enough to say yes. Nine times out of ten they didn't, just laughed, and I was left feeling a fool. Best thing is to get her on her own and ask her straight out if she'd like to go for a drink or a meal with you. And do it before someone else beats you to it.'

Eric's suggestion sounded easy enough for anyone but Harold. For him it felt like facing a firing squad. But he was determined to find the courage, take the bull by the horns and do it. And the next time he saw Eileen too. Feeling embarrassed, as a grown man, that he'd had to ask another man's advice on how to ask a woman out, Harold wanted to change the subject before he humiliated himself any further. Then something Eric had said earlier came back to mind. 'Did you say you were having a problem with one of your kitchen staff?'

'Yes, I did. He's new this year, and what a lazy so and so he's turning out to be! But I'm going to take a leaf out of your book, give him a warning, and if he doesn't pull his socks up by the end of the week, I'll see you about hiring a replacement.'

Harold then took his leave. As he was walking towards the door leading outside, Eric called after him, 'We still on for a drink and game of darts on Friday night? Unless of course you've a better offer between now and then,' he added meaningfully.

Harold hoped his resolve didn't wane and he had something else to do.

Marion arrived back at the caravan at just after six that night and as soon as she opened the door was asked the same question as she was every evening: 'Got a job yet that pays enough to get us out of this hovel?'

She angrily kicked the door shut behind her and took off her coat. 'Oh, for God's sake, Mother, how many times have I asked

93

you to give it a rest? As soon as I do, you'll be the first to know.' She fixed her eyes on the heater set to full, spewing out its stifling heat and nauseating fumes. 'Have you had that on high all day? I keep telling you that I can't afford a gallon of paraffin every other day and when that can runs out there's no more until pay day on Friday, and if I have to get dressed in the cold each morning for work and sit in the cold in the evening, through your selfishness, then I won't be happy, believe me.' She looked over at the two-ring burner and said accusingly, 'Haven't you even got the dinner started?' She fixed her eyes on her mother, sitting in her usual place at the front of the caravan. Marion's tone was sharp. 'Trip to the corner shop for our groceries all you could manage today, because you don't seem to have done anything else?'

Ida spoke sardonically. 'You wait, my girl, until you get old and just hope you haven't half my ailments. A trip to the shops might be a short walk for you, but with my legs, and especially carrying bags of heavy shopping, it's like walking up Everest! I've nothing left in me when I get back here to do anything else. Anyway, you can hardly call a warmed up tin of Irish stew, which looks as disgusting as it tastes, "dinner". You wouldn't feed a dog that muck.'

Then Ida could not control her sharp tongue and blasted out a tirade of anger at her daughter for her mindless actions that had landed them in their current dire situation. Marion had heard this same tirade so many times now she could almost repeat it word for word. As she busied herself with their meal, she fought to blank it out, just as she did the background crackle of interference on the wireless when she was listening to the old transistor she had picked up in a junk shop for a shilling.

Marion didn't know how much longer her nerves could stand living on top of her mother in such cramped conditions. She had thought it was bad enough when Ida moved herself into Lionel's house. But at least there Marion could escape from her domineering ways when they'd become too much by going to her bedroom or out to visit a friend or else getting Lionel to take her out somewhere. But the only bedroom in the caravan had been commandeered by Ida and now Marion had no friends to visit or husband to take her out and pamper her. Maybe she could bear it if there was a light at the end of the long dark tunnel of despair she found herself in. But as matters stood there was no end to it in sight and no hope to cling to that there ever would be.

Ida had obviously realised that Marion was not listening to her so she raised her voice several decibels. 'If you can't get a better-paid job in this Godforsaken backwater then what are you planning to do to get us out of here? I can't live like this any longer. The only hope I can see of us ever escaping this appalling life is if you find yourself a well set up man who can take us away from all this.'

Marion was struggling to get the tin of stew open with a blunt tin opener. Ida was still ranting on but what she had just said rang a bell in Marion's mind. Had her mother just come up with the answer to their problem? Get herself a well set-up man to lift them out of this situation they were in . . . Yes, it was the obvious answer, wasn't it? And thanks to a conversation she'd had that day she immediately knew of just the man who could do that for them. He didn't appeal at all to her physically, and his personality would no doubt prove very trying, but otherwise he fitted the bill perfectly and it was surprising what a person could put up with when needs must. Most older moneyed men would choose the blonde bombshell type they felt their money and status entitled them to, but that type of women would terrify the life out of the man she had in mind. The one who was going to be her saviour.

Marion was still very attractive, still had what it took to turn a man's head when she was all dressed up, could act the perfect hostess at dinner parties, the perfect companion at social functions, had all her own teeth and hardly any wrinkles . . . although how long that would remain the case if she continued living the hard existence she was, she didn't like to speculate. She knew how to flatter a man, how to make him feel special, and

95

was sure the man she had in mind could be easily bewitched once she turned her charms on him, considering his inexperience with the opposite sex. If she played this right, living in these dire conditions with hardly a penny to her name was very soon going to be a thing of the past. She knew it was best not to let Ida in on her plan. Her interfering mother would insist on being part of it and then ruin it, just like she had played a huge part in ruining her marriage.

She did have one problem to deal with, though, before she could put her plan into operation: getting Jill to drop her plan of bringing together the man and the woman he already had his eye on. Marion didn't know how she was going to go about that yet, but she would come up with something. And once she had, poor Harold Rose wouldn't know what had hit him.

CHAPTER ELEVEN

Patsy felt nausea rise up from her stomach to sting the back of her throat as a surge of panic seized her. What on earth was happening to her? She had believed she was coping well with the pressure of her job, but then she couldn't be, could she, or why did she keep making such stupid mistakes?

She was perched on a chair in Harold's office, and he was sitting opposite looking at her with an expectant expression on his face. Patsy had requested this meeting to put to him several changes she wished to make so as to improve the efficiency of her department. Before she had closed up her tiny office yesterday evening to go and add her support to the Stripeys on duty in the Paradise ballroom, Groovy's, and the several separate entertainment lounges, she had cast her eyes over the notes she had prepared for the meeting scheduled for eight thirty the next morning, to check for the final time that she had left nothing to chance. After all, this was her chance to show Harold what she was made of.

The Stripeys always congregated straight after breakfast in the area at the back of the stage where the dressing and props rooms were, so they could check the events scheduled for that day on the weekly chart pinned up on the noticeboard. After paying them a visit to ascertain all was well this morning, Patsy had left Dixie in charge during her absence and returned to her office to collect the manila folder in which she had placed the meeting notes the previous evening, then immediately made her way to the general office with a minute to spare.

Having politely refused Harold's offer of a hot drink, she opened the file to cast an eye over her notes and remind herself of her opening line, which she had laboured over to get just right . . . and then to her horror she saw the notes inside were not those she had prepared for the meeting but instead sheets of plain paper. How could this have happened? She knew without doubt that she had placed the unused paper back in the drawer and her notes in this folder.

And it wasn't the first time things had unexpectedly gone wrong for her. Lunchtimes for the staff were rotated weekly across the three sittings so one week a third of the staff were on the first sitting, a third on second, a third on the third, to ensure there were always enough staff members on duty to meet the needs of the campers not eating at the time. A new rota was made up every three weeks, which was then pinned to the Stripeys' noticeboard so as to take no chances of staff forgetting which sitting they were on at any given time. Thankfully, as Patsy had enough to be getting to grips with when she had first started her new job, Terry had already done the rota for the next three weeks so it was one job she hadn't had to worry about. Three weeks later she did.

Following on from the previous rota, she assigned each third of the staff to the sitting after the one they had just been on, and having rechecked that every member was accounted for and placed on the sitting where they should be, she replaced the schedule on the board. It was only when forty or so staff confronted her with the fact that their names were down for two sittings and others complained they were not on a sitting at all that it was brought to her notice she had failed miserably in her task. Good-naturedly the staff in question had put this down to her newness in the job but it still hadn't stopped her from feeling utterly humiliated about messing up such a simple task and the staff all knowing about it.

It was only a few days later that she'd discovered she had royally messed up again. Patsy had thought she was being efficient by taking a note of the sizes of the new Stripeys when they individually came to check in with her on first arriving. This took place over a period of one day as they all arrived at different times. When the last one had checked in with her, she then delivered the list to Eileen Waters so that she could have all the uniforms ready and waiting when the new members of staff turned up at the stores to collect them the next morning before they reported for their first shift.

Eileen had been very appreciative of Patsy's forethought in instigating this new procedure as in the past it had proved a nightmare to her when all the new Stripeys arrived together at the stores counter to collect their uniforms, with absolutely no information given in advance. The work involved in tracking down the different sizes of shoes, blazers, shirts and skirts, then having to fill in the appropriate paperwork, for dozens of people simultaneously, had been considerable and always gave Eileen and her staff an especially fraught morning. Patsy's new procedure meant most of this work could be tackled beforehand so all that needed to be done when the new starts arrived at the counter was to collect the uniforms that were already labelled with their name and hooked up waiting in alphabetical order on rails.

But to Patsy's horror it appeared that half of the sizes she had marked down against each new start were wrong, either far too small or much too big, and the same with the shoes. The result was that instead of easing Eileen's workload it had caused her more in sorting out Patsy's mistakes. To make matters worse, the name badges that she had laboriously made out for each new start with the aid of a stencil set were either misspelled or had the first and second names mixed up. Eileen had been very good-natured over the whole sorry business. Patsy had worked for her as a chalet maid when she had first started at Jolly's so the woman knew at first hand that she was usually a very conscientious worker. Like the Stripeys Eileen put Patsy's mistakes down to her newness at the job and over-anxiousness to prove herself worthy of her position

But those incidents were not the only reason Patsy was

becoming increasingly concerned. She had now lost count of the number of times since starting her new job when she had gone to get something in the office from the last place she had left it, only to find it wasn't there and nowhere else to be found. It was more frustrating than anything else and used up endless time she needed to spend elsewhere, but a few times the items in question had been needed by Stripeys to aid them in their jobs and she worried that her credibility as their leader was being eroded before she'd had a chance to build it. To make matters worse, those items had turned up later in places she felt positive she hadn't put them.

Harold had noticed that Patsy's face had suddenly paled and anxiety was filling her eyes. Bemused by this sudden change in her, he asked in concern: 'Are you all right, Patsy?'

Her mind whirled. She could escape her predicament by lying to him, saying that she had suddenly been taken ill and asking to postpone the meeting to another time. But then she risked him not being fooled by her excuse and beginning to have doubts about her competence to be leader of the Stripeys. If she told him the truth the same thing could happen. Then common sense took over. Patsy had over-prepared for this meeting in her need to make a good impression on Harold, so in reality didn't need notes to refer to as she knew by heart what she wanted to say.

She closed the file, took a deep breath and began her delivery. She explained to Harold how much time she wasted assigning each individual Stripey to a particular job every day, and then running around keeping an eye on them to make sure they were performing as they should. How much easier it would be if the Stripeys were formed into groups of about twenty with a team leader in charge of each. With a careful mix of personalities in each team, they should have a good spread of people and talents. Also a team leader would be better placed to note those who were not performing or behaving as well as they should be or even breaking any company rules, plus those who were due praise from the boss for a job well done. She then proceeded to inform Harold of all her ideas to improve or modernise the daily events themselves, plus the Stripeys' weekly shows.

Harold was listening intently, very impressed by what Patsy was telling him.

Meanwhile outside in the general office, as soon as the door to Harold's office had been shut for the meeting, Jill called across to Marion who was typing out a purchase order for stationery they were running short on.

As soon as she had her colleague's attention an animated Jill told her: 'Spilling the beans to you yesterday about my plan for bringing Harold and Eileen together proved to be a good omen. As I was on my way home last night I saw a poster advertising performances of *Death of a Salesman* by the Skegness Playgoers at the Pier Theatre. That gave me an idea. What if Harold and Eileen both received complimentary tickets supposedly from the theatre . . . a number of them are always sent out to promote the shows. It will just look as though this time their names came out of the hat together, so to speak. The tickets will be for the same performance, in seats next to each other.' She eyed Marion eagerly. 'What do you think?'

Marion was looking back at her blankly, fighting not to show her true feelings about the suggestion. Jill's idea might possibly work. But Marion herself had plans for Harold Rose, which didn't involve him getting together with Eileen Walters. Finding another candidate who fitted Marion's needs so exactly as Harold did would take time she wasn't willing to waste. Besides she no longer had the money to go to places where she'd usually meet men of the right calibre. Somehow she had to persuade Jill that her plan was far more likely to fail than to succeed, but she did have to be careful how she did it as Jill wasn't stupid.

Marion put a smile on her face and said encouragingly, 'I think it's a good idea.' She then added in a thoughtful way, as if it had just occurred to her: 'Mind you, it is reliant on them both attending the show . . . but what if one of them can't because they have other things planned for that night? And of course there is always the possibility that you have read their behaviour wrongly and they don't feel that way about each other. Then if they find out you were behind them getting the free tickets they might not be best pleased with you.' She was still trying to think of something else offputting to say but it was too late. Jill had taken an envelope out of her desk drawer and was getting out of her chair.

As she made her way round her desk she told Marion, 'I know I haven't read their behaviour wrongly. No plan is perfect, and after thinking long and hard about this one I believe it has as good a chance of succeeding as anything else. If it doesn't work, then it's back to the drawing board for me. I'm not going to give up until I've got Harold and Eileen together. Anyway I've bought the tickets now for Sunday evening, went straight to the theatre after seeing the poster, and I'm not going to waste them.'

She was waving an envelope at Marion which she then slipped into her dress pocket. 'I've got Eileen's ticket in this one, which I'm going to drop on her desk now as I know she's always out at this time in the morning, supervising the cleaning in the Paradise. And Harold is occupied too so I don't have to find an excuse to pop out. I'll put his in with his morning post later, and if either of them queries how the tickets arrived, I'll say they were hand delivered by an employee of the theatre.'

Marion's heart was racing. In her mind's eye she saw the light at the end of the dark tunnel going out. Panic flooded her. Jill was intent on delivering those tickets and somehow Marion must intervene and place Harold out of bounds to anyone else.

Jill had by now gone through the door leading to reception downstairs and was on the small landing with her back to Marion. Consumed with the idea of stopping her from fulfilling her errand, Marion saw only one way to do so. Without further thought she leaped up from her seat, sprinted over to the door, and, just as Jill was about to take the stairs, Marion gave her a shove in the back. Without waiting to see the outcome of her action, and ignoring her colleague's scream of shock and the dull thudding sounds as her body hit several steps while toppling down the stairs, Marion sprinted across to the back of the office, to the door leading into a corridor where the toilet facilities and accounts office were, yanked it open and disappeared through it. The door shut behind her just as she heard Harold and Patsy come rushing out of the boss's office to see what all the commotion was about.

After waiting in the corridor for a moment or two Marion returned to the general office and pretended to look surprised to see a worried Patsy standing just inside the outer door looking down. She hurried over to her and demanded, 'What's the matter, Patsy? I thought you were in a meeting with Harold?'

But before Patsy could answer a shout reached them. 'Telephone the nurse to get over here quickly and then call for an ambulance. Hurry, hurry . . . she's in a bad way.'

As Patsy turned to run over to Jill's desk and do Harold's bidding, Marion, putting a bewildered expression on her face, moved across to the place Patsy had just vacated. When she set eyes on the scene below she did then look genuinely shocked. Her aim had been to stall Jill from delivering the ticket, not to kill her! Terror filled Marion. She wanted to escape her dire living conditions, not exchange them for a prison cell. She called down to Harold, who was kneeling by Jill's crumpled body at the bottom of the stairs, his own face a ghostly white and looking back at her helplessly. 'She's . . . she's . . . not dead, is she?' Marion asked.

As she waited for his response it struck her that if the fall had killed Jill then no suspicions of involvement would taint herself as both Harold and Patsy could confirm that Marion wasn't even in the office when they arrived seconds after hearing Jill's first scream. If she wasn't as badly hurt as it appeared and did recall being pushed down the stairs, Marion should be able to convince her that her memory was playing tricks on her.

Just then Patsy arrived back and shouted down to Harold: 'Nurse Pendle is on duty today and she's on her way over. The ambulance is too.'

He went with Jill in the ambulance. Patsy meanwhile returned to her duties, the meeting to be resumed at another time. Marion had been left to man the office on her own. Selfishly, none of her thoughts involved Jill at all but were concentrated on how she was going to make Harold notice her in the way she wanted him to, starting the minute he returned from the hospital.

He did that at just after two, looking utterly wretched. As Jill's boss he felt he was somehow responsible for her accident. Marion immediately leaped up from her chair and hurried across to him, placing a hand on his arm. In a low voice she told him, 'You look done in. I've had the kettle on the boil ready for when you came back as I thought you'd be in need of a strong sweet cup of tea. I suspect you won't have eaten either so I could go and have a tray made up for you in the kitchen?' It was obvious that Harold appreciated her concern for his welfare, which was just what she'd intended him to do, but he refused her offer of food while acknowledging a cup of tea would be most welcome. It then struck Marion that she was showing all her concerns for Harold himself and none for Jill, which wouldn't help her present herself as the caring woman she wanted him to think her. She said, very tentatively, 'I've been afraid to ask, but how is Jill?'

He slowly exhaled before he told her, 'She's in a bad way, Marion. Both legs are broken and her right arm as well. One broken rib, three cracked. She's covered in bruises and has concussion. When the doctor asked her what happened, all she said was that the last thing she remembered was standing at the top of the stairs about to go down. She can't actually recall where she was going or why. The last thing she remembers is sitting at her desk typing up the minutes of the meeting after it had finished.'

Good, thought Marion. And long may it stay that way! 'Oh, thank God her injuries aren't life-threatening,' was what she said.

He flashed her a wan smile as he made his own way around his desk and wearily sat down.

Marion left him then to make his tea and moments later

returned and placed it before him along with a plate of digestives. While she'd been away Harold seemed to have composed himself, realising that he was not personally to blame for what had happened to Jill and still had work to do. He thanked Marion for the tea, took a sip of it before saying, 'I have no idea yet how long Jill will be off work for. It'll be a while anyway. I need to get someone in to cover for her while she's off. I'll call the agency, but in the meantime . . . I know it's an imposition to ask you, as you're only a temp yourself . . . but could you manage to keep the office running as best you can until they send someone?'

Marion saw a great opportunity here for herself in more ways than one, and wasn't about to let it slip through her fingers. By acting as Harold's right hand she'd have unrestricted access to him. Her spontaneous action of earlier might have proved very detrimental to Jill but was doubly beneficial to Marion herself. Who said that crime didn't pay?

'I'm quite capable of stepping into Jill's shoes until she is well enough to return to work, if you should wish me to, Mr Rose.' She purposely used his title, despite the fact that in general staff were all on first-name terms, in order to show him she had the discretion to decide when professionalism was called for. 'I'm a qualified shorthand typist and ran the office in my last job. I do have testimonials I can show you. And of course it's not as if I'd be doing the job blind as I've worked alongside Jill for a few weeks now, so I know how the office operates. Though I wasn't privy to all the work Jill did as your assistant, I can't imagine it will be very much different from what I did for my last boss, and I'm a fast learner. I will need someone else to undertake my present duties and can see to that for you, if you wish me to.'

He took off his glasses and gave them a wipe then put them back on and said, 'Yes, of course, I am aware of your qualifications. I'm so sorry they slipped my mind. I'd be grateful if you'd stand in for Jill until she's fit enough to return and I'll leave it to you to organise a temporary assistant from the agency. And while you're on to them, please ask them to adjust your hourly rate accordingly.'

Marion wanted to punch the air in jubilation. This day had first started as dismally as all the others she had lived through since Lionel had called time on their marriage, but it was set to end as one that marked an upturn in her life.

Harold was continuing, 'In the circumstances Jolly's are lucky the agency sent you instead of the young girl we requested to replace . . .' he couldn't recall her name at that moment so continued ' . . . the junior who decided she didn't like it here.'

'I can't imagine anyone not liking working for Jolly's. And you are such a great boss to work for.'

Her compliment made Harold go hot under his collar.

He gave a cough as he made to busy himself with his work. 'Er . . . um . . . very nice of you to say so. Well, I must get on.'

Marion smiled as she left the office. Harold Rose was going to be a pushover.

A while later Harold had gone to find Patsy to tell her his response to the ideas that she had put to him that morning and Marion was working away at Jill's desk, which she had already cleared of any personal items, now seeing it as her own. She came to realise then that there was still one matter that might prevent her from getting her claws into Harold. Although she had put a stop to any chance of Eileen and Harold getting together via Jill's interference, there was still the possibility that Eileen could take it upon herself to be the one to approach Harold. She needed to be got out of the way too, and as a matter of urgency.

A while later Marion was presented with the ideal opportunity when Eileen came into the office looking worried.

Marion had found it impossible to adopt Jolly's philosophy of a less formal, more friendly approach when greeting visitors, which went totally against her college training, so her approach now to Eileen was stiff and formal.

'What may I do for you, Miss Walters?'

Eileen shot her a taken-aback look, she not used to being addressed by the office staff or bosses with such formality, before saying, 'Well, I've just heard about Jill. Such an awful accident. I came to enquire from Harold if there is any news on how she is?'

Marion looked perfectly sincere when she said, 'Mr Rose isn't in but I can tell you what he told me himself after returning from the hospital. Mrs Clayton's injuries are not life threatening but it'll be a while before she'll be fit enough for work. In the meantime I'm taking care of her duties. I'll make sure Mrs Clayton receives your good wishes for her speedy recovery. I'm sure Mr Rose will wish me to organise a collection for flowers from the senior Jolly's staff and I'll make sure I don't miss you out.'

All the time she was talking, Marion's mind was churning in search of a plan of action. Then in a flash of inspiration it came to her just how she could get Eileen out of her way. She asked, 'Was your visit just to enquire after Mrs Clayton or is there something else I can help you with? Oh! But first, I wonder if you could help me? As Mr Rose's personal assistant as well as office manager, I shouldn't really be breaking a confidence but my instincts tell me I can trust you. You see, he has asked me to book a meal for two for tonight. He didn't have to tell me but I knew it was for him and his girlfriend. Well, it wouldn't be for him and another man as he asked for the table to be in a secluded corner and for flowers to be on the table!'

She pretended not to notice the stunned expression that appeared on Eileen's face at this information or the tears of distress that glinted in her eyes.

'I have to say, he's kept it quiet about having a girlfriend but that tells me he must be serious about the woman. Anyway, he left the venue to me as long as it was reported to serve good food and wine. But the trouble is that it seems to have slipped his mind, with all this bother over Mrs Clayton, that I haven't been in this area long so I wouldn't know a decent restaurant here. The last thing I want to do on my first day in the job is foul up and ruin his evening. I mean, for all I know he could be planning to propose to her tonight, couldn't he, considering he wanted a table in a secluded corner and fresh flowers on it? So you couldn't recommend somewhere suitable, could you?'

Eileen's whole world was disintegrating around her. Before she had realised how deep her feelings for Harold were, she had been happy enough with her life. On reaching forty she had come to terms with the fact she wasn't destined to be married or to have children; any hopes she had once harboured of achieving either or both, she had managed to bury and content herself with what she had. Her job with Jolly's was something she enjoyed immensely, and she had the camaraderie of the staff; she had her flat, only one-bedroomed and small but it was enough for her; she enjoyed reading and was an active member of the library along with having her own good collection of books; she had a radio to listen to, a large collection of LPs from a wide variety of artists to play on her record player, a black-and-white television, so she was never really lonely. If she needed company she had a couple of married friends from her youth that she would go and visit, and her sister's children to hug and spoil should she ever feel broody. But over the past year Eileen's feelings for Harold had made her unsettled, realising that there was a void in her life which this quiet, kindly, thoughtful man would fill perfectly. All her instincts told her that they were destined to be together and would suit each other perfectly. From his manner towards her she had truly believed her feelings were reciprocated but due to his shyness she would need to be patient and wait for him to pluck up the courage and ask her out. She had waited a lifetime after all so a while longer she'd felt she could bear.

Now to learn that his feelings for her were in fact no more than friendly, as his affections had been captured by someone else, felt like a knife had ripped open her chest and a hand was clutching her heart and squeezing it tight. She feared drowning from the tears of misery she was unable to shed openly as she couldn't let Marion see how devastated the information had left her. Eileen needed to get out of here and go somewhere private where she could release her unbearable anguish.

She managed to say, 'I'm so sorry, I can't help you there. I don't go out to dinner except to the houses of friends. Please excuse me, I have suddenly remembered I have to be elsewhere.'

As she hurried out Marion urgently called after her, 'You won't ever tell Harold that I betrayed his confidence, will you? Or he could sack me.'

Without turning around Eileen called back, 'No, no, trust me, I won't say a word.'

As she disappeared through the door, Marion lips curved into a sly smile. She was well aware of just what an effect her lies had had on Eileen but felt no sympathy for her. She was stupid woman not to have realised that by waiting for Harold to approach her first, she was risking someone else snatching him away.

Out in the courtyard Harold was about to open the door leading into reception. He was smiling to himself. Patsy's face when he'd informed her moments ago that her ideas were very well thought out, and just what was needed to breathe new life into the department, had been a joy to behold. The beam of delight in her eyes could have lit a room and for a moment he'd thought she was going to kiss him. He was glad she hadn't, though, as he wouldn't have known how to handle that.

As he'd been walking around the camp in his search for Patsy the full horror of Jill's accident had hit him, making him realise that no one could ever predict what life had in store for them; it could suddenly change out of all recognition. How would he be feeling now had that accident happened to Eileen and she had died as a result, without him ever telling her how much she had come to mean to him? That she was, in fact, the only woman he had ever met he'd felt he could have a relationship with? Eric was right, life was too short to let fear of rejection stall him from possibly being with the woman he had come to feel so much for. Surely requesting the company of a lovely woman like Eileen couldn't be compared to facing the barrel of a gun or a naked man rampaging around the camp? Besides, should he have read the signs wrong and Eileen didn't reciprocate his feelings then he knew without a doubt that she was not the sort to belittle him in any way, so in truth his fears were all of his own making.

He reached a bold decision. Eileen would be in her office over in the maintenance building. Her staff would have left for the day at four-thirty and she would be alone, dealing with paperwork, until her own finishing time arrived at five-thirty. As soon as he had paid a visit to Marion to check that nothing needing his attention he would pay Eileen a visit and ask her out as he had meant to do for such a long while now.

A sense of pride in himself filled Harold then. Like a man with a purpose he pushed open the door into reception and was just about to step inside when someone came rushing out.

It took a moment for the two people concerned to gather their wits. Harold was the first to. On seeing just who the other person was, his heart began to race. Having made his decision only moments ago finally to ask Eileen out, he realised there was no point in prolonging the agony. Now was as good a time as any. He took a quick look around, glad to see there was no one within earshot, then fixed his eyes on Eileen's and was just about to open his mouth when she beat him to it.

Harold was the very last person Eileen had wanted to cross paths with right now; she needed to avoid him as much as possible for a good while until she'd had time to bury her feelings for him and accept the fact that he would never be hers. It wasn't his fault that she had fallen for him and he didn't deserve her cold austere manner towards him now, but she had to act like this for her own self-preservation. Brusquely she said, 'Please accept my apologies, Harold, I wasn't looking where I was going. If you'll excuse me, I must get on.'

He was confused. He couldn't understand why Eileen was acting so off hand with him as he felt positive he'd done nothing to warrant it. She was already walking away and he stepped after her to catch her arm, pulling her to a halt. 'Eileen, is something the matter?' he asked.

She wrenched her arm free as though his touch had burned her. Yes, something is, she wanted to scream at him. I love you but you love someone else. And why she told him what she did then she could only put down to her own hurt pride in case he was aware of her feelings for him and was being nice to her just because he felt sorry for her, a plain, thin woman, the wrong side of forty, who'd had romantic notions for a man way out of her reach. 'Nothing is the matter. I'm just in a rush as I'm going out with a friend tonight and I've some things I must do before I leave. If I don't hurry, I'll be late meeting him.'

Harold froze. She had said *him*? Eileen was meeting a man? And he must be someone special as she didn't want to keep him waiting. His heart felt in danger of crumbling inside him. How stupid he had been to believe a woman like Eileen would not have other men vying for her affections. He'd let his own fear stop him from making a bid for her a long time ago and as a result he'd lost her to someone else.

She mistook the look of heartbreak in his eyes for that of shock that a nondescript woman like she was had managed to get herself a man. Containing the avalanche of miserable tears was no longer a possibility. Just before the dam burst she dashed off back to the privacy of her office, to weep for her loss.

Upstairs, Marion had just placed a folder containing the letters she had typed out and that needed Harold's signature on his desk ready for him when he returned. She looked out of the window to see if she could spot him so that she could have a cup of tea ready for him and so happened to witness the exchange take place below. Judging by their body language it didn't take a genius to work out that the meeting wasn't a friendly one, at least not on Eileen's part.

As Marion made her way back to her own desk a satisfied smirk lit her face. Now the way was clear for her to claim Harold and he would become a saviour to her mother and herself.

Patsy was still feeling euphoric after Harold had told her he liked her ideas and that she had his permission to put them into practice. She was humming happily to herself as she dealt with matters needing her attention before she made a start on formulating a plan to put her new ideas into operation without causing any disruption to the campers.

She had been checking over the daily events schedule for tomorrow, making sure the staff assigned to run each individual event were qualified to do so and the sort to impart their experience to the new Stripeys assigned to work alongside them. Satisfied she had done her best so that all ran smoothly, she went to pin the schedule back on the board on the wall behind her desk when the drawing pin stabbed the end of her finger and blood spurted over the paper. 'Damn and blast,' Patsy exclaimed, annoyed by her own clumsiness.

Dixie just happened to have arrived at the office door then. She had been on tenterhooks all day, praying with all her being that her attempts to sabotage Patsy's meeting with Harold had worked. Judging by Patsy's outburst just now, Dixie was convinced that it had.

Fighting not to show her delight, she placed her hand on Patsy's shoulder and in a voice laden with sympathy, said, 'Oh, I am sorry, Patsy, that Mr Rose wasn't impressed by your ideas. Hopefully he won't be thinking too badly of you and believing he made a mistake in giving you the job. I mean, after all, you are new to the entertainments side and maybe it's too much responsibility for you, especially after all the mistakes you've made since you started.' She stopped herself in time from mentioning the notes mix-up this morning as she wasn't supposed to know about that.

Patsy was shaking her head at her. 'You've got it wrong, Dixie. Mr Rose was really impressed with my ideas, all of them. He's instructed me to start putting them into practice straight away. I've already made my list of those Stripeys I think would make good team leaders and tomorrow morning, after the meeting has finished, I want to gather the show team together to run over ideas for some new routines. I was blaspheming when you arrived as I stabbed my finger with a drawing pin and got blood all over the daily events schedule.'

Dixie was inwardly seething at this news. It was apparent to her that getting rid of Patsy and snatching the job of Head Stripey for herself wasn't going to be as easy as she had thought. But regardless, Dixie would carry on trying to thwart her new boss until finally one of her ploys succeeded. She wasn't going to let an upstart like Patsy Mathers get the better of her, she'd be damned if she would.

In a performance worthy of a Hollywood Oscar she enthused, 'Oh, that's fantastic news. Congratulations! I knew you'd do it. I'll help you all I can, you know that.' Help you all I can to make a mess of it, she thought nastily.

Her bad mood wasn't helped by the fact that she was on duty in the Paradise lounges that night, along with another Stripey. Dixie felt he had all the personality of a limpet; she actually felt physically disgusted each time she came face to face with him and was forced to look at the molehill-sized spots that covered his face. Gareth Nuttall was actually a very pleasant, accommodating young man, whose spots were in fact just a few adolescent pimples at the sides of his nose, but as he possessed nothing that attracted Dixie she was as unkind about him as she was about any other male she found unworthy of her notice.

Time passed slowly for her tonight. Plenty of people had been using the lounges but those in the quiet ones just wanted to be left alone to catch up with the newspapers, play whist, watch the television or chat amongst themselves. They were not interested in playing board games, which Dixie was glad about as she hated playing them. She had therefore been bored all evening, spending the majority of it idly chatting with any of the half a dozen or so bar staff in the lounge and, when she could be bothered, helping the waiting staff deliver drinks around the three separate lounges the bar serviced.

There was no one more grateful than Dixie was when twelve o'clock arrived and all the entertainments came to an end.

She was already in bed reading a women's magazine, still too furious about her failed plan to go to sleep, when Val arrived at just after one. She almost fell through the door, having joined other staff members for a couple of drinks after their shift had ended.

She flopped down on the end of her bed and kicked off her shoes. A look of delirious joy on her face she told Dixie, 'I've had the most wonderful night.'

Dixie glanced at her scornfully. How dare Val have had a good night when hers had been one of the most tedious she had ever endured? 'Don't be stupid, Val,' she snapped. 'You were on duty in the ballroom tonight, so don't tell me you had a good time, dancing with all those old fogeys.'

Val gave a hiccup before telling her, 'But I do enjoy entertaining the oldies and so do most of the other Stripeys, Dixie. They can be such fun. A few old couples tonight had us in stitches, showing us their rendition of the sand dance. And I tell you this, some of them are fantastic at doing the jive. One old boy swung his missus right under his legs, then pulled her back. He couldn't manage to throw her over his head as he was ancient, at least sixty. Anyway, that's not the reason my night was wonderful.'

Dixie sighed. 'Okay, I give in. What made your night wonderful then?'

Val flashed her a triumphant look. 'Well, a new barman started today. He's gorgeous. Tall and blond and with a body to die for.'

Dixie snorted. 'And this coming from a woman who had a crush on Freddie Garrity of Freddie and the Dreamers, and thinks Herman of the Hermits fell in love with her just because he pecked her on the cheek after his performance here on the opening night of Groovy's the year before last.'

'Oh, Dixie, how could you? I admit Freddie isn't what you'd call a dreamboat but he is *so* cute and a really nice man. And it was a kiss . . . all right, a peck, but not on my cheek . . . on the lips that Herman gave me after the show. Anyway, Jamie really is a dreamboat. You should see his muscles! Picks up a crate of Newcastle Brown like it weighs a feather. I think he's taken a fancy to me as he was winking and smiling at me all night.'

Dixie said immediately, 'Well, of course, that will all change when he claps eyes on me.'

Val scowled at her. 'Not necessarily. You might not be his type.'

'Don't be stupid, Val. What man could resist me?' Dixie's eyes narrowed purposefully. 'I shall look forward to checking out this Jamie to see if he's as gorgeous as you reckon he is.' She then shut her magazine, dropped it beside her bed and snuggled down under the covers. 'Now hurry up and get into bed, I want to sleep. And be quiet about it.'

As she shut her eyes Dixie's bad mood lightened a little. She hoped that the new barman was her idea of gorgeous and not just Val's. If he was then the poor man wasn't going to know what had hit him tomorrow night. She could do with a distraction to help take her mind completely off her feud with Patsy, and this Jamie sounded just the thing to do it.

CHAPTER TWELVE

S tanding side by side, Harold and Eric were both staring in utter dismay at the scene before them.

The back end of the large camp kitchen resembled a bombsite. Wisps of acrid smoke were still rising from smouldering timbers that had crashed to the floor when part of the ceiling caved in. Several of the huge gas stoves over this side of the kitchen were covered in thick layers of ash and blackened with soot; likewise metal workbenches and hanging pans and utensils. The doors of the food stores, cold stores and fridges were wide open and the enormous amount of foodstuffs each held were all suffering from varying degrees of fire damage. Water from the hoses was still dripping and the black-and-white-tiled floor was swamped with filthy water and floating debris.

Scraping a hand threw his hair, heedless of the fact that his actions made it stick up wildly, Harold uttered: 'What a bloody mess!'

Eric shot him a startled look. Whatever the circumstance he had never before heard Harold blaspheme, however mildly. He said, 'Whoever is behind this meant to cause as much damage as they could, not just to the kitchen itself but all our food stocks by opening the stores and fridge doors. The food is ruined.'

Harold sighed heavily. 'I just thank the Good Lord that whoever is responsible obviously didn't know that they set the fire not long before the security guards were due by the kitchen on their rounds of the camp. If they had set it any earlier or later the fire would have spread throughout the rest of the kitchen and the restaurant too, and if this is bad enough, that would have been catastrophic for us.'

Eric pulled a knowing face. 'I bet you a week's wage it's those orphan kids that are responsible. I told the police sergeant as much before you arrived. You should have got rid of them, Harold, while you had the chance. I did try and warn you that a telling off would be like water off a duck's back to kids like them.'

A man approached them then. He was dressed in a suit over which he wore a fawn macintosh. He lit a cigarette before addressing Harold. 'Inspector Morton,' he introduced himself before he continued speaking. 'Those lads your chef told my sergeant about couldn't have started the fire, Mr Rose, as since you took them to task for misbehaving, the staff in charge of them have made sure none of the kids has been let out of their sight. At night they've all been sleeping in the same chalet and the staff have taken it in turns, on four-hour shifts, to make sure they don't get up to no good. I've questioned the staff on shift tonight and they are adamant that none of those boys left their bunks.' The look Harold shot Eric told him that he'd been wrong and his warning to them had worked after all. 'Do you know of anyone with a grudge against Jolly's or Mrs Jolly personally?'

Harold shook his head. 'Absolutely not. I can't imagine anyone having a grudge against Mrs Jolly.'

The inspector scratched his head. 'Well, I can't see what anyone would have to gain from setting fire to your kitchen except to cause you grief. My lads have had a thorough check around and we haven't found any clues whatsoever, not even what was used to jemmy the back kitchen door open with. It's my opinion that this was caused by drunken louts from Mablethorpe or some village roundabout, who thought that breaking into your kitchen would be fun. Maybe they didn't actually start a fire intentionally but after they had tipped your food stores upside down, thought they'd better scarper before anyone caught them. They could have been smoking and accidentally dropped a cigarette.

They could easily have got in through the hedge at the back of the derelict farmhouse and left the same way.

'Butlin's have had trouble with locals breaking in and rampaging around their camp after pubs have shut at night and had to tighten their security, so you're not on your own. Thankfully the damage is less than it could have been, thanks to your security guards.' He gave a loud yawn before adding, 'Of course, we'll do our best to find out who did this but with what we have to go on . . . well, I couldn't hold out much hope. Please do telephone me at the station if anything comes to light that you think could be of use to us in catching the culprits. I'll be in touch if we come up with any leads.'

Harold thanked the man and the police officer went on his way. Harold then stared around, mortified. Whatever the police said, this was a major catastrophe. He heaved a worried sigh and said to Eric, 'I'm at a loss as to what to do. It's two o'clock on Saturday morning. In six hours' time we'll have thousands of hungry campers wanting their breakfast before they go home, then thousands more arriving and expecting their dinner at twelve. How on earth are we going to feed them? Apart from the baker, milkman and egg supplier who deliver daily, all our other commodities are delivered on a three-day or weekly basis. If memory serves me right, you're had the three-day delivery of meat and vegetables this morning, so getting that amount again at short notice, and considering it's Saturday . . . I don't think we stand a chance. The dried goods we might fare better on. Replacing the food all depends on whether I can contact any of our suppliers on a weekend and see what they have in their own stocks or can call in to help us out. But what's the good of having the food if we've no means to cook it? It's going to take at least a week to get this kitchen back up to scratch.'

'At least,' Eric agreed worriedly.

Harold's brain worked desperately, searching for a way for the camp to keep functioning, but having a cooked meal provided three times a day, freeing themselves, especially the woman, from the chore, was one of the pivotal reasons people chose to holiday at the likes of Jolly's. He told Eric: 'We have no choice but to shut the camp until the kitchen is back in use again. I shall have to telephone Mrs Jolly and inform her about this. I feel terrible for letting her down. She put all her trust in me to look after her camp while she's away and I let this happen.'

'And how have you let her down? Tell me how you could have stopped those mindless cretins from doing what they did? You couldn't, and that's what Drina would be telling you too if she were here.'

Harold knew Eric was right but nevertheless snapped angrily, 'Did those drunken louts not stop to think for a minute what repercussions their bit of fun would have on others? People will be getting up soon, all excited about their holiday, packed ready to go, only to learn it's been cancelled when they arrive at the coach station.'

At that moment an idea was striking Eric. He grabbed Harold's arm, exclaiming, 'Hang on, we might not have to close the camp while the repairs are done. The restaurant wasn't touched by the fire so that'll just need a thorough clean-up to rid it of the smell of smoke and I know Eileen will rally her troops to see to that. Replenishing the food is going to be a headache, as you said, but when all's said and done Jolly's gives their suppliers a huge amount of business and they'll not want to risk losing it so will bend over backwards to help us.'

Harold eyed him, seeming puzzled. 'But aren't you forgetting that we have no facilities to actually cook the food on, Eric?'

He grinned. 'We will if I can manage to pull a few strings with my old muckers. Listen, you go and see what you can do about the food supplies and leave the rest to me.' Without explaining further he turned and made his way around and over mounds of debris to his office, which thankfully had escaped the fire. Unlocking the door, he squashed his bulk inside and started searching through his desk drawers.

Harold couldn't for the life of him see how he could have the answer to their predicament so felt it would be very inter-esting indeed to find out just what Eric had in mind. He then stood for a moment looking around at the chaos before giving himself a mental shake. What was he doing, standing here like a village idiot? If Eric did somehow manage to perform a miracle, then his efforts would all have been a waste of time if they had no food to cook.

Three hours later Harold heard the sound of heavy vehicles coming through the entrance gates. He had become so immersed in what he had to deal with that what Eric was up to meanwhile had been put to the back of his mind. Harold had just replaced the telephone receiver after speaking to one of their suppliers of sausages, having got the poor man out of his bed the same as he had all the other suppliers he had managed to get hold of since leaving Eric to his secret mission. Once all the suppliers had learned what had happened they all readily agreed to deliver whatever stock they could to the camp as soon as was physically possible, and in respect of fresh stuff, as Jolly's had no fridges or freezers in use, they would deliver new supplies daily for the duration. The vehicles rolling into the camp now therefore couldn't be any deliveries of food as there hadn't been time for the suppliers to have organised them.

He jumped up from his seat and ran over to the window to stare agog as a parade of canvas-topped army lorries drove through the gates. The lead truck pulled to a stop by the fountain dominating the middle of the courtyard, the rest halting in a line right behind. Harold was just about to go and see what on earth the army was doing here when he spotted Eric plodding along as fast as his huge bulk would allow him from the direction of the camp restaurant and kitchen building. Panting heavily, he arrived at the driver's side of the lead vehicle and spoke briefly while pointing a finger over at the large expanse of grass to the front of the restaurant and kitchen block. The vehicles all moved off in that direction while Eric himself hurried after them.

Bewildered, Harold rushed out of his office, down through the dark reception area, out of the door, across the courtyard and on down towards the large grass area at the front of the restaurant building to stare at the hive of activity going on before him. A dozen or so squaddies had already piled out of the trucks and several were unloading the cargo while others were unrolling lengths of canvas and others sorting through lengths of poles.

Eric himself was standing beside another man who seemed to be in charge as he was giving instructions. Harold tapped Eric on the shoulder, demanding, 'What's going on here?'

'The cavalry has arrived! I did try to telephone and let you know but your line was permanently engaged and I had no time to come over, with all I've had to do before the trucks arrived.' Eric introduced the other man as Sergeant Rawlins and Harold shook his hand, telling him he was very pleased to see him. In fact he'd never been more pleased to see anyone in his life. Eric then went on: 'I thought this wasn't going to happen at first as I couldn't find the notebook I keep the telephone numbers of my old mates in, but thankfully it was in the bottom drawer of my desk under a pile of stuff. Anyway, they weren't happy about being woken up at two in the morning when I phoned, I can tell you, nor were their wives, but once I told them our situation and what I was after, they soon jumped to attention.

'They called a couple of their old cronies at the camp in Catterick, then those old mates did the same at another camp, and to cut a long story short, a few strings were pulled and unpaid debts called in, so to speak, and hey, presto! We have a kitchen. Well, we will have once the squaddies have erected it . . . six kitchens to be exact as one was no good considering the numbers we have to cook for. The equipment is antiquated as it was last used during the war and it'll all want a good scrub as it's been in store since then, and the tents might be a bit moth-eaten after all this time, but it'll all do the job until our own kitchen is repaired. Don't worry, I cut my teeth using equipment the same as this to feed a platoon of ravenous soldiers in Cyprus so feeding Jolly's hordes will be a doddle. We will have to hope that the weather is kind to us for the duration but should it turn then Sergeant Rawlins is leaving us enough tenting equipment to erect an undercover passage from the serving tent to the restaurant.'

Harold was dumbstruck. An army field kitchen! Eric was a genius to have thought of this. Thank goodness he had still kept in touch with his old army pals so was able to call on them. Harold didn't know how they in turn had managed to get their superiors to agree to loan this equipment and the use of the squaddies to help set it all up but maybe it was better he didn't. He gave Eric a hearty clap on the back. 'I don't know what to say. You've certainly performed one hell of a miracle. I don't know how the campers are going to react to this, though.'

Eric chuckled. 'Believe me, the campers won't give a monkey's uncle how their food is cooked as long as their bellies are filled three times a day. Anything has got to be better than having their holiday cancelled.' He took a quick look at his watch. 'Time is ticking and there's still lots to do. Oh, Harold, better get the coke stocks topped up as those stoves, once I fire them up, are hungry beasts.'

As Harold began to hurry back to the office to continue ringing around those suppliers he hadn't yet managed to contact and order tons of coke, his eyes caught sight of the activity that was going on inside the restaurant. The army of chalet girls, foaming buckets, mops and scrubbing brushes in hand, were working away cleaning the tables and floor. And there was Eileen, up a ladder washing down the walls, along with several others of her staff doing likewise. He knew without Eric having to tell him that once the restaurant was all spick and span, Eileen would then have her maids moving on to help him get the old kitchen equipment sparkling ready for use. And after all this they then had hundreds of chalets to prepare ready for the new arrivals once the leavers had vacated. For a moment he stopped and looked at her, working away. Her job was to supervise her staff doing the work so she didn't have to roll up her sleeves and get stuck in alongside them. The man who had captured her heart was one lucky chap indeed. Harold was just sorry it wasn't him.

Thankfully the food lorries started rolling in one after the other at just after seven. Having no more suppliers to contact, Harold ran over to see how matters were progressing by the restaurant and what he could do to help. By now the sergeant and his squaddies had erected all the kitchens side by side, allowing Eric to come and go through flaps in between, to check on his staff and see if all was going well. At the end of the kitchen tents stood a servery where the food would be collected by the restaurant staff and loaded on to trolleys to be transported over the short expanse of grass to the restaurant. All the equipment had been cleaned by Eileen and her chalet maids and the dozen massive stoves fired up and ready for use, only a couple needing a bit of fine tuning by one of the mechanics in the maintenance crew, which considering the stoves had been in storage for nearly twenty years was another miracle. The sergeant and his squaddies having done their bit were on their way back to their base in Ollerton, but would return and collect their equipment when it was no longer needed.

All the rest of the staff . . . Stripeys, sous-chefs and assistants, nursery nurses, bar workers, maintenance crew, ground staff, mechanics, three electricians, two carpenters, camp photographer, all the shop staff and even Sam the donkey man . . . had been woken from their sleep and brought in to help and were labouring together, to get everything ready for the first breakfast sitting at eight o'clock.

Harold was humbled by the loyalty of all the staff in pulling together to achieve what they had. Drina Jolly was certainly reaping the benefits now for the way she insisted her staff be treated, with respect and consideration, as human beings not numbers. Harold doubted that other companies who just saw their staff as commodities would ever have been able to motivate them in a dire situation like this. Out of respect for Drina Jolly they had worked hard and without complaint to save the company from potential ruin.

CHAPTER THIRTEEN

Harold had just finished using his private bathroom to tidy himself for work, discarding the clothes he had hurriedly put on the previous night when security had summoned him to the camp, when he heard noises coming from the general office and realised that while he had been in the bathroom Marion had arrived for work. Out of respect he went out to meet her and inform her what had happened the previous night. He had just finished telling her when the outer door opened and a man entered the office. He was short and balding, his features sharp, eyes beady. He looked down-at-heel in a shabby top coat over a shiny brown suit and well-worn shirt, a grease stain on his faded tie. He had a camera case slung over his shoulder.

Before either Marion or Harold could speak the man said, 'No one was on reception so I came straight up. Ron James from the *Skegness News*. Mrs Jolly here? I'd like to interview her about the fire you had last night.'

Marion started to respond but Harold beat her to it. 'Mrs Jolly is not available. I'm the manager, Harold Rose.' He hadn't given the press getting hold of this news a thought, with all other matters occupying his mind. Suddenly being confronted by this man while unprepared caused Harold to feel very anxious. He fought to quash this, aware that if the reporter detected he was nervous in any way, he could see that as a sign of guilt or a cover-up in progress. Harold must say nothing that this man could twist and sensationalise, as the press were notorious for doing. The result could be detrimental to the good name of Jolly's.

He courteously asked the man to come into his office and Marion to make him a strong coffee and, after asking Ron James his preference, a cup of tea for him.

As Marion went off to do his bidding she was feeling miffed to say the least. This morning she had attacked her quest to snare Harold with the precision of a military campaign. Previously she hadn't taken too much notice of what she had worn for work but now it was a different matter. Thankfully she still had the expensive wardrobe she had amassed while with her husband so could at least look the part of a well set-up woman even if she wasn't any longer. Wanting to look efficient yet still feminine, she had dressed in a snug-fitting pencil skirt and white blouse with frills around the collarless neckline, which continued on down the front and around the cuffs of the long sleeves. Her shoulder-length hair she had backcombed for body, then smoothed into a smart French roll. On her feet she wore low black leather courts. Her makeup was light and she had sprayed herself with Tweed eau-de-cologne. All that trouble she had gone to this morning yet Harold hadn't seemed to notice! Nor had he commented on the small bunch of flowers she had bought from the flower seller outside the bus station, spending precious money she could ill afford, to put on his desk whilst he was in his private bathroom in an effort to show him how thoughtful she was.

But the working day had only just begun and she was adamant that before she left for home that evening he would notice her, and in the way she wanted him to.

Inside the manager's office, Ron James was looking at Harold questioningly, pencil poised ready to write. But instead of asking Harold about the fire, he surprised him by saying, 'I had a holiday once at a camp like this when I was a nipper. I went with my parents.'

Harold thought that this was a good sign, the reporter having experienced for himself the delights of a place he'd come to write an article about. He smiled. 'Good memories you have of that holiday then?'

Ron pulled a face and shook his head. 'Nah . . . I hated every minute of it, couldn't wait to go home from the minute we arrived. It was a small camp on the Norfolk coast. It poured down every day, the chalet we were in was damp and the mattresses on the beds like lying on bare boards. There were cockroaches in the showers and the food was terrible, overcooked and tasteless and the same every day. A gristly sausage and beans for breakfast, fatty boiled beef, lumpy mash and soggy cabbage for dinner, stodgy pudding and lumpy custard for afters, and for tea, tongue or shoulder ham salad, bread and marge and tinned fruit cocktail. The so-called entertainment was the same every day too: exercise routines one after the other in the morning, sports in the afternoon or a ramble through the woods, and in the evening we kids were put to bed while our parents went to the club house, which was a wooden hut, to have a drink and a dance to music played by an old chap on his organ. The place closed down about four years after it opened, went bankrupt, which was no surprise to me or I suppose to any of the other unfortunates who chose to holiday there.'

Harold's heart sank as he listened to this. He tried to restore a modicum of good will in Ron James towards holiday camps by saying, 'Well, camps have improved leaps and bounds since those early ones, as you can see here at Jolly's.'

Ron didn't respond, just launched off. 'So this major fire you had last night that gutted the whole restaurant and kitchen building . . . We received information that it was started by an angry mob of campers in protest because they were dissatisfied with the food served up here. "No better than pigswill" to quote our source. Have you any comment?' His voice had an accusatory tone to it.

'Yes, I certainly do have a comment, Mr James. I don't know where your source got their information from but it's inaccurate.'

Harold could see disappointment cloud the man's beady eyes. For a local paper whose main articles were usually no more sensational than who had been crowned the local beauty queen, the old lady who had tripped up on an uneven paving slab or the theft of a farmer's prize bull or tractor, this news was juicy indeed.

'Are you telling me that the information we received was a hoax?'

'Not all of it. We did suffer a fire last night but certainly not of the magnitude your source is claiming. It was no angry mob that started it and it was contained to the back part of the kitchen. It's the police's opinion that it was more than likely started by youths out for a bit of fun.'

'Oh!' Harold could tell the man was disappointed that the truth wasn't as sensational as his source had led him to believe it was, but regardless his brain was ticking over, determined not to leave without some sort of story for his readers. 'But still, the damage to the kitchen will take time to repair and if you can't feed your punters then surely this means you'll have to close the camp meantime? A lot of holidaymakers are going to be disappointed, aren't they? It will be a big operation for you, won't it, organising the sending home of those holidaymakers here and cancelling the holidays of the ones due to arrive? This is not going to be good for Jolly's business reputation, is it?'

'On the contrary, Mr James. Thanks to an ingenious idea of our head chef's we will manage to keep operating with little disruption to our campers while the kitchen is undergoing the necessary repairs.'

Ron James's eyes betrayed his interest. 'And just what was this ingenious idea?' Before Harold could answer, he had put his pencil inside the notebook, shut it and stood up. 'Better still, why don't you show me?'

At this request Harold tried not to show his anxiety. A while had passed since he'd visited the makeshift kitchen and he prayed that nothing had transpired to give Ron James reason to write a damaging article.

* * *

127

As they drew near the restaurant building, to Harold's surprise, mingled with the animated chatter of the milling campers, he felt sure he could hear the distant sound of a piano playing and people singing. As they began to pass the restaurant Harold took a tentative look through the windows that lined the whole side of the massive, building, where up to just over three and a half thousand campers at a time in high season ate their three daily meals. He was mortally relieved to note that the diners he could see were tucking in and seemed to be enjoying their food. So that meant the kitchen was functioning at least. As they drew nearer to the end of the building, to Harold's confusion the sounds of piano playing grew louder as did the singing.

As they turned the corner he took a deep breath to steel himself for what he might find. He was vehemently hoping to see happy campers coming and going from out of the folding glass door at the front of the restaurant building, and waiting staff toing and froing with loaded trolleys of plates of food ready to serve and dirty plates and crockery ready for delivery to the washing tent.

And that was just what he did see, and more besides.

Sitting on the grass by the open folding doors was the upright piano that the Stripeys used in their end-of-week shows and several members of the entertainments team had clearly raided the chests of show costumes and were dressed 1940s style, several in army uniforms. A group were gathered around the piano, one playing and the others, among them Patsy, singing popular war-time songs. Another group was dancing or smooching together. All the campers Harold could see, both outside the restaurant and inside, seemed to be thoroughly enjoying the entertainment laid on for them. Patsy had obviously arranged it off her own bat in an effort to warn the campers of the unorthodox cooking arrangements. Harold was very impressed with her impromptu actions and would tell her so at the first opportunity.

Standing on the periphery alongside Harold, Ron James was

looking around keenly and jotting down notes on his pad. Finally he said, 'Well, I didn't know what to expect, but it wasn't this.'

It wasn't possible by his tone to tell whether Ron James thought Eric's idea ingenious or saw it as undermining the holidaymakers, expecting them to accept their meals being produced by such an unorthodox method. Perhaps he thought they should be making a stand against it. Regardless, Harold felt Eric's idea had saved Jolly's from a costly catastrophe and it was apparent by what they were viewing now that it was working. He told the journalist, 'We can always rely on the staff to rise to the occasion when faced with unusual circumstances that could affect the wellbeing of our campers. We pull together to do what is necessary to give our campers a holiday to remember.'

Ron said matter-of-factly, 'The ones here now and on their way will certainly remember this one.'

Harold looked at him sharply. What did he mean? That the campers would remember their holiday with Jolly's in a good way or a bad one? He wished the man would put him out of his misery and enlighten him as to what sort of article he proposed to write, detrimental or laudatory.

Just then he felt a tap on his arm and turned to find a man and woman with two young children standing beside him. The man asked, 'I'm sorry to bother you but are you one of the people who run this place?'

Harold turned fully to face the new arrivals, worried about why they had approached him. 'I'm Harold Rose, the manager, yes. How may I help you?'

The woman said, 'Oh, we don't need help. I just saw you, hoped you might be something to do with the management, and wanted to tell you that it's our first time at a holiday camp and we've all had a great week so we'll definitely be coming back. The kids don't want to go home this morning, and neither do we. We're going to start saving for next year straight away. Anyway, we're not on our own, 'cos everyone we've been sitting near in the restaurant is saying the same. We all think that what you've come up with to cook the meals after the fire in the kitchen last night is absolutely brilliant and we've loved the forties entertainment while we were eating. My husband reckons his breakfast tasted much better this morning, cooked in an army tent like they used to during the war. Not that he hasn't enjoyed all his other breakfasts though,' she added hurriedly. 'Anyway, we thought we'd just tell you. Now we'd better get off to finish our packing or we'll miss our coach. See you next year.'

Harold was so pleased that the young couple had taken the trouble to give him this favourable opinion and hoped that the reporter had been listening. He turned back to ask if he'd seen enough but to his shock the space Ron James had occupied was empty. Harold's eyes darted frantically around, wondering where he had gone, but couldn't see the man anywhere. Then he noticed one of the reception girls hurrying over to him. When she joined him she informed him that that Marion had asked her to find him as she couldn't come herself and leave the office unattended. Mrs Jolly was on the telephone for her weekly update.

And Harold had a lot to tell her. He was in a quandary. Did he ask the receptionist to ask Marion to ask Mrs Jolly to telephone him back, which was against usual practice of always taking a phone call from his boss, or did he respond to Drina and leave the reporter free to roam the camp, talking to whomever he wished? Harold took another look around and still couldn't see hide nor hair of Ron James who, for all he knew, could already have all he needed to write his article and had gone back to his office to write it. Harold decided to follow his principles and honour his boss, and hurried off to his office to take the telephone call.

CHAPTER FOURTEEN

At just before three that afternoon Harold lifted his eyes from a brochure he was looking at as Eric lumbered into his office.

The big man looked tired but at the same time exhilarated. As he parked his huge frame on the seat before the desk, he pointed a podgy finger at the booklet in Harold's hand and said: 'I see the management is shirking while we minions do all the work.'

Harold smiled. 'I was just looking at what the competition is offering. Up to me to keep an eye on what's going on in other camps, what prices they are charging, what new attractions they are introducing, that kind of thing, and if I think we should be concerned, report my findings to Drina. This is the brochure for a new camp opened up near Whitley Bay.'

'And is it a threat to us?'

'Well, it's only half the size of Jolly's and has no funfair, only slot-machine arcades, and it's not on the beach but set a little way inland, so I don't think it's any competition.' He then eyed Eric in concern. 'Not here to report anything wrong, I hope?'

He shook his head. 'On the contrary. The kitchens are functioning really well. It's a bit cramped in the tents and staff are getting under each other's feet, but we're managing. I've heard no complaints from the campers over the quality of the food. So far, so good. I was on my way to find an empty staff chalet and have a couple of hours' shut-eye before next shift begins, but then there's a danger that if I fall asleep I might not wake up until tomorrow morning so I thought I'd come and thank you instead.'

Harold frowned. 'Thank me for what?'

'For sending that weasel to see me without giving me any warning.'

The frown deepened. 'Weasel?'

'I should have said ferret, the way he was nosing around for information.'

Harold looked at him blankly for a moment before he twigged who Eric was referring to. 'Oh, you mean the reporter. So that's where he got to! He never mentioned anything about wanting to interview you. But of course he'd want to speak to the brains behind the improvised kitchen. What did you tell him?'

'Nothing I could be hung for. Or I hope not anyway. Reporters seem to have a knack of getting things out of you without you realising, don't they? He asked how I came up with the idea. Well, how do you explain how you come up with any idea? When you're looking for a solution to a problem, it just comes to you or it doesn't. He was interested in my background. What for, I've no idea. Maybe he was hoping I had a past that would make his story more meaty.' Eric gesticulated with his hands as if displaying a banner: 'MURDERER MASQUERADING AS A CHEF AT A HOLIDAY CAMP. The thing he was most interested in, though, was wangling a free breakfast out of me. Once I'd got one dished up for him, he disappeared off into the restaurant and I never saw him again.'

Harold sighed. 'I've been worried about any damage the article could do to Jolly's reputation and it's going to be a long wait until Monday when the paper next comes out. But as Drina said when I told her, we have no control over what Ron James writes, and if it is detrimental then we have no choice but to trust that not everyone believes what they read in the newspapers and Jolly's reputation precedes it. Doing our best for our campers is where our priorities lie. Drina was pleased that we had done just that, and against the odds.'

Harold then lapsed deep into thought.

Eric asked, 'Something wrong?'

He gave himself a shake. 'Oh, er, nothing . . . well, nothing I can pinpoint. It's just that Drina wasn't her normal self today. I know she was upset about what happened to Jill. She asked me to keep her informed and said that I was to make sure we did all we could to help speed her recovery, but I don't think that was the main thing on her mind.'

'What is the latest on Jill?' Eric asked.

'When I telephoned the hospital a short while ago, they told me that she's in a lot of pain but is stable. She'll be in hospital for at least six weeks as they won't be letting her out while she's still in her plaster casts and can't fend for herself. As long as nothing here prevents me, I'm planning to go and visit her this evening, take her some flowers from us all and see if there is anything she needs, although her husband has that covered.'

'Give her my best,' Eric told him. 'So, Drina. What do you think is bothering her then?'

'As I said, I don't know. It was nothing she referred to, just that she seemed a little distant.'

Eric shrugged. 'Well, she's got a lot on her plate, getting her new camp up and running.'

'Mmm. But when I asked her how matters were progressing there, she told me that Rhonnie and Jackie between them were doing an excellent job and all was on course for the opening at the beginning of July, with bookings looking very promising. She said Artie was fine and doing a great job setting up the new maintenance team down there. You've got to be right, Eric, it's just that she's got a lot on her plate and is a little tired, that's all. She did tell me she was very proud of the staff here for all pulling together to make sure everything went as smoothly as possible this morning, considering it's a busiest day of the week with all the changeovers. She asked me to make sure they were made aware of her gratitude. As for you, Eric, she says that you deserve a medal.'

Eric beamed and said, tongue in cheek, 'So I do, but I'll settle for a cup of tea. With a drop of whisky in it. I know Drina likes a tipple herself and keeps a bottle in the drinks cabinet . . . good stuff an' all, better than I could afford. Purely medicinal, of course, to help keep me awake being's I'd only just nodded off last night before I got the summons from security about the fire. The same went for you, so I bet you could do with one yourself.' He heaved himself off his seat, saying, 'I'll ask your new secretary to make the tea while I get the whisky. She isn't a bad-looking woman for her age. What's her name?'

Harold looked taken aback. 'What new secretary?'

Eric eyed him back as though he was stupid. 'The one out in the general office, sitting at Jill's desk.'

'But that's Marion.'

Eric raised his eyebrows in surprise. 'Really! I didn't recognise her. She must have done something to herself. Was it her that put the flowers on your desk?' he asked, nodding at the vase containing the flowers Marion had bought that morning.

Harold looked at them for a moment. 'Oh, she must have done. I hadn't noticed.'

Eric laughed. 'Only got eyes for Eileen. That reminds me, have you asked her out yet?'

Harold shook his head, sadness in his eyes. 'No, and I won't be.'

Eric shook his head in frustration. 'Oh, well, if you're not going to swallow your pride . . .'

Harold cut in, 'It's nothing to do with that. Eileen already has someone.'

Eric looked stunned and said disbelievingly, 'I don't know where you heard that from. She's not the type of woman to have her eyes on someone, which she clearly has on you, while involved with someone else at the same time.'

Harold sighed. 'I agree, she's definitely not, so it must have been wishful thinking on my part, believing that she liked me. I'd made up my mind after our chat that I was going to summon the courage and ask her out, Eric. I bumped into her yesterday, there was no one in earshot, and I was just about to when she told me herself she hadn't time to chat as she

134

wanted to get her work done so as not to keep her date waiting. She mentioned *he* so there is no disputing it was a man she was meeting. But she was really . . . off . . . with me, like I'd done something that she was upset about, when so far as I know, I haven't done anything to upset her in any way.'

Eric scratched his head, bewildered. 'That's not like Eileen, to be off with anyone. She's the most amenable woman I know.' He tried to bolster his friend by telling him, 'Well you know what they say? Plenty more fish in the sea.'

There might be, but none would match up to Eileen in Harold's eyes. He needed to come to terms with the fact that she was never going to be his. He needed to keep his mind busy to stop it from dwelling on her. 'Fancy a walk around the camp?' he asked Eric.

The big man pulled a face. 'I've not had my cup of tea with my medicinal tot in it yet.'

Harold stood up. 'We'll get one from the kiosk . . . minus the whisky of course. Might help to blow your cobwebs away.'

Out in the general office Harold informed Marion he would be gone for about an hour and where he was off to and she watched them both leave with a sense of deep frustration. She had vowed that she would make a start on ingratiating herself with Harold before he left for home that evening but, despite several attempts, as yet the man seemed blind, deaf and dumb to her womanly wiles. She had been very careful to be subtle with her efforts, knowing she could frighten a man like him off if she was too blatant. So flashing her thighs when she sat down to take shorthand or her cleavage when she leaned over the desk to pass him his tea, actions that would have had other men champing at the bit, were not on the agenda with Harold. She confined herself to shooting him a winning smile at every opportunity; made sure he got a waft of her perfume; acted very in awe of the way he had resolved problems caused by the kitchen fire, even though he'd credited Eric with deserving all the praise; without asking him had taken it upon herself to have a meal brought up for him at dinnertime, knowing he'd

135

had no breakfast . . . which he did seemed gratified by and thank her for, so she supposed at least that was something. But he'd not once made any comment about her appearance and nothing at all about the flowers she'd put on his desk either. Harold, it seemed, was not going to be quite the easy catch that she had thought he would be. Normal tactics were not going to work on him so to snare him she was going to have to come up with something different.

While she continued with her work, she thought about what else she could do to chivvy proceedings along. There was a tap on the door then and a young woman came in.

Marion was about to ask her what she could do for her when recognition struck. 'What are you doing here?' she asked, puzzled.

The newcomer responded in a sulky voice, 'Miss Abbott sent me. I'm your new temp.'

'Bit of a funny time to be sending a temp to start work, three on a Saturday afternoon, but I suppose that's better than nothing. I thought you worked in the agency office, though?'

I did, Sandra Millington thought, until you tricked me into sending you on a job that Miss Abbott hadn't personally sanctioned. Believing what Marion had told her, that her boss would be extremely impressed by her using her initiative, Sandra had proudly told Miss Abbott what she had done, expecting praise for being so enterprising. But her boss hadn't seen her actions like that at all, and insisted Sandra had been undermining her. She had immediately sent the girl packing. Because she had been sacked from her job she hadn't been able to get another one since, so her parents were furious with her too as they relied on her board money to supplement their own meagre incomes. Ever since Sandra had had no money to buy her own necessities or go out and socialise with her friends.

She was well aware that Miss Abbott was only giving her this chance of work because no other young girls on her books would take on a job that involved weekends and travelling a distance outside town, Jolly's being situated in the countryside.

Her former employer had resorted to Sandra in desperation. As soon as she had received the telegram asking her to contact Miss Abbott as a matter of urgency, Sandra's mother had sent her round immediately, warning her that if she messed up this opportunity of work she would send her daughter to live with her aunt Beryl, a humourless, austere woman who had a farm deep in the wilds of Northumberland. Even working under the woman who had caused her such problems through her own selfishness was preferable to living with Aunt Beryl, which was the only reason Sandra had agreed to take the job.

'I did work in the agency for a while, but it was only until I got some office experience and Miss Abbott thought I had enough now, so here I am,' Sandra lied.

Marion wasn't fooled. Miss Abbott seemed the unforgiving sort to her. Unforgiving . . . But not averse to using Sandra as a stopgap to earn the agency its fee.

Marion said coolly, 'You can stay, Sandra, so long as you understand that, dare cross me like you did Miss Abbott and you'll be out on your ear.'

Despite her disdainful manner towards the young girl, Marion was actually relieved to see her. Trying to cover two jobs had left her no time to devote towards luring Harold into her clutches. As soon as she had finished instructing Sandra in what was expected of her, though, she meant to concentrate on her campaign.

Later Marion was searching the desk drawers for a pencil sharpener when she came across the envelope containing the theatre ticket Jill had been planning to give to Harold after she'd delivered Eileen's. An idea to further her campaign struck her. If Jill had been of the opinion that her plan would work to bring Eileen and Harold together, then why wouldn't it for Marion and Harold?

Marion called across to Sandra, who was busy typing addresses on a pile of envelopes, and told her, 'I want you to run me an errand on your way home tonight.'

Sandra looked worried. 'I can't be late home for my dinner

137

as my mum gets cross if it's ruined, and she'll be wanting to know how I got on here.'

Marion cocked an eyebrow at her meaningfully. 'Well, if you don't do me this errand then you'll be telling your mother that you didn't get on very well.'

The girl got the gist. Upsetting her mother over a ruined meal was far preferable to life in the wilds with Aunt Beryl. 'What do you want me to do?'

'Go to the box office at the Pier Theatre and get me a ticket for tomorrow night's performance. Just the cheap seats will do, but if they haven't any left get whatever you can. Just don't come in tomorrow without one.' She added the threat with a smile on her face but her eyes told Sandra she wasn't joking. Marion then got up and went into Harold's office to put the envelope containing the ticket Jill had got him on his desk.

Marion was out of the office paying a visit to the Ladies' room when Harold returned. On his way in he introduced himself to Sandra and told her that he hoped she would enjoy working for Jolly's and not to hesitate to seek him out should she need any help and Marion not be available at the time. She could tell from that short speech what a nice man he was, one who would see her as a person and treat her with respect, not like Miss Abbott or Marion Frear, like she was their personal lackey, someone with no life of her own, who could be threatened with the sack should she not jump to attention. She would love her job here if she were working directly with Harold Rose, she realised. But no chance of that. Regardless she had no choice but accept her situation and hope in the future a job would come along where she needn't dread going in each morning because she lived in fear of her immediate superior.

Inside his office Harold came across a plain envelope addressed: 'Private and Confidential, for the Manager, Jolly's Holiday Camp'. Having no idea what it might contain he slit it open and pulled out the contents. It was a ticket for a showing tomorrow night at the Skegness Pier Theatre. There was a note attached to it that read: '*With compliments of the management*'. He thought how nice it was of the theatre to include him in the list of complimentary tickets sent out to local business people. The last time he'd been to the theatre was with his mother and he hadn't been since as he felt self-conscious going to places people went to in couples or groups. Now he was more confident within himself it wasn't such a trial to him. Providing nothing happened at work to prevent it, he would take advantage of the ticket and go, he decided.

A while later Marion told Sandra to make them all a cup of tea, instructing her how Harold and she liked theirs. Armed with the tea tray containing three cups of tea and a plate of biscuits for Harold as Marion had instructed, out of respect for the pecking order, Sandra made her way straight into Harold's office to give him his first, for which he graciously thanked her.

As she made her way back to her desk Sandra wondered if it was just a coincidence that the boss had a ticket on his desk for the same performance, at the same theatre, that Marion had told her to obtain a ticket for on her way home tonight.

CHAPTER FIFTEEN

Patsy gave a yawn and stretched herself. She had caught up with her paperwork and, after the long day she had had due to the kitchen fire, would have liked nothing more than to go back to her chalet, collect her things for a shower and then have an early night. Not that she had had an early night or taken advantage of her weekly afternoon off since she had started her new job; it had been far too hectic keeping the department running while she implemented a proper office system and formalised the new ideas she'd had approved by Harold. Before she did finish, the same as she did every night, she made a tour of the Paradise to satisfy herself that all her staff were coping all right and had no need of her to help them. So after tidying her desk in the tiny office, she took her ring of camp keys from her pocket and swapped them over with the office key hanging on its hook on the wall, put on her Stripey jacket, locked the office and made a start on her rounds.

First she paid a visit to Groovy's and satisfied herself all was well there, stopping for a moment or two after checking on the staff to watch the dancers enjoying themselves and trying to remember the last time she'd had a night free to dance it away with her friends, though she couldn't. Then she made her way through all the lounges and Carousel bar area and on in to the Paradise ballroom. The vast room was heaving but not as much as it would be in a couple weeks once high season got underway. At least at the moment it was possible to make her way around the room without having constantly to ask people to excuse her.

There were twenty staff members on duty that evening in the ballroom. She observed that most of them were on the floor dancing with campers, the rest sitting at tables chatting to them, some fetching drinks from the bar when the army of waiters and waitresses were otherwise busy. Satisfied all was well, she went to make her leave but decided she would have one drink before she did.

As she arrived at the bar she saw Dixie sitting on a stool at the far end. She didn't see Patsy as her whole attention was focused on one of the barmen. He must be a new staff member as Patsy hadn't seen him before. He was about her own age, she judged, twenty-four or -five, tall with honey-blond hair that fashionably skimmed the top of his shoulders. And those shoulders, like the rest of him, rippled with muscles. But it was his face that Patsy found she couldn't take her eyes off. He was the most handsome man she had ever seen in her life. The nearest she could liken him to was Robert Redford. She had seen him in the film *Butch Cassidy and the Sundance Kid* and had thought then that no man could ever top him for looks, but somehow this barman did. He was the sort Patsy always envisioned when reading a bodice-ripping novel, the sort where the hero carried the heroine off into the sunset at the end, and like every woman who read them she'd fantasised about being in that man's arms.

Obviously Dixie thought the same as Patsy saw she too couldn't take her eyes off him. It was her night off tonight and the pretty girl was looking very attractive in a pair of snug-fitting lime green Wrangler jeans and a blue, pink and lime green striped polo-neck jumper. She had styled her long blonde hair into two pigtails, each secured with an elastic band just below her chin. Her makeup was pale and even from the distance Patsy was she could see thick black false eyelashes curling at least an inch away from Dixie's eyes. Patsy wondered how she could see through them.

Patsy watched the girl trying her best to catch the young man's interest. Whether he was just oblivious to her fawning all over him or playing hard to get wasn't clear, but at the moment

Patsy felt the girl's efforts were wasted and if she wanted him that badly, she ought to try another, more subtle approach. Patsy then smiled inwardly, thinking who was she to be advising another woman on how to grab a man's attention, considering the lack of experience she herself had in that department.

There were several other bar staff behind the counter all busy with customers. The new barman Dixie had her eye on was sliding the base of clean wine glasses on to the slots above the counter, but as soon as he saw Patsy waiting to be served he immediately came over to her, gave her a bright smile and politely asked what he could get her. She considered herself off duty now so asked for a glass of white wine. Next thing she knew Dixie was beside her, obviously seeing her chance to ingratiate herself with the new barman by engaging him in conversation while he was dealing with Patsy.

She said to Patsy breezily, 'Everything all right?' Before Patsy had chance to respond Dixie's attention was fixed on the man again. She was giving him an engaging smile and saying, 'You're new here, aren't you? My name is Dixie. I'm Assistant Head Stripey. If you want someone to show you around then I'm your girl. Actually, if you fancy a drink after work in my chalet, I can fill you in on a few things. Number two-o-one in the staff block.'

As he put Patsy's drink down in front of her, the young man replied, 'Thanks for the invitation but after the early start this morning, by the time my shift finishes, I'll just about have enough energy to get myself into bed.' Dixie opened her mouth, about to suggest another night, but he stopped her by fixing his attention on Patsy and telling her the price of her drink, making it obvious that to him the subject was closed .

As she fumbled in her jacket pocket for money, Patsy was very conscious that Dixie was fuming about him turning down her invitation. It was apparent that the young woman was not used to being rejected, something made worse in this instance by the fact that it was in front of witnesses. Patsy searched for something to say to Dixie in an effort to soften the blow but couldn't, so thought it best to pretend she hadn't heard the exchange as she'd been concentrating on trying to find her money. Finally she took everything out of her pocket, found the half crown she was seeking and handed it over. The barman, whose name she had noticed from his badge was Jamie, immediately left with it to go to the till at the back of the counter.

Vicky Smith, one of the Stripeys who were new this year, then arrived at the counter, looking flushed from dancing. Seconds later another new Stripey who had started at the same time, Trevor Briggs, also came up to the bar, though he stood a little distance away from them.

Both of the newcomers were an enigma to Patsy. Vicky was a nice-looking young woman, with an easy-going personality. Patsy had observed her picking up the rudiments of her job very quickly and just a couple of weeks into it she needed very little, if any, supervision, and was in fact guiding her fellow starters if they began to flounder when their team leader was otherwise occupied. To Patsy she was displaying all the traits of someone who had what it took to gain promotion. She had therefore felt that despite Vicky's short time in her job she would make an excellent team leader. On being approached about the promotion, though, Vicky had politely refused, telling Patsy that she didn't want the responsibility and was quite happy with her job as it was. Patsy had been most surprised by her reaction, feeling positive the girl wasn't the type to be led when she was given an opportunity to lead and wondering if there was some other reason why she had declined. But Patsy had had no choice but to accept her decision.

Trevor Briggs wasn't at all a good-looking young man. He was slightly built and no more than five foot seven. His nose was far too big for his face and his eyes set too close together. His hair was carrot red and freckles covered his pale skin. It wasn't his looks that bothered Patsy, though. How could she judge others by their looks when she was lacking herself in that department? It was his personality that confused her. When he was doing his job in front of the campers he was the life and soul of the party, never shying away from tackling anything that meant keeping the campers happy even if it proved an embarrassment to himself, but while off duty and amongst his fellow workers he kept his distance, seemed very introvert, didn't show any signs of wanting to mingle with them and make friends. To Patsy he was like two different people. But regardless, he more than adequately did the job he was paid for and that was what Patsy primarily cared about.

As she accepted the change Jamie gave her, she smiled at the newcomers and said to them, 'The campers are obviously putting you both through your paces tonight. The last thing you needed really, after our very early start.'

It was Vicky who answered. 'They're a lively lot, but then that's what they come here for, isn't it, to enjoy themselves? And it's our job to make sure they do. Could I have a glass of water, please?' she said to Jamie now that he had finished dealing with Patsy. Then she called over to Trevor: 'Can I get you something, Trev?'

The young man looked wary for a moment before he answered. 'Oh, er . . . yes, please. I'll have a glass of water too.' He then, seemingly reluctantly, came over to join the other three at the bar.

It was impossible to believe that a few moments ago this nervy young man had been throwing himself whole-heartedly into the hokey-cokey.

Armed with their glasses of water Vicky and Trevor returned to the dance floor. Jamie went off to serve other customers. Patsy said, more to herself than to Dixie, 'It's such a waste.'

Dixie had heard her but was still aggrieved over Jamie's rebuff, made worse for her as it had been in front of her boss. For once Val hadn't exaggerated a man's attributes and Jamie was everything she had proclaimed him to be. He was certainly a sight for sore eyes and had made Dixie's widen when she had first clapped them on him. But was the man blind? She was every man's dream woman and he should feel honoured that the likes of herself had singled him out. Then it struck her. Of course,

144

he had to be the old-fashioned type, who felt he should be the one to make the first move. Well, at least she had let him know that an advance from him would be welcomed by her. Now she would just have to be patient until he did the deed.

She looked quizzically at Patsy and asked, 'What's a waste?'

Replacing her belongings in her pocket, Patsy looked puzzled for a moment before realising she had spoken out loud and replying, 'Oh, I just feel it's a waste that Vicky Smith wouldn't consider becoming a team leader when I offered one of the positions to her. She would have been really good at it. To me she's got all the marks of someone who'll go far. Still, I have to accept that she's happy doing what she is and doesn't want the responsibility.'

Dixie turned her head and looked back over the dance floor. Through the crowds she spotted Vicky Smith chatting amiably to several campers around a table. Her suspicious mind began to whirl. Dixie wanted to get on in life and couldn't understand anyone who didn't. She didn't believe that Vicky Smith was happy being just another Stripey. She'd obviously a reason for turning down Patsy's offer. Then a thought struck Dixie. Was that because Vicky was after something better for herself? Like Dixie's job, for instance? Dixie was complacent enough to believe that none of the staff posed a threat to her . . . how could they when she was the best-looking woman on the team and outshone everyone when it came to talent? . . . but then she wasn't going to stand by and allow an upstart like Vicky Smith to steal her job off her, if that was indeed what she was after.

She stayed for a while longer, hoping that Jamie was noticing the appreciative looks she was getting from men who came to the bar and hoping her flirtation with them was making him jealous, before shooting Jamie himself a long lingering look as she left to return to her chalet. Before she did go back, though, she had an errand to do. Making sure that she wasn't in Patsy's eyeline, she skirted around the tables edging the dance floor until she found Vicky. Secreting herself behind a pillar, Dixie caught her eye and beckoned her over.

Dixie was the boss's assistant so the young woman immediately responded to her bidding, arriving with a smile on her face and raising her voice above the noise of the music and campers' jollifications to say, 'Hello, Dixie. Everything all right?'

She nodded. 'Yes, as far as I'm concerned. I just thought you needed to know that my job is not up for grabs.'

Vicky eyed her in bewilderment. 'I don't understand why you're telling me this?'

'Just so you know.'

Vicky's brow furrowed. 'Do you think I'm after it then or something?'

'Well, are you?'

'No, I'm not,' she emphasised.

Dixie smiled at her. 'Well, that's all right then, isn't it?' She pushed her face forward and fixed Vicky's eyes with her own in a warning. 'Just so you know, though, I shall be keeping my eye on you, lady, and if I think for a minute that you're getting delusions of grandeur then you'll be out of here quicker than a frog catches a fly. Patsy's new to her job and she relies on me to keep her straight, trusts my judgement. You get my drift?'

Vicky nodded. 'Oh, yes, very clearly. Let me assure you, though, Dixie, I am not after your job or any other job in the team. The job I have suits me just fine. But if you are still here when I am in a higher position than you, then it will be you who needs to watch her back.'

With that Vicky spun on her heel and went back to work, leaving Dixie staring after her wondering what she had meant by that remark. Was she after Harold's job, was that it? Dixie issued a snort. The girl was mad if she thought she could land his job, while a mere Stripey. She still wasn't quite convinced that Vicky wasn't after her job, though. Dixie felt she had better watch her own step in future, not sneak off for so many breaks, and must conceal the boredom she often felt so that Patsy would not be tempted to replace her with Vicky.

Over on the dance floor, Vicky looked across at Dixie as she weaved her way through the tables to disappear in the throng, and a secretive smile crept over the watcher's face. That bully of a girl had laughed at her announcement that she would need to watch herself when Vicky was in a position to get her sacked, believing that the likes of her would never achieve such an aim, but should Dixie still be around when she did do just that then Vicky would make her smile on the other side of her face.

Dixie had been vigilant to make sure Patsy couldn't witness her exchange with Vicky but she hadn't taken into consideration the other Stripeys on duty. Trevor had been in the middle of waltzing with an elderly camper . . . she was at least forty . . . when he had spun around and spotted Dixie and Vicky deep in conversation. He immediately wondered what it was about. Not him, he hoped. He had worked a lot alongside Vicky since starting here, so was Dixie quizzing Vicky about him? But he knew he hadn't done anything to arouse suspicion, he'd been too careful, to the point of keeping his distance from all of his colleagues when not in a work-related situation. Then as he had spun around again and caught sight of the pair, their manner towards each other struck him and he realised they were having, not an argument as such but certainly an altercation and it was a personal matter and nothing to do with anyone else. As a spin took him out of their line of vision he breathed a sigh of relief. His secret was safe and he intended to keep it that way.

Back at the bar there was a lull and Jamie headed over to where Patsy was sitting, sipping her drink, her attention on the dancers enjoying themselves. He leaned on the bar and said to her, mimicking the voice of Humphrey Bogart: 'So what's a good-looking broad like you doing in a gin joint like this?'

She turned to look at him, grinning. 'Same as you . . . working.'

He cast his eyes over her before saying, 'Head Stripey.'

She gawped. He was not only devastatingly handsome he was psychic too. 'How did you know?' she asked.

He laughed. 'It says so on your name badge.'

Of course it did. Patsy giggled. She liked a man with a sense of humour. Then she asked him, 'And how are you liking your job with Jolly's?'

He fixed his eyes on hers and said meaningfully. 'Very much so.'

If she didn't know better she would have said he was flirting with her, but in her experience women like her didn't attract his sort when he could easily land himself the prettiest girl in the room. She suddenly gave an involuntary yawn. 'Oh, do excuse me. It's been a long day.' She glanced at her wrist watch and saw that it was just coming up to ten thirty. 'I'm going to call it a day. Goodnight, Jamie,' she said to him, and slid her long body in an ungainly manoeuvre off the tall bar stool, just managing to steady it before it fell over. She flashed a glance over at him to see him chuckling at her antics. She thought it best to leave quickly then before she embarrassed herself any further in front of him.

CHAPTER SIXTEEN

Marion's lips tightened in disappointment when she approached the end of the pier and viewed the theatre. She handed her ticket to the usher at the door and went inside. This venue was a far cry from the sort of establishment she'd thought she would be patronising tonight. The sort of theatre she was used to attending when she had been married always had an elaborate foyer, sweeping stairs leading up to the gallery, and plush red velvet-covered seats, with ushers dressed in gold-braided uniforms guiding patrons to theirs. This place was not much more than a glorified hut. When Marion looked down, through the gaps between the floorboards she could see waves rolling several feet below. Still, the venue wasn't as important to Marion as the person she was going to meet here tonight.

Believing it was what she perceived as a proper theatre she was attending, she had dressed herself in a pale green taffeta, figure-hugging, knee-length evening dress with a mink stole slung around her shoulders. She wore her hair coiled up into an elaborate French pleat. Observing the more casual attire of the rest of the crowd, she felt out of place. But then overdressed or not, she knew she looked stunning and Harold couldn't fail to think so either when he clapped his eyes on her.

When she'd been getting herself ready earlier Ida had tackled her like the Spanish Inquisition, demanding to know why she was dolling herself up like she was, where she was going and with whom, why wasn't Ida invited too, and why was Marion spending precious money on nights out when they were living in such squalor? She had managed to fob her domineering mother off with a tale that it was a ticket only do courtesy of Jolly's, just as a treat for the senior staff, one of the perks of the job, and it wouldn't be costing her a penny. Ida's mood had lightened a little when Marion had given her a half-pound box of Terry's All Gold chocolates, two bottles of barley wine and a new copy of the *People's Friend* to keep her company while her daughter was out.

Marion had deliberately arrived at the theatre as soon as the doors opened, not wanting to chance Harold seeing her before she was ready for him to. Once inside she found a dark corner in the foyer where she could observe those coming in as she knew there was a chance that Harold wouldn't turn up at all should he for any reason decide not to accept the complimentary ticket, and if that was the case then she wasn't going to stay herself when her whole reason for being here was negated. She willed him with all her might to appear, though, as coming up with another plan as good as this one to begin her entrapment of him was going to take some doing. She needed him in her clutches as soon as it could be managed and then the current miserable existence would be over for her mother and herself.

A while later, her eyes were beginning to ache after continually searching for one audience member in particular. Just as she was giving up hope of him coming there he was, easing himself inside the door in his usual unassuming manner. Harold might not be at all a charismatic or good-looking man but she thought he did look very smart tonight in a dark blue blazer, white shirt and pale blue slacks. She slunk further back into the shadows until he'd gone through the door into the auditorium, then hurried after him so she could see where he was sitting. From the back of the large room she watched as he took his seat on the left-hand side towards the front and was pleased to note that hers was on the other side towards the back. That meant she was able to execute the next part of her plan without him spotting her before she was ready. It was all well and good perfecting a plan but it could not always account for the actions of others. Ideally she wanted Harold to visit the bar during the interval but in the event he decided not to, she had a backup plan ready.

The events on-stage were just a background blur to Marion as she willed the time to pass until the interlude. The programme stated that it would take place at the end of act three at eight forty-five and finally, when Marion's wrist watch told her it was eight forty, she excused herself to the six people seated next to her, much to their disgruntlement, then stood at the back of the auditorium with her attention turned towards the area where Harold was sitting so that when the lights went up she could observe what he did.

A couple of minutes later the cast took a bow as the third act ended and the curtains came down for the thirty-minute interval. Marion's eyes never left the back of Harold's head as she waited to see what he intended to do. As the row of people next to the aisle on his side started to leave their seats, Harold rose and followed them. It seemed he was going to the bar but just in case he intended to buy an ice cream off the confectionery and cigarette woman who had just appeared at the front of the stage, and then return to his seat to consume it, Marion stayed put. As soon as she saw him turn to head up the main aisle, not down, she hurried off to the bar, secreting herself behind a wooden pillar just inside the door to await his arrival.

He came in moments later and went over to the bar, which at the moment was four deep in people. She bided her time until she could see he had reached the actual bar then excused herself to the people behind him, making out she was not pushing in but joining her companion at the bar. Finally manoeuvring herself beside Harold, she pretended to be trying to catch the barmaid's attention then made a display of seeming to notice the identity of the person by her side and exclaimed loudly, to be heard over the noise of the throng: 'Why, Harold, how lovely to see you.'

At the sound of his name he spun his head and looked at the woman beside him blankly for a moment before recognition struck and he responded, 'Marion. It's . . . er . . . nice to see you too.'

She asked him, 'Are you here with friends?'

'Er . . . no, no, I'm on my own.'

She feigned a look of sympathy before she said, 'Me too. Since my marriage broke up and I moved to Mablethorpe to put distance between us, I haven't yet managed to form a social circle. I wouldn't normally attend something like this on my own but it was either that or miss the production.' She wanted to bring his attention to her so in a jocular manner continued, 'I'm rather overdressed for this kind of theatre but it's been a while since I've had an excuse to dress up.'

At her prompting he cast his eyes over her. She did look very glamorous, as if she'd stepped out of a fashion magazine. Eric had not failed to notice that Marion was an attractive woman and he was right, she certainly was. Out of the corner of his eye Harold could see several men nearby looking at her very appreciatively and then at him. He knew they were wondering what such an attractive woman was doing with a plain-looking man like he was, obviously thinking that they were a couple.

He realised Marion was talking to him and apologetically said to her, 'I'm sorry, I didn't catch that.'

She shot him a winning smile. 'I said, it's not the same, though, is it, coming to the theatre on your own as you've no one to share the experience with?'

He had to agree. 'Er . . . no, no, it's not.'

Just then the barman approached and asked Harold what he could get him. Harold started to order half a bitter for himself but then, being the courteous man he was and considering Marion was on her own, asked her if she would like a drink. She graciously requested a gin and tonic and while he paid for the drinks told him she would try and find them a table.

The tables were all taken by then so they had to stand by the back wall. As soon as Harold joined Marion and she had thanked him for the drink, she asked, 'Are you enjoying the play?'

He nodded. 'Very much so. And you?'

She heaved a forlorn sigh. 'Well, I wish it were possible for me to, but you see I have a lady beside me who is constantly whispering to her friend about what's going on, and to make matters worse constantly rustling sweet papers too. Other people have asked them to shush but she seems a law unto herself and has taken no notice. Before the interval is over I'm going to ask one of the ushers if there are any empty seats left so I can swap. I just hope it's not a full house so I can at least enjoy the final two acts.'

Harold fought his conscience. The seat next to his was vacant and he really should offer up this information to her, but then he didn't want to make her feel obliged to take it just because he had bought her a drink. But as the honest man he was he had to tell her, then it was up to Marion whether she took that particular seat up or not. 'Well, er . . . the seat to one side of me is unoccupied.'

Before he could say anything else she exclaimed in delight, 'You're my saviour, Harold. Oh, I'm really looking forward to the second half of the play now.'

He felt he didn't deserve her praise as, after all, it wasn't really he who was her saviour but the person who had decided not to claim the seat.

An hour later, encores taken and the curtain finally coming down, Marion enthused, 'I did enjoy that. Didn't you, Harold? What did you think of . . .' She then broke off and looked at him expectantly. 'Look, if you haven't any need to rush off home, how about we find somewhere to have a drink and discuss the play?'

Before he had chance to respond she had stood up and was making her way down the row of seats towards the aisle.

As they came out of the theatre, Marion feigned a stumble and, just as she hoped Harold automatically caught her arm to steady her. She thanked him and added, 'My high heels are no good for walking along the pier. Too many gaps between the boards. Would you mind if I held on to you until we arrive at the end?'

Whether he did or didn't, before Harold could reply Marion had hooked her arm through his and they were strolling back down the pier, he feeling uncomfortable at the intimacy of the situation. A short while later they were in a hotel sipping drinks and again he felt out of his depth as Marion had chosen to sit next to him at the table and not opposite like he'd thought she would.

Over another couple of drinks they at first discussed the play and Harold enjoyed listening to her interpretations of what the writer had intended the audience to feel at certain parts and her thoughts about the skill of the actors in bringing his characters and words to life. It was nice for him to have someone listen to his own observations in return. And then somehow the subject came up and he found himself listening to the sad tale of Marion's marital breakup. How her husband, a successful businessman whom she had absolutely adored, had cheated on her with a succession of women despite her being a loyal wife, and after twenty years of marriage had decided he wanted someone younger than her. He had made it impossible for her to stay in their home and made sure she had left with only her personal possessions and a few pounds in her purse. She had chosen to leave her home town as the thought of bumping into her ex with his new woman was too distressing for her, and that was how she had ended up in Mablethorpe. Thankfully she had her secretarial skills to fall back on so was able to find work to pay her own way but unfortunately the wage she earned wouldn't stretch to a place of her own so she was forced to lodge with an elderly lady until such a time as her fortunes changed.

He felt sorry to hear that her husband could treat her so shoddily and hoped her circumstances did indeed improve enough that she could afford a place of her own.

She knew by his manner that she had completely taken Harold in with her fabricated story and achieved the reaction from him that she had hoped to. Now he had listened to her tale, though, she wanted him to see her as a sharing kind of woman so turned the conversation to him. She knew better than to ask him any personal questions so instead asked, 'What's the latest on Jill? It must be awful for her, lying in her bed in such pain and not being able to do anything for herself. Would it be impertinent of me to visit her one evening, do you think? A fresh face, so to speak. I could put her mind at rest that I'm doing my best to cover her job until she returns.' In truth her only reason for wanting to see Jill was to satisfy herself that the woman attached no blame to Marion for her fall down the stairs.

Harold told her, 'I propose to drop into the hospital tomorrow evening and I will certainly ask her.'

Marion was aware that it was after ten thirty and felt it was time to bring the next stage of her plan into motion. She drank the remains of her gin and tonic, adjusted her stole around her shoulders and picked up her handbag. 'It's time I went back to my lodgings. Thank you for a lovely evening, Harold. I trust you've enjoyed it too.' Standing up now, she leaned over and gave him a friendly peck on his cheek, before adding, 'I hope you don't think I'm being presumptuous but maybe we could do this again sometime. I really would like that.'

Then she turned and left him staring after her, finding it hard to accept that she had enjoyed his company enough to want to spend more with him. He hadn't made her laugh with his anecdotes as he hadn't got any, or regaled her with interesting stories; in fact he'd been rather nervous all night, not finding himself able to relax at all in such a good-looking woman's company. Throughout their time together he had been wondering if she was finding him utterly boring but just couldn't think of an excuse to get away from him until it was time to go home. It was more than likely that her parting words hadn't actually any substance to them, just Marion being polite, as after all he was her boss and it wouldn't do for them to be working so closely together and there be any awkwardness between them.

He downed the last of his drink and began to make his own way home. He did feel guilty at not offering to see Marion safely to her door, but then had been so taken aback by her parting words the thought hadn't entered his head until it was too late. As he walked down dark streets through town to the outskirts where his house was situated, he had to admit that his evening had been the more pleasurable for sharing it with her. But deep down he knew that during their time together he hadn't been at all fair to her as his thoughts had been on another woman, wishing it were she who had watched the play with him, been clinging to his arm on the walk down the pier, she he'd been buying drinks for and chatting with in the hotel afterwards.

Marion almost skipped her way back to the dilapidated caravan, so pleased was she with how matters had gone between herself and Harold. It couldn't have better in fact as far as she was concerned. She meant to give it a couple of days then she would cast her web a little wider in his direction.

CHAPTER SEVENTEEN

The next morning Harold was in a quandary, not knowing quite how to greet Marion after spending time socially with her the previous evening, but he needn't have worried as she treated him with the same respect she always had and made no comment whatsoever about the events of the previous evening.

At just after eight o'clock the next morning, Harold was nervously sitting at his desk with a pile of daily newspapers in front of him, knowing that Ron James's article would be in the local one that he'd purposely arrived early to read. His nervousness was due to just what tone Ron James had taken when constructing his story about the kitchen fire. So it was the *Skegness News* he selected first and he didn't need to flick any pages in search of the piece as it was on the front. Blazed across it was the bold headline **CHEF SAVES THE DAY AT JOLLY'S HOLIDAY CAMP.**

As Harold read the article his nerves evaporated while enormous relief set in. Ron James had written nothing detrimental to the business. In fact, exactly the opposite. He was full of praise for the way that Jolly's had turned the potentially damaging situation into a triumph, thus saving thousands of holidaymakers from being sent home, their dream holiday in tatters, and it was all down to the brilliant idea of their resident head chef. Harold couldn't wait to inform Eric that he was a local hero. He wondered what his friend's reaction would be? Drina would be both relieved and delighted that her beloved camp had suffered no ill effects from the drunken louts' escapades and thanks to Ron James's article in praise of them, they might possibly see their sales boosted.

Before he went to inform Eric of his celebrity status Harold decided to scan through the nationals first as he liked to keep up with the news going on in the rest of the country and out in the world beyond. After his visit to the big man he then intended to continue with the daily camp inspection round, not forgetting too that Patsy was implementing a new idea of hers this morning in the Paradise and he was very keen to see how that went down with the campers. On looking though the national newspapers, Harold received an even bigger shock. It seemed that Ron James had sold them the story and Eric wasn't only a local hero but a countrywide one. Harold wouldn't be needing to tell Drina that the article was after all favourable as she was probably reading it for herself.

A short while later he was saying to Eric, 'You obviously made a great impression on the reporter. His article positively sings your praises.'

Normally, unless it was a matter of life or death, no one would interrupt Eric while he was overseeing his army of staff in the mammoth task of producing thousands of meals for hungry campers. It was a precisely timed operation and any delays at even one stage of the process could result in that sitting over-running, and if that sitting happened to be the first one, then the timings for the remaining two would be out of sync too, meaning lots of unhappy campers with nothing else to do but wait around for their meal to begin.

Like all the other makeshift tented kitchens, the section Harold was in now was a hive of activity. Trays of bacon, sausages and eggs were sizzling on the tops of stoves, along with huge pans of bubbling baked beans and tinned tomatoes, assistants monitoring their cooking process. Other staff were overseeing the buttering of piles of toasted sliced bread, yet more were plating up. Eric would normally be keeping an eye on the operation but this morning his eyes seemed to be elsewhere, focused on one young man in particular, and the normally even-tempered chef was rattled to say the least. The young man causing his black mood was holding a box of sausages while staring at Eric with a gormless expression on his face.

Eric barked at him, 'You were sent to fetch those sausages ten minutes ago from the store tent, Steven. They should be all separated by now and frying in the pans. Did you have a quick nap while you were in the stores tent or a fag around the back?'

The young man gave a slight shrug of his shoulders. 'I couldn't find 'em.'

Eric roared, 'What! You couldn't find boxes marked "sausages" in bold letters.'

The kitchen assistant responded sulkily, 'Well, they weren't in the place they should be. Whoever offloaded them when they were delivered by the butcher this morning stacked 'em in the area alongside the fruit and veg and not in the area marked for fresh meat.'

Eric shook his head in frustration. 'Wasn't it you who offloaded the sausages and bacon from the butcher's delivery van this morning? Look, just get them separated and in the pan and quick about it, before we have a riot on our hands for keeping the campers waiting for their meals.' As the boy went off to do his bidding, Eric said to Harold, 'That young man always seems to have his head up his arse. Give him the simplest of instructions and he manages to cock it up. He's the one I mentioned to you the other day and I've given him the benefit of the doubt for long enough. He'll have to go, Harold, before I end up strangling him.'

Harold nodded in understanding. 'I'll get Marion to go through the pile of applicants that we marked as suitable for kitchen work. Look, I knew this was a bad time to collar you so I'll call back later. I just wanted to let you know the good news about the article.'

Eric shot him a look of derision. 'Good news! For the camp, yes indeed, but certainly not for me. I'm going to be ribbed something terrible by the rest of the lads in the darts team on

Wednesday night. I can't miss it as it's a crucial match. You'd better make sure you're there to help take some of the flak off me.'

Harold had at first been extremely reticent when Eric has suggested last year that he come along with him to his local on a Wednesday or Friday night to watch him play darts, by way of getting the withdrawn man to start socialising instead of sitting on his own at home every evening. Despite his protests Eric wouldn't take no for an answer and on the first few evenings had arrived at Harold's house to collect him until he was satisfied Harold would turn up without being shepherded by him. Harold at first felt very intimidated by the others, they in turn thinking he was viewing them all as beneath him despite Eric's insistence the man was just extremely shy, and it took a number of weeks for the others to start including Harold in their circle and for him to feel comfortable being accepted into it. Now he wouldn't miss these sessions, apart from when work prohibited him, thoroughly enjoying the bawdy banter between the men and the other teams they were playing against, even though for most of the evening he would be fighting to hide blushes of embarrassment when the drink-fuelled men's language became very colourful, especially if they were losing. Harold hadn't yet ventured so far as to try and see if he possessed any talent for actually playing the game, still not quite confident enough in himself, but it was a mission of Eric's one day to get a set of darts in his hands.

'Work permitting, I'll be there,' Harold assured him. 'I'll leave you to it and get on with the inspection round.'

As Harold set off, over in her office Patsy was feeling both nervous and excited. As part of her plan to update the entertainment the daily Bingo session had been replaced with a version of the popular television game show of *Take Your Pick*, which Patsy had renamed *Pick Your Choice*, and it was going to be trialled today at ten thirty. The camp carpenters had done an exceptional job of making the ten small boxes, fastening them together to shape a pyramid that held the prizes and painting numbers on them from one to ten . . . the top prize being ten pounds and the rest vouchers of certain denominations to spend around the camp, such as the hairdresser's, gift shop, photographer's and food outlets. Patsy herself and the three Stripeys she had chosen to aid her this morning, including Dixie, had been practising hard to make sure it all ran smoothly, but it was the audience's reaction that was paramount; depending what that was the game would become a regular inclusion or not.

If all went well this morning she was going to trial her version of *Double Your Money*, renamed *Double Your Prize*. Her nerves over the audience's reaction were not as acute, though, as her worry over what Harold Rose's would be. He was aware of what was planned for today and therefore was bound to make an appearance to see for himself how it was going down with the campers. Viewing this as a major test of her suitability to be in her job, Patsy had planned the game with extra-meticulous care . . . it being very much at the forefront of her mind that the mistakes she had made in the past when implementing new ideas could have proved disastrous for her, but thankfully hadn't. Patsy was confident that there wasn't anything more she could have done to make sure nothing could go wrong this time.

It was now half an hour until the event was due to start, the audience already arriving to take their seats. Having collected an envelope from her desk drawer containing all the questions she had painstakingly prepared, Patsy made her way backstage. The staff were eagerly awaiting her arrival, all very animated, excited at being part of something new, and she was gratified that those involved had made sure there was nothing left to do so Patsy felt it wouldn't hurt for them to put in a bit more practice to pass the time until curtain up.

'We'll have a run through of the "yes, no" interlude,' she told them. 'Jenny, you can play the part of a contestant. Lennie, you can be the glamorous assistant,' she told the tall, lanky young man with a chuckle. 'Dixie, can you please watch us carefully and let us know if we are making any errors?'

While the others took their places in the wings of the stage,

Dixie hid a smile of self-satisfaction. She was full of glee after seizing another opportunity to engineer Patsy's downfall. Since she had revealed her plans for the new games, Dixie had been trying to find a way to sabotage them in a way that would make Patsy herself look ridiculous in front of the audience, but hadn't been able to. She had almost conceded defeat when late yesterday afternoon she had been with Patsy in her office. Another Stripey had interrupted them with a problem he was facing which Patsy needed to go off and sort out for him. During the few minutes she was gone Dixie had exchanged the question cards Patsy had painstakingly come up with for blank ones she took from the stationery cupboard. She had then slipped the written ones into her own pocket and ripped them all up later, putting them in a bin on her way back to her chalet that night, knowing that Patsy wouldn't discover this before the game was actually about to start, when it would be too late for her to rectify the situation.

The questions and answers were the most important part of the game. No questions and answers, no game. There would be no choice for Patsy but to confront the audience and tell them the event was cancelled, due to . . . well, Dixie couldn't wait to hear what excuse Patsy would make, but regardless she was in charge and would be blamed. The audience wouldn't be very happy, though. And far more important, neither would Harold Rose.

She watched with great interest now as Patsy opened the envelope she was holding and took out the pile of cards inside. Her eyes then widened, her jaw dropping open in shock at seeing the top card was blank. Then her eyes widened further, her jaw dropped wider, when she flicked through them to see they were all the same.

Patsy's mind fought to take it in. Coming up with the questions hadn't been at all easy. She had made sure she had more than enough to cover a fortnight, two shows, one each week, so that those people staying for two weeks would not be subjected to the same questions at both shows. Satisfied she had enough questions of the right calibre, she'd then transferred each question and its answer on to postcard-sized cards in clear bold writing so they were easy to read while on stage. Now all she had were blank cards.

Dixie's voice broke into her thoughts. 'Anything wrong, Patsy? Only you look very worried.'

As the honest person she was, Patsy was just about to come clean when a thought struck her. If she had put the blank cards in the envelope then the ones she had written on must still be in the stationery cupboard.

She told them all, 'I've made a slip up. I've left the cards with the questions and answers on in my office and brought blank ones with me instead. I just need to pop to my office and exchange them. I won't be a tick.'

She rushed off.

Back in her office she opened up the stationery cupboard but to her astonishment there was no bundle of cards in there at all.

She slumped down on her chair, completely and utterly mystified. She replayed over and over in her mind everything she had done in respect of the cards on arriving in the office yesterday morning. She was positive that she had put the written cards into an envelope, putting that into her drawer and the blank ones into the stationery cupboard, but if that was the case then why weren't the blank set of cards in the stationery cupboard now? Then it struck her that what she must have done due to her tired state was not pick up both bundles of cards yesterday morning before she had left the chalet for work but just the blank bundle and put them in the envelope on arriving at work, believing them to be the written ones. Therefore the written ones must still be on her bedside table in her chalet. If she hurried she would just about make it there and back behind the stage before the curtain was due to go up.

Jumping up from her chair, she dashed out of her office.

Then minutes later she slumped down on her bed in despair. She had searched every nook and cranny but there was absolutely no sign of any cards, written on or blank.

She felt as if there was a noose around her neck and she was just about to be led before the crowd for a public hanging. What on earth was she going to do? No questions, no game. She was going to look utterly incompetent, not only in front of the campers but Harold Rose as well. And she had thought she had been so meticulous! There was nothing for it but to come clean. If she was lucky Harold Rose wouldn't sack her but demote her back to nursery assistant.

She was just about to lock the chalet up behind her when another thought struck. She had originally written all her questions and answers out on sheets of paper before transferring them to the smaller cards for use on the stage. She had been looking for the cards, not the sheets. Where had she put those when she had finished with them? She searched her memory regardless of starting to believe she couldn't trust it, and remembered folding them up and putting them in the waste bin because as far she was concerned she didn't need them any longer. She prayed that Jan hadn't emptied the bin in the meantime. She shot back inside the chalet to the waste bin, which was kept by the small chest under the wall mirror just inside the door.

On top were some dirty tissues, a couple of empty crisp packets, a biscuit wrapper, a ball of hair collected from a hair brush, and . . . lo and behold, underneath it all the folded sheets she was desperate to find. With a surge of relief rushing through her, she hugged them to her chest, mouthing, 'Thank you, Lord.'

She arrived back behind the stage, clutching the sheets tightly in her hand, with only a minute to spare before the show was timed to start. 'Sorry, I can't understand what on earth I've done with all the cards I wrote out, but I can't find them anywhere. Luckily I found the sheets I first wrote the questions and answers down on instead. Reading off these won't look as professional as cards would have done, but it's better than having to cancel the show. There isn't time now to have another run through but it's not like we haven't practised several times already. Right, we had better get ourselves into position for curtain up.'

All were happy to oblige except for Dixie. Yet again that

woman had managed to thwart an attempt to make her look unsuitable for the position she was holding. But she was determined not to give up her quest to get Patsy removed from her job and win it for herself.

The laughter and cheering during the show and the enthusiastic clapping at the end told Patsy how much the audience had enjoyed this replacement for Bingo. But they weren't the only ones. Harold had slipped inside the doors to the Paradise just after the show had started and enjoyed it so much he had stayed until the end. Patsy was overwhelmed by his praise when he sought her out afterwards, and his announcement that he was looking forward to seeing the next idea brought to life. Being the person she was, she explained to him why she had used sheets and not cards to read her questions off, but he told her that if that had been the only problem she had faced while instigating the new venture then she should count herself lucky. And, after all, she had overcome it and not let the campers down. He then laughingly told her that it was sod's law the cards would now turn up in the place she least expected to find them. Unfortunately, though, Dixie had already ensured they wouldn't so Patsy was left with the laborious task of writing them all out again.

CHAPTER EIGHTEEN

Jill held her breath and steeled herself in an effort to control the pain she knew she was going to suffer as the nurse slipped her arm around her back and as gently as possible eased her up the bed then positioned pillows around her to make her as comfortable as possible. Having finished her task the young woman smiled down at her and said, 'Well, that's you all ready for visiting time, Mrs Clayton. Is there anything else I can do for you before we open the doors to let everyone in?'

'There's something you can do for me, nurse,' the woman in the next bed piped up. 'Get me a large gin and tonic. My husband is coming in and I need something to help me put up with an hour of his miserable face.'

Jill tried not to laugh, aware of how much she would hurt if she did, as the nurse responded pan-faced: 'I could do with a stiff drink myself after the morning I've had running after you all. At least you only have an hour to cope with your husband when I have eight every day to put up with you lot.'

As the young nurse walked briskly off down the long ward the woman in the next bed then asked Jill, 'You expecting anyone in this afternoon?'

She shook her head. 'Not that I know of. My mother-in-law, thank goodness, had a church meeting to attend this afternoon about arranging flowers for a wedding this Saturday so I'm spared her company today. She's a dear, bless her, but such a fusspot and drives me insane with her constant fussing around me while she's here. I've got plenty of magazines to keep me occupied though.' Not that it was at all easy to read them with only one able limb to hold anything with. Still at least she could sit up in bed now and knew what time of day it was, unlike two weeks ago when she was first brought in with no memory of where she was or how she'd got here, suffering unimaginable pain from injuries received from her fall.

Both women then automatically turned their head to look down the ward towards the doors. The sound of feet pounding the floor resounded. It was made by the visitors who swarmed in, armed with their bunches of flowers and carrier bags of gifts.

Not expecting anyone, Jill wasn't looking out and had just picked up a copy of *Woman's Own* to finish reading an article she had started earlier when a voice said to her, 'Hello, Jill. How are you?'

Her head jerked up and on recognising her visitor a smile of pleasure lit Jill's face. 'Eileen, how nice to see you,' she said, putting down her magazine.

Eileen put a couple of new women's magazines and a bulky brown paper bag down on the over-bed table, which at the moment was positioned by Jill's feet, saying, 'I bet you're sick of grapes but I didn't know what else to bring you, and you might have already read those magazines . . .'

Jill cut in, 'I appreciate whatever you've brought me, thank you, Eileen. Please grab a chair and sit down. The tea trolley will be around soon so we can have a gossip over a cuppa.' She waited for a moment while Eileen took off her coat and pulled a visitor's chair next to the bed to sit on. Jill was desperate to ask her if anything had happened yet between her and Harold but couldn't as neither Eileen nor Harold had mentioned anything about their attraction towards each other.

Eileen was saying, 'I wanted to come and see you before now but wasn't sure if you were up to visitors apart from family, so that's why I waited. How are you feeling, Jill? Terrible accident, just awful. Do you remember anything about it?'

'Only that I was standing on the top of the stairs about to go down them. Then nothing after that. I have this niggle though.'

'Niggle? What about?'

'Well, that's it. I don't know. It's just that I have a feeling something happened when I was at the top of the stairs, it's there in the back of my mind, but as hard as I fight to grab hold of it, it won't let me. The doctor told me that things could come back in fits and starts or else they might not at all. I can't even remember where I was going.'

That wasn't quite true, in fact. She did remember something now. Jill's husband had found an envelope in her cardigan pocket when he had come to wash her clothes after the accident. It had Eileen's name on it and when he had asked Jill on his next visit if he should take it to the camp, to make sure Eileen received it, in her fuddled brain a memory had stirred and slowly several pieces of the puzzle had come together. She had been on her way to put the envelope on Eileen's desk. It contained a ticket for a performance at the Pier Theatre. She was going to put the same thing on Harold's desk. It had been a plan to bring the pair of them together as they didn't seem capable of managing it for themselves. Jill couldn't tell her husband that, though, or he would see her as interfering in other people's lives. She couldn't tell Eileen for the same reason. Jill had told him to throw the envelope away.

Now she told Eileen, 'I had a surprise visitor yesterday evening. Marion came in to see me. I thought that was very good of her. She assured me that she was doing her best to keep everything running smoothly until I came back. I have to say, I hardly recognised her. She never wore makeup, dressed quite so smartly or styled her hair like that when she was working for me. Mind you, she did mention that she was getting over a broken marriage and when you're going through heartache like that you tend to lose sight of yourself, don't you? Anyway, she's got an agency assistant in to help, apparently, and told me the girl is proving her worth.'

Eileen smiled. 'I've had a couple of dealings with Sandra when she came over to my office to bring the wage slips and collect paperwork from me. She seems a nice young lady.'

'Well, hopefully she'll continues doing a good job for us and I can offer the post to her permanently when I return.' Jill paused for a moment before she told Eileen, 'When she was here, Marion did say something that didn't seem right to me.'

'Oh, what was that?' Eileen asked, intrigued.

'Well, she asked me if I remembered anything about the accident. When I told her the same as I did you, she said she was sorry she couldn't be of help in triggering my memory as she was not in the office at the time but paying a visit to the Ladies'. But, you see, unless it was a matter of life or death, I would never leave the office unmanned for even a minute. So, it begs the question why I was going off wherever it was to and not waiting for Marion to return.'

'Mmm, that is odd, isn't it?'

'Yes, it is.' Jill felt that this was the right time to bring Harold into the conversation, as they were talking of visits from people at work. Hopefully while he was the topic of conversation Eileen might let something slip that would allow Jill to ascertain whether they had begun a relationship or not during her absence.

'Harold has been in to see me several times,' said Jill. 'The poor man feels so responsible for my accident even though it had nothing to do with him. He's such a caring person, isn't he?' She expected Eileen to agree with her and was surprised when she didn't, which Jill thought odd knowing of the other woman's feelings for him. She continued, 'He told me about the fire. Mindless hooligans, what on earth were they thinking of? What if their bit of fun killed someone? Harold told me the rounds by security have been upped from two to four during the night, but apart from that there's not much the camp can do to stop outsiders finding a way in. Let's hope this was a one-off. Anyway Chef Brown came up trumps, didn't he, with his idea of the army kitchens or Jolly's could have been facing a disaster. It was all in the papers and Chef's now heralded as a hero.'

Eileen smiled. 'Yes, he's rather embarrassed about it all. The repairs to the camp kitchen should be finished in a few days so it will be back to normal for us then. When do you think you'll be allowed home, Jill?'

She was disappointed that raising the subject of Harold had not brought forth a hint from Eileen that anything had transpired between them. Usually women couldn't wait to divulge information of such a sort to another female whose listening ear they had. Maybe, though, that was because there was nothing to tell. But was it Jill's imagination or had she seen a flash of sadness cross Eileen's face when Harold's name was mentioned? Usually when his name occurred in conversation her eyes would light up.

Jill gave a fed-up sigh. 'Not for another four weeks at least, until my casts come off and I'm walking with the aid of sticks and can fend for myself a bit. Ada, my mother-in-law, was insistent she could manage to come in every day and look after me, but she's such a tiny thing that the doctor worried it would be too much. Oh, it's all so embarrassing, Eileen! People have to help you do such personal things . . . If only I had broken just the one leg I could have hobbled around on crutches, but with an arm and two legs in plaster that's not possible. It's not so bad in here really, though. At least I have Nancy in the next bed and she's such a card. The nurses are all lovely and can't do enough for me.'

A bell rang announcing the end of visiting time and Eileen rose. 'Well, if it's all right with you, I'll come again on my afternoon off, work permitting of course.'

Jill couldn't stop herself from saying, 'I will look forward to seeing you. But don't mind me if you have a date with a nice man you have a fancy for.'

Eileen shot her a strange look, as if to say, Why did you say that? but didn't make any comment. 'Is there anything I can bring you?' she asked instead.

Jill smiled. 'Just yourself, Eileen. I've enough magazines, grapes and chocolates to stock a shop. Oh, I didn't mean to sound ungrateful for the mags and grapes you brought in today.'

Eileen chuckled. 'It's cream cakes from the bakery next time then.'

Jill watched her as she walked back down the ward. All her instincts were telling her that something had happened to upset Eileen greatly and Jill wondered what it was.

Back at Jolly's, having checked that the Stripeys on duty had no problems, Patsy was making her way back to her chalet where she intended to have a shower then settle herself down on her bed and have a good think about possible changes to the end-of-week shows. She bumped into Janice, her chalet mate, coming the other way. She was a short plump girl with a sunny nature. It was her night off tonight and she was all dressed up for an evening of fun.

Jan's face lit up on spotting Patsy. 'Congratulations! I heard through the grapevine how well the new game show went this morning. And I've overheard loads of campers saying how much they enjoyed it.'

'Yes, it did go well, I'm glad to say. Well, apart from the fact that I mislaid all the question cards I wrote out. Thankfully, though, I managed to find the sheets I copied them down from so managed to avert a disaster.' Patsy heaved a worried sigh. 'I seem to have gone to pot since I started this job. I've lost count of the times now I thought I'd done something and found I hadn't, or put things in a certain place and found them missing when I went to get them. I'm beginning to wonder if it's all too much for me.'

Jan shook her head. 'It's a big job you've taken on, so much responsibility, and no one is perfect. I shouldn't be too hard on yourself. Anyway, aren't you going to celebrate your success of today with a drink? I'm meeting a few of the other nursery nurses in the Paradise before we go down to Groovy's. Why not come and join us?'

'I appreciate the offer, Jan, but I planned to do some work . . .'

Jan cut in, 'For Pete's sake, Patsy, you haven't had a night off since your promotion. Have you not heard of people working themselves into the grave? How do you know that not giving your brain a rest is what is causing your forgetfulness?'

171

Jan had a point. It wouldn't hurt Patsy to set work aside for a couple of hours, give her brain a rest from it. 'I'll just come for a drink, though, as I'm not in the mood for dancing.'

Jan smiled. 'Well, hurry up and get ready then. I'll have a drink ready for you on the bar.'

Wearing a brown and cream maxi peasant dress with thick bands of cream-coloured lace around its square neck, puff sleeves and the bottom of the skirt, and with her hair hanging loose to her shoulders, Patsy quickly put on some makeup then returned to join Jan and the others at the bar in the Paradise. It was very seldom that Patsy wasn't the tallest of the women in a group and tonight was no exception. She was a good four inches above the tallest of the others. She wasn't the largest built by any means as one of the girls was a good couple of dress sizes larger than her size sixteen but that didn't stop Patsy from feeling like an Amazon.

They all greeted her enthusiastically, pleased she had joined them, and true to her word Jan had a half-pint glass of cider waiting for Patsy on the bar. With the drink in her hands, Jan proposed a toast. 'To the success today of your new game show. Well done, Patsy!'

They all clinked glasses and cheered.

A couple of drinks later the other girls were beginning to make signs that they were ready to move on to Groovy's. Patsy was undecided whether to go with them or not. The couple of glasses of cider she had drunk had relaxed her. She was enjoying the company of the other girls, realising how much she had missed socialising with them since her need to prove herself in her new job had overtaken her life. She loved to dance, especially in a place like Groovy's that always provided such an electric atmosphere. Trouble was, though, she was desperate to start working on the new comedy sketches for inclusion in the Stripeys' shows and the evening really was the only time she could give such matters her full attention.

She decided she would finish her drink and go back to her chalet and was just about to tell the girls that she wouldn't be joining them in Groovy's when Jamie, along with several other male members of Jolly's staff, came in. Patsy hid a smile as her companions' eyes fixed on him and his group weaving their way through the throng of campers towards the bar.

'He's gorgeous, isn't he?' uttered Jan. 'I wouldn't say no to a romp in the hay with him, that's for certain.'

'Me neither,' murmured the others.

Neither would Patsy but he was unlikely to return the sentiment when he could have his pick of any of the girls who caught his eye.

Mandy, a pretty dark-haired girl who worked in the souvenir and sweet shop, said, 'I'm going to go and ask him if they all want to join us in Groovy's.'

The rest of them admired her bravado and stood back and watched as she went up to ask him. Jamie seemed to be refusing, nodding towards the pool table as if their plans included a couple of games. Then he lifted his eyes and glanced away from Mandy towards the rest of them. Realising he was catching them all staring back at him, Patsy included, they all quickly cast their eyes down, pretending they were chatting among themselves regardless that they all knew he must have seen them.

A moment later Mandy returned, looking very pleased with herself. 'They were off to play pool but they're coming with us now instead. They're just getting a drink then they'll be over.'

Several minutes later the men joined them. There were nine of them altogether and Patsy noticed Trevor amongst them. They formed a circle and for the next few minutes jovial banter passed between the girls and the boys. Patsy couldn't fail to notice that everyone looked relaxed and seemed to be enjoying themselves apart from Trevor, who was standing a little back from the circle. He looked uncomfortable and hardly, if at all, joined in with the conversation.

Drinks all finished, Val suggested they have their next one in Groovy's. It was time for Patsy to take her leave. 'I need to get back to the chalet. I hope you all enjoy yourselves,' she said to Jan. 'I'll see you later.'

She made to turn and walk out when she was stopped short by a hand descending on her arm. She looked around to see that it belonged to Jamie.

He seemed dismayed. 'You can't go home.' Then, mimicking a Shakespearian actor, he gave her a mock bow and added, 'The night is yet young, fair maiden, and we're all going to have some fun.'

Before she could protest in any way, he was dragging her out of the Paradise and didn't release her until they were on the middle of the dance floor in Groovy's, bopping away to Tommy James and The Shondells' 'Mony, Mony'. Shortly afterwards the others joined them. Each time a record ended, Patsy made to leave the floor and each time Jamie blocked her way, insisting she stay. She thought no more of it than that he didn't want the group to break up and spoil his good time. She couldn't fail to notice that many other girls had spotted him and were trying to dance provocatively in his vicinity, eyeing him seductively in the hope of catching his eye. He didn't seem to notice, though. It wasn't until several more records had been played that Patsy suddenly noticed that Trevor wasn't with them. Jamie was beside her so it was him she addressed, shouting above the intro to Sly and the Family Stone's 'Dance to the Music': 'Where's Trevor?'

Jamie cupped an ear. 'Eh?'

She shouted louder. 'Trevor. Where is he?'

He stopped dancing to look around then brought his attention back to her, gave a shrug and said, 'I don't know.' He grabbed her hand. 'Come on, we'll go and look for him.' Like he'd pulled her on the floor a while before, he pulled her off. With Jamie still holding her hand, Patsy assuming so that they didn't lose each other, they weaved around the large dance floor, eyes darting everywhere for a glimpse of Trevor. They finally arrived by the bar having seen no sign of him and Jamie shouted to Patsy: 'We could have missed him. After all, it's a good crowd in here tonight. But I'm wondering if he didn't come down here when the rest of us did. He wasn't really keen on coming with us tonight anyway.'

Patsy frowned. 'But it's only polite to tell the people you're with that you're leaving.'

'Yes, it is. Trev's a nice enough chap but a bit of an oddball. I can't work him out, myself. When he's working he's the life and soul of the party, but outside work he's like a scared tortoise hiding in his shell. He hardly says anything unless he's no choice but to answer a question, and then it's barely more than yes or no. I gave him no choice but to come out tonight but I wish I hadn't now because it was obvious he wasn't enjoying himself.'

Patsy eyed him quizzically. Trevor was part of her team yet Jamie seemed to know as much about him personally as she did. 'You seem to know a lot about him?'

He laughed. 'It's amazing what a barman sees and overhears, as well as what people tell them. I might not have worked here long but I already know lots about people from what they've told me and snippets I've overheard. I could make a few bob through blackmail if I was that way inclined.' He laughed at the look on her face. 'I'm not like that, Patsy, let me assure you. Any money that comes my way is earned honestly. And talking about being honest . . . I know what I do about Trev because I share a chalet with him. And it's my guess that's where he'll be now, gone to bed, or else for a walk on his own, which he does most nights after work.'

Patsy laughed. 'Well, at least I know who to come and ask for information about any of my team I think is up to no good behind my back. Not that I think any are, they seem a good lot.'

'Do you fancy another drink?' Jamie asked her.

She shook her head. 'No, thank you. I've had enough for tonight.'

'Yeah, me too. What about a coffee from the kiosk?'

She eyed him quizzically. 'Don't you want to get back to the others?'

'Not particularly. I'm happy with the company I have.'

If she didn't know better she would have bet her last shilling he was flirting with her. 'I'd best be getting back,' she told him.

He grabbed her hand. 'Not yet you're not, until we've had a coffee.'

It seemed he was giving her no choice as he was leading her out of Groovy's and on up the stairs to the foyer. As they reached the top step she suddenly twigged just why Jamie had latched on to her and not one of the slim and pretty girls. She pulled him to a halt and told him: 'Look, go and see the office manager in the morning or when your shift allows, and ask for a form to fill in. When a vacancy comes up, I'll put in a good word for you.'

He frowned. 'Vacancy for what?'

She looked back at him, equally as bewildered. 'A job as a Stripey.'

'But I don't want a job as a Stripey. I'm quite happy as a barman, thank you. And why would you think I did?'

'Well . . . isn't that the reason you're . . . I can't think of any other way to put this, sorry . . . but sucking up to me, because I'm the Head Stripey and in a position to help you?'

He laughed. 'No, absolutely not! If I wanted a job as a Stripey, or anything else for that matter, I'm quite capable of getting it under my own steam. I'm with you because I like you, Patsy. Quite a bit, as it happens. I fancied you the moment I saw you. The only reason I persuaded the others to join your crowd and go dancing instead of playing pool tonight was because you were with them. I've been trying to summon up the courage all night to ask you out on a proper date with me. Well, of course, that's as long as you'd like to, that is?'

'But why ever would you want to take me out when you have the likes of Dixie making it plain she fancies the pants off you?'

He pulled a face. 'I wouldn't give the likes of Dixie the time of day. She might be pretty and have a good figure but she's nothing else going for her. I doubt she could hold a decent conversation unless it was about who's number one in the charts this week or what the latest fashion is. She's too short for my liking anyway.' Jamie laughed. 'I'd get neck ache looking down at her. I like tall girls, like you, ones I can look in the eye when I'm talking to them. And you don't need to plaster your face in makeup to help you look beautiful the way she does.' He then eyed Patsy expectantly. 'So how about it then, me and you going out on a date?'

She was staring blindly at him. Had he really just said he thought she was beautiful! There was nothing wrong with her hearing, so she most definitely had. Was it possible that a man such as he could find the likes of herself attractive? He was certainly showing all the signs that he did. And she was liking very much what she had found out so far about him. Looks aside, Jamie was caring, judging from the way he had responded to Trevor's disappearance; was not at all shallow, going by what he had told her he liked in a woman; was very attentive and protective, the way he had taken her hand so wouldn't lose her while looking for Trevor; and, an important quality to Patsy, he had a sense of humour. Had Jamie not been so handsome she wouldn't even be looking for any hidden agenda and certainly wouldn't be hesitating to accept a date with him.

She smiled at him. 'I'd like that very much.'

His face lit up with delight. 'Well, as you're in charge of your department, you can sort out your own evening off, can't you? My next afternoon off is next Wednesday. If you can take some time then we can make an afternoon and evening of it. We'll go into Skeggy, if you fancy? I've no carriage for me lady, so hope you won't mind using Corporation transport. Shall we say one o'clock at the fountain? I believe there's a bus into Mablethorpe just after.'

'I'll be there,' Patsy said.

'And I'll be seeing you meantime in the Paradise?'

She smiled.

Jamie took her hand again. 'Let's get that coffee.'

Later that night, as Patsy sat propped up in her bed, thumbing through a magazine, Jan arrived back and took one look at her before exclaiming, 'Good God, girl, you look like you lost a tanner and found a pound note! You went off with Jamie while we were dancing and we never saw either of you again after that. It's him, isn't it? It's him that's put that sparkle in your eyes and a silly grin on your face.'

Patsy chuckled and nodded. 'He's asked me out on a date. I'm seeing him on Wednesday. We're going into Skegness. And before you say it, no, it's not to suck up to me in order to get a job on the entertainments team.'

Jan looked hurt. 'I never thought that for a minute. As far as I'm concerned he's got good taste. I'm just miffed he didn't see in me what he obviously does in you.'

Patsy smiled gratefully at her. 'He does seem keen. I just . . .'

Obviously knowing Patsy well enough to realise what she was about to say, Val chided her, 'Eh, don't you start that. We're not all Twiggy or Julie Christie. Jamie obviously likes what he sees in you or else he wouldn't have asked you out. He's the sort who could land any girl he wanted.' She rubbed her hands together gleefully. 'Now we're got a week to plan what you're going to wear and how you'll do your hair. Because you, my girl, are going to look drop dead gorgeous on Wednesday, by the time I've finished with you.'

CHAPTER NINETEEN

'Now you know what you've got to do, don't you dare let me down.'

Sandra watched as Marion took her compact out of her handbag and snatched a quick look at her reflection. Obviously happy with what she saw, she replaced the mirror before getting up, collecting a pile of post and her notebook off her desk then making her way round it. She paused and in a warning voice said to Sandra: 'Three minutes, no more, no less.' She then continued into Harold's office.

Sandra's lips tightened with annoyance as she looked at her wrist watch, a Timex her mother had bought her last Christmas. Three times Marion had gone over what she wanted her junior to do, like she felt Sandra hadn't the brains to take in her orders on the first time of telling. Whatever her boss was planning to achieve inside Harold's office, she was certainly leaving nothing to chance. Sandra was intrigued to know just what it was but knew better than to outright ask her, but Marion was up to something, Sandra felt positive she was.

Inside the office, having given him the morning's post and relayed several messages to Harold, Marion was about to take her leave when, making out she was just enquiring out of politeness, she asked, 'Got anything nice planned for the coming weekend?'

He shook his head. 'Apart from my usual catching up with domestic matters at home, nothing in particular.'

'No, me neither,' she said in a slightly forlorn tone. 'Just domestic chores for me too. I did see an advertisement for a dinner dance at the Imperial Hotel on Saturday night that I would really like to go to, but it's no fun eating on your own and you can't dance without a partner, can you? Oh, well, never mind.' She made to leave, then as if the thought had just occurred to her, said. 'As you aren't doing anything special on Saturday evening, I don't suppose you would accompany me, would you, Harold?' Before he had chance to reply, she added, 'The do starts at seven thirty, so I could meet you at seven fifteen outside the Imperial. Oh, it will be such fun!'

Outside Sandra kept looking at her watch, not daring to be a second late in carrying out Marion's instructions, for fear of losing her job. Exactly three minutes had passed and it was time to act. Jumping up from her desk she shot over to Harold's office and precisely as Marion had told her to do, tapped on the door and called out: 'Sorry to disturb you, Marion, but there's a Mr Dillon on the telephone returning your call.' Sandra then scuttled back to her desk.

Marion said to Harold, 'Please excuse me. I must take this call. It's regarding replacement parts for the damaged kitchen cookers we're ordered. Mr Dillon was adamant he couldn't get them to us until a week on Friday and I told them that wasn't good enough and I had another firm lined up that could deliver by this Friday, so if he wanted our custom he'd better do likewise. That's him calling back to confirm the parts will be with us by Friday and the kitchen still on track to be back in operation for Monday.'

As she left Marion smiled to herself. Her plan had worked perfectly. Sandra had arrived just at the crucial moment so that Harold wasn't given any time to wriggle out of the suggested outing. And as an added bonus Marion had also proved to him yet again what a capable wife she would make him with the way she had dealt with Mr Dillon. Of course, that was all fabrication on her part. Arthur Dillon, a salesman with the company that supplied Jolly's cookers, had already sourced the parts they required and told her that they would be delivered by this Friday to be fitted by their engineers on exactly the day Chef Brown had asked for. She wondered how the salesman would feel if he knew how his name had been dragged through the mud.

Harold gazed after Marion as she left. Any man in their right mind would be euphoric that a woman like her had asked them to be her escort to a formal dinner dance at one of the best hotels in Skegness, where all the well-to-do of the area were bound to be present. He wasn't at all euphoric though. In fact, he was dreading it. No doubt Marion saw him as just a convenient escort for the evening, but even so he felt it was totally immoral of him to be in the company of one woman when his mind and heart were fixed on another. Regardless of how much he'd tried to put that woman out of his mind, it wasn't working. Marion had looked so happy about going to the function that he hadn't the heart to go after her and tell her that he was letting her down. It was only for a few hours and surely he could make out he was enjoying himself for that length of time.

CHAPTER TWENTY

Over in the Paradise, at the back of the stage Patsy was putting several Stripeys through their paces in a comedy sketch, one of several new ones plus some dance routines she had choreographed, which she was hoping the staff would be familiar enough with to include in the show on Friday evening. The sketch they were in the middle of practising at the moment was set on a farm and involved the farmer, his wife and a buxom milkmaid. It was hilarious so long as the timing was spot on. When the milkmaid was pushed over by the irate wife, the bucket of milk . . . which was full of small pieces of sparkly paper . . . went with her, tripping the farmer up in the process and then the wife herself. It had to be done smoothly or the whole sketch fell flat. Despite going over and over it numerous times the Stripeys involved could not get the timings right, and the normally even-tempered Patsy was beginning to lose her patience. Despite being perfect in past practices of the sketch, today Francine, who played the milkmaid, kept getting her position wrong, standing too far away for Mel, who played the farmer's wife, to push her over.

Patsy said, 'Look, let's leave the milkmaid sketch for the time being and revisit it later. In the meantime, let's practise the posh lady with the tramp on the bench. If you want to take your places, Julie and Ben.'

Standing next to Julie, Dixie hissed, 'You make sure you forget again or you know the consequences.'

Julie whispered back sharply: 'Don't think I'm stupid! I know that Fran is only mucking up her part because you've threatened her job, the same as you have done mine. It's not fair that you should get all the main parts in the sketches, Dixie.'

'It is when I'm the best actress out of all the Stripeys. Television scouts are always scouring the holiday camps up and down the country. It's only a matter of time before they come here, and when they do I mean to make sure they notice me. To be seen, I need to be visible . . . and I won't be if I'm stuck in the chorus line or playing a bit part, will I? Patsy's waiting for you to get in position, Julie. If you want to keep your job, remember what you've got to do.'

Julie shot her a look of pure hatred before she went over and plonked herself down on a wooden chest that was improvising as a bench for the practice. A few minutes later she was apologetically declaring to Patsy, 'I'm so sorry, I really am. I just keep going blank. Look, maybe it would be better if you gave the part to someone else.' Julie was conscious that Dixie was glaring at her as what she should have suggested was that the Assistant Head Stripey should do it instead.

Standing several feet away, Patsy frowned thoughtfully. Julie had been word perfect in previous run-throughs but today, like Fran, she was messing up for some reason. It was only two days before the new sketches were due to be played before an audience on Friday evening but after this morning's display she was starting to worry whether it was too soon to include them in the show. Trouble was, though, that posters had been put up in the Paradise foyer announcing the new-style end-of-week Stripeys' show and Harold was coming along personally to see how it all went so it was too late to postpone. It would be easy for her to hand the parts over to Dixie, who would readily step into the breach to save the day, but she was already playing a leading role in three of the sketches and several of the song and dance routines.

Quite how it had happened that Dixie was so dominant in the show Patsy wasn't sure but it was her own view that all the Stripeys in the theatrical team should take their turn at leading roles. That was how it had started out when she had first begun to practise her new ideas but then, without her being able to fathom just how, Dixie had gradually taken on the parts Patsy had assigned to others, after a series of gaffes, fluffs and people saying they did not feel up to performing. Patsy felt it wasn't fair to Dixie that she should bear the burden of virtually carrying the show and as their boss it was up to her to convince Fran and Julie that they were up to taking on these parts.

She said to them both, 'It's just first night nerves . . . or pre-show nerves . . . something like that. What's the saying? Practice makes perfect. So let's practise, again and again, until we are.'

Dixie glared darkly over at Patsy. That woman was the bane of her life! Not only had she stolen Dixie's job but now she was preventing her from following the road to greatness by her stupid need to play fair with all the others.

An hour later Patsy made her way to the office to take care of routine paperwork. Her encouraging words to Fran and Julie seemed to have done the trick and they had both played their parts without mishap since. Her confidence that the revamped show was going to be a success was restored.

She had just come out of the door at the back of the Paradise foyer and into the long corridor leading to the back-stage area, when she stopped short, her heart flipping a somersault, on seeing Jamie coming out of the double doors leading into the ballroom. She was still pinching herself that he had not only called her beautiful but asked her out on a date. Any doubt she had entertained that he might now be regretting asking her out was quickly dispelled as he seemed to sense her presence nearby, turned to look over at her, and blew her a kiss before he continued on his way.

She had barely got stuck in to office work when the telephone on her desk shrilled out. It seemed one of the several Stripeys on duty at the funfair down by the beach had fallen over and hurt her ankle and two others were having to support her the distance up to the nurse's office for it to be seen to. One fewer Stripey patrolling the fairground could be accommodated, but not three at one time. All the other Stripeys were busy elsewhere so that meant Patsy would have to go and fill in for the absentees until the two fit ones returned.

The funfair was heaving with young families and groups of teenagers. There were long queues for the assortment of rides and side shows, and popular music was blaring from the speakers dotted around. Apart from Patsy having to chastise two youths for riding around on bikes when cycling wasn't allowed in the funfair, nothing else seemed amiss. She was just passing the Waltzers, the cars spinning around with those they were carrying inside screaming with excitement or terror, when she jumped as a hand caught her shoulder. She spun round to face the young man whom she knew operated the House of Fun. He looked worried.

'What's the matter, Barry?' she asked.

'There's a woman collapsed on the moving bridge. I don't know what's up with her.'

With a sense of urgency filling her, Patsy told Barry to go and fetch the nurse. With him despatched she spun on her heel and shot off in the direction of the funhouse. On arrival she found a dense crowd of people blocking the entry and had to push her way through to the payment booth and then on up to the wooden steps that led inside. The funhouse was three storeys high. Patsy knew from previous visits that the moving bridge was situated on the second-floor balcony. To get there she had to overcome several obstacles first . . . not only the hordes of people already inside, but navigating her way through a turning barrel, a maze of mirrors, up a staircase whose steps revolved so that when a foot was placed on the first it slowly came down to lay flat against the floor, meaning the only way to negotiate them was to run up.

There was a normal set of stairs leading up to the second floor in another room that was almost pitch black and filled with hanging spiders and festoons of web-like material, and now and again a mechanical ghost would pop out of a niche in the wall and ghostly wails would fill the air, but in her haste to get to the stricken woman Patsy forgot about this. She gave a wail of fright and stood cowering for a moment as a figure shot out of a niche as she was passing through the room. On the balcony of the second floor a crowd of onlookers stood blocking her route. She had to push her way through.

In the middle of the bridge, which was made up of two sections that moved from side to side in opposite directions, a heavily pregnant woman was clinging to one of the handrails in an effort to keep her balance. She was intermittently panting while giving out groans of agony. A man was standing over her, one hand rubbing her back, the other clinging to the handrail too, to keep his own balance. There was a puddle of water by the woman's feet. Despite her total inexperience in such matters, Patsy recognised the signs of labour.

As she bounced her way over to the couple she could hear the man saying, 'There, there, sweetheart. It'll all be all right. Help will be here soon.' His attempts at soothing his wife were obviously doing nothing but irritating her as she kept nudging her elbow in his side by way of telling him to shut up.

As Patsy arrived the pregnant woman let out a loud wail of agony. Patsy looked helplessly at her for a moment, deciding what to do. She then addressed the crowd that had gathered around. 'Is there a nurse or doctor amongst you?' Their blank looks and shrugs gave her their answer. She then went to shout for the operator to turn off the motor to the bridge but realised that she had sent him to fetch the nurse. Patsy told the woman's husband, 'We need to get your wife off this bridge.'

The woman then bellowed, 'You can speak to me, you know, I am here! And tell that big lump to go. I don't want him here. I told him I was too near my time to come on holiday, but would he listen? We couldn't turn down a free holiday that his sister was offering us 'cos her son was struck down with mumps. "You've got three weeks to go, you'll be all right," was how that pig of a husband of mine convinced me to come.' She lifted one hand off the rail, heaved herself around and slapped her husband hard across his face while screaming: 'Well, tell that to the baby! It can't come yet as it's still got three weeks to go . . . you selfish bastard.' She then hurriedly turned back and clasped her hand tight around the rail, wailing out, 'I want my mam.'

Patsy asked the husband, 'Where does her mum live?'

'Leicester,' he replied.

A hundred miles away so fetching her here was out of the question. Patsy placed her hand on the woman's arm and said gently to her, 'We need to get you off this bridge to somewhere more comfortable. Nurse will be here in a minute or two so you'll be in good hands then.'

The woman let out another wail of agony then that seemed to go on for ever before it subsided enough for her to speak. 'I . . . can't . . . move. I . . . can't.'

Just then Barry came bounding across the bridge. He blurted out: 'Nurse wasn't in the surgery. There were some people waiting to see her and they told me she was called to deal with an emergency somewhere on the camp, something to do with a little boy falling off a swing.'

Patsy inwardly groaned in despair. 'Right, go back to the surgery and make sure Nurse knows to come down here immediately she gets back as there's a baby on the way. Leave messages with the people waiting, and a big note on her desk. Oh, and ring for an ambulance. And if you see any other Stripeys on the way, tell them to get themselves down here to help. A female Stripey, mind. Oh, and bring . . . er . . . towels and . . . er . . . whatever else is needed, in case the baby comes before the ambulance gets here.'

Barry eyed her helplessly. 'What other stuff do you want me to bring back?'

'I don't know. Ask a woman who looks like a mother waiting for Nurse in the surgery.'

He was bouncing back over the bridge when another thought struck Patsy. 'Barry!' she shouted after him. When he had stopped and turned to look back at her, she said, 'For Christ's sake, turn this bloody bridge off, will you?'

The pregnant woman had by now sunk to her knees, hands tightly clasping the bridge's handrail. She was groaning constantly. Her husband was kneeling beside her, and they were both bouncing up and down in unison. He was still trying to soothe her and she was still not receptive to his attempts. 'Will you bugger off and leave me alone?' she was yelling at him in between bouts of groaning.

The bridge came to a jolting stop and Patsy and the young couple nearly overbalanced with the suddenness of it. A Stripey then appeared through the crowd at the entrance to the bridge and rushed across to Patsy. She took one look at the crouching woman and knew immediately what was going on. 'We need to get her off here, Patsy, and lying down somewhere comfortable. Doesn't look to me like this baby will be long in coming.'

Patsy eyed her hopefully. 'Oh, Steph, do you know something about delivering babies? I mean, I haven't a clue. We've sent for the nurse but she's attending to an emergency so there's no telling when she'll get here, or the ambulance either.'

Steph looked worried. 'Well, I was with my mam when she gave birth to our Jenny, but I was only seven at the time and I was hiding behind the curtain so no one knew I was there. I remember the nurse ordering my dad to get a load of clean sheets and towels and boiling water.'

'What is the boiling water for?'

Steph shrugged. 'Haven't a clue except that the clean sheets were to put under my mum's bum while she was giving birth and the towels were to wrap the baby in when it was born. I remember thinking my mam was dying, the noise she was making.'

Patsy patted Steph's arm. 'Well, at least you know more about delivering babies than I do. Come on, let's try and get her moved to somewhere she can lie down, though this particular house is not built for comfort. Look, I'll get the husband to help me while you clear away all these people standing staring over like it's a freak show. Then let's just pray Nurse or the ambulance turns up before the serious stuff starts.'

Steph immediately started herding the gathered onlookers out of the funhouse while Patsy kneeled at the other side of the woman, placed one arm around her and said in a coaxing voice, 'What's your name?'

Her husband answered. 'It's Karen. Mine is Jeff.'

'Karen, we need to get you somewhere more comfortable.'

She groaned. 'I . . . can't.' With that she let go of the spars of the bridge and rolled on to the wooden planks, to lie on her side, arms cradling her massive swollen belly, whimpering, 'Oh, it hurts. It hurts so much. Someone make it stop. You tell that cretin he's never coming near me again. Oh, I want my mam . . .'

Patsy looked at her. There was no way they were going to get Karen off this bridge unless she was carried off and lack of space made that impossible even if they did get enough bodies together to achieve it.

Steph then arrived back and crouched down beside Patsy. 'That's the house cleared of campers and I found a Closed sign in the payment booth, so I've put it up.' She then looked down at Karen worriedly. 'I remember my mum was lying on her back with her legs up and the nurse was looking between them and telling my mum to push again. Should we get Karen on her back, do you think?'

Patsy nodded. She then shuffled on her knees to one side of Karen, just fitting in on the narrow bridge. 'Do you want to turn on your back and pull your legs up?'

'No, I just want to die! I can't stand this pain any longer. I don't want this baby any more.' Karen then seemed to change her mind and heaved herself over, pulling up her legs and urgently calling out: 'I want to push.' She then lifted her head, screaming as she did so, and gave an almighty push down, while the other three present gawped at her in shock.

Jeff suddenly jumped up and ran off, shouting, 'I'll go and see where that nurse has got to . . . and the ambulance.'

Patsy and Steph locked eyes, both aware that this baby was coming and they were the only ones to see it arrive safely as matters stood. As the senior Patsy felt it only right she should take charge despite not having a clue what to do except for what Steph had told her. Taking several deep breaths to steel herself for what she was about to do, she told Steph, 'You hold Karen's hand and support her as best you can while I . . . er . . . do my best at the other end.'

Patsy then shuffled on her knees to position herself between Karen's splayed legs. Whipping off her jacket, she placed it on the boards beneath Karen's legs and then pulled off the woman's knickers. Karen meanwhile was giving another hefty push, Steph holding her hand and telling her: 'That's it, hard as you can! Good girl. Now slowly pant until another contraction comes.' She looked over at Patsy, who was staring back at her impressed. 'That's what I remember the midwife telling my mum when she was pushing. Can you see anything?'

Tentatively Patsy ducked her head under Karen's skirt and took a look between her legs. 'Oh, my God! I can see the top of the baby's head.' She looked out from under Karen's skirt and said to Steph, 'What do I do now?'

The other girl shrugged. 'I don't know. I'd fainted by the time my mum was at this stage of giving birth to our Jenny. I presume you need to get yourself ready to catch the baby when Karen pushes it fully out.' Steph felt Karen's grip on her hand tighten convulsively. She yelped in pain and shouted, 'Get ready, Patsy, I think this is it.'

To Patsy's shock the baby's head emerged and then, before she could relay this information to Steph, Karen was heaving again and there was a baby in Patsy's waiting hands. As she pulled it out from under its mother's skirt, simultaneously taking the bottom of her own skirt with her to cover the child, she cried out: 'It's here! The baby is here. It's so . . . so . . . beautiful.' The baby then let out a wail and she leaned back on her haunches and cradled it to her, face wreathed in awe.

Karen was trying to ease herself up on one elbow. 'Is it all right? Can I see it? Please give it to me.'

Steph asked, 'What is it, Patsy, a boy or a girl?'

'A little girl,' Patsy announced in wonderment .

Next thing she knew the baby was being taken from her arms and Nurse Kitty Popple's rotund body was pushing her out of the way. 'Move yourself! And let me take a look at that child and see to the mother.'

A panting Barry then arrived. 'I've got the towels! The ambulance is . . .' He stopped mid-flow as the sound of a crying baby registered and stood looking down at the baby, cocooned for the most part in Patsy's Stripey jacket and white skirt in front of a crouched Kitty who was in the process of cutting the cord. He muttered, 'Oh, so you won't be needing them now then.'

A while later, Patsy and Steph were sitting with Kitty in her office, drinking a most welcome cup of tea. Barry was back operating the now re-opened House of Fun.

Kitty was saying to Patsy, 'I'm so sorry I was harsh with you when I arrived, but nothing else mattered then but making sure the baby and mother were well. I put a call in to the hospital and they are both doing fine.' She then eyed the two younger woman approvingly. 'You both did yourselves proud. If ever a woman goes into labour again on camp, I shall be sending for you two to assist me.'

'Not me,' said Patsy, going pale at the very thought. 'Once is enough, thank you.'

'Nor me,' agreed Steph. 'My hand will never be the same again. I thought at one time Karen had broken it, she squeezed it that hard.'

Patsy asked, puzzled, 'What happened to Jeff, the baby's father? I never saw him again after he ran off when she announced she wanted to push.'

Kitty chuckled. 'He was found propping up the bar in the Paradise, tipsy to say the least. Not sure whether he was drowning his sorrows or celebrating the fact he was about to become a father. He fell over three times making his way to the ambulance and when his wife saw the state he was in . . . well, let's put it this way, I wouldn't like to have been in his shoes from the hell she was giving him. The ambulance men shut the doors on them both and drove off.'

A voice reached them from the doorway. 'Is what I have heard right and you three have just delivered a baby in the House of Fun, of all places?'

They all looked across to see Harold standing looking at them expectantly.

It was Kitty who answered him. 'Well, I really can't take any credit as it was Patsy and Steph who did the honours. The baby was born safe and well by the time I got there.'

He smiled at the two younger women. 'Well done! Mrs Jolly will be so proud of you both when I inform her next time we speak. Of course, it goes without saying that I am very pleased with you both. I wish I could tell you to take the rest of the day off, it's not like you don't deserve some sort of reward for your actions, but when all's said and done we have plenty more campers to take care of. But please don't rush your tea.'

Harold left then and Kitty chuckled, 'All in a day's work, eh, girls?'

CHAPTER TWENTY-ONE

Friday at just after two thirty found Eric standing in the doorway of the large freezer, fighting to keep his temper in check. 'Steven, for goodness' sake, I asked you to put those trays of parboiled potatoes for the roasts this evening in the fridge, not the freezer. They're all frozen solid and when they defrost will turn black, so they're ruined.' The telephone in his office shrilled out but Eric ignored it. 'Look, lad, I think it's time we called it a day. I'll contact the general office and ask them to get accounts to make up what wages you're due and your cards ready for you to collect when you've packed up your stuff.'

The young man looked relieved. 'Thanks, Chef. I've hated every minute working here. I daren't give me notice in because me mam and dad would have killed me, being's I drove them daft to get them to agree to me working away from home.' He took off his large white apron and netting hat, putting them on a metal table and added gleefully, 'Ta-ra then.'

As he went out of the back door a young woman came in. Eric called across to her, 'No members of the public are allowed in the kitchens.'

She called back, 'Mr Rose sent me. He tried to telephone you but you didn't answer so he sent me across knowing you would still be here at this time.'

Eric went across to her. 'What's he sent you for?'

She was staring at him, appearing mesmerised for a moment, before she seemed to give herself a mental shake and replied,

'Mr Rose said you were after a new kitchen assistant. That's the job I came here to apply for, but I would have taken anything if it meant working at Jolly's. My name is Ginny . . . that's short for Virginia. My mother called me after the actress Virginia McKenna, her favourite film star. My mother's name was Theresa Holland.' She paused for a moment and Eric wondered why she seemed to be waiting for something; he couldn't imagine what. Then he reddened in embarrassment as Ginny grabbed hold of his beefy right hand, gripping it tightly and shaking it hard while she enthused: 'Oh, I'm so pleased to meet you, Mr Brown, really I am.'

Eric eased his hand out of her grip. 'Yes . . . well . . . it's nice to meet you too, Ginny. Er . . . have you experience of working in a catering kitchen?'

She shook her head. 'No, none at all. I worked as a shop assistant in my last job and I fancied a change. But I'm a quick learner.'

Eric scrutinised her. She was a pleasant-looking girl of around sixteen, of medium height, with a thick head of dark hair which she wore cut in a fashionable chin-length bob. She looked clean and neat and well presented. It was strange but there was something familiar about her, though he couldn't say what it was since as far as he knew he hadn't met her before. Despite her lack of experience she couldn't possibly be any worse than Steven.

'If I asked you to put a tray of parboiled potatoes in the fridge, where would you put them?' Eric asked her.

She looked taken aback for a moment before telling him, 'In the fridge.'

Eric chuckled. 'That's good enough for me. Make your way back to the general office and tell them I've set you on. They'll sort you out with accommodation, uniforms and a list of employee do's and don'ts. I'll see you bright and early in here at six in the morning.'

Her face beamed with delight. 'Oh, thank you, thank you so much. I'll be here on the dot.'

Eric watched as she left jauntily. Fate had certainly been smiling on him today, he thought.

Later that evening Patsy was making her way back to her chalet. After she had checked on the Stripeys to satisfy herself that all was well with them, she had been tempted to have a drink at the Paradise bar but didn't want to give Jamie the impression she was the limpet sort. She was counting off the time to her date with him in days, hours and minutes. It was months since she had had a bit of romance in her life, last August in fact when she had had a couple of dates with another of Jolly's employees, but it hadn't gone any further than that and afterwards she hadn't met anyone she liked enough to go out with. She wondered how long her dalliance with Jamie would last. Just the one date or dare she hope that they both enjoyed each other's company enough for another? It would be nice to have a man in her life, even just for a while. She realised that she was getting ahead of herself, though, and ought just to concentrate on her date and enjoy the prospect of it, not worry about what happened after that.

Travelling down the sparsely lit long path that crossed over a large expanse of grass at the end of which a high hedge hid the rows of employees' chalet's from the campers' view, she was humming happily to herself as she went over in her mind the clothes that Jan had selected for her to wear, insisting to Patsy that she looked great in them and Jamie would think so too. Patsy was still undecided, maybe she'd settle on another outfit . . . A sound caught her attention. It had come from somewhere to the right of her. She stopped and peered hard into the darkness. She worried it could be a fox, which were known to venture into the campsite after dark from the surrounding fields. She didn't at all fancy coming face to face with one as she wasn't sure if foxes attacked humans or not. Not seeing anything, she was just about to resume her journey when she heard the sound again. It was louder this time and she felt sure it was the noise made by stockinged or socked feet sprinting across the grass.

195

She peered hard in the direction the sound had come from and could dimly make out the shape of a human figure. It was not possible to tell whether it was male or female, but definitely dressed in dark clothes and carrying something. She peered harder. It looked to her like a large can, but then of course it was dark and could be something else or might not be anything, just the shadows making it look like the figure was carrying something. Judging from the way they were heading, she worked out that they had come from the main camp. Then the figure disappeared through a gap in the hedge leading inside the employees' compound. She stood in thought for a moment, wondering what the person was running from. Maybe nothing. Things always looked different in the dark and the figure she saw might not have been anything more sinister than an employee in a rush to get back to their chalet for as much sleep as they could before their next shift in the morning. Humming a tune again and with her thoughts back on what she would wear for her date with Jamie, Patsy went on her way

CHAPTER TWENTY-TWO

Harold couldn't believe his eyes. 'How on earth has this happened?'

Jack Masters, head security guard, gave a shrug of his shoulders. 'I dunno, boss. Could be a leak coming from the boiler and the oil has made its way into the water from underground possibly.'

Harold stared thoughtfully at the huge circle of oil, sparkling all the colours of the rainbow under the lights, in the large indoor swimming pool. 'Seems the logical answer, Jack, but we won't know for sure how the oil got in there until maintenance have done an investigation. If you'll get signs put on the doors that the pool is out of order until further notice, I'll alert maintenance.'

As Jack went off, Harold heaved a deep sigh. First the fire in the kitchen, which was only just back in operation after its clean-up, and now so soon afterwards this incident with the pool, which would have to be closed for several days while it was drained, thoroughly cleaned, the cause of the oil leak found and fixed, then the pool refilled again. And that wasn't all. Apart from the daily swimming sessions, many of the events centred around the pool organised by the entertainments team would have to be cancelled and alternatives found elsewhere on camp. Patsy was certainly going to be busy dealing with this on top of the fact that the revamped show was having its first airing tonight. He felt confident she could handle it, though, judging by her performance as Head Stripey to date. The cost of the repairs to the kitchen had proved expensive and now the pool clean-up and possible repairs to the leak meant further outlay. He prayed the camp had suffered its fair share of catastrophes for this season, and the rest of it . . . well, it was too much to hope it all ran smoothly but he could do without any further incidents of this magnitude at least.

A short while later Patsy was trying her utmost to appear like she was taking what Harold was telling her in her stride when in truth she was panic-stricken. At such short notice, she had no idea how she was going to fill several hours of scheduled events without a venue to hold them in.

It wasn't as if today wasn't busy enough without this additional burden as she had to oversee the final dress rehearsal for the show tonight, which was scheduled to take place between twelve thirty and two thirty this afternoon. Also the new costumes had to be collected from Eileen whose seamstresses had made them up, and after being tried on by the Stripeys concerned to check they fitted, any last-minute alterations taken back to Eileen, collected and again tried on. That was as well as Patsy's normal workload. She had no staff to call in to help her as she'd already had to juggle work around after ten Sripeys had reported being too ill for work this morning. As staff had to report to Nurse over any illness preventing them from working, Patsy knew they were all genuine.

She could tell that Harold was worried enough by the incident in the pool without adding to his worries by informing him that although she would do her best, what he was asking of her was virtually impossible to achieve in the time she was being given.

But she wasn't taking into consideration the fact that Harold was a very thoughtful man and it had already occurred to him that Patsy would need extra help to achieve what he was asking of her as well as cope with everything else she had to do today. She could have kissed him when he suggested, 'I appreciate that all your staff will be busy and you might not be in a position to pull any of them off from what you've assigned them to at such short notice, so would a temporary extra pair of hands be of any help to you? One of the receptionists or the office junior might be able to be spared for a while.'

Patsy smiled at him warmly. With someone helping her with the more mundane tasks, such as fetching the new costumes from Eileen, she stood a better chance of achieving everything else she needed to deal with. 'Whatever you can arrange, I'd be grateful of the help.'

'I'll see to it immediately.'

A while later Sandra was waiting in Eileen's office to be given the costumes she had come to collect. As she waited she became lost in her own thoughts. She was very much enjoying her temporary freedom from the office, being sent out on errands around the camp, and getting to see for herself what went on there. And for the first time in her working life she was experiencing what it was like to be appreciated by those in authority, as she had been pleasantly surprised by Patsy's grateful attitude towards her for what she had helped with during the last couple of hours. It was in complete contrast to Miss Abbott back at the agency, who had never actually smiled at Sandra in all the time she'd worked for her, let alone uttered a word of praise. As for Marion, everything that was done in the office had to be perfect, like she was trying to prove she was Wonder Woman, and woe betide Sandra if she fell short; no allowance was given for her youth and inexperience, and she was made to do the job all over again with a warning not to forget she was only temporary. This meant that Sandra was always on edge, fearing for her job and the wrath of her mother if she lost it for any other reason than Jolly's no longer had need of her temporary services.

Her thoughts were interrupted by Eileen coming into the office with a cup of tea in her hand, which she handed to Sandra. 'Sorry about the wait but the costumes are proving more intricate to make up than the machinists and I first envisaged. The last two are just being hemmed and shouldn't be much longer.' Then out of politeness she asked, 'So how are you enjoying your job, Sandra?'

A bright smile lit her face and she replied enthusiastically, 'Oh, I love it. Patsy's so nice. I wish she was my boss all the time. I've never had one who's made me feel she's pleased with the work I've done for her, like Patsy does.'

Eileen told her, 'I actually meant your job in the general office, Sandra. How you're enjoying that?'

The enthusiasm left her voice as the girl responded flatly, 'Oh! Yes, I like the work I do. All the people who come into the office are lovely and very friendly. Mr Rose is my favourite. He's very nice, isn't he? He's always asking me how I'm getting on and not to hesitate if he can be of any help to me. He keeps telling me to call him Harold as well but I find that difficult as he's so much older than me . . . and after all he's the manager of the camp so I feel I'm being disrespectful.'

Eileen thought it odd that as her immediate boss, Sandra hadn't mentioned Marion at all when she was praising her superiors. As Eileen was still fighting hard to quash her feelings for Harold, albeit it wasn't working, in an effort not to bring herself unnecessary misery now by talking of him, she didn't respond to Sandra's praise. 'Well, the lady who actually owns the camp likes us to think of ourselves as a family, all working together in a friendly atmosphere. Of course when protocol requires it, such as when they have visitors with them, we do show respect for the bosses by addressing them by their titles. If you do like your job, though, and your work is up to her standard, I know Jill will be looking for a permanent office junior when she comes back.'

'Is she nice?'

'Yes, Jill certainly is. As nice as Marion seems to be from what dealings I've had with her.'

Sandra replied, 'Oh, then I don't think I'll apply for the job in that case, if she's like Marion.'

Eileen looked at her strangely, wondering what she meant by that, but before she could ask Sandra to elaborate a middle-aged woman came in, her arms filled with costumes. 'That's them all done, Eileen,' she said to her boss.

Sandra downed the remains of her drink and stood up to take the bundle off her. 'Thanks for the tea,' she said to Eileen.

With that she left.

Eileen looked thoughtfully after her. Marion had come across to her as a pleasant woman, very willing to help with anything Eileen herself had asked, and she hadn't heard a bad word said about her by the other senior members of staff. Obviously, though, from what Sandra had said, or what she hadn't for that matter, she didn't think the same.

That evening at just after ten, Harold was standing with Eric at the side of the Paradise ballroom. The noise in the huge room was deafening due to hordes of campers clapping, stamping their feet, cheering and shouting for more.

'I think you can safely declare that the show is a hit,' said Eric. 'I loved it. That sketch with the two young men getting up to all those antics to grab that young woman's attention, and in the end she went off with someone else, was hilarious. The show was as good as some I've seen on the telly.'

Harold smiled. 'Patsy has done a grand job. And to think, I gave her the job by complete mistake believing she was someone else. Best mistake I've ever made.'

Standing in the wings, the tension that Patsy had been suffering since just before the show had begun finally left her at the response of the audience. They obviously liked what they'd seen and that was the most important thing. There had been a few fluffed lines and wrong steps, a couple of late entrances, but apart from that she thought all the performers had shone. There was still much she wanted to achieve and the audience's reaction to this attempt was giving her the momentum to forge on. She just hoped that Harold had enjoyed it as much.

In her attempts to bring Patsy down, Dixie should have been fuming at her success this evening. Dixie had, of course, had every intention of attempting to sabotage it in any way she could before the show had started, but due to the number of people backstage, getting themselves ready and taking the opportunity for a last-minute practice of their lines and dance routines, she couldn't risk doing anything for fear of being seen. At final curtain, she had manoeuvred herself into the centre of the row and a couple of steps forward, singling herself out from the rest and bowing and waving at the audience like the star of the show, much to the chagrin of the others who felt their performances had been just as good as hers. As the curtain came down and the rest left the stage behind it, Dixie slipped through the gap and waved royally at the crowd as she sashayed her way into the wings.

'You don't half think a lot of yourself,' Jenny hissed at her as she arrived backstage.

Dixie responded smugly, 'Praise where praise is due. I carried the show and you know it. The rest of you are nothing more than mere amateurs whereas I'm of professional standard.'

Her face tight, Jenny shook her head as Dixie waltzed off. She knew she wasn't the only one, far from it, amongst the Stripeys and beyond who fervently hoped that one day someone managed to bring that girl down off the pedestal she'd put herself on. Jenny prayed she'd be around to witness the fall from grace.

A while later Jamie beamed at Patsy as she arrived at the bar. 'Someone deserves a big drink for that fab show I've just watched, which I happen to know was all thanks to her inspiration. And I'm buying.'

'No, you're not. The honour is mine,' said Harold as he arrived beside Patsy. 'I'm extremely impressed. I'm just sorry Drina Jolly wasn't here to see it because she would be impressed with your efforts too. I shall certainly be telling her, though. Where did you learn to put on a show like that?'

'Just at school and in the Brownies. Me and my friends used to put on shows for our families . . . I know they dreaded it when we did as they were so bad.'

'They might have been then but definitely not now. You certainly have a talent for this.'

Patsy beamed then. 'I'm so relieved you liked it.'

'Liked . . . no. He loved it, same as I did,' Eric said as he joined Patsy and Harold. 'As I told Harold, the show you put on was better than some I've seen on the telly. If I'm speaking out of turn then I don't care, but the old shows were stale, same thing week after week, and that's why I stopped coming in to see them.'

Harold ordered the drinks. Once they had them, he told Patsy, who had now been joined by other members of the cast, 'We'll leave you youngsters to it.'

Sitting in the lounge together enjoying their pints of lager, Eric said to Harold, 'Got anything on tomorrow night? Only the darts team are having a friendly match with another team from the pub up the road, pie and peas afterwards, if you fancy it? The pie won't be as good as I make, of course.'

Harold looked uncomfortable. 'I would have liked to have come but . . . well . . . I . . . er . . . already have plans.'

Eric eyed him, taken aback. 'Have you!' As far as Eric was aware, the only social life Harold had outside the camp was when they had a darts match or shared a drink together in the Paradise such as they were doing tonight. Maybe Harold had built up his confidence enough to start forming his own social circle. He tried to sound casual but of course he was champing at the bit to know when he asked, 'Going anywhere nice then?'

Harold took a sip of his pint. 'Er . . . a dinner dance at the Imperial.'

Eric's eyes widened. A man or woman didn't go to a dinner dance on their own. Eileen's relationship with another man had obviously not worked out for her and at long last she and Harold had got together. He wondered which of them had made the first move, considering both of them had seemed too shy before this. 'I'm glad you and Eileen have finally sorted yourselves out. I'm sure you'll have a great night.' Then he chuckled before adding, 'I trust you'll be asking me to be your best man.'

Harold took another sip of his pint before responding flatly, 'If Eileen is attending the dance . . .' which he fervently hoped she was not as he didn't know how he'd get through the evening watching her in the arms of another man ' . . . it won't be with me. She is spoken for, remember.'

'Oh, sorry, I thought . . . It doesn't matter. So who are you going with?'

'Marion. And before you read any more into it than there is, she asked me to accompany her as she had no one to go with. She's new to Mablethorpe and doesn't yet know anyone on a social level.'

'Well, she could have asked me. I wouldn't have said no to a looker like her hanging on my arm.'

Harold wanted to change the subject and asked, 'How's your new assistant getting on?'

Eric took a swallow of his drink before he told Harold. 'She's all right. Keen, I'll give her that. She's off doing what I've asked her before I've finished telling her. She's getting on well with the rest of the kitchen staff and they all seem to like her. No complaints so far.' He paused for a moment, looking bothered before he added, 'But . . .'

Harold eyed him askance. 'But?'

Eric seemed to be about to tell him something but then changed his mind. 'Oh, nothing. Another pint?'

'No, thanks. I'd better be getting home.'

Eric eyed him knowingly and said flippantly, 'Of course, to get your beauty sleep for the big date tomorrow night.'

Harold just shot him a look, which was enough for Eric not to say another word on the matter.

Back at the bar inside the ballroom her eventful day had taken its toll on Patsy and she was stifling yawns. Finishing off her drink, she announced to the crowd of Stripeys she was amongst, all of them still euphoric after the reception they had received post-performance, that she was calling it a night and would see them all in the morning. Behind the bar Jamie overheard and called her over.

Dixie was part of the group and hadn't failed to notice. She moved nearer to the bar in the hope of overhearing what he could want to speak to her boss about.

Leaning across the bar, Jamie whispered to Patsy, 'Can't you hang on and I'll walk you home? Bar closes in ten minutes and it only takes me and the others about half an hour to clean up.'

She smiled at him. 'I really would have liked that, Jamie, and please don't think I'm being rude, but I'm so tired I'll probably fall asleep and collapse in a heap on the way home if I don't go now.'

'If that had had happened, I would have scooped you up in my arms and carried you the rest of the way and put you into bed.'

Just the thought of him doing that to her made her legs turn weak. She responded pan-faced, 'I never let a man see my tatty old pyjamas until I've been on at least six dates with him.'

He smiled seductively at her. 'Something for me to look forward to then.'

The way he was looking at her, with that warm light in his eyes, made her whole body turn to jelly.

He was continuing, 'Have a good sleep, Patsy, and hopefully I'll see you tomorrow, work permitting. Not long until Wednesday. I'm looking forward to it.'

So was she.

With narrowed eyes Dixie watched Patsy leave. Due to the noise in the room she couldn't hear a word of what was said between Jamie and Patsy. One thing she felt she knew for sure was that it wasn't anything of a romantic nature. A man of Jamie's calibre wouldn't look twice at the likes of Patsy. He was probably just congratulating her on the success of the show tonight, that was all. Dixie had been trying hard since she had arrived at the bar after the show to catch him on his own, so she could flirt with him and give him a chance to ask her out, but the bar was very busy and on the couple of occasions he had been free, as soon as she made to collar him he'd disappeared around the back. She knew he was doing that on purpose, purely to tease her by playing hard to get. She was confident that he wouldn't be able to resist her for much longer though. Give him his due, he'd held out much longer than any other man she had let know she was interested in him. Dixie admired a man with tenacity. It would be a change to be with one who didn't always dance to her tune.

CHAPTER TWENTY-THREE

With a face on her that would turn milk sour, Ida was sitting on the long caravan seat under the window, arms folded under her huge bosom, staring thunderously at her daughter.

Putting on a mink jacket over a scarlet, low-cut, full-skirted evening dress made of Chinese silk, and hoping a liberal spray of perfume over it had masked the musty smell the dress had acquired since being stored in the damp caravan, Marion paused in the act of sliding dainty black satin stiletto slingbacks on her feet, to shoot her mother a look of derision. 'If the wind changes your face will stay like that, Mother.'

Ida roared, 'Oh, so you expect me to be over the moon that you're leaving me on my own again on a Saturday night, to go off gallivanting? Not even a box of chocolates or bottle of stout this time to keep me company.'

'If you hadn't scoffed so much food this week and had been more sparing with the paraffin like I asked you then I would have had enough money to treat you tonight, so blame it on yourself. And for the last time, I'm not off gallivanting, it's a works do I'm attending.'

Ida snorted. 'Don't give me that claptrap, my girl. Think I was born yesterday? You don't dress yourself up like that to go for a drink with workmates. You've dressed tonight to impress a man.'

Marion had chosen her outfit with great care but having no full-length mirror at her disposal was unable to see for herself if she had created the effect that she'd wanted. Now thanks to her mother she knew she looked as striking as she had hoped. Her mother was always very sparing when giving out praise, and if Ida thought she looked impressive then Harold's eyes were going to pop out of his head when he saw his companion. But Marion still had no intention of letting her mother in on her plan to get them out of the dire situation they were in and risk her need to dominate everything.

'Well, of course I've dressed tonight to impress a man, Mother. I'm after getting myself a wealthy one to take us away from all this, remember? You never know who you might meet at a work do. For all I know, Billy Butlin has been invited.'

Ida's eyes lit up. 'He's got more than enough money to keep us in luxury. If he's there, you get to work on him straight away in case someone else sets their cap at him and you miss your chance.'

'Billy Butlin is happily married, Mother. I was just using him as a for instance. You can rest easy that I'm as desperate as you are to get out of here so I'm not going to let any chance slip through my fingers. Now if you want company while I'm out, why don't you go over and see the lady that lives on her own over the other side of the site, or maybe offer to babysit for the young couple next door while they go to the pub together for an hour, to give them a break.'

Ida balked at the thought. 'I wouldn't lower myself to associate with the scum who live here.'

Marion reminded her, 'You live here, Mother.' She picked up a black satin evening bag and slipped the silver chain handle over her arm. 'Don't wait up.' She opened the caravan door and stepped carefully down the rusting steps on to the rutted mud below, thankfully dried as it hadn't rained recently.

Over the other side of town, Harold was struggling to tie his dickie bow before the freestanding mahogany mirror that matched the rest of the furniture in his bedroom. Although he could afford to have his suits handmade, out of loyalty he chose to buy all his clothes from the local men's outfitters; his mother had taken him there thirty years ago to buy his first pair of long trousers when he had started at the senior school.

Tonight he was wearing a formal black suit, white dress shirt, black dickie bow . . . once he'd got it tied . . . black cummerbund around his middle, and black leather shoes. From his top pocket the corner of a white handkerchief was poking out. After several attempts and just as he was of the mind that he'd have to settle for an elasticated bow, he finally managed to tie the bow so that it sat just right between the points of his collar. Turning from the mirror, he went across to the dressing table to pick up his wallet, which he put in his inside jacket pocket. It was on his mind to have a brandy to afford him some Dutch courage to help him face the next few hours, which he wasn't looking forward to at all, but he decided against it. He wasn't a drinker as such and didn't want to risk showing Marion up by not being in control of himself. He ought to leave now or he risked her arriving outside the Imperial Hotel without his being there to greet her, which to Harold was not the gentlemanly thing to do.

He arrived a good ten minutes before Marion. When she joined him she looked so glamorous and self-assured he couldn't help but feel that the other people going to the dance must wonder why such a woman was with an ordinary-looking man like him. It made him him feel mortally uncomfortable. His awkwardness escalated when Marion kissed him in an affectionate way on his cheek and hooked her arm through his, just like a romantically involved couple would. She must be very pleased to be here at the dance, thought Harold.

They were seated at a large round table with five other couples. The men he found the bumptious sort, all drinking double malt whisky or brandy, smoking fat Cuban cigars, and fighting to outdo each other with their bragging about business deals or golf handicaps. The women too competed to prove themselves top dog, bragging about of the size of their houses, the jewels they owned, the private schools their children attended. When the men found out that Harold was only a manager of a business and not the owner they ceased to include him in their conversations, which other men would have felt insulted by but which suited Harold as he didn't at all like shallow sorts. He was surprised, though, that Marion made it clear she wasn't interested in being drawn into the women's circle, considering she had told him that she was trying to build a social life for herself. Instead she focused all her attention on him, asking him questions about himself, such as how he liked to spend his social time, what books he enjoyed, foods he liked, music he preferred to listen to. He assumed she was feeling obliged towards him for him providing her with an escort but all the same he wished her questions weren't quite so personal; he felt they were inappropriate considering that when all was said and done he was her boss.

He was glad too when the meal ended and the dance band came on. All the men on their table asked their wives to dance and Harold felt obliged to ask Marion. Dancing he didn't mind, his mother, a proficient dancer herself, having taught him in their living room when he was a boy. He knew he wouldn't make a fool of himself and embarrass Marion. The band was good and so were the male crooner and the female singer. The songs were all from the late forties and fifties, an era Harold was particularly fond of. He was surprised that Marion turned down offers to dance from other men, and felt compelled to tell her that he wouldn't be offended in the least should she accept, but regardless she made it clear she preferred to partner just him. Again he felt that this was out of a sense of obligation to him and thought she was wrong to miss out on the chance of meeting new people.

During the evening, he at times took a furtive look around but saw no sign of Eileen and was grateful for that. He couldn't help thinking, though, how different the evening would have been for him had she been his partner. Even with her dressed in the sort of finery Marion was wearing, he wouldn't have felt outclassed by Eileen; she wouldn't have probed him about personal matters but waited until he had volunteered them to her; he wouldn't have felt awkward holding her in his arms during the slow dances but would instead have been fighting the desire to hold her even closer; and he wouldn't be looking forward to the evening ending, but wanting it never to be over. It came down to the fact that Eileen was his type of woman, the sort he felt comfortable with, and Marion, for all her good looks and self-assurance, wasn't.

As they queued to collect their coats, Marion impressed on him just how much she had enjoyed the evening . . . almost as if trying to prompt him to ask her out on an official date. She seemed to be disappointed when he didn't. Outside the hotel, a queue of taxis stood waiting in the rank and he offered to get her one but she refused, saying she preferred to walk, so he felt obliged to offer to walk with her. Asking him where he lived first, she told him that she wouldn't feel comfortable taking him so far out of his way, then thanked him once again for taking her out tonight and said it would be nice to do it again sometime. Before he had a chance to respond to this she had turned and walked off.

It was a jubilant Marion who made her way back to the dilapidated caravan site. The evening had proved a total success so far as she was concerned. During conversation she had managed to glean enough personal information from Harold to move her plan along significantly, to the point where she could get him to propose to her.

CHAPTER TWENTY-FOUR

Patsy's face was screwed up in deep concentration. 'Stop pushing me, Jamie. This is a major decision you're asking me to make and I need to think carefully. I can't do that when you're constantly asking me to hurry up.'

He raised his hands in mock surrender. 'All right. All right. I agree, it is a life-changing decision and I'll leave you in peace to make it in your own time.'

Several moments later Patsy said, 'I've made my decision. I'll have a steak pie with my chips, please.'

Both the chip shop assistant and Jamie looked mortally relieved and so did the crowd of people queuing to be served behind Patsy and Jamie in the shop on Skegness front.

'Thank goodness for that,' he said. 'If it takes you this long to decide what to have for your supper, then I dread to think how long it would take you to consider a really life-changing decision . . . like whether to accept my proposal of marriage or not.'

She laughed, not taking his comment seriously. After all, this was their first date together. As far as she was concerned it had been fantastic, she had enjoyed their day out more than she could remember enjoying any other man's company, and all because it had been Jamie with her. Right from the moment they had met at the fountain in Jolly's courtyard he had made her feel that he wanted to be with her, had been attentive towards her but without being overbearing or controlling, and she'd felt at ease in his company. They had caught the bus into Mablethorpe then one to Skegness, and like other tourists had strolled together arm in arm along the promenade, had a paddle in the sea, lost their pennies in the arcades and had fun on several rides in the funfair. A busman's holiday of sorts for them both, Jamie had joked. As a memento of their day he had bought her a Kiss Me Quick hat, and as soon as she had put it on, he had, but quick it was not. Amid crowds of other day trippers, he had taken her face in his hands and kissed her long and tenderly, and Patsy had been a willing recipient.

During their time together they had learned much about each other, both delighted to discover that they had much in common as well as much they did not share. He loved liver and onions where she balked at the thought. He did not at all like jazz or trad music whereas some of it she did. He had three siblings whereas she was an only child. He had gone to a grammar school, she to a secondary modern. His favourite colour was blue and so was hers. They both loved dancing. They both liked to play ten pin bowls. They both loved the countryside and one day would like to live in it.

She responded to him, 'I wouldn't need to dither any over my reply to your proposal. I know now what I'd say.'

He eyed her keenly. 'And that would be?'

She tapped the side of her nose in a teasing manner. 'That's for me to know and you to keep guessing at.'

The assistant placed their parcels of food on the counter and before Jamie could put his hand in his pocket to fetch out his money to pay, Patsy had handed the woman two half crowns. To still his protest she told him, 'You haven't let me pay for a thing all afternoon so this is my treat. And if you don't like it, that's tough.'

He chuckled. 'Oh, I do love a feisty woman.' He collected their parcels off the counter, gave Patsy hers and put a liberal sprinkling of salt and vinegar on his. 'Thank you, Patsy, my stomach will appreciate this.'

They sat on a bench overlooking the sea, the late-evening sun sparkling on the water as they chatted easily together as they ate. She told him about her beloved parents, her father a factory worker and her mother a part-time school cook. They'd both cherished her as their only child, supported her in whatever path she chose as an adult. She told him how she had landed at Jolly's at the age of sixteen and how her plan to be part of the team entertaining the campers has been brutally quashed by a thoughtless Head Stripey. Now, after years of working her way up, she had landed herself her dream position.

He in turn told her of his close-knit family, himself the youngest of three brothers and a sister growing up in the busy public house their parents had run in the middle of a rough area of Nottingham. His parents now owned their own very popular public house set in several acres in the beautiful Peak District countryside, serving food in its restaurant cooked by a renowned chef and also catering for weddings and functions. His siblings had gone their own way, forging good careers for themselves, only Jamie showing an interest in the family business. His father was planning to buy another pub about ten miles away from his with its own restaurant, function room, and also a separate hall in which to hold regular dances and entertainment evenings. He had asked Jamie if he would like to take over the management of it, with a very generous salary and a share in the profits. Too good an opportunity for Jamie to turn down and he had readily agreed but, as he had never done anything else but work for his father, while the sale was going through he'd wanted to spread his wings a little away from his parents and that's what had brought him to Jolly's for the season.

Despite their meal being long finished and the sun beginning to disappear below the horizon, they would have chatted on had a passing couple not been discussing the time. They realised then they needed to get to the bus station to catch the last service to Mablethorpe or it was a long walk home for them.

In Mablethorpe the last bus from the station that night that went by the camp didn't leave for another half an hour so they headed into the station to find seats while they waited. Several other people were already filling most of the benches while waiting for their buses to arrive. They noticed that there was a space next to a man over the far side of the station. His head was bent and he seemed to be studying his hands, lost in thought.

It wasn't until they were almost at the bench that Patsy recognised the person sitting on it. 'Look, Jamie it's Trev.' As she sat down next to him she said, 'Hello, Trev.'

'Hello, mate,' said Jamie, sitting down the other side of him.

Trevor's head jerked up and he looked from one to the other of them, his eyes nervous, before he said, 'Oh, hello.'

Patsy couldn't understand why he would be disconcerted to see them both. As his boss she had always treated him in a friendly manner and she couldn't imagine Jamie treating him in any other way either. Maybe she was mistaken and it hadn't been trepidation in his eyes that she had seen but surprise. 'Are you waiting for the bus back to the camp too?' It was an obvious question and Patsy felt silly for asking it. 'Where are the others?' she said, looking around.

'Others?' he asked her, bemused.

'The others you've come out with . . . people from Jolly's?'

'Oh . . . er . . . there are no others. I came to Mablethorpe by myself.'

'Couldn't have been much fun on your own,' said Jamie. 'What did you get up while you were here then?

He and Patsy both looked shocked when Trevor snatched up a bag by his feet, jumped up and announced, 'I'm going to walk back to the camp. If I'm back after you, Jamie, I'll be as quiet as I can so as not to wake you. 'Bye, Patsy.'

With that he hurried off out of the station.

Patsy and Jamie looked at each other blankly for a moment before she said, 'That was strange. He obviously didn't want to tell us what he was up to in Mablethorpe tonight, did he?'

Jamie thoughtfully scratched his chin. 'No, he didn't.'

'He's a strange one, there's no getting away from that. People come to work at a holiday camp to make friends and have a good time, but Trev doesn't seem interested in either, just likes to be on his own out of work. Do you think that could be because deep down he's shy and finds it difficult to make friends?'

'Could be, I suppose.'

'Well, do you think he might open up to you about it if you had a chat with him when you're in the chalet together? If you could get him to talk about himself he might admit how difficult he finds it to mingle with others and then you could try and persuade him to accept some help from us.'

Jamie smiled at her. 'Anything for you, Patsy.' He then eyed her fixedly. 'As you are in such a helpful mood, maybe you can help me with something that is bothering me.'

She looked worried. 'Oh! Yes, of course I will, if I can. What is it?'

'Well, it's just that we only get one afternoon and evening off a week and for me to wait seven days before I see you again is too long. I know I see you sometimes during work, but I can't give you a kiss and a hug when we're opposite sides of the bar, can I?'

She answered, straight-faced, 'You're presuming that I want to see you again, let alone kiss you.'

He looked worried. 'Yes, I am, aren't I?' Then he said earnestly, 'But you do, don't you, Patsy? I really like you and I've enjoyed myself with you today . . . best date I've ever had in fact. I'm not wrong in thinking you've enjoyed being with me, am I?'

She shook her head. 'No, you're not wrong. I've had a great time too and next Wednesday does seem a long way off. We'll just have to snatch what time we can together in between our days off.'

'Well, for me it won't be as much time as I'd like, but I'll settle for that. Oh, here's our bus.' Jamie took her hand and told her, 'If you behave yourself, I'll let you sit near the window.'

Patsy felt like she was walking on a cloud as she made their way over to the bus with him and then giggled and playfully slapped his arm after he'd slapped her backside as she stepped on board before him.

* * *

215

Back at the camp Dixie returned to her chalet and Val only had to take one look at her to see she wasn't in the best of moods. 'What's up with you?' she asked.

Dixie flopped down on her bed and began to pull off her shoes, leaving them where they dropped on the floor. 'I'm pissed off, that's what I am. It's my night off tomorrow and I decided I was going to spend it with Jamie. If it wasn't his night off then I'd get him to change it,' she said, as though she just had to snap her fingers and everyone would do her bidding, no matter what chaos it caused others. 'Only when I went to the Paradise bar on my break to see him as I was on duty in Groovy's, I found out that his night off was tonight. I had a scout around and couldn't see him anywhere so he must have gone off camp.'

Val hid her delight when she informed her, 'Yes, he did go off camp and not on his own either.'

Dixie shot at her, 'What do you mean?'

'Me and Paula saw him going out the gates and heading off towards the bus stop just after lunch. With Patsy.'

Dixie's eyes bulged in shock. 'With Patsy!' Val could see her thoughts racing before she snapped, 'It was just coincidence they were going off to catch the bus together. No way would a man like Jamie be going anywhere with the likes of Patsy, he'd never live it down with his mates, not being seen with an ugly lump like her.'

Not for the first time, Val thought that Dixie was being grossly unfair in respect of her opinion of Patsy. She might not be the prettiest of women but she was far from ugly, and she might be tall and well made but she was a thoroughly lovely person, didn't possess a spiteful bone in her body, wasn't shallow or full of her own importance. If only the same could be said of Dixie. Val knew better than to voice that to her though. She said, 'For all you know she might be Jamie's type.'

'Don't be stupid, Val! Not when he could have the likes of me. No, it was just coincidence they met up and walked out of the gates together.' Then Dixie's eyes lit up as a thought struck her. 'No, it wasn't. I'll tell you what it was. Jamie set this up

216

on purpose, making it look like he was off somewhere with Patsy when he wasn't really. He did it to make me jealous 'cos he knew it would get back to me.'

'Well, they did look pretty cosy together, and he was holding her hand.'

Dixie snapped furiously, 'You must need glasses. He wasn't holding her hand, they were just walking close together and it looked like they were.' She threw herself on the bed, and folded her arms around the back of her head, looking up at the ceiling. 'I thought I'd made it obvious to him that I wouldn't say no if he asked him out. I'm fed up with playing games. I'll put the man out of his misery and ask him myself tomorrow night.'

Val looked at her. She knew she wasn't mistaken in what she had seen. Jamie and Patsy had been holding hands and looking very much together. She strongly believed that Dixie was about to make a complete fool of herself when she asked Jamie to take her out, and in Val's opinion no one deserved it more. She just wished she could be there to witness it and she knew many others here at Jolly's would enjoy the sight too. Dixie had treated too many of them appallingly through her misguided belief that she was better than everyone else.

CHAPTER TWENTY-FIVE

The next morning, Harold had hardly stepped into his office when Marion was informing him that Jack Masters, head security guard, was here to see him.

As she had done previously, Marion made no reference to their evening out together and he knew that was because she was being careful to avoid gossip among the staff. He was grateful for that and hoping that after Saturday night she would realise that he wasn't the sort she needed to help her build her social circle.

Immediately Jack Masters arrived, Harold knew something was seriously wrong by the grave expression on his face. 'I hate to tell you this, Harold, after the kitchen fire and the oil in the swimming pool, but we've another disaster on our hands now.' He then tried to soften the blow by adding, 'Well, my wife is always saying that things come in threes. This is our third so hopefully that's it for the time being.'

Harold would have preferred not to have anything go wrong. 'What's happened, Jack?'

'We've got an invasion of mice in the cinema. Skittering about all over the place, they are. Thankfully I saw them before the cleaners did or else they would have woken the whole camp up with their theatricals. You know what women are like. Scream blue murder at spotting a teeny money spider, don't they?'

Harold exclaimed, 'What!' He ran a hand through his thinning hair. Maintenance operated a rodent patrol to keep the prospect of any invasion from rats or mice, wasps and such like, at bay, regardless that it was a constant battle with the camp being surrounded by open countryside on three sides. No matter how good the preventative methods, no season went past without reports of a mouse or two finding their way into campers' and staff chalets and inside Jolly's buildings. Wasps' nests could appear seemingly overnight in chalets' eaves. But what Jack Masters was reporting now in the cinema was of different proportions. Where had such a huge number suddenly come from? The maintenance men had never been able to uncover how the oil in the pool had got there. They had found no leaks in either the pump or boiler room. Harold hoped they could find out where the rodents had originated and how they had got into the building so that they could prevent this from happening again on such a scale. He was no expert but as far as he knew mice lived in small groups so how come so many had come together now? And what wasn't making sense to him was that they weren't all running amok around the camp but all together in one building.

He told Jack, 'I'll get on to maintenance . . .'

Jack cut in, 'With due respect, I've already done that as I came across this problem at just after seven this morning before you arrived for work when I went to open the place up. Every available man is in the cinema now, trying to catch the little blighters. Maintenance have put a sign up saying the cinema is closed for urgent repair work.'

Harold doubted the cinema would be back in use for a couple of days until the mice were all disposed of, the place given a thorough clean-out and all cables and such like checked to make sure no mice had decided to nibble through them and possible fires result. The hordes of cinema-goers planning to attend the showings today and tomorrow were going to be disappointed and he hoped they would take the fact well as there was absolutely nothing Harold could do by way of holding them elsewhere. He was just grateful that the mice had found their way into the cinema and not the Paradise building, leaving the campers with nowhere to go for their evening entertainment.

219

'Thanks, Jack. I appreciate all you did.'

Jack left and Harold immediately got on the telephone to Patsy, to explain what had transpired and warn her to prepare for the fact that there were going to be far more people attending the Paradise ballroom that morning and afternoon and a good possibility of the same tomorrow due to the temporary closure of the cinema.

A couple of hours later, having dealt with matters that needed his immediate attention, Harold felt he ought to go and show his face in the cinema and see how the maintenance crew were getting on. He thought he may as well do the daily inspection round while he was out.

He'd just reached for his jacket off the back of his chair when Marion appeared. 'There's a man from the council to see you, Harold. He hasn't an appointment but says it's a matter of urgency.'

The council had obviously heard of the mouse infestation and a health official had come to check that Jolly's clean up operation was underway and no threats were posed to the campers.

'Send him in, please, Marion.'

The skinny middle-aged man who entered was wearing a shabby beige mac over his grey suit and holding a clipboard. He introduced himself to Harold as Mr Pickles.

Having asked him to take a seat, Harold said to him, 'I assume you're here regarding the mouse infestation and to check we're tackling the problem to the council's satisfaction. Though I must say, you have heard about it pretty quickly as I didn't myself until a short while ago.'

Mr Pickles cut in, 'I don't know anything about any mouse infestation. I'm here because of a serious complaint we've received from one of your holidaymakers. It's regarding the derelict farmhouse on site.'

Harold eyed him in surprise. He'd received no complaints from any campers regarding the farmhouse 'Oh! What about it?'

'Due to the state of it, it's only a matter of time before someone gets seriously hurt there. The complainant had taken a walk one day during their stay over by the farmhouse and, despite its having a secure barrier around it and signs up warning the public not to trespass, they were worried that children, youths out for fun, or tramps even, could get in there and end up in a life-threatening situation. Before I came to see you, I've been and had a look to validate the complaint and have to agree that the farmhouse is in a very poor state, and the outhouses too. My recommendation is that the buildings need to be demolished and with immediate effect.'

Harold was concerned. He knew Drina was aware that sooner or later she had to make a decision about what to do with the farmhouse and outhouses and realised that they would have to be demolished one day. She had been putting off that decision simply for sentimental reasons, for the farm's associations with the old farmer who used to own it. He had sold it to her father at a knockdown price after his sons had abandoned him. It seemed the decision to relinquish it had now been made for her.

'Oh, I see. I'll get hold of Mrs Jolly, the owner, as soon as possible and inform of her this development and take her instructions, then let you know what they are.'

'I'm afraid it's in the hands of the council now, Mr Rose, because of the severity of the situation. We will instruct a firm to carry out the works, to make sure there are no delays, and we'll be billing you for the cost. I'll get back to the office now to make the arrangements.'

Harold made to stand up to shake his hand but the man had turned away and was making his way out.

Harold was surprised when Drina answered the telephone in her rented cottage down in Devon as he had thought by now she would have been off overseeing the works to her new camp, which had been the next place he was going to try and get hold of her. He could tell by the tremor in her voice that the news was deeply upsetting to her but she also wasn't surprised as she knew that the demolition of the buildings was long overdue. He felt this blow was enough for her to deal with in one day so decided not to inform her yet of another camp catastrophe. Hopefully the mice would be dealt with by the time he did.

That night Dixie was on duty in the Paradise lounges along with six other Stripeys, to make sure all the campers were well catered for. In truth she couldn't give a damn about the campers or anything else at that moment. All she wanted was for Patsy to come by on her usual nightly check. After that Dixie could make her escape and collar Jamie to inform him she was wise to his game of playing hard to get and he should finally ask her out, like she knew he wanted to.

In the quiet lounge, a group of middle-aged people stopped her as she passed their table, requesting she join them to make up the numbers for a game of whist, they being one short. She didn't like card games in any guise but through gritted teeth told them that she'd be delighted to, intending to find an excuse and leave once Patsy had been in.

Several games later, now fighting hard to appear as if she was enjoying herself when in truth she was bored rigid, Dixie got her wish when out of the corner of her eye she saw Patsy come into the lounge. As soon as Patsy had left again after speaking to several campers who waylaid her and also checked with her assistant that all was well with her, Dixie made her own excuse to escape from the card game, saying she needed to pay a visit to the toilet. Then seeking out one of her fellow Stripeys on duty in the lounges, she told them she had an urgent errand to attend to, didn't know quite how long she'd be, and said that should anyone of a senior level come looking for her for any reason while she was gone, they were to cover for her. She left the Stripey in no doubt she'd make sure they suffered if they didn't. She then made a quick visit to the Ladies' toilets to check her hair and makeup then slipped down the stairs to Groovy's, bypassing the main disco in favour of the cellar.

Catching Jamie's attention at the busy bar for a talk without interruption was nigh on impossible, so cleverly she'd thought she would catch him on his own in the bar stockroom, which he would visit at intervals during the evening to restock with bottles. The stockroom was out of bounds for any other personnel but bar staff, given the value of the stores, so she just had to make sure that no other barmen who came in caught her before she had a chance to get Jamie on his own. She chose a place to hide behind a stack of barrels where she had a clear view of the door so she could see who was coming in as soon as they switched on the light just inside the door.

Several barmen from the various bars arrived to fetch bottles of spirits, mixers and change barrels, but Jamie did not. During the time they were present Dixie hardly dared to breathe or move a muscle for fear of discovery. Finally, after a wait of nearly an hour, Jamie appeared, heading straight over to a rack of shelves holding bottles of vodka and gin. He nearly jumped out of his skin when he heard an unexpected voice, its tone seductive, say, 'Hello, Jamie.'

He was bemused to see Dixie emerging from her hiding place. 'What are you doing in here? You know the cellar is out of bounds to everyone but bar staff.'

She stood very close to him and ran a hand down the front of his black barman's waistcoat in a seductive manner. 'What do you think I'm doing?' she said in a teasing voice.

He took hold of her wrist and removed her hand while responding with a knowing look in his eye: 'Stealing drink for a party you're having later.'

She disdainfully answered, 'If that's your idea of a joke it's not funny. You know damn' well why I'm here, Jamie.'

He looked puzzled. 'I can assure you, I don't.'

She snapped, 'Oh, enough of the games, Jamie.'

He shrugged. 'What games?'

'You know exactly what games I'm talking about. The way you avoid talking to me at the bar by pretending to be busy. And yesterday, aiming to make me jealous by pretending to take Patsy out. You knew you'd be seen going out of the gates together and that it would get back to me.'

'I wasn't pretending. Behind the bar, I was busy. And I can assure you that making you jealous yesterday was the last thing on my mind.'

'Oh, what was then?'

'Not that it is any of your business, but I was hoping that my date with Patsy went well and she'd want to see me again.'

Dixie looked stunned. 'You really took Patsy out on a proper date?' She shook her head in disbelief. 'You with Patsy! No, you're joking, you've got to be.'

'And what do you mean by that?'

Dixie snapped, 'Well, let's face it, she's got a face like the back end of a bus and she's a big lump to boot.'

Jamie scowled darkly at her. 'I suspect that you don't see any other women but yourself as beautiful, you're that vain.' He shook his head at Dixie, a look of utter derision on his handsome face. 'You really are a nasty piece of work, aren't you? In my eyes you don't measure up to Patsy in any way whatsoever. She's the most beautiful woman I have ever met, both outside and in, and I fell in love with her the first time I clapped eyes on her. But Patsy or no Patsy, I wouldn't lower myself to talk to the likes of you, let alone take you out. You might make some men drool over you but you don't attract me. Now I've got better things to do than waste my time talking to you. If you're got any sense, you'll get yourself out of here sharpish before someone catches you and you're sacked for being somewhere you shouldn't be.'

With that he grabbed two bottles of vodka, spun on his heel and walked out, switching the light off and shutting the door behind him.

Dixie was in utter shock about what had just transpired. No man she had set her sights on before had turned her down and especially not because they had fallen for a woman like Patsy. Jamie must have been lying, saying to her that he'd fallen for Patsy. He was with her for a reason, something she had that he wanted. That could be the only explanation for him choosing her when Dixie herself was in the offing. She struggled to work out his motive. Then it struck her. Money. He must have found out that her family were wealthy and Patsy . . . not that anyone would guess by the cheap clothes she wore . . . was his way of bettering his life from the lowly barman he was to what marriage into a prosperous family would bring him.

On that score she couldn't fault him. If Dixie believed she could get what she wanted out of life by marrying an unattractive man whose father was rich then she wouldn't think twice about it. What a fool Patsy was to be taken in by Jamie, believing he loved her when in truth he just saw her as his meal ticket. But then never before having had a handsome man show her attention, she would have been swept off her feet by him and hung on his every word. Dixie was miffed that she wouldn't now be the envy of all the other women on the camp for landing herself the best-looking man or get to enjoy his great body under the bedclothes, but sooner or later another Jamie would turn up and she wouldn't let anyone stand in her way of getting him for herself . . . for as long as she wanted him, that was.

When she returned to her chalet that night she was prepared for Val's onslaught about how she had got on with Jamie.

Without batting an eyelid or feeling any shame whatsoever for her blatant lies, Dixie told her: 'I collared him in the bar stockroom and told him I was wise to his efforts to make me jealous by flirting with Patsy and he admitted it all right and asked me to see him tonight after work. I refused, told him that I didn't put up with any man playing games with me and he'd lost his chance. It's his loss. He begged me to change my mind but I wouldn't.'

'And was he upset?' Val asked her.

'Yes, of course he was. Do you need to ask?'

Jamie hadn't looked very upset to Val, in fact just the opposite, when she had seen him just a short while ago while on her way to the chalet. He'd been sitting on a bench next to Patsy in one of the children's play areas. They were eating packets of crisps and drinking from a bottle of fizzy pop together, looking very much like a couple in love. She knew Dixie's whole tale was a lie. Jamie had turned her down in favour of Patsy but Dixie would never admit to this. Val would give anything to tell the others and make Dixie a laughing stock but daren't for fear of what Dixie would do to her by way of retaliation. All she said to keep favour with her was, 'Well, you certainly taught him a lesson not to mess with you then.'

Dixie snorted. 'Yeah, I did, didn't I?'

CHAPTER TWENTY-SIX

'What do you think then?'

Harold swallowed before he answered. 'Yes, that was nice. I enjoyed it. A real change from meat and two veg. What did you say it was again?'

'Spaghetti bolognese. The dish originates from Italy.'

'I've never had foreign food before.'

'Well, now you can claim you have. And I'll make a curry for you to try. I have an army buddy who was out in India during the war and he learned the proper way to make it. It's a spicy meat dish served with rice.'

Harold looked aghast and said faintly, 'Meat and rice pudding together?'

Eric gave a belly laugh. 'No, boiled rice. It's delicious, believe me.'

Harold asked, 'So was a mate of yours in Italy during the war?'

'No, I got the recipe out of a women's magazine. And before you say anything, I only read the recipe pages. It's a great way to come up with new ideas that I can adapt for mass production.'

Harold admired that trait in Eric, his continual search for new recipes to give the campers a variety of meals during their stay, something more inventive than Brown Windsor soup, Spam and chips. 'And you can produce enough to feed the campers within budget?'

'I can.'

'Well, let's give it a try one night and get their reaction.'

Eric looked pleased. He asked, 'And what did you think of

me putting lemon curd in my roly-poly instead of jam? I take it you liked that too, since you cleared your plate.'

'I did like it, Eric. Very much. As you know, I have rather a sweet tooth. I think the campers would like that for a change too. I . . . er . . . wouldn't mind another piece, if there's any going?'

As Eric busied himself cutting Harold another slice off the sample roly-poly he had made, he asked, 'How's the mice problem getting on?'

'Sid reported to me just before I left on my camp inspection round earlier. He's confident his men have caught all of them but they have laid traps where the campers won't see them just in case they missed any. They had started to make a meal of some of the cabling in the projection room, which is being changed, so hopefully they'll find nothing else and the cinema can be reopened tomorrow. They caught forty-three mice altogether. Sid has no idea where they all came from and can't find anywhere in the building where they could have got in except for a small window at the back that was off its latch. Security must have missed it when they did their rounds. But then the mice would have had to climb up the wall to access it. It's a complete mystery.'

Eric put the dish containing the slice of roly-poly he'd cut before Harold, his face thoughtful. 'There's no one you can think of who has a grudge against Jolly's, is there?'

Just about to put a spoonful of pudding in his mouth, he paused it mid-air. 'Not that I know of. Why do you ask?'

'Well, it's assumed that the kitchen fire was started by drunken louts but you never discovered how the oil got in the pool and now can't find how the mice got in the cinema. It was just a thought that crossed my mind, that they were all done deliberately.'

Harold replaced the full spoon back in the dish, eyeing Eric meanwhile. 'I never thought of that. But why would someone do it? If the things that have happened are not acts of God, so to speak, why would someone go to all the trouble of plotting and carrying the plans out for no apparent gain, and risk being caught and facing the consequences? We haven't received any demands for money and threats that the sabotaging will continue until we pay up.'

Eric shrugged. 'That's a good point. It's got to be God having a laugh at us then.'

Harold smiled at Eric's quip. 'It wouldn't hurt to put all the staff on the alert to be vigilant for anyone acting out of the ordinary. I'll ask the managers in the meeting tomorrow to ask their staff.' He then picked up his spoon before Eric could say anything else to stop him eating. A couple of minutes later the bowl was empty and Harold patted his stomach and issued a satisfied sigh. 'That was good, Eric. Thank you. Now I'd best get back to work before I ask you for another piece. It really is very more-ish.' He made to get off the stool he was sitting on at the metal table in the kitchen when he changed his mind, instead asking, 'As you haven't said anything to me to the contrary, I take it your new kitchen assistant is working out?'

Eric hesitated for a moment before he answered. 'Yes, she's doing well. I've no complaints.'

Harold eyed him. He knew Eric well enough to see that he was holding something back. 'But?' he said.

Eric looked at him blankly for a moment, rubbing a hand over his chin before he ventured uncomfortably, 'This is going to sound . . . well, I don't know how it's going to sound to you . . . but I think Ginny's got a crush on me.'

Harold gawped. 'A crush!'

Eric pulled a hurt face. 'Don't looked so shocked that a young thing could have a fancy for me. I'm in my prime, I'll have you know. Well, I admit I could do with losing a little . . . a lot of weight , but I'm still a fine figure of a man and not that bad-looking.'

'I apologise, Eric, I didn't mean you to think that your notion that a young girl could have a fancy for you was ludicrous. But it was the last thing I expected you to tell me. What makes you think Ginny's got a fancy for you?'

'I keep catching her looking at me with a sort of funny look on her face. She's always asking me what I consider personal questions about myself that an employee really shouldn't be asking her boss. What family I have . . . what town I come from . . . what I like to do in my spare time . . . how I became a chef. The sort of things you'd only be asking someone you were interested in. She doesn't bluntly ask me these questions, you understand, just starts chatting to me and drops them into conversation.'

'She's probably the nosy sort,' Harold said.

Eric shook his head. 'She doesn't quiz any other member of staff about their personal life. Or I've never heard her anyway. She's always first in, and I have to tell her to leave at night as she always seems to be reluctant to go. She's so eager to please me all the time. If that's not a crush, what is, Harold?'

He got off his chair. 'Well, as far as women are concerned, I'm the wrong person to be asking for advice, as I know next to nothing, but I'm sure it's just a passing phase and she'll soon turn her attentions to someone her own age. If she doesn't and you still feel uncomfortable with her attentions then you'll have to have a private word with her. Anyway, I'd best get off now and go and see how Sid and the crew are getting on in the cinema.'

Eric watched Harold leave and heaved a sigh. Most men having long left their youth behind would be flattered by a young girl's attentions towards them, especially a pretty girl like Ginny with a bubbly personality. But Eric wasn't at all. It just made him feel mortally uncomfortable. He liked women of his own age. He knew Harold was right and that if it carried on he'd need to have a word with her before his other staff started to notice . . . that's if they hadn't already assumed he was having relations with her and he became the talk of the camp, which would mortify him. He hoped her crush died a death before that needed to be done, though, as the thought of tackling Ginny over such a delicate matter was just as mortifying.

Harold walked around the back of the kitchen and restaurant building to get on the main thoroughfare that would take him to the courtyard and on to the cinema. At the same time Eileen was making her way down the path from the laundry, her destination too the courtyard, where she proposed to carry on out of the gates to the bus stop as she was on her way to visit Jill.

Harold and Eileen spotted each other long before they met up at the intersection. Since Marion had led them both to believe the other person was romantically engaged elsewhere, they had purposely avoided contact with each other, except for events such as the fortnightly management meeting. During that they had avoided looking at each other and conversed when they had no choice but to do so and only on Jolly's business.

As they arrived at the point where the paths joined, Harold politely dipped his head and said in a stilted fashion, 'Hello, Eileen. How are you?'

She responded matter-of-factly, 'Very well, thank you, Harold. And yourself?'

'Very well too, thank you.'

In uncomfortable silence, they continued walking side by side along the path to the main courtyard.

It was apparent to Harold that Eileen was obviously going off camp somewhere as she was dressed very prettily in a summery green and yellow flowered shift dress with a green cardigan over it, white low-heeled sandals on her feet, over her arm a white handbag. He was inwardly torn apart at the thought that she was going to spend her free time with her special man friend whom Harold wished with all his heart was himself.

Eileen was finding the encounter absolute torment. Walking side by side with Harold was unbearable to her when all she wanted to do was run off and put a safe distance between them so she could fight to rid herself of the visions that plagued her: Harold with his arms wrapped around the woman who had managed to capture his heart, kissing her passionately instead of Eileen.

Their purgatory finally ended when they arrived in the courtyard.

After a brisk goodbye Eileen began to walk away. Harold did something then that he couldn't fathom and afterwards felt foolish for: he called after her, 'I hope he's taking care of you and makes you happy, Eileen.'

She stopped and spun on her heel to ask him who he was talking about but Harold was already walking off towards the cinema building.

Propped comfortably against her pillows, Jill looked over apprehensively at the door as she heard the sound of shoes pounding down the corridor outside. Several days ago the doctors had decided she was well enough to be transferred to the Mablethorpe Cottage Hospital for the rest of her convalescence, which was far more convenient for her family and friends to visit. Her husband Dean had told her the previous evening during his regular nightly visit that his mother was planning to come and see her this afternoon. Jill had seemed pleased by this news and told Dean she would look forward to it, but secretly she was dreading it. Dean's mother Ada was a dear little woman with whom Jill got on very well, but she was a fusspot and Jill knew she would spend the entire hour exhausting her with incessant chatter and worrying. Jill felt guilty for feeling as she did as she knew her mother-in-law meant well. The door opened and she prepared herself for the onslaught. In Ada bustled, carrying a loaded gondola basket.

'Hello, dear. And how are we today?' she addressed Jill as she put the basket down on the visitor's chair by the bed and took off the thick winter coat she wore despite the fact it was a lovely sunny day outside. She laid it over the back of the chair then proceeded to take a bottle of syrup of figs out of the basket, which she put on top of Jill's locker.

Jill smiled warmly at her mother-in-law. 'I'm fine, thank you, Ada.' She eyed the bottle of syrup of figs which would go the same way as the others Ada had insisted on bringing in since her daughter-in-law's hospitalisation: into the waste bin, as apart from the fact it tasted disgusting to Jill, she didn't

232

need it but hadn't the heart to say so. 'And thank you for the medicine.'

'My pleasure, dear.' Ada beamed back. 'I thought by now you'd have finished the last bottle.'

She then took several battered-looking women's magazines out of the basket, putting them on the bed and telling Jill, 'I borrowed these from Mona next door whose daughter works at the doctor's surgery. She passes them on to Mona when they replace them with new ones. There are some pages missing out of them where people have ripped out articles and coupons but there's still plenty left for you to read. Mona would like them back when you've finished with them as she's not read them yet.'

All the magazines were ages old and Jill had read them new but wouldn't tell Ada that. 'Please thank Mona for me and assure her I will take care of them and return them to you when you next visit.'

As she eased her ageing body down on to the visitor's chair, Ada started fretting, 'Now them nurses are looking after you all right here, aren't they? What's the food like? Has the doctor told you yet when your casts are coming off so we can organise your return home? I told Dean that he'll have to make you up a makeshift bed downstairs as you won't be able to get up the stairs for a bit. And that woman he's got in to do the housework while you've been in hospital will need to be kept on until you're properly up and about again. Oh, do you know, dear, you don't look very comfortable. Let me give your pillows a plump.' Before Jill could tell her that a nurse had done that just before visiting hour started and she was perfectly comfortable, Ada was out of the chair and standing at the top of the bed, telling her, 'Now you lean forward so I can get to the pillows.' Jill did as she was told, leaning forward as far as she could while Ada stretched her short body over the bed behind Jill's back and proceeded to give the pillows a vigorous bashing. As she was in the process her elbow sharply jabbed Jill in her back.

'Ouch!' Jill exclaimed.

Ada stopped what she was doing to look worriedly at her. 'Are you suffering a spasm, lovey? Don't you move, I'll fetch a nurse to give you something to ease it.'

Before Jill could stop her she'd hurried over to the door, pulled it open, and in her rush to get help for Jill, collided smack, bang with Eileen who was about to come in. Gathering her wits, Ada bellowed at her, 'Outta me way! My daughter-in-law Jill is having a spasm and needs urgent medical help.' Eileen immediately stepped aside and Ada bustled past her and off down the corridor.

Eileen hurried over to Jill's bedside. She was still leaning forward, trying to keep herself in place by using her good hand to clutch the side of the mattress.

'Oh, Eileen, thank God you're here. Can you arrange the pillows behind me so I can lean back?' Eileen put down her handbag and a carrier bag she was holding by the bed and proceeded to arrange the pillows while Jill continued saying: 'My mother-in-law means well but I wish she'd leave well alone. She insisted I needed my pillows plumping when they were fine as they'd just been done.'

Eileen looked bemused. 'So why has she gone off to fetch a nurse, insisting you're in agony?'

She had finished her task by now and gently eased Jill back against the pillows while she answered, 'When Ada was sorting the pillows she elbowed me in my back. Her elbows are really sharp and for someone so tiny she didn't half give me a wallop. Thank goodness it wasn't enough to topple me out of the bed or I dread . . . Oh!'

Eileen looked at her sharply. 'What is it, Jill?'

But Jill never heard her. The sharp poke in her back had made a memory surface from the depths of her mind where it had been hiding since her accident. She was back in the office, just about to make her way down the stairs. Returning to the present, she looked at Eileen with troubled eyes and told her, 'I know how I came to fall down the stairs. Someone pushed me in the back, Eileen. My mother-in-law doing it just now reminded me.'

234

Eileen was staring at her, stunned. 'But who would do such a thing? And why? How could someone have pushed you down the stairs when you told me that you were in the office on your own at the time?'

'I know,' Jill said, frowning in puzzlement. 'But I was pushed, I know I was.' She lapsed into thought for a moment before she said, 'Harold was in his office with Patsy, having a meeting with the door closed. That left myself and Marion. She said later on she was in the Ladies' when I fell. I told you I couldn't understand why I would have left the office unattended. I would never do that unless it was a matter of life or death.'

'What is the last thing you remember?' Eileen asked her.

Jill lapsed into thought again for several long moments before she said, 'I just remember Marion and I were discussing something . . . I can't remember what though.' Of course she did remember, but she wasn't about to tell Eileen. 'After that it's a blank until I woke up in hospital. The doctor did tell me my memory could return at some time but there's no saying when or even if that will happen. If there was a life or death situation happening in the camp, I would automatically have told Marion to interrupt Harold's meeting and tell him about it while I rushed off to see what I could do. Nobody's mentioned anything like that to me, though, since the accident happened. So if there was nothing important going on at the time, why didn't I wait to go off on my errand until Marion came back from the Ladies'? Oh, unless . . .' Her voice trailed off as she eyed Eileen meaningfully.

Eileen said, aghast, 'Are you thinking that Marion lied and wasn't in the Ladies' at all when you fell? That she was the one who pushed you?'

'Someone did, Eileen. I can feel that pressure in my back like it just happened. She was the only one who could have done it. It was Marion who pushed me, I know it was.' Jill's eyes filled with hurt and bewilderment. 'But why would she do such a thing? I've never given her any reason to want to harm me. The fall could have killed me, couldn't it?'

'Yes, it could have,' said Eileen gravely. 'I've not had that much to do with Marion but when I have she was pleasant enough and seemed efficient at her job . . . she's a bit formal in her manner, I have to say, but doesn't make her a would-be murderess . . .'

Jill had a sudden thought then and cut Eileen short by exclaiming, 'That's it! She's after my job. With me out of the way she can prove to Harold she's better than me, and he'll keep her on and tell me he doesn't want me back. Will you go and have the nurse telephone the police and tell them I want to report a crime?'

'Oh, but you can't do that!' exclaimed Eileen. 'You have no evidence that it was Marion who pushed you. You couldn't have seen her do it, so it'll be her word against yours. We need something concrete to go to the police with before they'll take you seriously.' And despite her heartache over Harold, Eileen could not allow anyone to think he would consider acting in an underhand fashion like that. 'Harold would never act so shoddily as to sack an employee while they were recovering from an accident that happened at work and replace them with someone else, no matter how much better that person was at the job. He's a man of integrity.

'Anyway, Jill, no matter how desperate Marion may be for a job, would *you* risk going to jail for murder to land one? Why do you think she would? And it wasn't like her temporary employment was ending, she already had a job, so why would she take such risks to get yours?'

Jill sighed. 'You have a point. So if she's not after my job, what other reason could Marion have for wanting rid of me from the office? If I can find out that I will have something to give the police, won't I?'

Eileen shrugged. 'I've no more idea than you have. I still can't believe Marion is capable of doing such a despicable thing. As I said, when I've had dealings with her she's always come across as a nice enough woman. Mind you, I was talking to Sandra, the young girl that's the temporary office junior at the moment, and I did get the impression she wasn't that fond of Marion when I asked her how she was enjoying her job. But then, I suppose I didn't like all the bosses I worked for when I was young, as all they seemed to do was bark orders at me and tell me off when I didn't get something right.'

Jill nodded. 'Yes, me too.'

They sat in silence for a moment, trying to come up with a way to establish Marion's guilt and bring her to task, but nothing occurred to either of them.

Eileen finally suggested, 'Maybe if we both think hard as we're going about our business we just might hit on it between us.' And she welcomed having something to help take her mind off constant thoughts of Harold.

Jill said sardonically, 'Thanks to Marion, I've got plenty of time for thinking, haven't I?' Just then they heard the noise of the door opening. Jill whispered, 'That'll be Ada coming back with the nurse. Don't talk any more about this in front of her. My husband is an easy-going man but if he learned I knew how I came to fall down the stairs, and suspected who was responsible, he wouldn't wait to have it out with her and then we really would be in trouble! Hopefully we'll both come up with some possible reasons and we can confer on your next visit.'

The nurse and Ada arrived by Jill's bedside. The nurse announced, 'Mrs Clayton, your mother-in-law said you were in a great deal of pain. Do you need me to fetch a doctor?'

Jill smiled up at her. 'I had a stitch in my side, that was all it was, Nurse. I'm fine now. I tried to tell Ada not to bother you but she was so worried about me she left to fetch you before I had a chance to.'

Ada bristled. 'Better safe than sorry.'

'Yes, of course,' said the nurse, and left them to it.

Ada addressed Eileen. 'I think Jill has had enough excitement for one day. She is supposed to be resting.'

Jill exclaimed, mortified by her mother-in-law's behaviour: 'Ada!'

Eileen smiled good-naturedly. 'I was just about to leave. I'll see you on my next afternoon off, Jill.

'I'll look forward to seeing you,' she told her meaningfully.

Eileen collected her handbag from the floor and made to leave then stopped as she remembered something. She leaned down to pick up the carrier bag she'd come in with, out of which she pulled a white confectionery box which she held out to Jill. 'The cream cakes I promised to bring you the last time I visited.'

Before Jill could take them, Ada did, saying, 'How kind of you. The tea trolley should be here any minute so we'll have these with a nice cuppa.' She then added dismissively, 'Thanks for coming in and safe journey home.'

Both the other women looked at each other, then burst out laughing.

Ada looked at them with a puzzled expression on her face. 'And what's so funny?'

Neither of them felt inclined to enlighten her.

CHAPTER TWENTY-SEVEN

'I don't believe that you're leaving me on my own for the third time in three weeks on a Saturday night!'

Marion calmly met her mother's angry eyes. 'Believe it, Mother, because I am. Now I've already told you that one of the women at work is having a few friends round for a bite to eat and she's invited me to make up the numbers. I'm only going as there might be a well set-up man there who's looking for a wife. Once he meets me he won't need to look any further, will he? And we'll have found our way out of this mess.'

Ida scoffed, 'You've been looking for a bloke for three weeks now and haven't met anyone yet.'

'Wealthy men don't grow on trees, Mother. I'm doing my best.'

'Well, I don't think you're trying hard enough. I can tell you now that you're not going to meet the likes of Lionel at a fellow worker's bite to eat do. Men like we're after you landing go to dinner parties in big detached houses . . . that's the sort of party you should be getting yourself invited to. Or go to dinner dances at good hotels and for drinks at posh bars where the moneyed lot go. Or what about joining a marriage bureau? They'll do all the work for you and save you a lot of time and trouble.'

'You seem to have forgotten, Mother, that I don't move in the same circles any longer. Those things you suggest I do all cost money that we haven't got, or don't you think that's what I'd be doing?' It was on the tip of Marion's tongue to tell her mother that she had already found the perfect man for her plan and was now in the process of ensnaring him, but she managed to remind herself just in time that if she wanted this plan to succeed then her interfering, manipulative mother was the last person to let in on it.

Ida was looking at her closely. 'If your Mr Money Bags does happen to be at the do, then he won't look twice at you as possible wife material in the sort of clothes you'd wear to fetch the shopping in on a Saturday morning.'

Her mother was right, he wouldn't, but Marion wasn't going to a party. The part of her plan she was carrying out tonight did not require her to dress to kill, like the other occasions had, so she was just wearing a pair of smart but casual navy slacks and a pale blue tie-neck blouse with a cream linen jacket over the top. She lied, 'No one there will be dressed up as it's just an informal get together and buffet. Now I'd best go or I'll be late. If you've nothing to do but sit on your backside having a good moan about your miserable life, then you could be more useful and give this place a going over.' She knew that her suggestion would fall on deaf ears. Since they had landed in this dire situation, for which Ida blamed Marion entirely, by way of punishing her daughter she didn't do any housework at all unless she was absolutely forced to.

As Marion let herself out, Ida called after her, 'The least you can do is bring me some food back. Anything will do as it's got to be better than the tasteless cheap rubbish we're eating at the moment.'

Over the other side of Mablethorpe, Harold was settling down in his armchair with a tumbler of Glenfiddich, to listen to *In Town Tonight* broadcast on the BBC Home Service. As the introductory music began, he took a sip of the whisky, leaned his head back against the chair, rested his legs on a footstool and closed his eyes. It was a few weeks since he'd had a whole Saturday afternoon and evening off and he meant to enjoy it as he might not get another for the next few weeks with the extra work the demolition of the farmhouse would create for him. He also hoped that the telephone didn't ring to disturb his weekend with reception or security needing him to go in and sort out a problem only he could resolve.

It wasn't the telephone ringing that was to disturb his evening but a knock on his front door.

He wondered who could be calling on him. Never having been the most sociable of men, callers to his house were infrequent, the majority being door-to-door salesmen trying to sell him something he did not want or the odd elderly neighbour to request his help with the changing of a light bulb. He would always oblige if he could.

The knock came again, more urgently this time, and reluctantly he put the tumbler of whisky down on the side table beside his chair and got up to answer it.

He was stunned to find Marion on his front doorstep. It struck him immediately that something was dreadfully wrong. Fear blazed from her eyes and she was shaking, her hair was wild and the pocket of her jacket was ripped. He asked in bewilderment, 'What on earth has happened to you, Marion?'

Tears burst from her eyes and she threw herself at him, burying her head in his shoulder and stammering, 'Oh, Harold, I was so frightened. I thought he was going to . . . to . . .'

Harold urged her, 'What! Who did you think was going to do what to you?'

'The . . . the man who attacked me.'

He felt her go limp against him and was afraid she was going to faint. 'You'd better come inside and sit down,' he told her.

As he took her inside, she clung to his arm as if afraid to let him go. In the lounge he sat her down in the armchair he had just vacated and went over to the fireplace to turn up the gas fire, then switch off the radio. Perched on the edge of the chair, still visibly shaking, she held out her hands towards the warmth. She didn't look physically hurt in as much as he could see no blood on her clothes, but regardless he asked her, 'Did the man hurt you, Marion? Do I need to fetch a doctor?'

She insisted, 'No . . . no, I don't need a doctor. I managed to get away before he . . . he . . .'

'I'd best telephone the police.'

She shook her head and insisted, 'There's no point in calling them. I didn't get a good look at him. It all happened too quickly. Could I have a drink, please, Harold?'

He felt mortified for not already having asked her. 'Oh, yes, of course, of course. Tea . . .'

'Something stronger, if you have it. I don't mind what.'

He hurried over to a sideboard against the wall across the room, bent down to open one of the doors and took out a bottle of Napoleon brandy and a tumbler.

Marion watched Harold as he unscrewed the top of the bottle and poured out a good measure into the tumbler. She suppressed a smile. She couldn't have picked a better subject. This man was so gullible, believing every lie she was telling him. But then she was putting on a faultless performance, and should Patsy have been here to witness it she'd be badgering Marion to take part in the Stripeys' show sketches. She quickly removed the smirk from her lips and assumed her previous look of shock as she saw Harold was about to return with her drink.

Making her hand shake, she accepted it from him, placed the glass to her lips and took a large gulp, pulling a face and shuddering as the liquid hit the back of her throat as she swallowed it down. She eyed him gratefully. 'Thank you, Harold. That's made me feel a little better.'

He perched in the armchair opposite, looked at her earnestly and said, 'I feel strongly that I ought to fetch a doctor to look at you and tell the police to find this man before he attacks another woman and she doesn't get off so lightly.'

'No, I told you, Harold, I'm not hurt, just shaken up, that's all, and we would only be wasting police time. I can't tell them anything about the man as he was behind me and I never saw his face. If I could just sit here for a minute, I'll be fine and then I'll leave you in peace.'

He sighed and said, 'If you're sure.'

She swallowed back her drink, then stared down into the glass with a look of regret on her face that it was empty, hoping he would take the hint and ask her if she'd like another. Being the polite man he was, he did. With a full glass now in her hand, she took a sip of it, before saying to him in apparent sincerity, 'I'm so very sorry for disturbing your evening, Harold, but I had nowhere else to go. I couldn't go back to my lodgings in this state. My landlady is a dear sweet old lady but the nervy sort, and if I told her what had happened to me she'd never rest in her bed again for panicking that there was a brute out there somewhere who might break in and murder her.'

Marion put down the tumbler on the occasional table at the side of the sofa then clasped her hands together, wringing them as though distraught, and her voice had a tremor to it when she relayed to him what had supposedly happened to her earlier.

'I was feeling very down this evening, alone in my room with only a book for company, and I thought a walk would help lift my mood. Not often we get such warm evenings at this time of year. There was hardly anyone about and I was really enjoying my walk around the town, looking in the shop windows.'

She paused for a moment then apparently forced herself to continue. 'I . . . I was just passing by an entry between two shops when suddenly an arm clamped round my chest and a hand was over my mouth and I was being dragged backwards into the entry. I tried to fight free but he was too strong and I was thinking that this was it . . .' she gave a small sob and a shudder before she went on ' . . . that the man was going to rape and possibly kill me. But then it was like a miracle as where this other man came from I have no idea, but I just heard this shout of, "Oi, what's going on?" Next thing I knew my attacker had released me and was pelting out of the entry towards the sea front. I ran the other way. I never stopped, I just kept going, until I couldn't run any more. I hid behind a wall until I'd got my breath back. I just wanted to get back to the safety of my lodgings. But as I told you earlier, I couldn't return in the state I was in and upset my dear landlady. I thought there must be a church nearby where I could go and sit and compose myself so I set off in search of one and then I saw the street sign. It

243

was the road where you'd told me you lived. Knowing what a kind man you are, I thought you wouldn't mind if I took sanctuary with you for a short while.' She eyed him then, worriedly. 'You didn't, did you, Harold, mind me turning to you for help?

Her story was utterly shocking to him. He just could not understand the mind of men who thought nothing of using force against women to satisfy their sexual needs. He felt so sorry for Marion, having suffered such a terrifying ordeal. Thankfully for her she had come out of it relatively unscathed, whereas other women weren't so lucky.

He answered, 'No, no, of course I don't mind. Stay as long as you need to. When you're ready, I'll run you back to your lodgings in my car.'

Lodgings that didn't exist. 'I wouldn't dream of putting you to any more trouble than I have already. I'd be grateful if you could order me a taxi.' She saw he was about to protest and stopped him by saying, 'Please, Harold, I insist.'

He relented. 'As you wish.'

She took another sip of her drink, before she said, 'I really don't know how I'm going to repay you for your kindness tonight, Harold.

'There's no need, really.'

'My mother always taught me that one good turn deserves another.' Before he had a chance to insist that no repayment was necessary, as she must not leave without creating an opening for the next stage of her plan, Marion quickly added, 'Your home is lovely. It's very cosy and comfortable. You have good taste, Harold.' In truth she felt like she'd stepped back into the 1930s, a time when brown seemed the fashionable colour. The walls were papered in a muddy brown and cream patterned paper, the three-piece suite was covered in brown moquette, brown and cream curtains hung at the large bay front window, a huge sombre Axminster rug covered the wooden floor; the fireplace was covered in brown and cream speckled tiles, its mantel littered with an assortment of pottery figures and silver-framed photographs of family members. As soon as she moved in as Harold's wife this room would be cleared and redecorated in her own taste, along with the rest of the house, decided Marion.

Harold told her with a proud light in his eyes, 'The credit belongs to my mother. It's all her doing. When Father bought the house before they married, they made a pact between them that he took care of the outside and she everything within.'

Marion froze, her heart thumping thunderously. Mother! She hadn't bargained on having a mother to deal with. How stupid of her not to have taken that into consideration when she was perfecting her plan. What if his mother wasn't gullible like her son, but astute? Within a short space of time she could see through Marion's act . . . She now faced starting from scratch while still living in her rusting metal hovel with her own insufferable mother.

As she was contemplating the possible repercussions Marion was still aware that Harold was talking about his mother and something he was saying now resonated. *People had loved her and she'd been very popular in the vicinity.* Her low spirits rose. He was talking about his mother in the past tense. She was dead! Marion quashed the urge to whoop with joy. Relief flooded through her. Her heart rate returned to normal. The shards of her tattered plan flew back together. She lied to him, 'I'm sorry for your loss, Harold. Your mother sounds like she was a remarkable woman,' She grabbed the tumbler off the table and downed the last of her drink. 'I feel composed enough to face my landlady now. May I please use your bathroom to tidy myself up while you call me a taxi?'

Ten minutes later Harold showed her out.

On the doorstep, Marion laid a hand on his arm and said, 'Thank you again, Harold. You really are a lovely man.' She then stood on tiptoes and kissed his cheek before she turned and hurried off down the path to join the taxi waiting for her by the kerb.

Harold thoughtfully watched her go. She was very resilient. A short while ago she had gone through an ordeal that would have reduced most women to shivering wrecks. Yet he had definitely seen a spring in Marion's step as she had hurried off down the path just now, which told him that she was already managing to put her attack behind her. He was pleased that she appeared to have such strength of character, for her own sake. He did wish, though, that she didn't feel she needed to repay him for the hand of friendship he had offered her tonight. He would have to be a callous, hard-hearted man indeed to have turned any woman away from his door who was in the state Marion had been in when she'd knocked on it. But also he was far from comfortable about her display of intimacy towards him on departure. Her lips had lingered on his cheek for far longer than the peck of gratitude required. To him, that kiss had been more the sort a person gave another they were very fond of! But then, he reasoned with himself, it was probably just him making too much of things, thanks to his inexperience with women.

How very much he wished that kiss had been delivered by another.

'So, how are you enjoying your cruise?'

Patsy issued a contented sigh. 'It's wonderful, Jamie. If ever I go on another cruise in the future, it will never match up to this one. So where is this picnic you promised me, along with my cruise?'

He laid down one of the oars of the boat in which he was rowing Patsy around the camp boating lake, fished in his pocket and pulled out a packet of salted peanuts, tossing them over to her. 'Make sure you save me some.'

She immediately tossed them back to him. 'You can have them all as I hate nuts of any kind.'

He fished in his pocket again. 'Then it's a good job I brought these along with me too,' he said, tossing her a packet of Walker's cheese and onion crisps.

She caught them and smiled at him. 'You remembered these are my favourite flavour.'

He was pulling on the oars, looking behind him, conscious he was close to the bank and not wanting to crash into it. 'Well, you eat them at your own risk.'

She frowned. 'Why?'

'Because you risk me not kissing you again tonight. I hate cheese and onion crisps and I'll still be able to taste them on your breath.'

She tossed the bag back to him. 'I've suddenly gone off cheese and onion.'

He dropped both oars and crawled over to sit next to her in the stern of the boat. He put his arm around her, pulling her close. 'Pleased to know a kiss from me means more to you than a bag of crisps.'

'Every time,' she said meaningfully.

They shared a tender kiss, then both rested against the stern, gazing up at a cloudless sky, stars twinkling brightly, a crescent moon casting a thin path of light across the water. The manmade lake had been designed to look like it was a natural one, with stretches of mature trees and shrubs around uneven banks planted with flags, reeds and bullrushes. It had a small island thick with shrubs and trees in the middle. A path ran alongside the part of the lake that carried on up to the courtyard one way and down to the funfair and beach the other. It was a very romantic setting at night in the moonlight.

It was after midnight that late-June evening and the air had turned chilly but neither of them seemed to notice; the only thing they were aware of was that their time together tonight must soon end or neither of them would be fit for work tomorrow. They shouldn't in fact have been out on the lake after the boats had been tied up for the night earlier that evening, but as Jamie had laughingly explained to Patsy as he had expertly picked the padlock at the mooring stage, how else was he to fulfil his promise to take her on a cruise after work that evening? There were prominent signs on the landing stage warning that no persons were allowed on the lake without the boating staff present so in fact they were breaking camp rules. If caught they could be reprimanded, but that fact wasn't as uppermost in Patsy's mind as wondering just how Jamie knew how to pick a lock.

When she'd asked him, he'd told her that one of his father's chefs was a reformed burglar, having served time in prison for his string of crimes, who had taught him how to do it as a young boy when he'd lost the key to the padlock on his bike. She had ribbed him that he was handy to know then just in case in future she needed a safe cracking open. He had responded that unfortunately padlocks was his limit, but he did know a man who could handle most safes.

Sighing contentedly, she said to him, 'The sky is so clear. I feel as though I just have to reach out my hand and I can grab a handful of stars. I've never seen them shining so brightly before.'

'Well, I hate to put a dampener on it, but the sky won't be like this for much longer tonight as there's a storm coming in and it's going to rain all day tomorrow.'

Patsy groaned. 'That means an extra busy time for my team, keeping the campers happy with entertainments indoors. Thankfully the cinema is back in use after the mouse invasion or we'd be really pushed for space to hold everything. Jamie, not only are you an expert padlock picker, you can forecast the weather too?'

He chuckled. 'The chap on my transistor told me when I was listening to it as I got ready for my shift tonight after tea. So how are the plans for the new sketches coming along?'

'Not as well as I'd hoped. The one with the two males dressed up as two old dears in the corner shop just didn't work when it was acted out and neither did the one with the two kids having their dinner. So it's back to the drawing board for me but I've got plenty more ideas. I saw a sketch that Morecambe and Wise did on their telly show that I happened to catch as I was passing through the television lounge the other night and I think I can adapt that to go on the stage.'

'And I'm sure you will,' he told her with conviction. 'Have you never wanted to go on the stage yourself?'

'Oh, yes, of course I did. When I was young it was my ambition to dance and sing on stage, and it was a huge blow to me to find out when I came here for an interview to join the Stripeys that I hadn't got what it takes. Still, I am lucky that I've had the chance to be part of the backstage crew and I love every minute of it, just as nervous that the show will go well as those about to go on-stage before the curtain goes up. When you were young, what did you want to be when you grew up?'

'Run a pub like my dad. Never wanted to do anything else. I suppose I'm one of the lucky ones who will have their child-hood dreams come true. I . . .' He suddenly stopped talking as he lifted his head to peer across the lake towards the far bank the boat was drifting towards.

'What's the matter?' Patsy asked him.

He whispered, 'Remember we've been asked to look out for anyone acting suspiciously around the camp, especially after dark?'

She whispered back, 'Yes, it was a direct request from Harold Rose. We managers were told that they now think that kitchen fire might not have been caused by louts larking about, but set deliberately. So was the oil in the indoor swimming pool and mice in the cinema, and it must be someone on the camp who's the culprit as all these things have happened in the early hours of the morning and in each case a back window was found off the latch. Except for the kitchen incident where the back door was jemmied, but then that was the only way in as there is no window on the back wall to sneak in through. But why have you mentioned this now?'

'Because I can see someone over there, walking along the path in the clearing between those two clumps of trees. See?' he said, pointing

Patsy looked across in the direction Jamie was referring to, seeing the shadowy figure too. 'Oh, yes.'

'What do you think he or she is doing out at this time of night?'

She chuckled. 'Well, we're out, Jamie.'

'But we're together and they're on their own.'

'Well, they're probably just taking a walk as they couldn't sleep. I've done it often enough in the past, especially on hot sticky nights.'

'Yes, but it's not one of those nights, is it?'

'No, but they don't look suspicious to me. I mean, all they're doing is walking around the boating lake path and we can hardly report someone for doing that.'

He peered harder. 'It's definitely a man and it looks like they're carrying something.'

She peered too. 'Oh, yes. It looks like a bag of some sort. Hang on, I'm sure that's Trev.'

'Now you mention it, the man does remind me of him. But it won't be Trevor. I asked him if he was going along to Kevin's chalet after work as it's his birthday and he's invited all the bar staff and the Stripeys on duty in the ballroom and anyone they want to bring with them, as long as they bring some drink with them of course.'

'You never told me we'd been invited for a drink?'

He leaned over and kissed her nose. 'That's because I was being selfish and wanted you all to myself.'

She smiled. 'Oh, that's all right then. So what did Trev say?'

'That he had things to do tonight in the chalet so wouldn't be going.'

Patsy still felt sure the man was Trev and looked again towards the path skirting the lake. But Trev or not, the man was no longer visible to her, having disappeared into the night.

She turned to Jamie and said, 'I've been meaning to ask you . . . did you manage to have a man to man chat with Trev?'

'I meant to tell you that I did. Last night, in fact, after I saw you back to your chalet. There's not much to relate and what I did manage to wring out of him was like getting blood from a stone. He was getting ready for bed when I got in so I started chatting about this and that, then I got on to the subject of work and how much I was enjoying my job and asked him if he was enjoying his. He said yes, he did.'

'Did he say whether he felt I was a good boss to work for?' Patsy asked.

'Oh, fishing for compliments, are we, Miss Mathers?' Jamie responded with a twinkle in his eyes.

'No, no, not at all,' she insisted. 'I just like to know that my team think me fair, that's all.'

'And how else would anyone think of you? I've never heard any of your staff say a word against you, and people often don't realise I'm in earshot when they're having conversations at the bar. Anyway, he didn't say any more than I've told you. So then I asked him if he was missing his family at all. He didn't answer. So I asked him about his friends. He said no, he wasn't. I did tell you it was like getting blood from a stone. Anyway I tried one last time to try and find out why he keeps such a distance from the rest of the staff by saying that I supposed he didn't miss his friends back home with all the new ones he's made here at Jolly's . . . and as you and I know he hasn't made any.'

'And what did Trevor answer?'

'He didn't. Just got into bed and turned his back and that told me our conversation was over.'

Patsy sat in silence for a moment before she said, 'It's obvious he doesn't want you probing him about his life then. Has he got something to hide, do you think?'

'Maybe he's got nothing to hide but he's a private sort of person.'

'Mmm. Yes, maybe he is. My mum always told me that it's a mistake to expect everyone to act like you would. Just because I couldn't manage without my friends in my life, doesn't mean to say everyone feels like that.' She then fought to stifle a yawn of tiredness, not wanting Jamie to think that she was bored.

She failed as Jamie did notice. He said, 'Best get this ship back to shore and you home to bed.'

Patsy smiled warmly at him. 'I've had a lovely time, thank you, Jamie.'

'Me too,' he assured her.

CHAPTER TWENTY-EIGHT

The next morning Harold raked a hand through his hair in despair as he let out a despondent sigh. 'How did it happen, Jack?'

Jack Masters shrugged. 'I've no idea. It started to rain about four in the morning and there was a wind but it wasn't stormy. The last bad storm we had was when Dan was killed last year, and even then the rowing boats on the lake didn't break their moorings and sink.'

'So are we saying that this must have been done deliberately?'

'I can't see how it can have been anything else. Forty boats just don't sink on their own.'

'We were beginning to suspect that the other things that have happened recently were deliberately arranged too, but after this I don't suspect any more. I know. All the staff have been asked to be vigilant and if any were out and about late last night then they would have reported back by now if they'd witnessed anything amiss, and your men too would have told you if they'd seen anything untoward while doing their rounds. I can't understand what the perpetrator is gaining from this. I don't know what else we can do to try and catch them other than what we are already as we've no idea where they are going to strike next. I shall speak to Mrs Jolly and see what she advises. I haven't mentioned the plague of mice to her yet because I felt she had enough on her mind at the time, having just broken the news to her about the farmhouse, but I've no choice now. Thank you, Jack. I'll get on to maintenance to deal with it. I suppose it's one consolation that it's raining today so this won't cause any disruption to any campers wanting to go on the boating lake.'

After speaking to maintenance he then tried to get hold of Drina but had no luck. Harold was getting concerned that he hadn't heard a word from her after their last conversation when he had informed her about the farmhouse demolition and she'd said to him she would think of how best to handle it from Jolly's point of view and call him back to tell him what she would like him to do. He hoped she'd telephone him soon as the work was scheduled to start tomorrow and if he didn't hear from her before then, he'd just have to use his own initiative and hope he was doing right by her.

The news of the latest incident to befall the camp was flying around the staff breakfast tables that morning but Patsy wasn't to learn of it until much later as, due to the rain, she had only been in the restaurant long enough to grab a couple of slices of toast and some tea, which she took to her office to consume there as she had a lot to see to before the campers descended en masse at nine thirty inside the Paradise. Regardless of the weather prohibiting outdoor activities they would still expect to be entertained.

Patsy had devised what she called her 'rainy day plan', and today was the first time she would be implementing it so she was feeling nervous.

Dixie had been delighted when she had seen what the weather was throwing at them on first getting up. Under Terry's reign all that had happened on days like this was endless bingo games in the Paradise ballroom and lounges, plus non-stop showings of comedy films in the cinema. Those campers not wanting to participate in either were left with the indoor pool or staying in their chalets to while away the time until the weather improved.

Dixie had no reason to believe that Patsy wouldn't do the same as Terry had on days like today so she was under the impression that she was in for an easy time because, with so many people congregated together, no one would notice when she slipped away for lengthy periods to have a crafty cigarette or even return to her chalet for a nap, which she could certainly do with doing today as she didn't get much sleep last night thanks to a good-looking camper she had taken a fancy to. Besides, she felt she deserved an easy day as she had hadn't put a foot wrong work-wise since she had started to worry that Vicky was after her job . . . despite the young woman's denials . . . putting Dixie's plans for her future in jeopardy. So she had decided not to give Patsy any reason to consider replacing Vicky with her, and it had all proved very tedious and tiring doing her job properly all the time. A day off from it would come as a welcome relief.

Dixie breezed into Patsy's office after breakfast that morning, intending to impress her by offering to instruct the team leaders on her behalf as she knew the drill for bad weather days. But she was to get a nasty shock when Patsy thanked her for her offer but declined as she was implementing her own plan of events today. She told Dixie that she would like her to oversee all the games she had planned for the lounges along with the team of Stripeys she would send over to help her, and would she make a start by collecting all the board games, Ludo, Snakes and Ladders, Tiddly Winks, Scrabble, Monopoly, et cetera, from the Stripeys' storeroom at the back of the stage and then set them out on the tables, ready and waiting for when the campers started piling in. In the games room, she wanted pool and table tennis tournaments and darts matches arranging, and Stripeys assigned to oversee the games. Patsy herself was going to be overseeing a continuous run of stage games and quizzes in the Paradise ballroom but periodically she would come over to the lounges to check with Dixie that there was no problem she needed any help with, meaning that for Dixie there wasn't going to be any chance of skiving off at all.

Her easy day in tatters, Dixie wandered off in a sulk, her resolve to find a way to get rid of Patsy once and for all rising higher.

Mid-morning, satisfied that all was in hand and the campers happy with everything that had been laid on to entertain them until the weather improved, Patsy snatched a few moments to grab an orange juice from the bar in the quiet lounge, for once using her position to slip behind it and not wait her turn amongst the queues. In the anteroom at the back of the bar she was surprised to come face to face with Jamie, who was in the process of fetching a crate of mixers to restock the bar with.

His delight to see her beamed from his eyes as he put down the crate and grabbed her tightly to him. 'Hello, you,' he said. 'Come for a kiss?'

Patsy chuckled. 'No, orange juice, but being's you're here . . .'

The kiss never happened as another barman appeared, telling Jamie, 'Hurry up with those mixers or we'll have a riot on our hands.' He disappeared back behind the bar again.

Jamie dropped his arms from around her and bent to pick the crate up, telling Patsy, tongue in cheek, 'Oh, well, you'll just have to contain yourself until later. Help yourself to an orange juice.' He indicated with his head for her to take one out of the crate he was holding, which she did. Having told her she would find a spare bottle opener on a shelf beside her he then made to leave, but stopped as something struck him. 'Oh, what do you think about the sinking of the boats down at the lake last night?'

She looked puzzled. 'I haven't heard anything about the boats being sunk.'

'You haven't! I'm surprised as it was all everyone was talking about in the restaurant at breakfast this morning.'

'Yes, well, some of us didn't get time for breakfast, with all they had to do towards entertaining the campers during this awful weather. So someone sunk all the boats down at the lake. But why would they do that?'

'Search me. Probably some brainless idiot who thought it was funny. But it must have happened after we left last night.' His face clouded over. 'I'm just worried someone might have seen us and thought we did it.'

'Well, if they did, they'd have reported the fact by now and we'd be facing a Spanish Inquisition from the boss.'

Jamie's face brightened. 'Oh, yes, so we would. That's all right then. Have to go, see you later.'

As she took a swallow of her drink out of the bottle, a memory flooded back to Patsy of her and Jamie lying in the boat under the stars and seeing a figure walking down the path on the other side of the lake. She had been positive it was Trevor. They had been asked by the hierarchy to be on the alert for anyone acting suspiciously around the camp at night because of all the incidents that had occurred recently. But Trevor hadn't been acting suspiciously, just walking down the path like he was out for a stroll, so she hadn't considered that he might be the one behind the incidents. But what if he'd come down to the lake to sink the boats and seen herself and Jamie already there, so when she had seen him walking down the path he was just going off somewhere to hide until they left?

And hadn't Jamie told her that most nights Trevor went out for a solitary walk after he'd finished work? Was that because he was sussing out the best place for his next attack? And then she remembered the incident a while back when she had been making her way home after finishing work and had seen someone running across the grass, carrying a bag or something, who kept looking back as if they were worried about being followed, to disappear through the hedge and into the staff chalet compound. Had that person been Trevor too? Come to think of it now, the figure she had seen that night had been about his build, of medium height and slim.

Trevor must the camp saboteur. All the evidence against him was telling her he was.

It made sense to her now why Trevor behaved as oddly as he did. He was keeping his distance from the other staff as he didn't want them to be badgering him to join them socially when all he wanted was to be left alone to carry out his dastardly acts against the camp. And there was that night when she and Jamie had come across him in the bus station in Mablethorpe and Trevor hadn't looked at all pleased to see them. As soon as they had asked what he had been doing he'd announced he was going to walk home. Was that because he'd been buying something he needed to assist him in his next attack and that was what was in the bag he'd been carrying?

What didn't make sense to her was why he was doing this. What grudge could he have against the camp that would warrant him causing it such damage? But she knew it was her duty to report this to Harold Rose. Then she realised that she hadn't any proof to offer against Trevor, only her suspicions. She needed to obtain proof to substantiate her claims. There was nothing for it but to keep a close eye on Trevor and catch him in the act the next time. All the acts of sabotage had been carried out late at night and as Jamie shared a chalet with Trevor it was going to be relatively easy to monitor him and be on hand to get the proof she needed to put a stop to his antics before one of them turned nasty and irreparable damage was caused.

CHAPTER TWENTY-NINE

M arion was sitting in Harold's office taking dictation. Her mind was only half on the job in hand, just sufficient to do what Harold required of her without fault while the other half was focused on the future. This coming Saturday to be precise. She had planned how the evening would go down to the last minute detail, but what she couldn't plan for was whether Harold would be at home or not. If not then she would have no choice but to postpone matters to the following weekend, but that meant another week spent living in intolerably cramped conditions.

The fact that she couldn't control this part of her plan was causing her a great deal of frustration, hence the reason why, on hearing someone tap on the door and open it, she spun round in her seat and snapped at the uninvited newcomer: 'Excuse me, but you can't just waltz in here unannounced during a private meeting. Did the junior outside not tell you that? If . . .'

A broad smile splitting his face, Harold cut in. 'It's all right, Marion. This lady can interrupt any private meeting she likes.' He rose from behind his desk and hurried around it to greet the visitor. 'How lovely to see you, Drina. What a nice surprise,' he enthused, taking her hand and shaking it warmly. Where most employees would be anxious and unnerved by the unexpected appearance of their boss, Harold wasn't taken aback at all, but genuinely pleased to see her. He then introduced Marion. 'Drina Jolly, this is Marion Frear who's covering for Jill while she's recovering.'

Marion had never given any thought whatsoever to the absent owner of the business but had not expected her to be a small, dumpy, homely-looking woman in her mid fifties, the sort she would expect to find in a kitchen fussing over a meal for her family, not presiding over a business the size of Jolly's. Unlike Harold, Marion wasn't at all happy about Drina's sudden appearance. Women of all ages, shapes and sizes had an inbuilt instinct for knowing when another woman had a particular interest in a man, regardless of how hard that woman tried to conceal it. The last thing Marion wanted was for Drina Jolly to suspect she was interested in Harold in any other way than on a work level, or his boss could easily joke with him that he had an admirer in his temporary secretary. By the way Harold always spoke of Drina Jolly, it was very apparent he held her in high regard, so anything she told him he would take serious notice of. Harold might be reserved by nature but he was intelligent, and any remark of that nature might just be enough to tip him off that Marion's intentions towards him were not as innocent as she had led him to believe they were and that she was seeing him as much more than a boss.

Damn the woman, thought Marion. Why did she have to make her visit right now and not in a week or so when it would be too late for her to warn Harold that his office manager was interested in him? It was hard enough for Marion as it was to keep her thoughts focused entirely on her work when she was constantly anxious over the outcome of Saturday night, due to its importance to her own and her mother's future. Now, thanks to this woman, she had the added problem of watching her every move to make sure she gave nothing away.

As she accepted Drina's proffered hand Marion said in a formal tone, 'I'm very pleased to meet you, Mrs Jolly.'

All Drina's instincts were telling her that Marion was not as pleased to meet her as she was making out. She wondered why. Nor was Drina at all impressed by Marion's snappy remark to her when she had arrived in the office. She hoped this was not the other woman's normal attitude when addressing visitors or staff who arrived unannounced, and made a mental note to query this with Harold when they were on their own.

He said to Marion, 'We'll finish the correspondence later. Would you be kind enough to ask Sandra to make a pot of tea for us?'

Before Drina's arrival, she would have smiled at him and responded to him in a soft, almost seductive voice, but now Marion kept it strictly businesslike: 'Yes, of course, Harold.'

She went out and shut the door behind her.

He said to Drina, 'It really is good to see you. You look well.' He hesitated for a moment before he added, 'Er . . . is everything all right down in Devon?'

She assured him, 'Everything is fine.' She placed her hand on his arm and said knowingly, 'You're anxious to learn why I'm here out of the blue but too polite to ask me. Let's sit down and I'll explain.'

He thought she'd take her rightful place as the owner of the company and sit behind the desk, but instead she surprised him by heading over to the visitors' area by the drinks cabinet and sitting down in one of the armchairs there.

Drina made herself comfortable then heaved a sigh of relief. 'I've missed this place, Harold, more than I ever thought I would. It's so good to be back.'

He was now sitting down on the sofa by the side of the armchair and at her words a wave of sadness washed through him. When Drina had first asked him if he would run the camp on her behalf while she was overseeing the opening of her new one in Devon, he was always aware that one day she would return to retake her place at the helm back in Mablethorpe. It seemed that day was now. Running this place had been a trial to him at times but one he had come to enjoy immensely as his confidence in himself had grown. People no longer saw him as a failure of a man, but as someone of worth. But what did Drina's return mean for him now? There was only room for one manager of the company and his old job as its accountant was now handled by a very capable man who had Drina's trust, and she wasn't the sort to sack anyone for no good reason just to make way for someone else.

Harold tried to sound upbeat, masking the sadness he was feeling, when he told her, 'I'll have my desk cleared for you as soon as you need me to.'

She frowned at him quizzically. 'Why would I need you to clear your desk?' Then she realised. 'Oh, Harold, I haven't come back to take over the running of the camp again. I'm more than happy with the man who's doing that now. But you've got enough of a job with the day-to-day running of things here without being expected to cope with any more. I've returned to keep an eye on the farmhouse demolition and see to whatever comes up in connection with that. I have to be honest and admit that is not all I've come back to do, but it gave me a good excuse.'

There was a tap at the door and Sandra arrived carrying a tray. She put it down on the long coffee table before them and, with a nervous smile on her face, said, 'There you go. Tea for two. Can I get you anything else?'

Drina answered, 'Not at the moment, thank you.' She smiled warmly at the girl. 'Sandra, isn't it?'

The youngster looked shocked that the owner of the company knew the name of a mere temporary office junior. 'Yes . . . yes, it is.'

'Are you enjoying working here at Jolly's?'

The girl's eyes widened in surprise that the boss would care whether she did or not. 'I do.' She flashed a shy glance at Harold before she added, 'I like working for Mr Rose, he's very nice.'

Drina hid a smile. 'Yes, he is, isn't he? Well, thank you again for the tea, Sandra.'

Both Drina and Harold hid a smile then as the girl did a little curtsey before she turned and left them.

The fact that she hadn't said she enjoyed working for Marion wasn't lost on Drina. She leaned forward and poured out two cups of tea. After handing Harold his, Drina went to take a sip of her own then stopped to put the cup down on the table, saying, 'I know it's a bit early but I could do with a drop of whisky in mine, just as a pick me up after my long journey.'

She made to get up but Harold stopped her, saying, 'I'll fetch it for you.'

A moment later he was sitting back down with a half-bottle of Teacher's whisky in his hand, which he passed to her. Drina put a measure in her cup then said, 'You'll join me, won't you?' She added, tongue in cheek, 'You'll be needing a pick-me-up too after the shock of seeing me walk through the door.'

Not a shock to Harold, more like the return of a comfort blanket. He told her he would, though, and held out his cup for a tot.

'Did you come up on the overnight sleeper?' he asked. 'I wish you'd let me know and I would have had a car meet you.'

'There was no need as I drove myself up. I split the journey by staying in a hotel last night and continued on this morning. It's a long way and I won't do that journey again in a hurry on my own.'

He was eyeing her in surprise. 'You drove!'

She laughed. 'I learned while I was in Devon. The camp there is like this one, situated five miles from the nearest town, but it has no buses running past so if I needed to attend any meetings there I always had to ask Artie or one of the staff to drive me. I decided to take lessons, and lo and behold, I passed the test first time. I encouraged Rhonnie and Jackie to learn too and now they're both whizzing down the narrow Devon lanes in their own cars. Artie wasn't happy about me driving all the way up here on my own, he wanted me to wait until he could come with me, but the demolition starts tomorrow. I need to see the place one more time before it's gone for ever, for sentimental reasons.'

Harold totally understood, aware that the farmhouse was her last connection to the man who'd set her father and herself on the road to a prosperous future. Without his sale of the farm to them it was unlikely they would have achieved the success they had. 'And the Devon camp looks set to do well?' Harold asked.

'Very. Surpassing my expectations. It was fully booked for the first week of opening and is for the rest of the season . . . in fact, we have a waiting list for cancellations. The new camp has been Rhonnie's saviour. As you know, she saw her life as over when Dan died. She adores little Danny and is a wonderful mother to him, but even her son wasn't enough to lift her out of the doldrums. Although I thought an upmarket camp for the middle classes was a good idea, the main reason I went ahead with it was because I hoped that encouraging her to take an interest in helping me with it would bring back Rhonnie's zest for life. To give her a further incentive, I signed the camp over to her, lock, stock and barrel. It would eventually have become hers anyway when I die, same as this place will.

'Rhonnie's in charge now, Jackie's her assistant, and along with the staff they handpicked between them, they've got the camp going from strength to strength. Of course the clientele is completely different from the holidaymakers here and their expectations and demands sometimes defie belief. Here the top complaint from the campers is that the sink plugs are missing because someone has stolen them. At the Devon camp the guests complain very vocally if the water in the indoor pool is not quite warm enough for their liking or if one of the camp masseurs kept them waiting for their appointment because they weren't finished with their last client. But then, they do pay well for their stay and we have the same aim there that we have here: to give our guests a holiday they'll never forget. Then hopefully they'll come back year after year.

'So my job down there is done and for the most part I've been left twiddling my thumbs. Artie knew how much I was missing this place. This is where my heart is, Harold. It was he who suggested it was time for us to return. I can't wait to be back in my own bed again.'

Despite the fact that Drina could afford to buy virtually any house in the area, she and Artie lived in a small two-bedroomed workman's cottage about a mile from the camp as when they got together that was all Artie could afford. He'd told Drina he would not live with her if he couldn't hold his head up, knowing he'd provided the roof over her head. The last thing she would ever do to the proud man she loved more than life itself was demean him, and so she'd readily agreed.

'We want to spend more time together, pottering around the garden, going out in the car, that sort of thing . . . but we're not yet ready to throw in the towel completely. So I was wondering if you could have a word with Sid Harper, find out if he's willing for Artie to help out in maintenance again for a few hours a week, doing general jobs? But please make quite sure Sid knows that Artie is not in any way after taking charge of that department,' Drina told Harold.

'Yes, of course I will. I'm sure Sid will be pleased to find Artie as much work as he wants when he's ready.'

She took a drink from her cup before she went on. 'I want to assure you that I have no intention of interfering with your job, Harold, now I'm back. All I intend doing right now is keeping an eye on things in respect of the demolition, to make sure nothing inconveniences the campers or the staff in any way. Then when it's over, I intend to investigate some plans I have for the use of the cleared land. But never forget that I am nearby should you need me, Harold. You have managed without me since I've been away so I can't imagine you'll be calling on me much in the future. I would, however, like to accompany you on the daily inspection rounds now and again, if you wouldn't mind?'

Harold was relieved to learn that he needn't start looking for another job. He was intrigued as to what plans Drina had in mind for the land to be cleared but knew she would enlighten him in good time. 'Of course I wouldn't mind, I would be glad of your company. I was planning to do today's inspection round as soon as the weather improved.'

She laughed. 'Oh, Harold, a bit of rain never hurt anyone . . . let's go now!

'And I know it's not a good time for him, but maybe we could call in on Eric as I'd like to say hello and personally thank him for coming to the rescue over that kitchen fire. If we're lucky he might have something tasty for us to eat, he usually does.

'And of course I know Patsy, she was working here for a few years in Joe's time before I took over on his death, but considering she was thrown in at the deep end as Head Stripey . . . it's all right, I won't tell her that she got the job through a mistake on your part as it's not good for anyone's morale to find out something like that. But to me it was a very fortunate mistake on your part as apparently Patsy has done marvels in improving the camp entertainment and I'd like to thank her myself for all she's done. Her job can take her anywhere in the camp so if we don't come across her during the tour, I would appreciate it if we could drop by her office. Oh, I nearly forgot in my excitement at having a look around the camp . . . is there anything you need to update me on since we last spoke?'

'Well, there is, as a matter of fact, and I hope you'll forgive me for not telling you before because at the time I thought you'd suffered enough of a blow by hearing the news of the demolition.' He explained about the mouse infestation and then this morning's discovery of the sunken boats. Taking all the other incidents that had befallen the camp over the last few weeks into consideration, he had concluded that apart from the kitchen fire, which the police still believed was caused by drunken youths who'd broken in for a joke that went wrong, they couldn't just be a run of bad luck. They had to have been done deliberately by the same person, though the reason why was a total mystery to Harold.

Drina sat in thought for a few moments before she said, 'I can see why you've come to the assumption you have after the latest incident this morning and have to agree with you, that it must be the same person behind it all. And like you, Harold, I can't see what that person is gaining from doing what they are apart from causing us strife and a great deal of expense.' Drina's eyes narrowed shrewdly. 'Don't you think it's odd that the fire was started not long before the security guards were due to check the place during their round?'

Harold frowned quizzically at her. 'You mean, the starting of the fire was timed to be stopped by the guards before it spread? That it wasn't drunks having fun but the same person as was behind the other incidents? I feel stupid for not considering that before. I was just so relieved that the guards discovered the fire before it spread to the rest of the building, I suppose I just accepted the police's conclusions as after all they are the experts.'

Drina lapsed into thought again for a moment before she gave a heavy sigh. 'You've done all you can to catch whoever the culprit is. All we can hope is that they've had their fun and the sinking of the boats is their final action.'

'Yes, let's hope,' agreed Harold. 'Shall we set off on the round then?'

She said eagerly, 'Yes, let's.'

As soon as they left the kitchen after paying a call on Eric during the tour of the camp, Drina said to Harold, 'I've known Eric a long time now and I know that man has something on his mind that's bothering him. There's a good chance that you know what it is, Harold, as you two are good friends. I wouldn't wish to alter that, so I'm not going to put you in a compromising situation by asking you to tell me. I just want you to know that should Eric need any help with his problem in any way whatsoever, then he's not to be afraid to ask me. Oh, but wasn't that piece of treacle tart he gave us just delicious? There's no denying that that man knows how to cook and I am so lucky he chooses to work here at Jolly's.'

Later that afternoon, the relentless rain still battering down on the umbrella over her head, Drina stood in the midst of the jungle of weeds on the uneven cobbles of the farmyard. The house before her was in varying stages of decay and looked bleak and neglected, rainwater gushing down its broken gutters causing rivers of running water on the cobbles below. She hadn't visited the house for a while and during her absence more of the roof on one side had caved further in so nearly all of the left-hand side of the attic was roofless, exposing rotting beams with long-abandoned birds' nests clinging in their corners, and she could see that the hole in the bedroom floor was now a much wider gaping void, the fallen debris from it dangerously piled in the room below that had once been the parlour.

For a moment, though, Drina's mind's eye saw the place as it used to be when she had first arrived here with her father all those years ago, in desperate hope the owner would allow him to park a caravan on a field, having been turned away from other farms countless times before just because they were Romany. The house had had a neglected air about it even then, some repairs long overdue, but it was still in a habitable condition. Lonely and old, penniless Farmer Ackers, having long since been deserted by his sons who'd selfishly gone off to make lives for themselves elsewhere, had tried his best to manage the place single-handed, and failed miserably. That was until Drina's father had befriended him and come up with an idea to earn them both some money, making the old man's remaining years so much happier and rewarding for him than they ever would have been otherwise. She seemed to see her father then, making his way up the long muddy track from their caravan to the house of an evening, carefully carrying a bowl of his homemade rabbit stew by way of thanking the old man for his kindness in letting them stay. While the old man ate, he and her father would sit in his kitchen, passing away a couple of hours together, and that was how their friendship began. Then a vision of herself as a girl rose before her, on her way home from school, skipping down the path past the farm gate and on down several fields to the one where their old rusting caravan was parked by the stream. In all weathers Farmer Ackers would be waiting for her at the gate, his old body leaning heavily on it for support, and they would share a few words about her day before she carried on.

Her thoughts then returned to the present and she saw the house as it really was now. The person who had reported its dangerous condition was right to do so. Despite her sadness, she was relieved and grateful that the decision to seal its fate had been taken out of her hands as she knew she would never have been able to do it herself. In a short space of time the house and its barns and outbuildings would no longer be here, but regardless of what came to replace it on the soon-to-be-cleared land, nothing could take away her memories of this place.

Patsy did not get a chance for the rest of the day to talk in private to Jamie so it wasn't until he had finished his shift and was walking her home, the rain finally having stopped, leaving warm moist night air behind, that she was able to explain her worrying thoughts and conclusions to him over Trevor possibly being the camp saboteur.

He listened intently and when she had finished, exclaimed, 'Blimey, yes, it does all point to it being him, doesn't it?' Jamie scraped his hand through his hair. 'I would never have thought it of Trev, though. He's so . . . well . . . timid and withdrawn except when he's working. But you're right, we do need proof to back up our claim that's it's him before we go shouting our mouths off.'

Patsy was warmed by hearing him say *we* and not *you*.

'How will we get proof?' Jamie enquired.

After she'd told him, he said, 'Seems you've got it all worked out. Right, let me get this straight. Starting tomorrow night, as soon as Trev finishes his shift, you're going to follow him back to the chalet and keep an eye on him, see that he doesn't leave before I join you as soon as I've finished up at the bar. If he does go out before I get there, you're going to be following him with your camera ready. If he does anything incriminating, you take photographs and then run like mad to find security in case he turns nasty at being caught as he's bound to notice the camera flash going off. Then you come back here to let me know you're all right as I shall be worried if I turn up and find you're not in your hiding place.'

Patsy smiled at him. 'You really care about me, don't you?'

Jamie said in all seriousness, 'I might do, just a bit. Anyway, if he doesn't go out before I get back, you're free to go to your chalet and get some sleep. I'll put something against the door in ours so that if Trevor does decide to go out when I'm asleep, it will make a noise and wake me up. Then I'll follow him and take pictures with my camera if he's up to anything.'

'And then run like mad to find security in case he turns nasty?'

'Oh, come on, Patsy. Trev's the weedy sort and no match for me. He can turn as nasty as he likes but he'll be wasting his time.'

'Well, all the same, just be careful.'

Jamie smiled at her. 'You really care about me, don't you?'

She replied matter-of-factly, 'I might, just a bit. So we know what we've both got to do?'

'It seems like it. Just one thing?'

'Oh!'

'Until all this Inspector Clouseau malarkey is over one way or the other, when do we find time to get together for a good snog?'

Patsy laughed. 'Don't worry, I'll make sure we find time.'

CHAPTER THIRTY

When Drina arrived at the farmhouse at just after nine the next morning, there was no sign at all of the deluge of yesterday as the July sun was beaming down from a wispy cloud-filled blue sky and had dried up all the standing water. The abundance of flowering weeds, briar roses and thick hedges of thorny brambles were now looking lush and green, having been replenished by the much-needed soaking.

Several workmen were already making preparations for the demolition to begin. A flat-backed lorry had flattened a path through the weeds and was parked in the middle of the yard, piled with tools for the job waiting to be offloaded.

Drina approached one of the workmen and asked where she could find Mr Brady, the owner of the company instructed to carry out the demolition works. She was told he was around somewhere and found him in the barn assessing the rusting farm machinery, piles of rotting straw and other rubbish needing to be removed before the actual levelling of the building could begin.

Drina went up to stand by him, holding out her hand in greeting as she introduced herself.

Reg accepted her proffered hand with a smile of greeting on his own face while giving her hand a firm shake, telling her how pleased he was to meet her. He was pleasant and polite in his manner towards her all the time he was informing her about his plans to tackle the work, allaying any worries that it might impact on the staff or holidaymakers.

But to Drina's mind his eyes told a different story. They held a look of contempt in them when he fixed them on her, almost of hatred, though why he should harbour such feelings for her she had no idea because as far as she could recollect she had never met him before and during their time together she had been as pleasant and polite towards him as he had her. She could only think that maybe he was angry that he had been given no option by the council but to take on a job he didn't want to do, albeit Jolly's were having to pay a large amount of money to him for the work.

He was the second person she'd met since she got back who did not seem in any way as pleased to see her as they said they were.

Drina decided to leave him to it after letting him know that she intended to visit the site on a daily basis.

Reg watched her walk away until she disappeared from view around the corner of the derelict farmhouse. She seemed a nice enough woman on the surface, but her veins ran with the blood of a race who were nothing more than murderers and thieves and the scourge of decent human beings as far as Reg was concerned. One of her kind had been the cause of the death of his beloved daughter and this woman's own father had fleeced a defenceless old man out of his farm, denying his sons their rightful inheritance. Well, she wasn't going to benefit from that for very much longer. Two filthy Romany gypsies had committed crimes and gone unpunished but at least one of their kind was going to be made to pay for them, and if that was the best justice Reg could obtain then so be it.

On the walk back to the main courtyard Drina diverted to pay a visit to the laundry to reacquaint herself with Eileen. This time she was left in no doubt of her welcome as Eileen made it very apparent that she was delighted to see her. Drina had always liked the other woman very much, found her to be pleasant and helpful, and knew she was a fair leader of her army of staff who all found her good to work for. After sharing a cup of tea and a catch-up chat with Eileen, Drina left her and went to join Harold in the restaurant to review camp business.

That afternoon she paid a visit to Jill in the cottage hospital. As she walked into the small ward, carrying a large bouquet of flowers, she was surprised to find Jill already had a visitor with her.

With a smile on her long narrow face, Eileen, who had just arrived herself, greeted her as she arrived by Jill's bedside, saying, 'Well, how lovely to see you again today, Drina.'

Drina? As in Drina Jolly! Jill had never had the privilege of meeting the owner of the camp in person before and was having difficulty believing that a woman in her position would put herself out to visit the office manager in hospital, when she must have better things to do with her time. But this small, dumpy woman with her homely face and greying hair cut in a bob, dressed in an off-the-peg plain yellow shift dress, Jill would have judged at first sight to be just an ordinary housewife, someone's favourite auntie, someone kind to tell all your troubles to, never the owner of a prosperous business. But how Jill wished now that she had asked a nurse to wash her hair and put a fresh nightdress on her and a dab of lipstick, so as to look more presentable before meeting her employer for the first time.

Jill was in a very relaxed position, slumped back against the pillows, and out of respect for her boss she tried to inch herself upright by digging her casted arm into the mattress while she levered herself up on her good hand. But due to the weight of the casts on both her legs, she didn't move an inch.

Thinking that Jill was uncomfortable, in pain even, Drina thrust the bunch of flowers she was holding at Eileen, who hadn't seen what Jill was trying to do as her attention was still focused on their boss, and stepped across to the side of the bed, to slip her arm between the pillows and Jill's back, saying, 'Let me help you.' And she started to ease Jill further up on the pillows.

Mortified that her boss should be helping her in such an intimate way, Jill exclaimed, 'Mrs Jolly, you shouldn't be doing this. I can manage, honestly.'

Drina stopped what she was doing and looked enquiringly at her. 'And why shouldn't I help you?'

'Well, er . . . you're the boss of the company and . . .'

'And what? It's beneath me to do such things? At the moment I am not your boss, I am a woman, helping another woman who needs assistance.' She began once again trying to inch Jill higher.

Eileen had by now dumped the flowers on the bed table and was around the other side. She slid an arm around Jill's back too and helped Drina pull her up into a comfortable sitting position. That achieved between them, they plumped up the pillows to better support her.

When they had finished, Drina looked down at Jill, smiled and held out her hand. 'Can I now tell you I'm pleased to meet you?' And she added jocularly, 'Is that permitted between a boss and her employee?'

Jill chuckled, 'Yes, it is.' She accepted Drina's hand with her uninjured one. 'I'm very pleased to meet you too, Mrs Jolly.'

'It's Drina, dear. Makes me feel so stiff and old, being called by my title. I'm sure Harold has told you that I like all the senior staff to address me by my Christian name. May I take a seat for a moment? I've new shoes on and they're still a little tight and playing havoc with my bunions.'

'Yes, yes, please do,' Jill responded, feeling mortified that she hadn't already asked her to make herself comfortable.

With Eileen and Drina now seated beside each other, Drina told Jill, 'I apologise for dropping in unannounced and I don't mean to stay long and intrude on your time with Eileen. I know Harold has been visiting you as he has kept me updated on your progress, but I wanted to see for myself.' She smiled. 'Not the best way for me to meet you for the first time but it is good to meet you at last.'

'Yes, you too,' said Jill.

'So any news of when you'll be going home?' Drina asked.

'My casts come off next week, and as soon as I can get about on crutches or sticks I'll be allowed home. Hopefully not long after that I'll be fit enough to return to work.'

'And we'll look forward to having you back. Such a terrible

accident you suffered, and thank goodness it wasn't even worse.'

Jill and Eileen passed a look between them before Jill said, 'Yes, at least I'm alive to tell the tale. It's very kind of you, Mrs . . . Drina, taking the time and trouble to come in and see me, considering Eileen told me just before you arrived here that you only came back today and you must have so much to see to after your absence.'

'Hardly anything to do with the day-to-day running of Jolly's, dear, Harold has seen to that. And coming to see you was important to me, to check that you're on the mend and are not in need of anything. Naturally I came at the first opportunity.'

Jill smiled. 'I appreciate that, thank you, but my family are looking after me very well.'

Drina stayed for a few minutes longer and then, after telling Jill not to hesitate to ask if there was anything Jolly's could do to help with her recovery, she left.

As soon as she had, Jill eagerly demanded of Eileen, 'Did you think of any reason why Marion might have wanted me out of the way?'

Eileen shook her head. 'No, I'm afraid not.'

Jill's face fell. 'No, me neither.' Then she added with conviction, 'But I know it has to be Marion who pushed me and she must have had a reason for doing it. I won't give up until I figure out what it is so I can go to the police and get her charged for attempted murder.'

On her way back to the car park Drina was very thoughtful. She had noticed the look that had passed between Jill and Eileen when she herself had mentioned what a terrible accident it was that Jill had suffered. She wondered what lay behind that look.

CHAPTER THIRTY-ONE

L ater that night over in the camp, armed with her camera that she had loaded with a new film and flash bulb, Patsy was discreetly following Trevor as he made his way back to the chalet he shared with Jamie. As he let himself inside she secreted herself in the dark shadow to one side of the chalet opposite.

Half an hour later Jamie joined her. They shared a kiss before she told him, 'Trev came straight back after work and is still in there, so it's over to you. What are you going to do to make sure he doesn't sneak out while you're asleep?'

He lifted up a carrier he was holding. 'Well, all I could think of was to leave this bag of empty beer bottles right outside the door so he can't avoid stepping on them if he sneaks out. They'll make quite a racket clanging together so they're bound to wake me, but I'll pretend that it just roused me and I've gone back to sleep. If he doesn't go out tonight then I'll make sure I'm the first out of the door in the morning so I can hide them to use tomorrow night. If he does happen to leave in the morning before me, I'll just make out I don't know anything about the bag of bottles being left on our step and say it must have been one of the other staff leaving them for us to bin, saving them the trouble.'

Patsy looked impressed. 'I would never have thought of that. Well, if anything does happen during the night, you make sure you come and tell me before we both go to work. In a way I hope it doesn't because I'd hate to lose Trev off the team. He's such as good dancer, the women are always queuing up to partner him.'

275

They shared another kiss and reluctantly parted to go their separate ways.

Trev did not leave the chalet that night or the following two nights but on the third night, a few minutes after arriving back after his shift, Patsy observed him come out of the chalet. He had something slung over his shoulder, which she assumed to be a bag. He headed off towards the boundary hedge that shielded the staff chalets from the view of the rest of the camp. As soon as he was a short distance away, with adrenalin pumping through her, Patsy emerged from the shadows to follow him.

Although it was a clear night there was no moon, so she only had the intermittent lamps to aid her and at times the path was in virtual darkness. In order to keep Trevor in sight, she had to follow closer to him than she would have liked. After travelling down the path that crossed over the large expanse of grass splitting the main camp from the staff chalets and maintenance buildings, it became obvious he was keeping a look out for anyone spotting him as he kept stopping and glancing around, and at such times Patsy had to throw herself to the ground so that he didn't see her, aware that she was going to be covered in bruises come morning. Finally he arrived at the fork in the path. One branch of it led over to the courtyard, the other down past the sports courts and fields and the boating lake, eventually ending at the funfair down by the beach. He took the path to the beach. As he'd already sabotaged the boats on the lake a few nights before, Patsy wondered just what he had it in mind to sabotage next. And what was his motive?

She had followed him past the sports facilities and now he was skirting the boating lake, approaching a curve in the path as it followed a clump of trees and shrubs. Rounding the bend, Trev disappeared from view and she quickened her pace, fearing he could head off the path and she would lose him. At the bend she hid herself behind a tree then gingerly peered around it. She couldn't see any sign of Trevor. He'd completely disappeared. She came out from behind the tree and stepped back on to the path, and at the same time from the other side of the

276

tree out jumped Trevor, brandishing a thick length of branch like a weapon.

As Patsy let out a shriek of shock, Trevor cried out: 'Why are you following me?' Then it seemed to occur to him who his pursuer was. He lowered his arm and said in astonishment, 'Patsy! It's you that's following me. But why?'

Her mouth opened and closed fish-like for several moments before she stuttered, 'I . . . I . . . I wasn't. I was . . . er . . . just taking a walk and happened to be going the same way as you.' She took a deep breath and a look around, saying lightly, 'It's a lovely evening for a walk, isn't it?'

He was looking at her suspiciously. 'But I sensed someone was following me right from when I left my chalet, and when I kept turning around to see who it was there was no one there. So if you weren't following but just taking a walk and going the same way as me, then why didn't I see you?'

Patsy stared at him blindly. She'd no plausible answer for that. It seemed that she had no choice but to tell him the truth. He would then know he'd been sussed and make a run for it, and the bosses would never know why he'd done what he had, but at least she had stopped him doing whatever he had been going to do tonight and there'd be an end to his campaign of destruction. She eyed the thick branch in his hand, which she was worried he might use on her out of anger once he knew that the game was up. 'Okay, Trev, I'll tell you why I was following you, but put that branch down first.'

He looked down at it like he'd forgotten he was holding it and dropped it on the ground. Patsy took a deep breath and said, 'I . . . well, me and Jamie, know you're the one behind the bad things that have been happening in the camp.'

Trevor looked taken aback. *Things that have been happening*? Oh, you mean like the other day, the sinking of the boats on the lake, and the oil in the pool . . . those things?'

She nodded. 'Yes.'

He frowned, seeming deeply puzzled. 'But why would you think I was behind them?'

277

'Because . . . well, Jamie and I were on the boating lake the other night and we saw you walking by, carrying a bag. Then next morning we heard that the saboteur had struck again and sunk all the boats on the lake. Then we realised that when we'd seen you, you must have been there preparing to sink the boats but saw we were there so went off to hide until we'd gone.'

He was gawping at her in amazement. 'And you're putting the blame on me for doing all the things just because I happened to be walking by the lake that night, carrying a bag?'

'No, not just because of that. It's the way you are.'

'The way I am! What do you mean?'

'Well, people work here to make friends and have a good time away from home. But you haven't made any effort to make any friends, and when people make an effort to make friends with you, you run a mile. And Jamie says that you're always going off for walks after your shift most nights, and so we could only think that that was to suss out, then carry out, your next attack against the camp.

'Just about the same time as the attacks started, I was on my way back to my chalet after finishing work one night when I saw a figure running across the grass, looking very suspicious indeed and carrying something, which could have been a bag. Later, when I thought about it, the person I saw was built like you, and the morning after that was when the oil was discovered in the pool. And then that night when Jamie and I came across you in the Mablethorpe bus station, you couldn't get away quick enough when you realised that he was about to ask what you'd be up to there. That's because you were getting things you needed for your next attack, or up to something you didn't want us to know about at any rate, or else you'd have told us what you'd been doing. And besides, as a Stripey you'd have no trouble finding an excuse to be in any of the buildings you'd chosen to attack if someone stopped and asked you why you were there. It would have been easy for you, leaving a window open or a door on the latch so you had no difficulty getting back in at night. You're the saboteur, I know you are. What we can't work out is why you're doing it?'

Trevor was staring at her, dumbstruck. He then pleaded, 'But I'm not the troublemaker, Patsy. I'm not, I swear it. I go out at night and keep myself to myself because . . .' His voice trailed off as he stepped over to the tree, leaned his back against it and slid down until his backside reached the earth below. Then legs to his chest, chin in his hands, he started to cry.

Mortified, Patsy squatted down beside him and laid a hand on his knee. 'Because of what, Trev?'

He wiped a hand across his eyes, sniffed and told her, 'All I've ever wanted to do is dance, Patsy. I can't remember wanting to do anything else since I saw a film my gran took me to as a boy. It was an American dance film called *Stormy Weather*. Bill "Bojangles" Robinson and the Nicholas Brothers were some of the dancers in it. As I watched them tap dancing across the screen, their feet barely seeming to touch the floor, that was it for me. I was hooked. I went home and asked my mother if I could go to dance classes because I wanted to be a dancer when I grew up. There was a woman in the village who used to dance on the stage when she was younger, down in London at the Windmill and Palladium Theatres, but when she became too old for that she came back home and taught dance in her front room to local children. It was all girls, though.

'My father had died just after I was born, in an accident at work, and we'd had to move in with my gran and grandpa as Mum couldn't afford for us to live on our own. She worked in a local factory that made brushes, on a machine that put the bristles into the heads, but she didn't earn that much. My grandpa was an invalid so he and Gran were managing on a bit of state pension. I could tell Mum was really sad when she sat me down and told me that she was sorry but she couldn't afford to send me to lessons. She said she'd do her best to teach me herself and that if ever things changed and there was money to spare, she would pay for me to learn properly. My gran cleared a space in her parlour, used some of the pennies out of her Christmas savings jar to buy me a pair of old shoes from the pawn shop, and my grandpa nailed metal strips on the soles and heels. Then my mum use to sneak over to the teacher's house and peep through the window to watch what she was teaching her pupils, so Mum could come straight back and show me.

'My mother couldn't dance to save her life. It was quite funny watching her try to show me how to do the steps. I used to practise them over and over, and Mum or Gran would take me to see all the old dance films that were shown at the cinema on a Saturday afternoon, and I would memorise some of those steps and try to copy them myself. I was in the parlour practising and making up my own dances every chance I got, but I did go out with my mates to play when my mum insisted as she said it wasn't good for me, staying in all the time. I never told my mates why I didn't come out with them after school every night. I knew they'd only laugh at me and call me a sissy, so I just told them I had to help my gran with the chores. I used to put on shows for my mum and grandparents and they were always telling me how good I was and saying it was a shame they couldn't afford for me to go to a proper dance school and learn to dance professionally.

'Then when I was thirteen Gran died, and not long after Grandpa too, and we had to move out of their house because the landlord put the rent up and Mum couldn't afford it. All she could afford on her wage was a small one-bedroomed flat upstairs at the back of an old Victorian house. I slept in a recess in the kitchen. Despite the fact there wasn't much room, Mum made a space in the tiny living room so I could still practise my dancing, but the people underneath us complained about the noise so I had to stop. Mum sat me down and told me that it was probably for the best as she knew she'd never be able to afford to send me to dance lessons and I ought get used to the idea that, like all the other lads in our village, it was the local factory for me. But I just couldn't give it up. I lived for my dancing and life was just miserable for me when I had nowhere to practise. I certainly wasn't going to forget my dream of dancing on the stage, I was determined not to. Not all dancers are professionally trained, it's their talent that gets them there, and I was hoping it would be the same for me.

'The only time I got to dance then, though, was when I was on my way home from school with my mates. While they were kicking an old can or just larking about, I'd dawdle behind and practise my steps when they weren't looking, stopping as soon as I feared they'd catch me at it. I knew my life wouldn't be worth living if they saw me doing what they thought of as girl's stuff. One night I got carried away and they did see.' Trevor paused, making it plain by the expression on his face how painful the memory was to him. 'I lost myself in my own world. I was on a stage there, performing in front of a crowded house, and I was tapping and pirouetting around for how long I don't know . . . but then I realised my audience was laughing and sniggering and it brought me back to the present and there they all were, my mates and some girls who'd joined them, and then they were jeering at me, calling me a poof, a queer, a . . . a . . . nancy boy.

'I just stood staring at them, frozen. Until a few minutes before these were my mates, had been for years, yet now they were calling me these disgusting things because to them only queer types danced like I was doing. I tried to tell them that I wasn't, I liked girls as much as they did, I just wanted to dance and it was wrong of them thinking that all men who danced were homosexuals. I wasn't and I couldn't believe that all the men I'd seen in the films or on the variety shows I'd watched with my mum and grandparents could be queer either, but I couldn't make them listen to me.

'Then they started advancing on me and I knew what they were going to do to me, so I turned and ran like hell. But they caught up with me in the park and I was rugby tackled to the ground and some of the boys held me down while the others beat me black and blue while the girls just stood by, cheering them on. They only stopped because the park keeper happened to come along and then they all ran off, laughing. It was he who

281

got me home as I could hardly stand, but then he had to get back to the park so I had to wait until my mum came home from work to see to me. We were both sobbing as she cleaned me up. Thankfully the park keeper had come along before any long-lasting damage was done to me.

'But after that I suffered hell at school from nearly everyone as word had gone round that I was a queer. Even those who didn't believe it, and would have been my friend, daren't be for fear of what would happen to them. I had to go a different way to school each morning, and home every night, for fear that some of the lads would be lying in wait to give me another beating, which they managed to do a couple of times more before I left school. My mum went to complain about the bullies but all the headmaster said to her was: boys will be boys. My mum was beside herself but we couldn't move to another town as she couldn't afford that, so I had no choice but to get on with it. Her life became a misery too, being sneered at by other mums and talked about for having a queer for a son. She told me not to worry as her close friends knew the truth and she had broad enough shoulders not to take any notice of the others, but all the same I knew she was hurt for me.

'When I left school, I got a job in a warehouse but so did a couple of other lads who had been in my year at school, so straight away word went around from them that I was a poof and then my life at work was hell too. There was no point in trying to find work elsewhere as it wasn't a big place so chances were that anywhere I moved, I'd meet someone I was at school with. I was never going to be left in peace while I stayed in the village. No girls would look at me as they all believed the rumours that I was queer. I couldn't stand it any more, I'd reached the end of my tether, so I made my mother believe that after all these years my wanting to be a dancer was just a phase, which was over now. I threw my tap shoes away and all the books I'd got on dancing over the years, and started to go to football matches in the hope that my old mates would see me and want me to be their friend again. I was as miserable as sin but at least I wasn't being taunted and made a fool of every time I went out any more, and eventually it stopped at work too, when I got myself a girlfriend and took her with me to the works Christmas dance. I knew my mother was no fool and didn't believe me, but she had no choice but to accept what I'd told her.

'Then last March Mum was making spills from old newspapers one Sunday evening as she watched the television, so she'd have them ready to make the fires for the coming week. As she smoothed a sheet of newspaper out ready to roll up, she caught sight of an advertisement for workers at Jolly's, to start at the beginning of June. Amongst the list of jobs on offer were ones in the entertainments team. She was so excited, seeing this as my chance to achieve in a roundabout way my dream of dancing on the stage. She had no doubt that I'd be snapped up once they saw me dance. She told me that it might not be professional dancing on a theatre stage or in a television studio, but it would still be in front of an audience and wasn't that better than nothing? Oh, it was as if a load of fireworks went off in my head, like my birthdays had all come at once. Somewhere up there the Almighty was finally looking out for me. And sod the neighbours! I cleared a space in the living room there and then. With Mum cheering me on, I started to practise my steps, hoping I hadn't forgotten any and trying to come up with a routine for the audition. I posted off an application letter the next day.'

Patsy had been listening to Trevor's tale with a sense of great sadness. This poor young man had been made to go through hell by ignorant bullying people who saw him as something he wasn't just because he wanted to be a dancer. She urged him, 'Well, obviously you were successful and got taken on in the entertainments team, so why didn't you come and ask me to audition you to be a dancer in the shows?'

He sighed. 'I arrived at the camp on a Friday, and of course all us new entertainments staff were keen to see the Stripeys' show that night, me in particular as I wanted to see the standard of the other male dancers. But while I was watching, it struck me that there were males in the sketches but none of them dancing. I immediately believed that that was because they'd be seen by the rest of the male staff at Jolly's as queer and would have their lives made hell for them, like those bullies back home did to me. I was just so disappointed, seeing my last chance to dance gone as I wasn't going to risk having my life made a misery again. I know I can't act so I never bother applying to be in the stage shows at all. But at least I was getting to dance when I was partnering the campers and to me that was better than nothing.

'But then I found another place I could dance where no one could see me so I wasn't risking having my life ruined. A few nights after I arrived I went for a walk and wandered around the back of the funfair. There was a boarded-up area and on it some sheds, I supposed used for storage, but there was an area that hadn't anything in it and I saw it as a place where I could dance and no one need see me if I went after the fair closed for the night.

'I know it sounds stupid, pathetic even, but I could pretend I had an audience watching me and it would be like I was fulfilling my dream. I could buy a large torch and place that at the side of the space and pretend it was a stage spotlight. So most nights after work, I'd take my tap shoes and torch, that's what was in the bag you saw me carrying, and go down to my stage and dance until I dropped. My mum thinks I got a job in the entertainments team as a dancer and I just can't upset her by telling her the truth. That night you saw me in Mablethorpe, I'd gone to buy a new battery for my torch as it was running out. I couldn't tell you as you'd automatically have wanted to know what I needed a torch for. The other night when you saw me on the path by the lake, I was coming back from having a dance session down at the beach. That person you saw running across the grass one night was me too, but it was a fox I was running from that I'd seen on my way back from the beach.'

Patsy was beside herself with remorse. She was no better than those bigots who had hounded Trevor since he was thirteen.

Why had she assumed he was a saboteur just because he didn't act the way others did? How remiss of her not at least to try and find out why he'd acted as he had before accusing him of something he had no part in.

She told him, 'Trev, there are no male dancers in the shows at the moment because when I took over all the existing male dancers had left feet and couldn't dance for toffee, while all blithely assuming they could. I avoided upsetting them by telling them I wanted to try out an all-female dancing troupe for a change. Believe me, if I could find any males who could really dance, I would snap them up immediately for the shows.

'Look, Trev, you'll meet narrow-minded people wherever you go and in all walks of life, just like you'll meet people who don't see others as oddities, peculiar or queer because they are doing something out of the ordinary. I know at first hand what it's like to be taunted and ridiculed because of my height and the fact that I'm not a size ten, and it used to hurt me, I'm not denying it. I would shut myself in my bedroom afterwards and cry my eyes out for hours, threatening never to leave it again, until my mum gave me a good talking to and made me realise that that's how the bullies wanted to make me feel, because they got a kick out of seeing people miserable. She told me that if I never stood up to them, I'd spend my life being afraid of what others thought of me. That was when I decided that I wasn't going to let them do that to me any more and I started going to the places where I enjoyed being, whether they would be there or not. And if they were and did taunt me, I'd just ignore them, acted like their nasty words weren't getting to me, and they soon got fed up and left me alone.

'You're a grown man now, not that little boy any more who was no match for the bullies because you weren't wise enough then to know how to deal with them. As I see it, you have two choices. You can either pursue your dream career that some people believe is suitable only for women or homosexual men, and be prepared to stand up to anyone who mocks you for it, or you can go back and work in a factory and live the rest of your life never knowing if you'd have made it as a dancer.'

Trevor did not hesitate when he answered, 'But I can't stop dancing. I've tried but I can't.'

'Then stand up to the bullies and show them what you're made of.'

He said with conviction, 'I will. I shall dance on the stage, and if anyone taunts me or calls me names I shall ignore them, like you did.'

Patsy gave his knee a pat. 'Good on you.'

'Like my mum said, dancing here at Jolly's is still on the stage in front of an audience and that's all I've really ever wanted. Oh, but that's provided you think I'm good enough to be in the shows.'

She smiled. 'Well, we'll find that out when I audition you tomorrow. I'm no expert like those people who audition for the theatre but I know a good dancer from a bad one.' She paused for a moment before adding, 'I am so sorry that I believed you to be the camp saboteur. Tonight has taught me not to judge people just by the way they act.'

Trevor was about to say something else but just then there was the sound of running feet. Jamie, his face wreathed in concern, came charging around the bend in the track and nearly fell over when he spotted them both. He cried out: 'Oh, thank God, Patsy, you're safe!' He then bent over and placed his hands on his knees until he'd caught his breath before he straightened up and continued: 'I imagined all sorts when I found you weren't there in your hiding place and Trev gone from the chalet too. I've been practically all over the camp, trying to find you, just in case . . . Anyway, you're in one piece so Trev didn't turn nasty when you told him we'd sussed him out.' He then eyed his chalet mate darkly. 'So have you confessed to . . .'

Patsy cut in. 'Jamie, we . . . well, I really . . . got it wrong. Trev's not the one behind the attacks on the camp. That person is still out there.'

Jamie looked in confusion from one to the other of them several times before he asked Trevor, 'Well, if you're not the saboteur, where have you been going most nights after work with that bag over your shoulder? And why do you keep yourself to yourself, with no effort to make any friends?'

It was Patsy who answered Jamie's questions. 'He's been acting strangely because he's been worried people might think he was peculiar for spending time dancing alone down at the back of the funfair.' She laughed at the expression on Jamie's face and held up her hand to him. 'Come on, help me up and let's get back. It's late and I'm shattered. We'll explain everything on the way.'

CHAPTER THIRTY-TWO

The next morning, true to her word, as soon as the team meeting had finished, Patsy asked Trevor's team leader if he would send him along to her at the back of the stage for an audition as a dancer in the show. The team leader looked surprised as Trevor had never mentioned to him any interest in performing on stage. A short while later Patsy put on a track from a record that Trevor had selected and as the music began his feet began to tap, getting faster and faster until they seemed to be taking on a life of their own. Patsy watched, mesmerised and in awe. She was a big fan herself of American musicals, had watched many of them with her mother on a Saturday afternoon on their small black-and-white television, and to Patsy it seemed Trevor's talents were equal to any of the dancers she had seen performing in those films. Whether he would ever get the opportunity to show the world how talented he was, was beyond her control, but she could certainly make sure that the holidaymakers who came to Jolly's were enthralled by his brilliance.

She was so moved that she had great difficulty stopping herself from crying when the music finished and his performance came to an end. She had felt so guilty last night for accusing him of something he wasn't involved in, but now she wondered if that had been fate playing its hand, as if she hadn't then his dancing abilities might have never come to light. As the generous person she was, she so hoped that a show business agent did decide to come to Jolly's and witness his talents as she had no doubt whatsoever that Trevor would be immediately snapped up by them. It would be Jolly's loss but the stage's gain. A thought then struck her. Maybe she could do something to make sure that he did come to the notice of a show business agent rather than leave it to chance . . .

Trevor was still standing nervously on the spot on the stage where he'd danced his last step, waiting for her verdict. She came out from the wings and went over to him, put her hands on his shoulders and told him, 'I'm speechless, Trev. Your feet have wings.'

He asked her eagerly, 'Do you think that I'm good enough to be in the shows?'

'Good enough! Trev, you are *too* good for our shows. You shouldn't be asking me to consider you to dance in them, it's I who should be begging you to appear. I'm going to rejig the show to give you a spot on your own. There's not enough time for me to arrange it for this Friday's, but by next week certainly.'

His jaw dropped in shock. 'Really?'

She smiled. 'Yes, really. That routine you did for me just now would be perfect, but it'll be your spot and I am happy to let you choose whichever routine you wish to perform.'

'Oh, Patsy, Patsy, thank you so much!'

'I'll see you at rehearsal just as the tea dance finishes here this afternoon at four,' she told him. Then laughed as he jubilantly danced off the stage.

Dixie was having great difficulty hiding her fury from Patsy when later that morning she announced what a find they had in Trevor and said she was going to rejig the show to make way for a solo spot for him. The sketch she proposed to drop was the one Dixie featured most prominently in and which she felt showed off her acting skills the best.

Dixie had worked hard to get herself as much stage time as she could in her need to catch the eye of any theatrical agent who came along to check out the talent. She certainly wasn't going to let an upstart like Trevor shove her aside and steal her limelight. She would put a stop to him stealing her hard-earned stage time, just like she had done in the past with others who had posed a threat to her.

She waited for him to finish his shift that night and, after making sure there was no one else around, accosted him on his way back to his chalet.

His mind full of the routine he was going to perform in just over a week's time, Trevor almost jumped out of his skin when a hand grabbed his shoulder and a voice hissed, 'Oi, you, I want a word.'

He spun around and eyed his assailant in shock. 'What about?' he asked, bewildered.

Dixie spat at him, '*I'm* the star of the Stripeys' show, and I'm not having some jumped-up little shit like you come along and take that away from me! Now you'll go tomorrow and tell Patsy that you've changed your mind and don't want to be in the shows after all . . . or I'll make sure you lose your job. I'm Patsy's assistant, don't forget, and I will come up with something that gives her no alternative but to sack you.'

He eyed her wildly as old fears resurfaced, but then he remembered Patsy's advice that bullies must be stood up to and his promise to himself that he would never again allow his life to be governed by tormentors such as Dixie. Taking a deep breath, he grabbed hold of her hand and wrenched it off his shoulder, telling her, 'Go to hell.' Then, before his inner turmoil became apparent, he turned and ran off.

She stood staring after him until he disappeared through the gap in the hedge. No one had ever stood up to her before, her intimidating manner and threats to harm them in one way or another had always been enough for them to agree to do her bidding. She couldn't believe that this ginger-headed, ugly little man had done what all the others had been unable to and stood his ground with her, refusing to let her frighten him into obeying her. She might be very angry about this state of affairs but a part of her admired Trevor for standing up to her when so many others had failed.

* * *

Some distance away, on a bench by the outdoor swimming pool, Jamie had his arm around Patsy's shoulders, she resting her head against his as they sat side by side sharing time together before each retired to their respective chalet to ready themself for bed.

Patsy was happy in her job, happy with the way her life was now, but she was at her happiest when she was spending time with Jamie. He had long ago made her forget her inner worries that she was not pretty enough for him, too tall, too big, and now she was wondering what would happen to their relationship once the season came to an end, albeit it was still over two months away. She knew she had fallen in love with him and was dearly hoping they could keep things between them alive by writing letters and visiting each other whenever possible. Jamie had told her when they first started dating that his ultimate intention was to join his father in their family business. She wasn't sure if that would start immediately the Jolly's season ended. If it did, would their relationship stand the test? She was desperate to ask him but feared to in case his reply was not what she wanted to hear, and then she would be counting off the days before they said their goodbyes, knowing without doubt she would be left with a broken heart. Whoever she met in the future, to her they would never measure up to Jamie. He had everything that she could ever want in a man and she would for ever mourn his loss if they were separated.

Unbeknown to her, Jamie's own thoughts mirrored Patsy's. He might have only been dating her for a short space of time, but he had known from their very first kiss that she was the one for him; would never feel this way for anyone else. It was obvious to him that Patsy liked him very much, but as to whether that liking was enough for her to commit her future to him . . .

He couldn't make plans until he found out what she felt about him. To ask her bluntly how she felt would be unfair but he could always find out in a more roundabout way.

He kissed the top of her head and in a casual manner said, 'What will you be doing during the winter months, Patsy?'

'Going home and getting whatever temporary work I can until the season starts again.' She was afraid to hear what he was planning for the winter months but it would be rude of her not to ask him. 'What about you?'

Her heart sank as he told her what she hadn't wanted to hear. 'The pub my father is buying will be ready by then for me to start managing it.'

She tried to sound non-committal when she said, 'Oh, so you won't be returning to Jolly's next year then?'

'No. This is my one and only season. I have to say, though, I am glad I decided to come and work here, for more reasons than one.'

She lifted her head off his shoulder to fix her eyes on the fountain in the middle of the pool. 'So am I, Jamie,' she whispered.

He released his hold on her so that he could look into her eyes. 'You'll miss me, will you?'

She replied without hesitation, 'I will, very much.'

'Enough to come with me and help me run the pub?'

'You're offering me a job over the winter?'

'No, not a job, and certainly not just over the winter.' He paused to take a deep breath, praying that her answer to his proposal was the one he so much wanted it to be. 'Patsy, I'm offering myself to you as your husband. Will you marry me?'

This was the last thing she had expected to hear and for what seemed an age, to herself and him, she stared blindly at him, before an explosion of pure joy erupted within her. Flinging her arms around him, she cried out euphorically, 'Oh, yes, yes, of course I will!'

He grabbed her to him, showering her face with kisses until his lips found hers. The kiss went on and on until she had no choice but to push him away so that she could draw breath.

He held her in his arms again, with her head back on his shoulder, before he asked, 'Will you miss Jolly's, Patsy? After all, you've been working here for years.'

'I will, very much,' she told him with conviction. 'It's become like a second home to me. I've learned such a lot from all the different jobs I've done, and I've met some characters amongst the campers and the staff. I've made good friends too, but it will be easier to say goodbye to Jolly's than it would be to say goodbye to you.' She eyed him earnestly. 'I want to tell the world about us, Jamie . . .'

'Yes, so do I,' he cut in.

'But we ought to keep this to ourselves until the end of the season or it could unsettle the Stripey team. I've just won their trust and they're all working so well together, I don't want anything to change that.'

'I see your point. Okay, I promise to keep my gob shut. But I will be shouting it off once you give me the all clear.' Jamie tightened his arm around her. 'I love you, Patsy,' he told her.

'I love you too.' Then she added in all seriousness: 'But not enough to miss any more sleep. I could stay here all night with you, Jamie, but I've an entertainments programme to look after tomorrow.'

'And me a bar manager to keep off my back by not slacking.' He eased her gently from him, stood up and held out his hand to her. 'Come on, future wife, let me get you home.'

She felt like she was floating on a cloud as she accepted his hand and together they set off in the direction of the staff chalets.

CHAPTER THIRTY-THREE

The rest of the week passed without incident for the staff at Jolly's. When Friday evening arrived, no further attacks against the camp had happened, no camper had caused the staff any strife, nor any member of staff any problems for their managers, and the sun had been beaming down from a cloudless sky, which afforded everyone a sense of wellbeing.

Drina was feeling whole again as Artie had arrived from Devon the previous day, his Rover 3000 loaded down with the rest of their possessions, and apart from her daily visit to check on the progress of the farmhouse demolition she was spending the rest of the time with her husband, settling themselves back into their little cottage. She didn't intend to do anything else much until the following Monday when she meant to begin formulating plans for the farmhouse land once it was cleared.

Since Drina had spoken of her concerns for Eric, Harold had felt a strong need to offer his friend support. Work allowed Harold to return home at a reasonable time that evening, and he saw this as his opportunity to pay a visit to Eric and have a talk with him. He decided not to drive over but walk the short distance to Eric's flat, just fifteen minutes away. On his way he stopped to go into a corner shop to purchase half a dozen bottles of Double Diamond.

Eric was surprised to find Harold at the door as usually he never arrived at anyone's house uninvited. 'Nothing wrong up at the camp, I hope,' said Eric. 'No one has telephoned me if there is.'

Harold assured him, 'No, nothing is wrong. I just wondered if you fancied a bit of company, that's all.' He indicated the carrier in his hand holding the bottles of beer.

Eric smiled. 'Never been a man to turn any visitor away bearing the sort of gifts you've bought along. Come on in, mate,' he said, standing aside to give Harold just enough room to squeeze past his huge bulk and down the passage.

It was evident that a man on his own lived in the small flat as there were no fancy adornments or feminine touches whatsoever. Eric's idea of ornaments was a collection of miniature spirits bottles, all empty of their contents, lined up across the mantle on a near-identical 1930 fireplace to the one in Harold's own front room. Instead of a gas fire, though, it contained an old two-bar electric one. To one side of the fireplace was a sagging gold-coloured moquette armchair, with a foot stool before it, and positioned facing the fireplace an equally sagging sofa covered in a colourful but worn chintz material. By the other side of the fireplace on a teak-veneered coffee table sat a black-and-white television set, which at the moment was showing an episode of *The Saint*.

Relieving Harold of the carrier, which he put down on the stool, Eric left his visitor to take a seat on the sofa while he went into the kitchen to fetch a bottle opener and two half-pint beer mugs. A few minutes later he handed Harold a glass of beer and then turned off the television set and sat down in his armchair.

Once he was settled, Harold said, 'I apologise for disturbing your programme, Eric.'

With a twinkle of humour in his eyes, Eric responded, 'So you should. The Saint was just about to be shot by the baddie. I don't need to watch the end to know what's going to happen, though, as the Saint always gets himself out of any scrape he lands in.' He then eyed his friend shrewdly. 'Not that it's not nice to see you and the beers are most welcome, but what are you really here for?'

Harold took a swig of his beer, shifting uncomfortably in his seat. 'Last Monday, when Drina and I left you after our visit to the kitchen, she told me that she sensed there was something worrying you. She knows we're good friends so she asked me to offer you her help, should you need it. And the same goes for me, you know that, Eric.'

He tutted. 'That woman misses nothing,' he said in an affectionate manner.

Harold smiled and nodded. 'As my mother would have said, she's got eyes in the back of her head.' He took another sip of his drink before he ventured, 'I'm assuming it is the behaviour of your kitchen assistant that's still of concern to you?'

Eric nodded. 'It's getting beyond a joke, Harold. I've reached the stage where I wish I'd never got rid of Stephen. There's Ginny's hanging on my every word, I continually catch her watching me, the endless questions that she just shouldn't be asking her boss. And you know how when the shift finishes after dinner and all the staff get a couple of hours off, I usually take the chance to catch up with my paperwork, work out new menus, that sort of thing? Well, these last couple of days Ginny's done things to get out of leaving with the rest of them.

'Yesterday she tipped her handbag over the floor, making it look accidental, but took ages picking it all up. Then today, just as everyone else was piling out, she said she couldn't find her chalet key and wondered if it had dropped out of her handbag in her locker, so she shot off into the staff room and by the time she came back all the others had gone. I know it wasn't my imagination, Ginny was definitely trying to pluck up the nerve to say something to me both times. And each time, terrified what that might turn out to be, I panicked . . . excused myself, telling her I'd just remembered I had a meeting to be at, and shot off outside to hide behind the bins until I was sure she'd left. When she had, I sneaked back in and had a stiff brandy from the bottle I keep in my drawer . . . as you know, Harold, just for medicinal purposes . . . to calm me down. I had two, to be honest.

'I kept my distance from her during the tea shift, and as soon as it was over, told everyone to hurry and leave as I had

296

to get off myself sharpish tonight, so I didn't give her any chance to linger afterwards.' He drank back the glass of beer in one go, then leaned down to take another bottle out of the carrier, flipping off the top with the opener and pouring beer into his mug before going on. 'I know that I've only put the showdown off until tomorrow. Sounds pathetic, a grown man scared to face a young girl. I don't like the thought of hurting her, that's all, when I tell her I'm not interested in a relationship with her.'

Harold sighed. 'But you can't keep running for the hills every time you feel you're in danger of being on your own with her. You'll give yourself a heart attack. Look, you know I'm not the best person to be dishing out advice on how to handle women, but in my opinion you're going to have to put her straight some time, Eric, and wouldn't it be best for you both if you did it sooner rather than later, before she becomes any more infatuated and it's harder for her to get over you?'

His friend sighed heavily. 'Yes, you're right. I'll try and break it to her as gently as I can. I'll do it tomorrow. Can't say I'm looking forward to it, though. Thanks for coming round and making me see I have to face this, Harold. Sounds selfish of me but I just hope Ginny doesn't want to leave after I tell her I'm not interested in her in that way. She's a good little worker and I actually like her and would miss having her around. Another beer?'

Harold nodded.

Having made his decision to face Ginny and put her straight as soon as the dinner shift finished, early the next afternoon Eric tackled her about her behaviour. Ginny had not relented in her efforts to ingratiate herself with him all morning, to the extent that he was afraid he would lose his temper with her if he caught her watching him once more, smiling over at him or badgering him as to what job he needed her to do next, and all the time probing yet again for further details about him and his family. He knew that as soon as everyone left to enjoy the couple of hours of freedom between shifts, Ginny would find some excuse to stay behind and accost him. He was not mistaken.

As she had been doing for the last few days, she was the last to come out of the staff room and seemed to be searching through her handbag as she did so. Spotting Eric watching her from over in his office, she called, 'Can't find my chalet key. I must have dropped it somewhere.'

She had no more lost her key than he had lost his marbles. Eric took a deep breath before he called back, 'Ginny, both you and I know that you haven't lost your key, or anything else for that matter. You're stalling so as to make an excuse to spend time with me, just the same as you have these last couple of days. I think it's time me and you had a talk.'

Her face lit up and she eagerly babbled, 'Yes, I do too. I've been wanting to talk to you for ages now but just couldn't build my courage to. I've something important to tell you.' She had covered the distance to the office and her words were starting to trip over one another. 'You see . . .'

He held up his hand by way of a warning to her to stop, wanting to save her the embarrassment he knew she would suffer if he allowed her to spill out her feelings to him. 'No, I need to speak first.' Before he lost his nerve Eric continued firmly, 'Look, Ginny, this has to stop. Not that I'm not flattered that a pretty young girl like you has fallen in . . . well, whatever it is you do feel for me . . . but you should be falling for young men your own age, not the likes of me that's old enough to be your father.'

She cried: 'But that's just it! That's what I wanted to talk to you about. You *are* my father.'

His eyes nearly popped out of his head; he was stupefied by her announcement. 'What! But . . . but I can't be . . .'

'You are. I can prove it. Look,' she said, pulling an envelope out of her handbag. She opened it and slipped out the contents. 'It's my birth certificate and your name is on it as my father.' She thrust the certificate at him.

Eric was staring at her blindly, this information refusing to sink into his brain. Taking the certificate, he looked at it. And there it was in the registrar's neat handwriting, his name Eric Brown under the column headed Name of Father, and under the column headed Father's Occupation, Army Cook. The child's date of birth was 3 January 1953. Place of Birth, Beeston, Nottingham. The name of her mother, Theresa Holland. A name which meant nothing to him, like it hadn't when Ginny had mentioned her mother's name at her interview

Ginny pulled up the chair that Eric kept at the side of his office for visitors and was sitting so close to him that their knees were almost touching. She was looking at him earnestly as she informed him: 'You met my mother when you came to Nottingham to see your friend for a few days while you were on leave. It was a Monday night and she was with a group of friends celebrating one of their birthdays. She told me she saw you standing by yourself at the bar and couldn't take her eyes off you, you were so handsome. Then you must have sensed she was looking at you because you turned your head and looked over at her with your big brown eyes and she instantly fell in love. She said you told her that as soon s you'd clapped eyes on her, you fell instantly in love too. She told me that you were so funny, made her laugh so much, were the life and soul of the party, and so romantic too . . . just swept her off her feet. You spent the rest of the evening together and arranged to meet the next night. Then you spent the next three together before your leave was up and you had to report back to your unit. She told me that you didn't want to go and leave her but had no choice or you'd be facing a court martial for being absent without leave.

'You promised Mum you would write and come and see her again as soon as you could wangle more leave, and that you'd let her know when that leave was so that she could make arrangements with the register office for a marriage ceremony, and then you'd take her back with you to your base and they'd give you married accommodation and you'd live happily together for the rest of your lives. But she never heard from you again. Everyone tried to tell her that you'd just been using her for fun but she wouldn't listen to them. She knew you loved her and that the only reason you hadn't written or come back was because you were dead, killed in an accident while you were driving back to join your unit. You were the love of Mum's life, she never got over you. She died last year from cancer. She was a wonderful mum to me and I'll never stop missing her. She talked about you a lot, told me what a great father you would have made me had you not been killed. I used to pray to you every night, asking you to watch over me and Mum and protect us from harm, and before I ended my prayer I always told you how much we both loved you.' Ginny paused for a moment, a look of confusion and deep pain etching her pretty face. 'But you would never have heard my prayers in heaven, would you, as you weren't dead? I learned that you weren't from the article about you in the newspaper.

'As I read the story about the ex-army chef who'd saved the day when the holiday camp he was working at was damaged by fire, it didn't hit me at first that it was my father the story was about. Then your name registered. There couldn't be many Eric Browns, of the right age, who'd been a chef in the army, I thought. And that's why I came here to work and have been asking you those questions, so I could get to know about you while I've been trying to pluck up the courage to tell you who I am.' She paused before she asked him, 'Why didn't you come back for Mum and marry her like you promised?' She awaited his answer, hope and accusation visible in her eyes.

But Eric was still trying to digest the fact that this young girl wasn't after all infatuated with him but was his daughter . . . that he was a father. The story she had just told him about how he had met her mother had barely registered with him as yet. He said to her, 'Ginny, I'm sorry, but this has come as a huge shock to me. I need a bit of time on my own to take it all in. Then we'll talk, I promise you.' She did not move, obviously fearing that should she leave, he would disappear again. He reiterated, 'I'm not going anywhere, Ginny. I just need some time to take this all in.'

She got up. 'I'll wait for you to come to my chalet when you're ready. It's number three four one. I'll asked my chalet mate to leave us in privacy while we talk.'

She turned and left then.

Eric was unaware of the kitchen door closing after Ginny as he was lost in his thoughts. He was a father! It was incredible, frightening, terrifying to him in fact. He had no idea how to be a father. Where did he start? How did he suddenly love and feel caring and protective towards a seventeen-year-old girl who was a stranger to him? He looked down at the certificate in his hand, studying the birth details. And then he realised that Ginny couldn't possibly be his daughter as he'd never been to Nottingham, never even passed through the city. And there was the fact that from 1951 until 1954 he hadn't actually been in the country but serving with his unit in Cyprus. During leaves he'd stayed in the country and spent time with his mates at the beach, as his parents were both dead by then.

Parts of Ginny's story filtered back to him. She had said that her father had driven back to his unit after leaving her mother, promising her he'd return as soon as he could and then they'd marry. But Eric didn't drive. The only time he got in a car, it was in the passenger seat. Ginny's mother had described her father as being funny and romantic, the sort of man who swept a woman off her feet. No one who knew Eric well would ever describe him as having those traits. The description Ginny had given to him fitted his brother Jerry far better than it did Eric.

He froze rigid then, his heart hammering, thoughts in a whirl. Ginny's father was his brother! But why would Jerry use someone else's name before getting a woman into bed ? The Jerry he'd known had never had to make any effort to get a woman into bed with him, as they would be begging him to take them. Then it struck Eric. Of course! Because Jerry had been married at the time and, wrong of him as Eric thought it was, had needed to pass himself off as another, because he dare not risk his wife finding out about his adultery. Many of Eric's army buddies had been married and had affairs and, to him, they'd been sleazebags deceiving their wives, but his brother was unlike his army buddies who'd willingly got married. Jerry had been forced into it to save his own family from ruin. Eric realised Jerry's marriage must have been purgatory for him to have had to seek comfort in the arms of another woman. Tears pricked Eric's eyes at the thought of the great sacrifice Jerry had made for the sake of his family.

He was in a dilemma. For Alison to hear now that her husband had fathered a child not long after they'd had one of their own would be grounds enough for her to throw him out without a penny to his name, then all Jerry's years of sacrifice would have been for nothing. But then, didn't he need to know that he had another child? Didn't Ginny need to know who her real father was? Or was it best to let sleeping dogs lie? Eric could tell Ginny that he wasn't her father and had no idea who the man who had impersonated him actually was. But then what would that do to her, believing that the man who had fathered her was nothing but a liar who had used her mother for a bit of fun?

He tossed these problems around in his mind for several long moments in an effort to decide what was the best thing to do for Ginny. Then he made his decision. It wasn't up to him to decide her future. His brother was her father, so the responsibility was his.

CHAPTER THIRTY-FOUR

Over in the office Marion was working away typing out the next two weeks' worth of events for the campers on an A4 sheet of paper. Once finished, she would hand the chart over to Sandra who would copy it many hundreds of times on the Xerox photocopier, which had recently replaced the old Banda copying machine and come to make the lives of the office staff so much easier. Sandra would then fold the copied sheets into thirds to form a pamphlet. These would be handed over to the receptionists to give out to the new arrivals due in a week's time.

On the surface Marion appeared her usual efficient, calm and collected self, but inside she was spinning with excitement like a top. Now that she had everything in place, tonight she was planning to get Harold completely into her clutches, leaving him no room for escape. She had already found out that he was planning to be home all evening and so nothing lay in her way. By tomorrow morning she would be planning again, but this time it would be her wedding to him.

Her thoughts were interrupted by the arrival of Eric in the office. He didn't ask Marion to announce his presence to Harold, just told her he needed to see him urgently as he passed her desk and carried on into the manager's office, shutting the door behind him. Normally she would have been insulted that someone had undermined her position but she was far too preoccupied with thoughts of what tonight would hold to make any sort of protest.

Harold knew by Eric's whole manner that everything was not right with his friend when he stepped into the office unannounced, shutting the door behind him. 'What's the matter?' asked Harold.

The big man responded, 'I haven't time to explain now, Harold, as I've to get back to the kitchen for the tea sittings, but you told me I could count on your help if I ever needed it. Well, I need it now. Once I've got the staff organised I mean to put Paul Harrop in charge and leave early, about four thirty it will be, and I was hoping that you could get away at that time too and run me to Sheffield in your car. I need to see someone, you see, as a matter of urgency.'

And it must be if Eric was leaving his under-chef in charge; although Paul was a very reliable and capable young man, Harold had never known Eric hand over full responsibility for overseeing a service to him or any of the other under-chefs, no matter how desperate he was to leave. But Harold knew that Sheffield was Eric's home town so presumably this concerned friend or family. His own plans for a relaxing evening forgotten, he answered Eric without hesitation. 'Yes, of course I will take you wherever you want to go. I'll bring my car around to the back of the kitchen and pick you up at four thirty.'

Marion was to learn that her planned evening was in tatters when a while later Harold called her into his office and asked her if she would be kind enough to have Sandra deliver a note to the security office for them to find when they arrived to start their shift at nine, stating that he wouldn't be contactable at home this evening and wasn't sure what time he would be back but would contact them when he was.

Marion was fuming inside to be learning that tomorrow she wouldn't after all be planning her wedding. But she wasn't going to let this small setback upset her. She would just have to be patient until next Saturday. In the big scheme of things, what was another week?

* * *

On the drive over to Sheffield, a matter of three hours away from Mablethorpe, Eric told Harold Ginny's story. When he had finished Harold was speechless for a few moments before he said, 'The poor child. How do you think your brother will take this when you break it to him?'

'Well, he did the right thing by Alison. I believe that after he's got over the shock, he'll do the right thing by Ginny too.'

'And you know exactly where he lives?'

'Well, I'm hoping he hasn't moved. But when he came to tell us he was married, he mentioned that he and Alison would be living in the family home with her parents. Some start to married life, eh, living with your wife's parents? And it must be worse when you didn't actually want to marry the woman in the first place, and her father is the tyrant type who gives you no choice but to work for the family firm.'

They had arrived in Sheffield by now and Eric directed Harold through the streets of the steel-producing town, to an affluent tree-lined area, all the houses huge three-storey dwellings, in their own grounds and built from silver-grey stone. Only the wealthy could afford to live here. Harold parked the car at the kerb opposite the house Eric had directed him to and told his friend that he would wait for him here and to take as long as he needed.

Eric did not wish to make unnecessary trouble for his brother by turning up unannounced when he knew the likes of him were not welcome at the house, so he went around to the back. The door was opened to him by a young girl dressed in a maid's uniform. Behind her in the kitchen he could see a portly middle-aged woman wearing a large apron, whom he assumed was the cook, busy carving slices off a huge joint of beef. Behind her on the stove pans were bubbling, the heat and steam causing the cook to sweat as she went about her work. It was apparent that the occupants of the house were about to have dinner, but how well off must Alison's father be to afford a cook and a maid in this day and age? Eric thought.

305

The cook shouted sharply, 'Who is it, Bridie, calling us on us at this time of an evening when we're just about to dish up? If it's that lad of yours . . .'

'No, it's not, Mrs Lawson,' the maid hurriedly called back to her. 'After the telling off you gave him last time, and threatening to clip him round the ear with your rolling pin like that, Mickey wouldn't dare. You scared him to death. It's some bloke calling I've never seen before.'

'What does he want?'

'I dunno, I ain't asked him yet. What do you want?' she demanded of Eric.

'I'd like to have a word with Mr Brown, please.'

'Well, you can't, as the family have guests tonight and they're just about to sit down to dinner.'

'It's urgent,' insisted Eric.

The maid gave him the perfect excuse then. 'Oh, is it about the factory?'

'Yes, that's right, it is. No point in alarming the family until I speak to J . . . Mr Brown about it, so can you be discreet and get him here without the others knowing?'

The young girl looked intrigued. 'What's happened at the factory then?' she nosily enquired.

'Mr Brown, please,' Eric urged her.

She shut the door while she went off to fetch him.

Eric meanwhile nervously paced up and down, until he was stopped by the door opening and his brother's arrival. Jerry pulled it to behind him. He snapped at Eric, 'What's this about the factory that's so urgent my evening had to be disturbed? And who are you? You're not one of our employees.'

Jerry had hardly changed over the years. He was still handsome, with a headful of dark hair, still slim of figure. He was far better dressed, though, than he had been before his marriage, when his suits had been off the peg from a chain store in town, paid for on the never never. He was looking immaculate in a handmade black dinner jacket, dress shirt and black tie. Eric smiled at him. 'Don't you recognise your own brother, Jerry?'

For a moment Jerry froze and stared at him blindly, then he grabbed hold of Eric's arm and dragged him hurriedly across an immaculate lawn to a summer house. Inside he let go of Eric and demanded, 'What are you doing here? I told you when I came to see you all after I married Alison that I couldn't have anything more to do with you, and I warned you what would happen if I did. My father-in-law is not a man to cross, believe me, I've witnessed what happened to those who have.'

'Yes, I know, but . . .'

'No, buts, Eric. You can't be here and that's that. Mum and Dad are both dead, I know, I read the announcements in the local papers. But Alison's father would still ruin my life if he thought for a minute I'd gone behind his back. And then he'd cause you trouble as well, more than you could possibly imagine. He's a powerful man with friends in high places, and not the sort to easily forgive.'

Eric looked sad. 'I did think you might be glad to see me even though I promised I'd never contact you again. But twenty years have passed so surely . . .'

Jerry responded agitatedly, 'Nothing has changed, Eric. Now, for God's sake, what is it you're here to tell me? And hurry up about it before I'm missed. We've got important guests and my father-in-law won't be happy if I'm not there when the summons comes for us to sit down for dinner. He's a stickler for protocol.'

'Look, Jerry . . .'

'Jeremy,' he corrected Eric. 'I haven't been called Jerry since I married Alison.'

'I'm sorry, but of course I didn't know that. Well, you see, Jeremy, do you remember visiting Nottingham, Beeston to be precise, about eighteen or so years ago?'

His brother frowned quizzically at Eric, obviously not being at all clear why he would be asking him this, but regardless answered, 'I travelled a lot in the early days when I was first learning the business, but yes, I think I remember being sent by the old man to negotiate a better deal with a couple of factories in Beeston that supplied materials to us. It was his way of testing

307

me, to see what I was capable of. I returned back with a better deal than he could have struck himself. What of it?'

'First let me tell you that I don't blame you for seeking comfort in another woman's arms after being blackmailed into marriage, and I'm not angry with you for impersonating me as I realise when you did so you were in fear of Alison ever finding out . . .'

Jeremy erupted, 'What are you babbling about, man? Get to the point then go, before anyone sees you'

'Yes, sorry. Do you remember spending time with a woman called Theresa while you were in Beeston?

Jeremy pulled a packet of Dunhill cigarettes out of his pocket, lit one with a gold Rolex lighter, pulled hard on it and blew a plume of smoke into the air before he responded. 'Just about. Pretty little thing if I remember right.'

'You left her pregnant with your child.'

To Eric's shock Jeremy didn't bat an eyelid at what most would perceive as shocking news. Instead he gave a nonchalant shrug. 'And that's what you've come here to tell me, at the risk of ruining my life? Well, not my problem. That woman knew what she was risking when she opened her legs for me. She was more than willing, believe me.'

Eric felt disdainful of this crudeness about a woman charmed into having sex and his brother's absolute disregard for the child he had fathered. 'But don't you want to see your daughter, get to know her? I realise this must have come as a hell of a shock to you and you'll need time to get used to the idea that you have another child. But surely the girl deserves . . .'

To Eric's shock, Jeremy grabbed him roughly by his lapels and thrust his face close, snarling furiously, 'Now you listen here! I worked hard to get Alison pregnant and to marry me, so as to win myself the life I have now, and I'm not going to risk losing it for the bastard of some woman I can hardly remember fucking.'

Eric was reeling from Jeremy's revelation as well as his coarse language, which Eric doubted was used in front of his wife, children and father-in-law. 'But you told Mum and Dad and me that Alison purposely got herself pregnant, to trap you into marrying her?'

Jeremy smirked, letting go of Eric's jacket, and said smarmily, 'Bit of advice, brother. You shouldn't believe all you're told. When I met Alison I was heading for a life just like Mum and Dad's was, the same as all the rest of the families who lived on our street. Stuck in a miserable marriage with a wife constantly nagging that you haven't provided for her as well as she feels she deserves, scratting from day to day just to keep a roof over the family's heads, doing a job you hate in a dirty factory, lucky if you have enough left from your wages after paying out all the dues for a pint or two on a Friday night or a bet at the bookie's. I wanted better for myself without any idea how to get it. But I was determined to improve my life, no matter what. While I waited for something to come up, I amused myself by seeing how many notches I could carve on my bedpost.

'Just when I was beginning to give up hope that I was ever going to get myself out of my purgatorial life and feared I would end up like the rest, whether I liked it or not, Alison came along. I spotted her in a club . . . coming in with a few friends to slum it for a laugh, was my guess at the time. I found out through a mate that she was single and that her father was loaded. She was my ticket to the good life. All I had to do was get her to marry me. Well, for a man with my charm and looks, that wasn't too hard. As a bonus she was pretty and I fancied her rotten. I knew, though, that she would never see me as marriage material if she heard where I came from, or even if she did, I doubted her father would allow her to marry beneath her. So I invented myself a new background, learned to drop the slang when I spoke and how to use a knife and fork properly, bought myself a couple of good quality suits on tick, borrowed a few quid from the tally man, and went after her.

'She's no pushover, isn't Alison, and that's what I like about her, but she fell for my charms, hook, line and sinker, and my story that I was the only son of a once well-off businessman who had gambled away everything and left his only motherless son, without a bean to his name, to work in a factory. I said my father threw himself off a bridge when his debtors began closing in on him and he'd nothing to pay them with. Of course, I did sweat a bit in case her father decided to check out my story, when matters turned serious for us, but I must have been very convincing because he never did.' Jerry held out his arms. 'So here I am, brother, a man of means with a beautiful doting wife and two smart and good-looking children, both at private school, holidays abroad twice a year, a Rolls-Royce Silver Shadow to drive around in, and an obliging father-in-law who will be signing over the business to me when he retires in a couple of years. And yes, so I did play around a bit after I married Alison, but when you're a red-blooded man like I am it's hard to go without sex for a few months while your wife is pregnant and won't let you near her.'

Eric uttered, 'So what you told us about being made by Alison's father to have nothing to do with us after your marriage, as he saw us as not worthy to mix with his family and would ruin us if you dared to keep in contact with us, was all lies to get us out of the picture, for fear your true background would come to light and ruin your plans.'

Jerry gave a devilish grin. 'That about sums it up, brother. '

'Alison's father's not a man to be feared at all, is he?'

'I wouldn't say that I wasn't worried when he first discovered I'd got his little girl pregnant only weeks after we started seeing each other. It took me a lot of grovelling to convince him I would make a good husband to her and father to the child, and I did fear at one time he wouldn't give his permission for her to marry me as I couldn't provide for her in the manner he wanted, but since I agreed to his terms that I move in with them and work for him in the family firm, which was just what I wanted anyway, I've had him wrapped around my little finger.'

Eric was shaking his head reproachfully. 'I don't know you, Jeremy. I don't know you at all. You're not the brother I remember.'

He said almost proudly, 'I never was, Eric. You idolised me as your big brother and only saw in me what you wanted to. So now you know what the score is, you can leave here and never darken my door again. As for that girl . . . well, as far as she's concerned you're her dad, so how you get rid of her is up to you. But be warned, brother dear, that if you dare try and ruin my marriage and lose me what I've built up over the years by telling her the truth and pointing her in my direction, then believe me, it won't only be my life that's over. If I go down, I'll make it my business to take you with me.'

With that Jerry turned and ran down the stairs of the summer house and across the grass, to disappear through the back door of the house.

Eric stared after him. He couldn't believe that the man who had just left was the brother he had idolised since the day he was born and thought a saint for the last twenty years. In fact, he was nothing but a selfish, amoral individual who didn't care who he hurt in his quest to better his own life. Eric was ashamed to be related to him.

When Eric had made himself comfortable back in the car, Harold said to him, 'I gather from the expression on your face that all didn't go as well as you'd hoped it would.'

He sighed. 'No, it didn't at all, Harold. My brother made it clear he won't ever acknowledge Ginny as his daughter. He's not prepared to lose his marriage and his livelihood over a mistake he made years ago.'

Harold started the car and moved off. 'Oh, I see. Have you thought yet what you'll tell Ginny?'

'That I'll try and be the best father I can to her, that's what I'm going to tell her.'

Harold took his attention off the road just long enough to shoot his friend a look of pure admiration before he concentrated on getting them both safely back to the camp.

CHAPTER THIRTY-FIVE

'Mother, I didn't go out last Saturday night.'

Sitting in her usual place on the threadbare seating at the front of the shabby caravan, her huge flabby arms folded across her massive chest, fat legs splayed wide, Ida snapped at her daughter, 'And I'm supposed to be grateful for that, am I? For all the company you were last Saturday night, you might as well have gone out. No fun at all those games of knockout whist we played, you with a face on you like a slapped arse.'

Marion was putting the finishing touches to a light application of makeup, using the mirror of her silver compact, standing by the door to catch the light through the glass. 'I told you at the time, Mother, I was tired. The hours I work at Jolly's aren't exactly eight thirty to five, five days a week. I only get Sundays off and that's not a day of rest for me, is it? I have to give this place a good clean, take the washing to the launderette in town, iron my clothes for the week ahead, while you sit on your throne giving me orders.'

Ida said sulkily, 'I do my share but I'm not *exactly* a young woman any more, am I, so I help as much as I'm able.' And she was unable to resist having a jibe at Marion by adding, 'Living here is not doing my health any good, is it? So the longer I'm forced to live in this damp tin hut then the worse my health will get and the less I'll be able to do.'

Marion shot her a look of derision. Ida was much more capable than ever she admitted. Her idleness was down to her still making a protest against Marion for their situation, and until that improved her protest would continue. Well, soon she'd have a house to lord it over again and Marion would be quite happy for her to take over the running of it while she spent Harold's money and her time decorating and furnishing his house the way she wanted it. She'd also be building up a social life with the kind of people she had befriended when she'd been married to Lionel. Marion had been in a mood last Saturday night after her plan for that evening had been put on hold, which obviously her mother had not failed to pick up on, but her mood tonight was one of exhilaration at what the night ahead was going to bring, and she wasn't going to let her mother's nasty tongue spoil it.

'Yes, I know you help as much as you can. I shouldn't expect a woman of your age to tackle any more than you do,' Marion said sweetly. 'And I am working at getting us out of here.'

'Don't look like it to me from where I'm sitting,' Ida muttered. 'I've told you many times that you won't find the sort of well set-up bloke we need to take us away from all this, hobnobbing with the sort of people who work at that holiday camp.'

How little you know, thought Marion. She wanted to put her mother out of her misery and inform her of just how close they were to improving their life, but she still daren't risk Ida taking it upon herself to interfere in some way and manage to ruin it, especially at this crucial stage in proceedings. Marion could still do something, though, to get Ida to ease up on her constant badgering of her.

Touching up her eyelashes with a small brushful of block mascara, she said, 'Look, Mum, there is a man I've my eye on. He's a visitor to the camp, a friend of the manager, comes now and again to see him. He's not bad-looking, around forty-five, divorced and has his own business, big house somewhere across town where the better-off live. I know he's taken a fancy for me and I've let it be known to him I like him too, so I've a feeling that the next time he comes in he'll be asking me out.'

Ida looked pleased to hear this. 'Well, you'd better make sure you play your cards right with him then, my girl. Make him . . .'

'Mother!' she snapped. 'I know how to get myself a man, so please keep out of it. I don't want you interfering, you hear me?'

Ida looked insulted. 'Me, interfere? How dare you! I've never interfered in anything in my life.'

No, of course you haven't, Mother, thought Marion. If you hadn't constantly done so in my marriage to Lionel, then he might not have been so desperate to get rid of you and probably would have given me another chance after my affair.

She put her compact into her handbag and slipped on a green and yellow tweed waist-length jacket over a blouse, complementing the green slim-legged ankle-length trews she was wearing, then announced, 'I'm off. I've told you not to worry as I plan to stay overnight at Susan's because we'll be having a drink and you know what women are like when they get together. It's the early hours and we've no idea where the time has gone.'

'Well, it will drag tonight for me, being here on my own,' Ida grumbled. 'But you enjoy yourself and don't worry about me.'

She then thoughtfully watched as her daughter shouldered the ill-fitting caravan door open and slammed it shut behind her. As soon as she had walked away, Ida heaved herself off her seat, hurried over to the hook on the wall of the caravan just inside the door, took her coat off it and put it on. With her handbag over her arm and a pair of comfortable shoes on her feet, she let herself out of the caravan and followed after her daughter. Ida wasn't stupid and her daughter was kidding herself if she thought she was. She knew her daughter better than Marion thought she did. She had noticed over the past few weeks Marion lapsing into long periods of thought when she had been sitting of an evening thumbing through old magazines, her eyes holding a distant look. Ida had instinctively known that in her mind she had not been thinking about work or reminiscing over the past as she had said when Ida asked her what she was thinking about, but formulating plans. You only plotted when you had something to plot about. And it had to be over a man as nothing was as important to either of them as Marion snaring one who could lift them out of this life of hell. That story she had just told Ida about a man she had her eye on, who came in to visit the boss at work, was just a story and nothing more. Ida would bet her life on the fact that Marion had already snagged the man she saw as their saviour and was in the process of landing him. Well, Ida was her mother and it wasn't right of Marion to be keeping her in the dark about something so crucial.

Maybe she was trying to protect her mother by not telling her because she didn't want Ida to build up her hopes, only to have them dashed if matters didn't work out. But having some hope that her life could soon drastically improve was better than sitting here day after day, night after night, in this miserable rusting hovel, with only the lowest of the low as neighbours. It was better than no hope at all. She was desperately intrigued to see the calibre of the man Marion was in the process of luring; what type of house he lived in, for example, so that she could make her own plans for how she would arrange her bedroom, what furniture she would get Marion's new husband to buy her and such like. It would help her to endure the long hours of solitude while she was on her own and Marion was out at work, or when she went out pretending it was people from Jolly's she was meeting when really Ida knew it was this man. And that was why she was following her daughter now.

Ida was far more able physically that she professed and soon caught sight of Marion a few yards ahead, stepping carefully down the rutted path at the side of the scrapyard. Ida kept a discreet distance away as she followed her to the bus station. She was worried that Marion was going to be catching a bus and wondering how she was going to conceal herself on board, but then to her surprise Marion didn't make her way to any particular stop but headed to the lock-ups where people stashed their luggage for short periods while they whiled away time with a walk in the town or had something to eat. Standing before a set of lockers, Marion took a key from her pocket and opened

315

one while Ida was wondering what on earth her daughter could have stashed in there.

To her surprise Marion took out two laden carrier bags Ida could tell held food. Ah, so that was it. Marion was intending to cook her prey a meal. It was said that the best way to a man's heart was via his stomach and it seemed her daughter thought so too. Ida was impressed as that was just what she had done when she had been ingratiating herself as a young woman with Marion's father, cooking him meals to let him see that he would never starve with her as a wife.

She then followed after Marion as she left the bus station, walked through the town and on down several street before she stopped before a house in a tree-lined avenue. All the houses here were detached, three-storey Victorian villas with small well-kept gardens at the front, decent strips of land at the back. Marion put down her bags to straighten her clothes and smooth her hair before picking them up, unlatching the small iron gate between the low garden walls and passing though, kicking it shut behind her. She made her way up the short path then elbowed the doorbell.

A few moments went past before the door was opened by a rather ordinary-looking, bespectacled man, not much taller than Marion was, dressed casually in a shirt and blue V-neck jumper and fawn-coloured slacks. Not at all the good-looking man Marion had described to her mother earlier. But then, what did looks matter as long as this man had plenty of money in the bank? From where she was hiding behind a tree opposite, Ida thought the man appeared surprised to see Marion on his doorstep. But then maybe she was early and he wasn't expecting her yet.

After Marion had disappeared inside and the door had been shut, Ida stepped out from her hiding place to give the house opposite a more detailed appraisal. It was similar in style to the one they had lived in with Lionel but not quite so big and with not nearly so much space around it. But then it looked well kept enough and, knowing the rooms inside would be a good

316

size, she would have a decent bedroom to arrange her new furniture in and a nice big kitchen where she would make tea and cakes to feed her new friends with when she entertained them in the large lounge. Ida's smile of pleasure was almost lost inside her fat jowls. This would do nicely, she thought. The area was a decent one, the neighbouring houses within her view at the moment well kept too, and it wasn't that far to walk to the town for a browse around the shops or to buy what she needed with the money Marion's new man would be giving her.

Ida didn't mind so much returning now to the tiny damp dwelling on the miserable site, knowing that her time living there was soon coming to an end.

Harold had been very surprised to find Marion on his doorstep, laden down with bags of food. He had been disturbed from reading a book in his comfortable chair, a glass of beer to hand, when the bell had rung. In the week since he'd returned to the camp from Sheffield he and Eric hadn't managed to catch up so he thought it might be Eric coming to tell him how he was getting on with being a father to Ginny. To find Marion instead had thrown Harold. Before he could ask what she was doing here, she told him that she had so wanted to repay his recent kindness to her, she had decided to cook him a meal. Without giving him any time to protest, she had stepped over the threshold, passed him and gone on down the hall towards the kitchen. By the time he had shut the door and joined her she had already unpacked the bags and their contents were now spread out on the pine kitchen table.

She said to him, 'I've brought beer for you, the sort you like, and wine for me. I'll leave you to pour us drinks while I start on the food. I hope steak, salad and new potatoes, with Arctic Roll for pudding, sounds good to you?' She damned well hope so as it had cost her a good portion of her food budget for the week to buy all that and Ida wasn't going to be very happy living on not much more than tinned soup and bread until next pay day.

Harold had in fact not long since eaten, only beans on toast as that had been all he was of the mind to cook himself, and wasn't hungry but was far too polite to spoil Marion's attempt to repay him for his help. He fervently wished she hadn't as there really was no need to as far as he was concerned, and he'd so been looking forward to a relaxing evening, enjoying his own company and his book, later listening to a play on the radio.

After pouring her a glass of wine, not needing a drink for himself as he'd already got some beer waiting for him in the lounge, Harold showed Marion where to find what she needed to prepare the meal, then went off to set the table in the dining room.

As he was not a great conversationalist it was Marion who did most of the talking, regaling him with stories about places she had been, theatre productions she had seen and such like during her marriage to her husband, Harold just chipping in here and there as required of him while they ate together at the table. The meal she had produced was delicious, he couldn't deny, the steak cooked perfectly just as he had told her he liked it, the salad dressing she had made very tasty, the chips crisp on the outside, soft and fluffy inside. He had no room for the pudding she had brought along, but out of politeness he forced it down anyway. When the meal finished, as instructed by her despite his offer to help, he went to relax in the lounge while she cleared away. He had to admit that he liked having a woman fussing around him, had enjoyed the company, just that the woman concerned wasn't really the sort he found himself attracted to or at ease with.

During the evening he had started to feel uncomfortable as he felt sure that Marion was giving him the signs that she had feelings of a romantic sort for him. Just little signs he'd picked up on. How her hand had lingered on his when she had taken the glass of wine from him, and her look he felt sure had been a suggestive one; her general attentiveness towards him; her eagerness to hear from him that the food was to his liking. He hoped he was wrong as he didn't know what he would do if she did make a play for him; that wouldn't be welcome at all. It wasn't like he could make his excuse and leave. He just prayed it was his imagination that was playing tricks on him and Marion wasn't really flirting with him. It was his intention, though, after a suitable amount of time had passed, to encourage her to leave, professing himself tired after his busy week at work.

Having tidied up the kitchen, Marion joined him in the lounge with a glass of beer for him, wine for herself. He didn't really want another drink but felt obliged to accept it. Settling herself on the sofa, tucking her feet underneath her, she started chatting again . . . just general chit-chat that wasn't really of interest to him.

Then he felt himself relaxing. His body seemed to be sinking into the chair, he was finding it difficult to focus his vision and Marion's voice was fading further and further away from him . . . Next thing he knew he was waking up in bed, his head throbbing as if a thousand drummers were inside it. He was aware it was morning from the light behind the curtains. He put down his hand on the mattress beside him in an effort to help himself sit up, but instead of the sheet, his hand contacted something soft and warm. He pulled his hand back as if from a fire. He jerked his head around and his eyes filled with shock when he saw Marion lying beside him, one elbow bent, head resting in her hand, smiling at him tenderly, only parts of the sheet covering her nakedness. Automatically his eyes looked down at himself, to find with horror that he was totally naked too, no sheet covering any part of his body. He grabbed at the sheet and yanked it up over himself, right up to his chin.

'Morning, darling,' Marion said to him in a seductive voice. 'Did you sleep well?'

His thoughts were tumbling around in his brain, like balls in a bingo drum. He tried to speak, ask her what she was doing here, but his tongue seemed to have welded itself to the roof of his mouth.

319

'Well, you should have slept well after all the exercise you had last night,' Marion said to him meaningfully. 'I know I did. Oh, Harold, you really are a very sexy man. Or should I call you a very sexy fiancé?'

She held out her other hand, splaying her fingers out wide, the third one of which had a ring on it. He stared at it wildly. It was his mother's engagement ring! How had it come to be on Marion's finger?

She was looking at him with eyes brimming with love. 'Oh, Harold, you don't know how happy you've made me. I never dared hope that you would feel the same way as I did. I fell for you as soon as I saw you that first day in the office and you've no idea how hard it's been for me since, working so close to you, fighting to keep my feelings for you under control for fear of making a complete fool of myself, when all the time the only thing I've desperately wanted is for you to hold me in your arms, kiss me and tell me how much you love me too. When you unburdened yourself of your feelings for me last night, telling me that you had fallen for me too the first time you met me but were unable to believe that a woman like me could ever return them . . . well, I just wanted to burst with joy. To make sure I didn't think you were just saying these things to get me into bed, you went and fetched your mother's engagement ring, got down on bended knee and ask me to marry you while you slipped it on my finger. I couldn't have wished for a more romantic proposal, Harold. You really are a man with hidden depths.'

She ran her hand tenderly down the side of his face. 'I know I was worried about us taking things too quickly, but I have been lying here thinking while I was watching you sleep, and I agree with you: we're both old enough to know our own minds, so why should we wait to be together? I'll go to the register office first thing tomorrow morning as you asked me to since you have things to do at work, and I'll take the first available appointment for our marriage. Don't worry, I will take care of the birth certificate you gave me last night, it's safe in my handbag, and I'll return it to you as soon as I come back from the register office.'

Her eyes went to the clock on his bedside table then and she exclaimed, 'Oh, goodness, is that the time? I hate to leave you, darling, we have so much to talk about, so many plans to make for our future together, but I never expected to be out all night so my landlady will be worried about where I am . . . might even have the police out looking for me. I had better get back and put her mind at rest. I think she'll be sad when I tell her I'll be leaving her very shortly, but I know she'll be happy for me when she hears it's because I'm getting married and will be living with my new husband.'

He watched without a word as Marion slipped out of bed, unconcerned about displaying her nakedness before him while she went around the room, gathered up her clothes and put them on. When she was finished she came back to the bed, leaned down and planted a kiss on his cheek. 'I'll be back later, darling. We'll go out for dinner to celebrate our engagement.'

Harold was staring at her in horror. All these things that Marion had told him, he had no memory of whatsoever. The last thing he did recall was sitting in the chair, she on the sofa, listening to her talking . . . what about he couldn't recollect at this moment. He must have been blind drunk, lost complete control of what he was saying and doing, lost his mind even, to have professed undying love and proposed to a woman he had no romantic feelings for at all, then to have taken her to his bed and had rampant sex with her when he'd never had sex with a woman before because of his debilitating lack of self-confidence. But he'd never drunk himself into oblivion before. A bottle or two of beer or a couple of whiskies had always been his limit; any more and he'd be violently ill. Alcohol affected him that way, so how had he drunk himself into oblivion last night?

She was at the door now and sheer panic filled his being. He didn't want her to come back today, in truth he never wanted to see her again, but he needed to be on his own to think of a way he could get out of this. He finally found his voice and told her, 'No, no, I can't see you today as I have things to do.'

She looked totally disappointed. 'Oh! Oh, all right, darling. I have things to do as well. Tomorrow night then. You can cook me dinner this time. I'll see you at work tomorrow. Oh, and don't worry, I shall be as professional as ever while we're working together, but rest assured I shall be saving myself up to show you how much you mean to me as soon as we're alone!' She blew him a kiss and then disappeared through the door, leaving a waft of her perfume behind.

He sat up in bed, tightly clutching the sheet to his chest, heart painfully thudding, thoughts thrashing. But no matter how hard he tried he just could not find a way out of this situation. To tell Marion that it was purely an over-indulgence in alcohol that had made him say and do all those things he had last night would come as such a humiliation and shock to her, and from what she had told him of her feelings for him, break her heart even. His morals, all his beliefs in being truthful and honest to other human beings, rendered him incapable of treating Marion so callously. And also wasn't there a law over breach of promise, which meant should she choose to, as a woman scorned, Marion could sue him for retracting his proposal. That would be bound to be reported in the newspaper and everyone would see him then as a bounder and a cad for lying to her just to get her into bed. Therefore, he felt he had no choice but to honour his commitment to Marion, whether he liked the idea or not.

Full of misery, he covered his face with his hands and sobbed.

Marion meanwhile was walking jauntily down the street on her way back to the caravan site. She had arrived at Harold's house last night carrying heavy bags of food and a Mickey Finn she had obtained in a pub from a dirty-looking individual a couple of weeks ago. This morning she was leaving Harold's house with his mother's ring on her finger, in her handbag his birth certificate, so she could arrange their wedding, and an empty bottle that had contained the Mickey Finn which she had slipped into his glass of beer after their meal. A chuckle rose in her throat as she remembered her struggle to get Harold upstairs and into bed before he had completely passed out. Twice his legs had buckled beneath him and they had both nearly fallen backwards down the stairs. But eventually she had managed it, stripping him completely naked and taking a moment to admire his manhood, which she intended making good use of in future as she had learned her lesson and never again would she stray away from home and risk landing in the same situation she was in now.

She had then been free to search through the house for the items she needed to corroborate her fabricated story to him the next morning. But before she had stripped herself of her own clothes, scattering them around the bedroom to make it seem like he had been in a frenzy to get them off her and then doing likewise with his, she had emptied out all the bottles of beer she had brought with her, along with any of his she had found, as well as a full bottle of whisky she had taken from his sideboard, and left them for him to find after she had gone in the morning, so he would believe he had drunk all the contents.

Ida was waiting for Marion in her usual place on the bench seat and accosted her as soon as she walked through the door a while later. 'Good night?'

Marion smiled as she took off her jacket. 'Yes, very, thank you.' She felt it was now time to put her mother out of her misery, but with one stipulation. 'I'll tell you all about it as long as you promise me that you will do nothing whatsoever to jeopardise this. And I mean that. I will leave you in this caravan to rot and go off of my own if you mess this up for me. As it is, I've got the man I've been after in such a position he cannot get out of marrying me, but I haven't told him about you yet and if he suddenly found out I had a mother that I was responsible for, meaning that responsibility would then fall to him as my husband . . .' especially a dogmatic and interfering one like you that no man in their right mind would lumber himself with, she thought ' . . . he could find an excuse not to marry me and then all my hard work in landing him would be for nothing. I won't prevent you coming to see me get married but you will stay in the background until after the register is signed and I'm Mrs Rose. Then I will introduce you. Now do I have your promise?'

It would kill Ida not to meet the man who was to be their saviour and let him know that in future it would be she who was in charge of his household, and liked things done her way; not to demand she take over the organisation of the wedding; not to insist she had a tour of her new abode so she could plan where she was going to put the new furniture in her bedroom. But Marion's threat was enough of a deterrent to make her agree to her daughter's terms. Anyway she'd already seen where she would be living soon and had a rough idea what size her bedroom would be; had had enough of a look at the man who owned it to know that he wasn't the sort to battle against her for supremacy, so giving in to Marion's threat would cause Ida no lost sleep.

'Yes, you have my solemn promise. I won't step out of this caravan until it's to attend your wedding and move to my new address. Now how soon will that be, so I can start making plans for my new life?'

CHAPTER THIRTY-SIX

'What do you think of my idea of buying a lion, letting it run loose and terrifying the campers?'

Harold nodded distractedly. 'Yes, sounds good to me.'

'Right, that's enough,' Drina snapped, pulling him to a stop opposite the tennis courts, which were all full of campers playing games, mostly good-naturedly, though on one of the courts tempers were flaring over whether a ball was inside the line or out, which a Stripey was doing their best to calm before matters turned nasty. 'You haven't been listening to a word I've said since we starting the inspection round this morning. What's troubling you, Harold?'

He eyed her blankly for a moment. He hadn't realised that his depressed mood had been so transparent. He supposed he would have to tell Drina of his impending marriage to Marion; his boss deserved to be told in person by him, not hear it through the camp grapevine, which was bound to be spreading the news as Marion was at this moment at the register office in Skegness setting a date for the ceremony. As soon as she returned she wouldn't be able to keep such a big secret to herself and would need to tell anyone who would listen.

He took a deep breath before announcing: 'I'm getting married, Drina.'

She stared in surprise. 'Married? I had no idea you were courting someone.' Then her face broke into a broad smile and she warmly told him, 'Many congratulations, Harold. I'm so very pleased for you. Do I know the lucky lady? Does she work here at the camp, or did you meet her at some do or other?'

'Er . . . yes, you are acquainted with her. It's Marion.'

Drina frowned. 'Marion! I know no . . . oh, you mean Marion your temporary secretary?'

'Yes. I . . . er . . . realise we haven't known each other long but we don't see the point in a long engagement at our age, so Marion is at the register office now making the arrangements.'

Drina looked at him in surprise. She never would have put Harold and Marion together as a couple. Not that Marion didn't come across to her as a nice woman, and efficient at her job, but judging by the brief chats with her that Drina had had while passing through the general office, Marion had struck her as the type of woman who would like a man to possess a far more outgoing personality than Harold did, and one who enjoyed an active social life which Harold didn't. He would need to change the habits of a lifetime at an age when he was set in his ways in order to keep a woman like that happy. Still, opposites in personality did attract and it seemed in this instance that this was the case. Drina did however wonder why she sensed that Harold wasn't as happy about his forthcoming nuptials as she would have thought usual, but then he had always been a private sort of man, not one to show his emotions.

'This is so exciting, Harold. We haven't had a wedding at the camp since Rhonnie and Dan got married two years ago . . .' Her voice trailed off for a moment as a memory surfaced and she added distractedly, 'Such a joyous occasion. Those two were so much in love, with a wonderful future ahead of them both seemingly. We had no idea then that it would last not much more than a year.' She gave herself a mental shake and continued, 'I suspect you wouldn't want your reception in Groovy's like they did, so we'll find somewhere more suitable to hold it. The venue and the buffet will be my wedding present to you both. I shall speak to Marion and if she's amenable we'll work together on how she would like the decor of the room to be and her choice of food. After all, it will be her big day not mine.' Drina did hope as she spoke that one day a miracle would happen to free Artie from his bloodsucking wife so she could organise a big day of her own.

Harold detested being in the limelight so how he would cope with being in it for a whole wedding reception, and playing the happy groom when he would be feeling anything but, he had no idea. 'Oh, er . . . thank you so much for your offer but I . . . er . . . wouldn't want any fuss, really.'

Drina chuckled. 'Well, we'll see what Marion has to say about that, shall we? After all it's her special day, and it's up to her how much fuss she wants or doesn't want. The groom's role is to do as he's told.'

As Drina and Harold continued with the camp inspection tour, a jubilant Marion was sitting on the bus carrying her back to the camp. In three weeks' time, Friday 17 August at twenty past ten to be precise, her miserable life would be ended. Sooner even if the register office had a cancellation since they had promised her first refusal after being told that her beloved mother was terminally ill, and it would break her heart if she died before the wedding took place.

Marion felt no guilt whatsoever about deceiving Harold or about the life she was about to subject him to, being married to a woman who only cared for his money and not a jot in truth for him as a man, plus having a dominant, bullying mother-in-law to deal with, who would make his life a misery if he dared try and stop her from getting her own way over anything. All Marion cared about was that her own and her mother's future were now secured. The last few months had been extremely hard for her to live through and she felt she needed a holiday, and that's just what she was going to have. As soon as she was safely married to Harold she would get him to take her away, somewhere warm and expensive and definitely without her mother in tow.

* * *

Meanwhile over in the restaurant that dinnertime as they were eating together, along with several other Stripeys, Val asked Dixie if she had heard the news yet, having happened to overhear Patsy telling Trev.

'No, what news? I've been stuck down on the beach all day making sure none of the campers are drowning themselves and that the kids behave on the donkey rides, so I haven't heard anything.'

One of the other girls piped up, 'Oh, I've heard and it's really exciting . . .'

Val shot her a look to shut her up. She had started to tell Dixie this news and she wasn't going to allow anyone else to deprive her of the pleasure. In a roundabout way it would afford a morsel of retribution for the way Dixie had blackmailed her into giving up some of her more prominent places in the shows, in order to keep them for herself.

Dixie snapped, 'Is someone going to bloody well tell me what this exciting news is then?'

'Well,' Val began, 'I happened to be around when Patsy was telling Trev that she had managed to persuade a top London theatrical agent that it would to his advantage to travel up and see a sensational new dancer making his first performance in the Stripeys' show on Friday evening. From what she said I think she had a bit of trouble getting him to come, but finally he agreed. Wasn't it lovely of Patsy to take the trouble for Trev and help to get him noticed? Terry wouldn't have.'

Val was very gratified to see that Dixie had taken this news exactly as intended. She was so furious it was almost possible to see steam coming out of the top of her head. 'That fucking bitch,' she hissed. 'She's seen how talented I am yet she's never taken the trouble to get an agent up from London to see *me*.'

'Maybe that's because you believe you're far better than you actually are,' one of the other girls muttered under her breath.

Dixie flashed her eyes around the group she was sitting with. 'Who said that?'

They all knew but no one admitted it. One way or another, none of them felt they owed Dixie anything.

'You're all fucking jealous of me! Same as that bitch Patricia Mathers is. She can't sing or dance for toffee so she's jealous of anyone who can.'

'How do you come to that conclusion, after what she's done for Trev?' Val asked.

Dixie justified herself by hissing nastily, 'Because she's jealous of other *women* for having the talent she hasn't, you brainless idiot.'

'And how do you know Patsy can't sing or dance?' another girl piped up.

'Yeah, how? We've never seen her dance or heard her sing, so gave you a private performance, did she?' Val chipped in again.

'I know because she's never offered to show us how she wants us to dance certain steps when she says we're not getting it quite right or how to sing a song the way she feels it should be sung . . . she just explains to us. If she could dance or sing she'd not hesitate to show us how by doing it herself, would she, eh?'

Dixie had a point so they didn't challenge her explanation, just put their heads down and continued eating their dinner.

Dixie was too fuming to eat. Thanks to Patsy's decision to give everyone a chance in the spotlight, Dixie's own time in it now was severely depleted. The one time she had a chance to shine was when singing the main part of the song 'Somewhere Over the Rainbow' during a dance routine with several other girls, and as Patsy hadn't told the London agent to keep a special eye out for her then he wouldn't be aware of this in advance and might not take much notice of the rest of the show apart from Trevor's solo performance. But Dixie was damned if she was going to let a chance of being spotted by a London agent pass her by. There was no telling when one would come this way again.

All she had to do was get Trevor out of the picture while the agent was around so that when it came to be his turn for a solo performance he wouldn't be there to do it. Patsy would then have no choice but to get Dixie herself to fill the spot as none of the others would dare put themselves forward, knowing what she would do to them if they did.

Marion had a moment of fear not long after she had returned from the register office. Harold was nowhere to be seen and in her joy that her life was on the brink of drastic improvement she didn't pause to realise that he was making every excuse he could to stay out of the office. At the moment he was with the manager of the shops, looking over samples of new products and spinning out the meeting out for as long as he could. So when Drina arrived and asked for a private word in Harold's office, Marion panicked that somehow their employer had guessed that she was only using him as a meal ticket and had come to confront her about it. But then she reasoned with herself that Drina couldn't possibly have guessed anything of the sort as Marion had been so careful how she went about landing him that even Harold hadn't a clue.

When Drina offered to hold the reception at Jolly's and help her organise it by way of her gift to the happy couple, Marion was about to refuse, seeing the offer as an insult because so far as she was concerned her reception would be held in a top hotel, no expense spared, but then she thought better of it. She had no idea yet how much Harold was actually worth, but whatever it was, she had plans for much of it and relieving him of the cost of the wedding would mean that there was more left in the pot for her. She then purposely mistook Drina's offer, making out she believed it was to pay for all the wedding, and made it impossible for their employer to back out by thanking her so profusely for her generosity that eventually Drina was thanking her for being allowed to do it. If the register office did inform Marion they had a cancellation and could conduct the ceremony earlier, she wasn't going to refuse it for the sake of the reception. They could still have that, just not on the actual wedding day. She wouldn't rest completely easy until she had Harold's ring on her finger, and the sooner the better as far as she was concerned.

Drina left the general office in a state of confusion. She just could not work out how Marion could possibly have misinterpreted her offer to provide a venue and food for the reception for a proposal to fund the whole occasion. But Marion had been so overwhelmed with gratitude at her generosity that Drina hadn't the heart to put her straight. It seemed then that she had a wedding to arrange and not much time to do it in.

Before she returned to her cottage to jot down some ideas, she paid her daily visit to the demolition site. These visits were never happy ones for her because of her sentimental attachment to the place, but it was something she felt she had to face just to keep her eye on what was happening. The ruined outbuildings had now disappeared and the debris been removed, just the crumbling concrete foundations remaining. All the walls of the farmhouse were gone and the men were now in the process of shovelling the mountain of rubble that remained into the back of lorries to be taken away. Another few days and only the outlines of the outbuildings and a huge hole where the basement of the farmhouse had been, along with the uneven cobbles making up the yard, would be left to show that there was ever anything here.

Harold felt he owed it to his friend Eric to inform him personally of his forthcoming marriage. He waited until after the dinner shift had finished and the staff had gone for their break so that he could catch Eric on his own. Ginny might of course be with him, as part of their getting to know each other, but he felt the young girl wouldn't mind giving them a few minutes on their own.

There was no sign of her but Eric was busy in his office, checking off delivery notes against invoices to pass on to the accounts department. Harold had now seen Eric a couple of times since they had arrived back from Sheffield and he had definitely decided to take on the responsibility of being a father to his brother's illegitimate daughter, sooner than let her know that her true one had no interest in her. Eric had thrown himself into learning to be a dad, Ginny loving the fact she now had one, having grown up without, and the pair of them were growing closer as the days passed and they spent more time getting to know each other.

As soon as Eric saw his friend in the doorway of his office, he heaved his bulk out of his chair and said, 'Hello, mate, come for a coffee and a bit of cake? You're in luck as I made a Victoria sponge this afternoon, just in case you or Drina called in.' It was then that he noticed how drawn Harold looked. 'Doesn't seem as though you've been sleeping well, Harold. Anything up?'

He insisted, 'No, nothing at all. I've come to tell you something.' He then found that he couldn't. The same as when he'd informed Drina, speaking about his impending marriage only made it become more real to him and depressed him even further. 'Any chance of that cup of coffee then?' he said hastily.

Eric instantly knew that what Harold had come to tell him was something he wasn't comfortable with. 'Coming up. Just as you like it, strong, sweet and milky.'

Mugs of coffee made and standing before them on a metal preparation table, Harold still wasn't finding it easy to tell Eric his news so instead asked him, 'No Ginny today?'

'She's gone into Mablethorpe to buy whatever it is young girls do, with a few of the other female kitchen staff.'

'And how's it all going?'

'So far, so good. Do you know, Harold, having someone to care for is strange but as the days pass I'm sort of forgetting that's she's not actually mine. Drina's been in to meet her, of course. Unlike everyone else who believes Ginny is mine, I told Drina the truth and she has offered to be there for her should Ginny ever find she needs another woman to turn to for things dads can't deal with . . . you know what I mean.'

'I'm so pleased to hear that,' Harold told him in all sincerity. Eric said, 'And I shall be pleased to hear what you came to tell me, and voluntarily . . . before I have to throttle it out of you.'

Harold took a sup of his drink before he ventured, 'Well . . . er . . . I've come to tell you I'm getting married.'

Eric's reaction was the same as Drina's: one of utter astonishment. 'What? Married! Blimey, this is a bit of a surprise, to put it mildly. I didn't even know you were courting strong with someone, you dark horse. Oh, is it Eileen? That man she was seeing didn't work out for her and you two finally got it together?'

'No, no, it's not Eileen. As far as I know she's still seeing the man she told me about.'

'So who is she then and when is this wedding going to be?'

'I'm not sure of the actual date yet as I haven't seen Marion since she arrived back from the register office this morning . . .'

Eric erupted, 'Marion! Did you say, Marion? Your secretary . . . that Marion?'

Harold nodded. 'Yes.'

Eric stared blankly at him for several long moments while he digested this news. 'Well, congratulations, my dear friend. How did this all happen so suddenly?'

'Er . . . it just did. As you know, we've been out together a couple of times and she surprised me on Saturday night by coming round to cook me a meal by way of a thank you for . . . well, something I had done for her. And, well, the outcome is that we're getting married.'

Eric was looking mystified. 'But what I can't understand is how you got the courage to ask Marion to marry you when you couldn't even ask Eileen out on a date?'

'Oh, well . . . it seemed I had a little too much to drink.'

'Oh, the demon drink. Great for loosening tongues and helping us to do things we wouldn't normally. I have overindulged myself in the past, more times than I care to remember, but I've never gone so far as to ask a woman to marry me. Once to go to bed with me, though.'

'And did she?'

333

'No, just laughed and walked off. She's probably still laughing all these years later. I still feel embarrassed about it to this day.' Eric paused for a moment before he said, 'Look, Harold, I wouldn't be your friend if I didn't ask you this, but you're not marrying Marion on the rebound, are you? I know how cut up you were to learn that Eileen was serious about a fella she was seeing.'

'No, of course not.'

'No, I didn't think so as I know you're not a shallow man, Harold. So you'll be needing a best man then?' he said, eyeing his friend expectantly.

'Oh, I don't want any fuss, Eric.'

'I'm not offering to do a song and dance routine at the reception, Harold, but whether you don't want a fuss making or not, you'll still need a best man. Or for me to be one of your witnesses anyway.'

'Yes, of course I will. And I'd be delighted if you would be my best man. I'll tell you the date of the wedding as soon as I know it myself.'

Eric beamed, looking delighted. 'Then that's settled. I'd better get cracking on organising the stag do.'

'Oh, I don't think . . .'

'Eh, if you think I'm letting you get married without having a stag do, then you can think again. Just to please you, I promise I won't go over the top as I know you'd hate that. I'll get the darts lads together for a few pints, how's that suit you?'

Harold flashed him a wan smile. 'Yes, that sounds very acceptable.'

When Harold had left to return to his duties, Eric sat for a moment deep in thought. Harold was getting married to a very good-looking woman, one whom any man would be proud to have hanging on his arm. Inebriated at the time or not, for a man like Harold to have found the bravado to ask her to marry him, he must love her. So why was it then that Eric sensed his friend was not at all happy over his forthcoming nuptials?

334

CHAPTER THIRTY-SEVEN

Early that afternoon, Drina was sitting at the kitchen table in her cottage and had finished making a list of things she needed to do for the wedding when Artie arrived, carrying a large box. 'I've just about finished putting all the stuff away that I brought back with me from Devon. Where do you want me to put this?' he asked her.

'If I knew what it was, I'd be able to tell you.'

'It's that vase thing you bought in that pottery shop when we visited Truro for the day.'

'The one you hate, you mean?'

'Well, it is a bit hideous, you have to agree?' he said. putting the box on the table and pulling out a German-made Fat Lava vase glazed in green and orange, with animal heads as handles and relief panels with Aztec designs engraved on them. He held it up, pulling a face as he studied it.

'That style is all the fashion at the moment.'

'For people without taste,' he answered.

Drina leaned over and slapped him playfully on his arm. 'I've got good taste, I'll have you know. I'm with you, aren't I?' She looked for a moment at this well-padded, ordinary-looking man whom she loved more than life itself, and as much as she admired the vase, couldn't put him through coming face to face with it every time he went into the lounge. 'Oh, put it back in the box and store it in the cupboard under the stairs. I'll give it to the church the next time they have a bring and buy sale.'

He happily went off to do that and Drina returned to scan

her eyes down the list. Her eyes reached the item that read 'wedding outfit' and stayed there for several long moments. Shop-bought clothes were good enough but if a bride had the chance to have an expert seamstress hand-make her a gown that fitted her perfectly, she would be overjoyed. Drina knew just the expert seamstress to approach to make the outfit.

She got up, took a light summer cardigan from the back of her chair and slipped it on over her sleeveless belted shift dress. After hooking her handbag over her arm, she called to Artie, 'I'm going out for a bit, to do with wedding stuff. I shan't be long.'

He was inside the cupboard under the stairs, trying to move some of the clutter already in there around to make room for the box with the hideous vase in it, so his reply was muffled. 'Okay, love. Drive safely.'

Inside the camp laundry a short while later Lily Holmes, Eileen's assistant, was telling Drina, 'It's Eileen's half day this week, Mrs Jolly, so she's not here.'

'I'll catch her at her flat then.'

'She won't be there for a while as she told me she had shopping to do and a couple of other errands in town. Also she was going to call on Jill as she came home from the hospital yesterday and Eileen wanted to see how she was settling back in. She meant to visit Jill first before she did her shopping.'

'I was meaning to call on her myself and see how she was settling back in at home, so if I go now, that means I can kill two birds with one stone. Thank you, Lily.'

'My pleasure, Mrs Jolly. It's nice to have you back.'

'It's good to be back, Lily.'

Supporting her weight on two walking sticks, Jill beamed with pleasure on finding her caller was Drina. 'Oh, how lovely to see you.'

'I hope I'm not intruding but I wanted to come and see you, to find out how you're settling in back at home.'

Jill laughed. 'Not missing hospital food, that's for sure. My husband's glad to have me back home if for no other reason than that it was a long trek to come and see me every evening. Oh, I do apologise for keeping you standing on the doorstep. Please come in,' she said, using her sticks to allow her to stand aside while Drina entered.

As Jill made her slow, at times stumbling, progress down the short hallway of the 1930s semi and into the lounge, she said, 'Eileen arrived just moments before you. She's in the kitchen making tea. I haven't yet managed to do that by myself yet. In fact it's difficult doing anything really while I'm relying on these sticks to get me about.'

As they arrived in the lounge, Eileen was coming out of the kitchen carrying a tray of tea things. On seeing Drina she too beamed with delight and said, 'How lovely to see you. I'll just put this tray down and fetch another cup.'

Jill then regaled her two visitors with stories of the difficulties she was facing while the muscles in her legs strengthened. 'I just thank God we happen to have an outside toilet as it's no fun going up the stairs on my bum every time I want to go.'

The other two laughed at the vision she had conjured up.

It was a bit later when Drina finally got a chance to ask Eileen the question she wanted to. 'I'm glad you are here too as I wanted to ask how you'd feel about making a wedding outfit? A two-piece or dress and coat, something of that nature, for a register office wedding.'

Eileen's eyes lit up. 'Oh, for you, Drina? Yes, of course, I'd be honoured.'

'No, it's not for me. I don't suppose the news has quite got around yet, but Harold is getting married in three weeks' time. Not much notice, I know, to give you . . .' Her voice trailed off as it struck her that Eileen had grown very pale and was looking like the bottom had just fallen out of her world. 'Have I said something I shouldn't have, dear?' Drina asked her in concern.

Jill was sure she knew what had caused Eileen's distress, but as she wasn't supposed to know she didn't say anything. But she did feel very sorry for her.

This unexpected news had hit Eileen like a sledge hammer. Marion had told her a few weeks ago that Harold was serious about a woman he had been courting, but Eileen had never lost hope that it would fall foul at some stage and he might then look in her direction. But to be asked to make his bride her wedding attire . . . well, it was just unbearable to her and she wasn't sure if she could. But she would have to now, wouldn't she, as she had told Drina she'd be delighted to make the dress when she had thought it was for her employer? 'Er . . . no, no, nothing is wrong at all,' she insisted, forcing a smile on to her face when in truth all she wanted was to be on her own to nurse her pain. 'So who is the lucky lady?' she managed to asked.

'Marion.'

'Marion?' said Jill, taken aback. 'Marion who is doing my job while I'm off?'

'Yes. She and Harold obviously fell for each other as they got to know one another, working so close together.'

Eileen frowned. 'Marion told me that Harold was rather keen on a woman he'd been seeing but she never told me that the woman was herself. I wonder why she didn't want me to know?'

They both heard a gasp and spun round to look over at Jill, seated in the armchair opposite the sofa. She looked like she'd seen a ghost.

'What is it, Jill?' asked Drina.

Eileen had seen that look on Jill's face before and asked, 'Has another memory returned, is that it?'

Jill held up a hand and they realised she was requesting them to be quiet as she needed to think. They both sat in silence, watching her hawk-like until she finally said, 'That's why she pushed me down the stairs.'

Drina gasped with shock. 'Pushed you? Who pushed you?' she demanded.

'Marion,' Jill told her.

Drina looked bewildered. 'But what reason would she have for doing that? And how could she have pushed you when you were in the office alone? Anyway, if you suspected you were pushed and it wasn't an accident, why didn't you say so at the time so the police could make an investigation?'

'I only remembered I was pushed a couple of weeks ago, and it has to have been Marion who pushed me. Only if it was a matter of life or death would I leave the office unmanned, so Marion lied about that. She wasn't in the toilet when I fell, she was in the office. But as Eileen said when I had my first flash-back, you can't just go around accusing people of doing terrible things without any proof to back it up. It's my word against Marion's. I still have no proof as such, but thanks to something you both said just now, I'm sure I know why she did it.'

'Why?' asked Drina, intrigued.

'Yes, why, Jill?' asked Eileen. 'Because for the life of me, I can't think of a reason.'

They listened intently when she explained. 'I remember now where I was going when I fell. You see, I'm a bit of a romantic at heart and I just knew that you, Eileen, and Harold were in love with each other, but as the type of people you both are, neither of you could bring yourself to do anything about it. So I decided someone needed to give you both a nudge in the right direction.' She noticed that Eileen was looking uncomfortable and told her, 'I'm sorry, I don't mean to embarrass you, but I am right, aren't I? You do think a lot of Harold?'

Eileen cleared her throat before admitting, 'Yes, I do, very much so.'

Drina, who was sitting next to her on the sofa, laid a hand on hers in a compassionate gesture. 'I don't blame you, he's a lovely man and you're a lovely woman, Eileen. Jill's right, you and he are well suited to each other.'

Although it was no consolation to her, Eileen flashed a wan smile.

Jill went on talking. 'Just before my fall, I remember I was discussing you both with Marion, telling her that I didn't care that I might be seen as interfering but I couldn't stand it any more, seeing you mooning about over each other, so I had decided to do something about it. I had a plan and I was telling

339

Marion what it was. She was quite . . . well, horrible about Harold to me and made it clear she didn't find him attractive in any way whatsoever. I'm afraid I was rather angry with her for speaking about him so dismissively. I told her that he was a lovely man, kind and very thoughtful, the sort you could trust your life to. Okay, he might not look like a Hollywood film star, but not all women went for good looks above all. And Harold had a lot to offer a woman as he was a qualified accountant, had his own house and car, and I would have thought he'd a bob or two in the bank, never having married.'

Jill refrained from relating what Marion had said about Eileen as she didn't want to hurt her feelings any more given the battering they had just taken. 'Marion did apologise then for being so rude about Harold, and told me she didn't mean it, but I wonder now if that was just for my benefit. Anyway, my plan was to get Eileen and Harold together on their own for a few hours in a social setting, then hopefully during that time Harold would summon enough confidence to finally do what I knew he wanted to and ask her out. I'd bought two tickets for a show at the Pier Theatre in Skegness, seats next to each other, and I was going to slip Harold's on his desk with a note on it saying it was compliments of the theatre management, and the same with Eileen. That's where I was off to when Marion stopped me by pushing me down the stairs.

'I know from what she told me herself that Marion is divorced. Her husband left her for another woman and she ended up with nothing from her twenty years of marriage and can now only afford to live in lodgings. Can't be much fun that, can it? Living with an old dear by her rules. And she only has her own wage to manage on after being her own woman in her own home once. It would take her a long time to save up for the bond and first month's rent on her own place plus all the basics she'd need. It's my belief that after I told her about Harold being worth a bob or two, she saw him as good catch for herself, her meal ticket so to speak. That's why she needed me out of the way because if my plan had worked and I had managed to get

Harold and Eileen together then Harold would not have been available for Marion to get her claws into.

'I've got to be right as why else would Marion tell you, Eileen, that he was serious about a woman he was courting when that was a blatant lie? I'll tell you why: because she wanted you out of the picture too just in case you decided to approach Harold yourself before she'd managed to get him where she wanted him. In light of what she told you about him being serious about a woman, she probably told Harold *you* were seeing a man so he'd think his feelings for you were not returned and he was wasting his time hoping for a relationship with you. I know this must sound very far-fetched but it's the only plausible reason I can think of for why she would do such a dreadful thing to me.'

They were both staring at Jill agog as they listened to her story and when she had finished Drina said distractedly, 'Your conclusions do sound fanciful but also strangely plausible. They do perhaps explain why this marriage is happening so quickly. Because if she doesn't get that ring on her finger, and quick, Marion is afraid that Harold could find out somehow or even guess what she is up to, then her whole plan to get her hands on him would be in ruins.

'You hear of men sweeping women off their feet . . . well, it looks like Marion managed to sweep Harold off his. It can't be denied, she's a good-looking woman. They couldn't have been seeing each other until after your fall, Jill, which was what? Just over six weeks ago. The Harold I know wouldn't have reached the holding hands stage by then, let alone proposed marriage, so he must be totally besotted with her to be acting so out of character.'

Eileen looked sad that obviously she hadn't got what it took to have swept Harold off his feet, as if she had it would be she who was looking forward to marrying him in three weeks and not Marion. Regardless she asked Jill, 'Do you really think that Harold cared for me before he met Marion? I never dared hope that a man like him would look at me in that way.'

She answered with conviction, 'I do, yes. I have no doubt. He was like a puppy begging to be loved when you were around. I think he would be terribly embarrassed if he knew that, though.'

Eileen was looking deeply worried. 'Harold's not an unintelligent man and I can't bear the thought that it won't take him long to realise Marion has married him for his money and not because she loves him. Then he'd have to spend the rest of his life saddled with her. Don't you think it's only right that we warn him about Marion, and then leave it up to him whether he decides to go ahead with the wedding or not?'

Drina sighed. 'But we have no proof to back up our claims up about her, same as you don't, Jill, about your belief that she pushed you downstairs.'

The other two women murmured their agreement. Then they all sat in silence, each lost in their own thoughts.

Then suddenly Jill's eyes lit up and she excitedly exclaimed, 'Oh, but what if we could get Marion to admit she was only marrying Harold for his money? You know how it is: you're chatting away and before you realise it you let something out that you didn't mean to. I've done that many times. I was chatting away to my mother once, telling her about a weekend camping trip I'd been on. My parents were under the impression I was just with a girlfriend. This was before my husband and I were married, or engaged even. Before I knew it, I'd let slip the fact that while we were putting the tents up one of the poles snapped so we couldn't use it and all four of us had to share just the one tent. Well, my mother isn't daft and that was all she needed to hear to know that it wasn't just me and Jenny on that trip but our boyfriends too. The trouble I got in . . .

'And if we did manage to get Marion to let something slip about her motives for marrying Harold, we'd have proof to give him about just what sort of woman he's got himself involved with. One who was willing to cause me harm, even kill me, in order to get what she wants.'

Eileen said, 'That's a great idea, Jill. But surely Harold would have to be present to hear her incriminate herself or it would once again be our word again hers? It seems she's already got him in the palm of her hand so it will be easy enough for her to convince him that we're the liars, for whatever reason she can think of to tell him.'

Drina nodded her agreement.

They all lapsed into silence for a moment before Jill's eyes lit up. 'No, Harold wouldn't need to be present. Have you heard of those new portable recording machines that run on batteries?'

They both shook their heads.

'They're the latest thing. My husband has the use of one at work. I don't know whether they are actually for sale over here yet as it was the owner of the company my husband works for that brought a couple of them back from a trip over to America. One for his own use and one for his three senior managers to share between them. When he's really busy and no one else is needing it more urgently than him, my husband brings it home to record letters and all sorts of stuff on it, to take back with him to work for his secretary to deal with the next day. If I asked my husband, giving him a good reason why, I know he'd let us borrow the machine. He brings the recorder home at least twice a week for his own use so we shouldn't have long to wait. We'd have to work out how we're going to get close enough to Marion for it to pick up her voice. Then we'd have her confession recorded and could play it back to Harold, and there would be no more concrete evidence than that. And just maybe she might say something that would back up a claim to the police that she pushed me down the stairs and the police will charge her for her attack on me.'

'Oh, I like the sound of these new machines,' said Drina. 'I shall have to look into getting one for use in the general office.'

Eileen asked, 'So just how are we going to get Marion into conversation in the hope that she makes a slip?'

Jill replied, 'Well, the sort of woman to woman conversation we want to have with her is not the sort you have in an office. It needs to be somewhere private, a cosy chat over a cup of tea sort of thing, where there's no interruption to stop her from getting carried away, which hopefully she will.'

'That's just how it needs to be. Leave that to me,' Drina told them. 'I have every excuse to visit her at her lodgings over some urgent matter concerning the arrangements for the wedding that can't wait until the morning due to how little time I have to arrange it. During our conversation I could bring up the subject of how Harold and she got together, make out I'm really interested, and then hope that one thing leads to another and she tells me more than she means to, if not the first time of trying, then when I attempt it again. By the time I've finished with her she'll be looking on me as her best friend. Let's hope your husband, Jill, can manage to get hold of that recorder for us sooner rather than later. The wedding is in just under three weeks.

'Eileen, I don't expect you to make her wedding outfit in the circumstances. It's shop-bought for Marion. If we get our way, she'll never be wearing it anyway.' Drina paused for a moment and eyed them meaningfully. 'If this does fail, ladies, then I'm afraid . . .' She left the rest hanging in the air as she knew they understood very well they would have no other choice but to hope that Harold never came to regret his decision to take Marion as his wife, and Jill would just have to accept that her attacker would never be brought to justice for what she had done to her.

Two days later Jill had bad news for Drina and Eileen. Her husband had said that he wouldn't be able to get the recorder until the earliest a week on Monday evening, as one of the other senior managers had taken it with him on a business trip up to Scotland and wouldn't be returning to work until the Monday morning. That only gave them four evenings and three days to get a confession out of Marion before the wedding took place on the Friday morning. All they could do was hope that was long enough.

As the wedding date drew closer, Harold grew more and more depressed over just what the future would hold for him while married to a woman he didn't want to be with. He was getting plenty of practice as Marion insisted she come home with him every night after work and cook for him. Before she returned to her lodgings . . . despite the attack on her, she was still insisting she didn't want to put him out and was returning there each night alone . . . they would sit and talk for a while after the meal of their future together, or rather she would tell him how she was looking forward to keeping home for him, and how they'd sit together of an evening like she knew he liked to and listen to the radio together or else both quietly read. He had to admit she painted an appealing picture . . . if only the woman accompanying him on these quiet evenings in had been Eileen.

CHAPTER THIRTY-EIGHT

Patsy placed both her hands on Trevor's upper arms, fixed his eyes with hers and said to him, 'This is your chance, Trev, don't blow it by having an attack of nerves. You never know when you will get another opportunity like this.' She felt him shaking and wasn't sure if it was through excitement or fear.

'I know, I know, Patsy. I won't let you down, I promise.'

'It's not me you'd be letting down, it's yourself. You have a talent that the world deserves to see, not just the campers who come to our amateur shows. The agent's not arrived yet unless he's already somewhere in the audience and is going to introduce himself to us after the show ends, but he promised to be here tonight. So what do they say in show business . . . break a leg, or is it, don't break a leg? Anyway one of those. Now I have to go and check that everyone's ready for the opening number, so I'll see you in a bit.'

From her hiding place further back in the wings, Dixie waited a couple of minutes to make sure Patsy had left and no one else was around to witness what she was about to do, then taking several hurried breaths to make out she was panting from running, she dashed out from her hiding place and over to Trevor, who was in the middle of practising dance steps and was so engrossed in what he was doing he almost jumped out of his skin when he felt her tap on his shoulder.

Spinning to face her, he cried, 'God, Dixie, you nearly scared me to death.' After her attempt to bully him out of dancing in the show he was wary of Dixie trying another tactic to get her own way. He cautiously asked, 'What do you want?'

'Patsy has sent me to fetch you. She met up with the agent from London on her way to the dressing rooms and he told her that he can't stay long as he has to be back first thing tomorrow morning for an important meeting with one of his big clients. He had planned to stay overnight but can't now, has to drive back to London instead. He asked Patsy if there was somewhere private he could see you dance, then once he has he'll get straight off. The only place she knew that was suitable is one of the storage rooms off the corridor at the back. It's got some things stored in it but enough room for you to do your thing. Look, while I've got you here, I want to apologise for my behaviour the other day. I was only jealous of you. I am sorry, Trev. Anyway you coming with me or what?'

All he could think of now was his audition with the agent, hoping he wasn't going to let Patsy down. 'Yeah, yeah, 'course I am,' he said.

He followed after her as they hurried out of a door at the back of the stage. She led him to the last room just down from entrance to the foyer. The door leading into the room was slightly ajar.

With her hand on the door knob, Dixie opened the door a little wider, saying to him, 'In you go then. They're waiting for you. Come on.' She pushed the door open a little wider.

He made to step inside but then a strong gut feeling told him not to, though he wasn't sure why.

She saw him hesitate and urged him, 'What's up with you? I told you that the agent is pushed for time and you don't want to miss your chance with him through an attack of nerves, do you?'

He didn't so made to enter then again was stopped by a strong feeling that something wasn't right. Then it struck him. The room was in total darkness. If Patsy and the agent were inside waiting for him to join them, why wasn't the light on? He knew why. Dixie had lured him here to lock him in the room and get him out of the way so she could take his place.

After all Patsy's work in getting the agent here Trevor was damned if this selfish woman was going to deprive him of his chance to find out whether he did have a special talent or not. After suspecting Dixie wasn't a woman to give up easily, Trevor was cross with himself for not realising when she had first approached him tonight with her cock and bull story that she was up to no good. He lunged at Dixie, gave her an almighty shove into the room and pulled shut the door. Then fearing she would give chase and attack him in the corridor, still prohibiting him from showing the agent what he could do, he ran back to the wings as fast as his legs would carry him, surrounding himself for protection from her with the other Stripeys, who were now gathering in the wings for the show to start.

Inside the pitch-black room, a furious Dixie had scrambled up from where she had landed on the floor through Trevor's unexpected attack on her and felt her way over to the door. As she grabbed hold of the knob, meaning to turn it and let herself out, it came off in her hand, as she had intended it to do in Trevor's.

Realising her plan had backfired on her, through her own stupidity, she hysterically raged, 'NO, NO! Come back and let me out. COME BACK.' But deep down she knew the chances of being rescued at this time of the evening were remote.

Back behind the stage those involved in the opening number were lined up ready for the curtains to open in a couple of minutes' time. Patsy was with them, peeping past the side of the curtain to see if she could see someone who looked like a theatrical agent, while knowing it was highly unlikely she would spot him amongst the thousands of campers packed around the circular tables in the Paradise.

Conceding defeat, Patsy dropped the curtain and faced the line of entertainers chatting animatedly amongst themselves and was about to clap her hands to get their attention so she could tell them to go out there and bring the house down, when she realised someone was missing. 'Where's Dixie? she asked no one in particular.

They all responded the same way: they didn't know. She had got ready in the female dressing room and one of the girls did in particular remember seeing her as Dixie had taken her bottle of Miner's foundation without asking, but that was the last time anyone could recollect spotting her.

Patsy frowned. By now Dixie should be in the line-up for the opening act with the rest of them. She made a frantic search backstage and in the male and female dressing rooms, costume room and toilets too, but there was absolutely no sign of her. Hoping she had missed her during her search and Dixie with the others now waiting to make their stage entrance, Patsy dashed back to the wings. But Dixie was still not amongst them. She went over to speak to Darren, who was taking care of the sound system and lighting, to ask him if he'd seen Dixie. He said he hadn't. She approached Trev, who was practising his solo routine over the other side of the stage. He said he'd seen Dixie a short while ago but not since. By this time Patsy had no one else to ask, no places left to search.

During all her time of being in charge of the shows, Dixie had never been late for a stage entrance. Wherever she was it wasn't backstage as in her search Patsy had not left a cobwebbed corner in the darkest recess unvisited. So where on earth had her assistant disappeared to?

Patsy then realised that one missing from the troupe would not impact on the opening number in any way as it was a Tiller Girls routine, but all the other spots Dixie appeared in had been choreographed for a precise number; and of course there were all the sketches she played a role in. If Dixie didn't return and very shortly, who was Patsy going to replace her with?

She sensed a presence by her side and turned to see Vicky Smith, who was acting as the stage hand for this week's show. 'Are you ready for me to lift the curtain, Patsy?' Vicky saw her look of indecision and added, 'I'm sure she'll turn up. It's not like Dixie to miss a chance to be in the limelight.' Vicky wasn't being sarcastic but stating a fact.

Patsy sighed. 'That's why I'm bothered she's gone AWOL

without a word to anyone. I just hope there's nothing seriously wrong with her. I don't know what on earth I'm going to do, though. I can manage without her for the opening number but she's hardly off the stage after that and I've no one amongst the other on-duty Stripeys I can put in her place who knows all her dance routines and parts in the sketches.'

Vicky told her, 'Actually there is one person who does know them all.'

Patsy eyed her hopefully. 'You?'

She laughed and shook her head. 'No, you wouldn't catch me going on stage apart from to sweep up after the show's finished.'

'Who are you talking about then?'

'You. You choreographed the dances and wrote the sketches so no one knows them better than you do.'

Patsy nearly choked. 'Me! Oh, at one time I'd have been on that stage, giving it my all without a second thought, but the last time I performed in front of anyone was at my interview for a job on the entertainments team here eight years ago. Actually, no, that's not the last time I performed. I never got to at all because I was sent packing by the interviewer before I got chance to dance a step for him as it seemed I didn't possess the qualities they were looking for in a member of the team then. I haven't danced a step since . . . well, only to try out some steps of a new dance routine, and always when no one else is around.'

'Well, if you don't step into the breach, I wouldn't like to be in your shoes when you announce to the audience that the show is off.'

The sound of the audience growing restless reached their ears. Some of the campers were starting to slow clap, some banging their feet on the floor, and then some starting singing, '*Why are we waiting?*'

Patsy groaned. She really did not want to do this. It wasn't because she worried she would fluff her lines in the middle of a sketch or muddle her dance steps during a routine; as Vicky had reminded her, she knew every word and step better than the performers did. It was just that she was a good head bigger than the tallest of the female performers in the team at the moment and a good couple of sizes bigger built and knew she would stand out amongst them on stage like a sore thumb.

The noise from the other side of the curtain was growing louder. Pasty sighed. Regardless of the fact she was about to make the biggest fool of herself ever, for the sake of the show she had no choice but to substitute herself for Dixie before they had a riot on their hands. Dixie's costumes were not going to fit Patsy, though, and the only ones that might were old ones in a chest in the costume room that had previously been used by the male entertainers when a sketch required them to impersonate a woman. She would just have to hope that she could muckle something together that wouldn't look too out of place in each separate act she would be involved in. She had no doubt, though, that the audience were going to see her as no more than a comedy figure. But then, it was a light entertainment show, and better the audience laughed at her than not at all. She just prayed that Jamie was too busy in the bar to see her and be embarrassed.

She said to Vicky, 'You'd better crank the curtains open. Oh, before you go, Vicky, I never thanked you this morning for volunteering to be the stage hand tonight. Usually I have to tell someone as it's one of the least-liked jobs the Stripeys have to do. There's so much running about, they're exhausted at the end of it.'

'My pleasure,' she said before she went off.

Patsy watched her go. Vicky really was a nice young woman. It was such a pity she had no ambitions to improve her lot. Patsy then heard loud clapping and realised that the curtains were being opened and she had no time to be standing idling as she needed to go and sort out costumes for herself.

She did not fluff her lines in the sketches or make any wrong steps in the dance routines, but she was very aware that her build prevented her from being as light on her feet as the

351

others, so she felt like an elephant against them. Also it was embarrassing for her to be playing the parts of pretty young girls, as most of the sketches she was covering for Dixie called for, when she certainly was not. The audience roared with laughter when one sketch called for her to act demure, innocent and girlie, when in fact they were supposed to be heckling the villain who was trying to kidnap her before the hero of the sketch escaped from the bonds he was tied up in and managed to save her from a fate worse than death. But as the trouper she was, Patsy just gritted her teeth and got on with it. All during the show, though, she prayed that Dixie would return from wherever it was she had disappeared off to and relieve her from her purgatorial situation. But unfortunately for Patsy she didn't appear.

Trevor gave a flawless performance and was mesmerising to watch as he combined a mixture of tap, soft shoe shuffle, ballet and contemporary moves, and danced his way around the stage with the grace of an Giselle, his feet looking like they had a life of their own, to an upbeat version of the song 'It Don't Mean a Thing If You Ain't Got That Swing'. The audience's applause and shouts of appreciation, along with those of his fellow on-duty Stripeys in the ballroom, and backstage too, was deafening and, in Patsy's opinion, no more than he deserved. If the agent did not agree with her that Trevor had been born with an extraordinary talent, then he did not know real talent when he saw it.

There was one dance routine to go before all the performers took to the stage for the finale when they all sang 'We'll Meet Again', the audience encouraged to join in too. With all the noise those voices created, it was a wonder the roof of the Paradise building didn't lift off. Patsy was standing in place in the line-up in the wings, waiting for the act on-stage to finish and take their leave so as to make her entrance along with the others. The routine she was about to take part in was a rip-off from a scene in *The Wizard of Oz*. All of the girls involved were dressed alike in short gingham dresses with blonde wigs in pigtails curling out from the sides, huge blue bows at the ends, carrying stuffed toy dogs, only all Patsy could find in the chest to fit her was an old blue skirt and checked blouse so she knew she looked more like Dorothy's old aunt than a twelve year old. If that was not enough of a humiliation, she suddenly realised to her horror that at the end of the song, Dixie sang the last part solo. Patsy hadn't sung since being in the choir at school, apart from to herself sometimes, so really she had no idea what her voice sounded like when belting out a song with gusto. It seemed that she was about to find out.

As the song and dance routine progressed to the point of her solo performance, Patsy grew more and more nervous, colly-wobbles abounding in her stomach like a load of jumping beans. When it finally came time, she stood centre stage, took a deep breath, clung tightly on to the toy dog she was holding and opened her mouth. Throughout all the shows the audience was never quiet and the entertainers got used to the continual background hum. This was prevalent when Patsy began to sing but then suddenly she was conscious that it had stopped, as if she'd suddenly gone deaf, but then she could hear herself singing and the background music coming through the sound system. Mortification flooded through her. She had thought to herself that she didn't sound too bad but obviously the audience thought differently, that she was so appalling they'd all been struck speechless. But regardless she had to keep going to the end. To stop and run off the stage would not be setting her fellow entertainers a good example at all. Her solo lasted barely half a minute but to her it felt like hours. Finally she sang the last note and her ordeal was over. The rest of the girls then came to join her and form a line to take a bow. Simultaneously the silence in the ballroom was shattered by ear-splitting applause, clapping and cheering, on a par with that Trevor had received earlier.

Patsy was relieved to know that her solo hadn't marred the audience's appreciation of the rest of the routine.

As she arrived in the wings she was bemused to find herself

looked at in awe, receiving slaps on the back from some and exclamations of, 'Wow, Patsy! That's some voice you have.' She assumed they were being sarcastic and her response was, 'Okay, very funny. Let's get back on stage for the finale.'

Ten minutes later they were all trooping off again, the curtains being cranked shut by Vicky, but instead of everyone congregating in groups to congratulate each other that the show had gone well, they instead flocked around Patsy, some patting her on her back again, others simultaneously exclaiming, 'Wow, Patsy, you never told us you could . . .'

Before they could finish a loud voice boomed out, 'Miss Mathers? I'm looking for a Miss Mathers?'

Patsy spun around in the direction the voice was coming from and jumped up to see who it was over the heads of the crowd surrounding her. On the edge of this she saw a portly middle-aged man wearing a cashmere camel-coloured coat over a pinstripe suit and loud wide tie, his thinning black hair, which was obviously dyed, shining under the backstage lights due to the amount of Brylcreem it was plastered down with. He had a half-smoked Cuban cigar between fat fingers bedecked with large gold rings, several with huge precious stones in them. He was carrying an expensive briefcase. This must be the London agent.

Telling the staff to excuse her, she manoeuvred her way through the throng to meet him, greeting him enthusiastically with, 'Oh, you must be Mr Cohen.' She grasped his hand and shook it vigorously. 'Patsy Mathers. I am so pleased to meet you. Thank you very much for coming. What did you think of Trevor then? I told you it would be worth your while to make the trip up to see him. He is fantastic, isn't he? Just amazing. You do think so, don't you, Mr Cohen?'

He grinned at her, showing a gold tooth amongst a pristine set of white ones, obviously courtesy of a dentist. 'Calm down, young lady. Yes, I do. He's an exceptional young man. My trip up has been more than worthwhile. And call me Al.'

Just then Jamie arrived, having received permission from his boss to take five minutes to come and congratulate Patsy on her performance. He was behind her so she wasn't aware of him but he was close enough to hear what Al Cohen said to her next.

'And what about you, young lady? Your voice is incredible. Why didn't you mention that to me when you telephoned about Trevor? I nearly missed you singing as, having seen what I'd come for I was going to come around the back of the stage to meet him, do the business and be on my way. But thank goodness I decided to stay until the end. I've no doubt I can get you a recording contract tomorrow. I'm going to promote you as the next Dusty Springfield. I can get you gigs up and down the country no trouble, as the main attraction. Get you your own show on the television. The BBC and ITV will be fighting over each other to get you. How soon can you both be down in London? And where can we go for a bit of privacy to get the contracts signed? The sooner I get back to the city, the quicker I can make a start on the fabulous careers you've both got ahead of you.'

Jamie had heard enough. With a heavy heart he returned to the bar.

Patsy was reeling from this unexpected turn of events. 'Er . . . we could go to my office. If you would like to wait here, I'll go and find Trevor.'

Down the far end of the corridor, running down behind the back of the stage, Keith Williams had just slipped in through the door from the foyer. If Jamie could take a five-minute break to congratulate his girlfriend on the show she had just put on, then he could take five for a cigarette, although his break was unauthorised by their boss. The sound of banging and calls for help hit him as soon as he had shut the foyer door. He stood for a moment wondering where the sound was coming from, then realised it was the small storeroom just a little way further down. Someone must have got themself locked in there. He lit his cigarette first before he went to investigate. As soon as he turned the knob on the door and pushed it open, he was almost knocked down by Dixie in her rush to get out.

As she belted off down the corridor towards the back of the stage, he shouted after her, 'Oh, don't bother to say thanks then.'

Patsy was back from dealing with Al Cohen, who was now on his way to London, and was in the middle of thanking all the staff for their splendid effort when Dixie burst in on the scene and cried out, 'The show hasn't finished, has it? No, no, it can't have. Where's the agent? He needs to see me. He can't go until he's seen me.'

Patsy stepped out of the crowd to stand before her. 'He left a while ago, Dixie. Where have you been?'

She wailed, 'What! No, he can't have gone. He can't!' She started to stamp her foot in anger. 'It's not fair. It's not! This could have been my chance to make it to the big time. That agent would have snapped me up once he'd seen me dance and sing. I could have been the next Cilla Black. Now I'll have to wait for God knows how long for another to come up this way.' She glared darkly at Patsy and seemed to lose control of her temper then as she spat, 'This is all *your* fault.' She stabbed a finger into Patsy's chest and, like a woman possessed, shouted, 'You should have told the agent about me and not just Trevor. But you didn't, did you, because you're jealous of me. I'm everything you're not and you can't stand that, can you? You ugly fat lump! You know that job of yours should have been mine. I was Terry's second in command and it should have been given to me. I don't know how you did it but you stole it off me, I know you did. In exchange for sex, was it, with Harold Rose?' She sneered at Patsy as though she were a piece of dirt. 'How desperate you must both have been. For everything I did to make you look stupid and get my job back, you managed to end up smelling like roses. Well, I know now how you managed that, having Harold Rose in your pocket.' She stabbed Patsy hard in the chest again. 'Well, I'll get my job off you if it's the last thing I do, and get an agent up here to see me, you fucking fat bitch. I hope you rot in hell for what you've done to me!'

Patsy was so stunned to hear this tirade of pent-up anger and abuse coming from Dixie's mouth that she stood frozen in shock and would have taken the full force of Dixie's fist in her face next had not several Stripeys, seeing what Dixie was about to do, pounced on her, to hold her fast, preventing her from carrying out her attack on Patsy.

Dixie fought her jailers like a wildcat, kicking and flailing her body around, screaming at them to let her go, until they could no longer contain her. Freed from their restraint, Dixie then stared around her, saw how everyone was looking at her and realised what her loss of temper had made her divulge. She knew that her time at Jolly's was over and through no one's fault but her own. With fat tears spurting from her eyes, she crumpled to the floor and sobbed like a baby.

A while later, Patsy was sitting beside Jamie on top of the old wooden chest in the costume room. He had one arm protectively around her shoulders. She had her head resting on his chest and was crying. 'I can't believe it, Jamie. I had no idea whatsoever that Dixie believed I had stolen her job off her. I didn't, I promise you, Harold Rose offered it to me fair and square.'

'I'm sure he did, sweetheart. I know you well enough to realise you'd never backstab anyone to get yourself a job. Or anything else for that matter.'

She lifted her head enough to look at him and flash him a wan smile before she rested it back against his chest again. 'I thought I was going mad. I thought I was the one making all those mistakes, when all the time it was Dixie, hiding stuff and changing things in the hope that Harold would think I was incompetent and sack me so she could have the job of Head Stripey. I'm so shocked about what the other girls told me, and Trevor too: how she'd been threatening to use her position as my assistant to get them sacked if they didn't refuse prime spots in the dance routines and sketches, so that she had more chance of being spotted by an agent should one drop by. But actually going to the lengths of trying to lock Trev in that room so that she could take his solo spot for herself . . . well, I just can't take it in. I knew she was a bit full of herself but other than that I thought Dixie was a lovely girl and I really trusted her as my assistant.'

Jamie sighed. 'Well, she got her comeuppance tonight, didn't she? Where is she now?'

'She disappeared before I could speak to her.' Patsy sighed. 'I'd give her another chance if I could. But I can't keep her on as my assistant as I wouldn't be able to trust her any more. It's probably best for her she leaves and starts afresh somewhere else. I just hope she's learned her lesson: that it doesn't pay to treat people badly just to get your own way.'

'Let's not talk about her any longer as it makes my blood boil thinking what she was doing to you behind your back, to get your job. Good news about Trev, though.'

Patsy lifted her head, wiped away her tears with the back of one hand and smiled. 'Oh, just brilliant, isn't it? Al Cohen told him he's got a fabulous future ahead of him. I got so fed up with Trev thanking me for arranging an agent for him that I sent him back to his chalet to start packing. He's catching the first train to London tomorrow. I don't know how Harold Rose is going to take it, me losing him two members of staff in one night.'

'And is that when you will be leaving too, Patsy, with Trev tomorrow morning?' Jamie withdrew his arm from around her and took her hands, fixing her eyes with his. 'Look, I know about the agent wanting to sign you up too. I came to congratulate you on the show tonight and tell you how amazingly you sang . . . tick you off as well for not telling me you could sing like that . . . and I happened to overhear the agent telling you he wanted to make a star of you.' He heaved a deep sigh. 'I love you, Patsy, more than I thought it was possible to love anyone. I know you promised to marry me and we would run my dad's new pub together but this is a chance of a lifetime for you and I'm not going to stand in your way. I'm so pleased for you, really I am.' He smiled and said excitedly, although Patsy knew it was forced as the sadness in his eyes was unmistakable, 'Oh, just think, you're going to be staying in the best hotels, mixing with all those pop stars, worrying whether your latest record is number one still or dropped to number two that week.'

She said, 'I still can't believe that Al Cohen thinks my voice it good enough to get me a record contract, let alone my own television show.'

'Well, at least Dixie did one good thing tonight because if she hadn't tried to lock Trev up and take his place, you might never have got this opportunity.' Jamie then eyed her earnestly. 'But please, just remember, if you ever need me, I will always be there for you. You've only got to ring me.'

She studied his face for a moment before she replied. 'Should I ever need you, I won't be needing to telephone you, Jamie, I'll just give you a shout or come and find you wherever you are in the pub.' She chuckled to see the confused expression on his face. 'Al's offer is fantastic but compared to yours, there's no comparison.'

He was staring at her, shocked, not believing what he was hearing. 'You turned down the agent's offer?'

She nodded. 'I can't lie. Had I not met you, I would have jumped at it, but I have met you.'

'But don't you think you might come to regret turning this chance down, Patsy? It's not too late, you know, you could call him tomorrow . . .'

She put her fingers to his lips. 'I know I would deeply regret letting you go, Jamie. All the fame in the world, all the money, wouldn't make me happy if I didn't have you. You can't just switch love on and off. If I ever want to sing in the future, I can always entertain the pub punters to a song or two, can't I?'

He threw his arms around her and hugged her tight, then unashamedly started to cry. 'Oh, Patsy, I thought I'd lost you.'

She hugged him back and kissed his cheek before telling him, 'It'd take much more than an offer of stardom to get rid of me.'

They were sharing a passionate kiss when Jamie unexpectedly broke away and said, 'What was that?'

She'd been lost in the moment. All she'd heard was fireworks going off in her head. 'I never heard anything. Now where were we?' she said, pulling him to her. He was just about to respond when something distracted him. 'There it is again. It sounds like . . . someone knocking their foot hard against a beer keg, or one being tipped over, something like that. You didn't hear it?'

'No.'

'Well, I know I did. It seemed to be coming from below.' He looked down at the floor. 'What's under here?'

'I don't know. Groovy's? No, it will be the bar's stockroom, won't it? Oh, the noise you heard will be the security men doing a check around to make sure no one is still in the Paradise before they lock it up for the night. The noise you thought you heard will be them . . .' Patsy didn't carry on as something else more important had struck her. 'We'd better go before we get locked in, that's if we haven't . . .'

Her voice trailed off as she heard the muffled noise of breaking glass, a lot of it. 'Did you hear that?' she asked Jamie.

'I did. That was bottles breaking. Oh, my God, Patsy, I think the saboteur is at it again.'

Jamie jumped up off the chest. 'You go and find the security men and bring them to the cellar as quick as you can while I go and catch the beggar in the act.'

'Not bloody likely! He might be armed so I'm not letting you go in there and face danger on your own.' There were old sketch props piled in a corner and Patsy jumped over to pick up a battered cricket bat. 'Let him try anything on you and he'll get a taste of this,' she said, brandishing it menacingly in the air.

Jamie laughed. 'My heroine,' he told her. He grabbed up his own means of protection, which happened to be a rubber chicken and not what he'd meant to take: a tennis racket with some of its strings missing. He went to rectify his mistake and dropped the rubber chicken but then realised that Patsy had already left the props room. Out of panic for her safety, he shot out after her.

They entered the foyer together to find the place in darkness. It was obvious that the guards had already done their check in the Paradise, locked up and left. But not as thoroughly as they should have done as at least three people were still inside the building. Patsy and Jamie crept over to the door leading down into the cellar to find it ajar. Although the stairs leading down were in darkness, it was possible to see that some lights in the cavernous cellar below were on as there was a glow coming from there. The sound of breaking glass was much louder now.

Jamie made to head down the stairs but Patsy caught his arm, stopping him. 'Had we better not telephone the security office from the phone in my office as someone is always on duty in there if the other guards are out?' she whispered.

'But the attacker could escape meantime. Then he's free to strike again. We can't let this chance to stop him go, Patsy.'

She raised her bat in the air. 'Okay, let's go get him.'

They crept down the stairs, Jamie first, Patsy behind. At the bottom, Jamie stopped to poke his head around the opening into the cellar beyond, to assess the situation in the hope of making a plan of attack. Only one set of lights that ran down the centre of the cellar had been switched on so most of it was still in shadow. The sound of breaking bottles was still resounding. From where they were standing there was no sign of the saboteur, so Jamie stepped into the cellar, Patsy following. They both stared in shock at the sight that met them. Over by the stacks of full beer kegs several had been pushed over, their seals broken, the floor around swimming in beer. A couple of the kegs were still in the process of spilling their contents, making glugging sounds as the liquid poured out. From where they stood, they could see down the length of two of the corridors between four sets of the floor-to-ceiling wooden racks filled with bottles of drinks and bar paraphernalia. There was still no sign of the saboteur. From the direction in which the sound was, Jamie knew that the attacker must be somewhere in the corridor between the two racks just before the space where the kegs were stacked.

He turned and mimed to Patsy that he was going to try and surprise them by creeping down the opposite corridor and, in the hope that the saboteur was facing away from him, come up on him from behind and apprehend him before he had time to realise what was happening. If by chance the saboteur should escape before Jamie had chance to restrain him, then if Patsy hid herself at the end of the rack, Jamie would shout to warn her and she could wind the saboteur in his stomach with the bat, giving Jamie time to catch up with him and make sure he didn't get away.

It seemed a good plan to Patsy, so she nodded her understanding and while Jamie began to make his way down the corridor to the end of it, with her heart hammering madly, she got into place at the end of the rack, bat at the ready.

It seemed an age to Patsy as she stood there waiting for something to happen, with the breaking of bottles still resounding, then suddenly she jumped in shock as the sound of smashing glass abruptly stopped and a scream of fright rent the air. Panic struck that it was Jamie who had been attacked by the saboteur and with not a thought for her own safety, she let out an almighty cry and dashed around the side of the rack, bat raised high, heedless of the thick layer of broken glass she was running over. As she reached the two bodies struggling together against the racking she made to strike the smaller of the two over the head, recognising the taller of them to be Jamie, when he cried out, 'Stop, Patsy, I've got him. It's all right.'

The bat still raised, she saw that Jamie had the back of the attacker pulled against him, one strong arm clamped tight around their neck, the other clamping his arms together behind behind him and rendering them immobile. The attacker was dressed all in black with a balaclava pulled down snugly over their head.

Jamie told her, 'They won't escape me, Patsy, I promise. You can put the bat down now. Go up to your office and telephone security. I'll meet you in the foyer upstairs. Come on, you,' he said, giving the attacker a jerk by way of ordering them to get moving.

Bat now down by her side, Patsy made to do Jamie's bidding then stopped, intrigued to know just who the saboteur was. She stepped over and pulled the balaclava off the attacker's head. As the tumble of blonde hair that cascaded out of the balaclava came to rest to reveal the face of the culprit, Patsy gasped in utter shock and cried out: 'Vicky!'

CHAPTER THIRTY-NINE

With two beefy security guards standing watch over her, Vicky was sitting on the sofa in Harold's office, head bent low, studying her hands clasped in her lap. She hadn't said a word since her capture, despite being bombarded with questions by Jamie, Patsy and the two guards. Outside in the general office, Jamie was sitting in Marion's chair with Patsy perched on the edge of the desk beside him. Having summoned her from her bed, they were all waiting for Drina to arrive and take charge of the situation.

'Of all the people behind the attacks, I never would have thought of Vicky as the perpetrator,' Patsy said to Jamie for the umpteenth time since they had apprehended her.

For the umpteenth time he agreed with her. 'Nor would I, not in a million years.'

And for the umpteenth time Patsy said, 'Now I understand why an intelligent girl like her didn't want promotion. It wasn't worth her heaping all that responsibility on herself when she didn't plan staying any longer with us once she had achieved what she'd come here to do. What I still can't work out is just what had she to gain by doing what she did?'

And for the umpteenth time he responded, 'Me neither,' and gave a tired yawn. 'She'll have to come clean to Mrs Jolly when she gets here or the police will certainly get it out of her, so one way or another we'll find out eventually.'

'I suppose,' said Patsy, feeling impatient.

The door leading to the stairs opened and Drina arrived

followed by Artie. She looked strained, he deeply worried. Out of respect for their boss, both Jamie and Patsy stood up.

Drina smiled as she reached them. 'Thank you both for what you did tonight,' she said, then worriedly added, 'You could have been hurt. Thank goodness you weren't. I must find some way to reward you both.'

'There's no need, really,' Patsy insisted.

'No, there isn't, Mrs Jolly. We were just doing our jobs,' Jamie agreed.

'More than your jobs, much more,' Drina told them. 'Get off to bed now, we'll take over from here.'

Patsy and Jamie took their leave and Drina and Artie went into Harold's office.

Artie stood with the two guards, while Drina went and sat down beside Vicky, who was still sitting with her head bent, hands clasped in her lap. She looked at the girl for a moment before she asked: 'Are you going to tell me what this is all about?'

Vicky lifted her head and looked at her. 'If you'll allow me to make a telephone call, someone will come and tell you all you need to know.'

Her manner told Drina that she wasn't going to budge on the matter. Drina realised that if she wanted answers she had no choice but to agree to the girl's request. She nodded her head and gestured towards the telephone on Harold's desk. Vicky rose and went over to it, lifted the receiver and dialled a number. It seemed to be a while before she spoke into the receiver in low tones that no one else in the room could hear. Replacing the receiver, she returned to the sofa and sat back down again, telling Drina, 'He'll be here as quick as he can.'

He? Drina wondered just who this 'he' was but it was apparent that Vicky wasn't going to enlighten them. 'Well, it seems we have a bit of a wait on our hands so I'll make us some tea,' she said.

An hour passed by. The two guards were chatting together; Drina was sitting behind Harold's desk, looking through some brochures about other camps around the country that Harold had sent for so as to keep abreast of the competition; Artie had perched on a corner of the desk, drumming his fingers impatiently on it; Vicky was still sitting on the sofa with her head bent, studying her fingers, not having said another word since she had spoken to Drina after ending the telephone call. They all then gave a start as the door leading to the stairs in the general office was heard to open, followed by footsteps crossing the floor towards the office. They looked at the door, wondering who was about to enter.

Drina's eyebrows rose in astonishment when she saw Reg Brady walk in. She couldn't understand what a man who owned a demolition firm could possibly have to do with Vicky's attacks on the camp.

He immediately went over to the girl and placed his hand on her shoulder.

She looked up at Reg and smiled. 'Hello, Dad.'

'You all right, love?'

'Just annoyed I never got to finish what I started tonight. I know it would have worked this time if I hadn't been interrupted.'

Drina demanded of Reg, 'Vicky is your daughter, is she? And what does she mean, it would work this time? Whatever have I done to warrant you trying to bring my business to its knees?'

She was shocked by the look of pure hatred in his eyes when he said to her, 'We need to talk.'

'It seems we do,' she responded shortly.

She asked the guards to take Vicky outside into the general office. After assuring himself that Drina would call him if she needed his support in any way, Artie left too, shutting the door behind him.

With Drina seated behind her desk, Reg in the chair on the other side, she said to him, 'Just what is it I have done to you that is so bad in your eyes you would set out to ruin me?'

He shot back at her, 'It's not what you have done, but what your son has. Just to prove I have the right man, this is your son, isn't it?' he said, taking a photograph out of his pocket, slapping it down on the desk then pushing it across to Drina.

She picked it up and looked at it hard. It was a picture of the Waltzers ride at the funfair in Skegness. Frozen in time, people in the cars were waving and screaming as they whizzed around. On one side of the wide wooden steps leading up to the ride, a group of spectators stood waving and laughing at friends in the cars flashing past. In the middle a couple were entwined in each other's arms, kissing. On the other side, leaning against the rails, was a man smoking a cigarette, a young woman by his side. It was obvious the man and woman were conversing together. The woman was unknown to Drina but the man she certainly did recognise. It was Michael, her son. 'Yes, it is,' she told Reg.

'And that woman he's talking to is my daughter. He killed her.'

Reg's unexpected announcement shocked Drina rigid. 'Now look here, Mr Brady, my son certainly had his faults . . .'

Reg ferociously cut in, making Drina jump when he slammed one fist down hard on the desk. 'He might not have physically killed her but he was the one responsible for her death. Three years ago he took advantage of my daughter when she visited the funfair with a group of her friends. Sally went on some of the rides but refused to go on the Waltzers as it frightened her, so while some of her friends went on she watched from the sidelines. Your son was helping to run that ride at the time and went over to talk to Sally. He told her his name was Ray . . . since that was a lie it proves to me that right from the off his intentions were bad. Somehow he persuaded her to meet him when the fair closed that night. He took her down to the dunes, plied her with drink, then took advantage of her. Then after he had got what he wanted, abandoned her to make her own way home, but not before he'd stolen the money from her purse.

'About three months later Sally discovered she was pregnant. The poor girl was beside herself. If only she had come to us . . . But she was terrified of the shame this would bring on her family and felt she had no alternative but to have an abortion. The hag who did it used a dirty instrument, which caused septicaemia, and

367

Sally died in agony four days later. Her senseless death has destroyed us as a family, none of us will ever be the same again. I vowed on Sally's deathbed that I would make the man responsible pay for what he'd done. I visited the owner of the ride down at the fair, but by then Ray had moved on. The owner told me most of the time casual workers gave a false name anyway. I thought that was it, that I'd never get a chance to confront this man and somehow make him pay for what he'd done. We tried to get on with our lives without our beloved Sally. But you can't. It's always there with you, nagging away at the back of your mind, that the person responsible for your daughter's death is still living and breathing, with their life in front of them, when your child isn't.

'Then like a miracle last April one of Sally's friends was looking through some old photos and came across one from that night she hadn't looked at closely before. She knew the man in the photo talking to Sally was the one she'd met up with later, and gave the photo to Vicky just in case it might help us. Vicky didn't tell me about it right then as she didn't want to build my hopes up. She decided to see if anyone still working down at the fair recognised the man and knew his real name. She almost immediately found one who did. It seemed your son was well known. From the conversation Vicky had with his acquaintance it became clear that your son is an unsavoury character who has offended a great many people. My guess is that he's in hiding from some very powerful people and keeping his head low.

'Once again I was denied a chance to confront him, but now that I knew the family he belonged to it didn't seem right to me that he should have such a rosy future, one day inheriting a lucrative business, when he had denied my daughter hers. It was my hope that by systematically sabotaging certain areas in the camp, the impact on the campers would see them turn away in droves. And no campers, no business.

'Vicky getting herself a job in your Stripeys' team gave her liberty to be in most places on the site, not only to suss out the best areas to carry out our acts of sabotage but to implement them too. Each idea we came up with had the potential to ruin you, but your staff kept thwarting our plans or coming up with a solution to overcome the damage we had caused. It was so frustrating for us, to have all our hard work and planning proving to be to be a waste of time. So it became apparent that if we wanted to succeed in our aim, we needed to up our game.

'Tonight, not only was Vicky going to destroy all your drinks stocks, she was also going to set another fire, this time in the ballroom. There was no way you could carry on operating without any bar stocks, and even if you did get new supplies you'd have nowhere to serve the drink or entertain your thousands of campers. You would have had no option this time but to shut down the camp indefinitely, and with the cost of refunds, and the repairs, and with no money coming in mean-time, your son would be left with no inheritance to claim and we'd have justice for Sally.'

Reg paused to heave a sigh. 'I suppose now I won't be paid for the work I've done on demolishing the farmhouse, so I've lost a daughter and am grossly out of pocket as well. I thought that was clever of me at the time, getting a friend of mine who works for the council to make out they had had a serious complaint over the farm's state and then get me the job of demolishing it. He thought a lot of Sally and was only too happy to help. I strung the job out as much as I could, so the costs mounted. And of course it gave me an excuse to be on the camp should Vicky need me.'

Drina stared back at him for several long moments, trying to digest all she'd been told along with the overwhelming emotional pain she was suffering on learning of yet more terrible deeds her son had committed through his insatiable greed. Despite what this man and his daughter had done to her, Drina's heart went out to him in his loss, and although she was in no way responsible for Michael's despicable behaviour she nevertheless felt a margin of guilt as she was his mother.

She took a deep breath and told Reg, 'I can't express to you

369

how sorry I am for my son's behaviour, but you need to know that Michael is dead.'

Reg stared wildly at her. 'Dead!'

'He died last year, falling off the roof of the administration building while in the process of try to steal this business away from me. He'd found out, you see, that on his father's death he wasn't going to inherit a penny as he'd been cut out of Joe's will. In fact, my husband died after suffering a heart attack while catching Michael in the process of robbing the safe, which he still did then absconded with the proceeds without even calling for help for his father, leaving Joe to die. My son's attitude to life was that it owed him and he was prepared to sink to any depth of depravity to get his hands on every penny he felt he was due.'

Reg was still staring at her. He had been dealt a terrible blow by Michael Jolly but it seemed the young man's long-suffering mother had endured a lifetime of his despicable behaviour. Reg gave a deep groan of despair and uttered, 'So this has all been for nothing. I'm sorry to say this, but knowing the man who was responsible for my daughter's death is not around any longer is some small consolation.' He paused for a moment before saying: 'I owe you an apology. It wasn't right of me to take my anger out on you for what your son did. My only excuse is that at the time I craved any form of vengeance. Well, I suppose now you know what you do, you'll be wanting to call the police and have us arrested?'

Drina gave a deep sigh and momentarily closed her eyes, her thoughts whirling. By rights she should have Reg and Vicky Brady charged for all the damage they had caused, but she couldn't bring herself to as she felt they had both suffered enough at the hands of Michael. 'Please take your daughter home, Mr Brady. You'll understand that her employment here is terminated. I would, though, appreciate your finishing the demolition job and trust you will only charge me the price it should have been and not an inflated one.'

He was looking astounded that this woman wasn't going to

take any action against him or Vicky for the trouble they had caused her. It seemed inconceivable to him that a generous-hearted person like Drina could have given birth to such a callous individual as her son had been. Overwhelming guilt rushed through Reg at the realisation that while he'd thought he'd been punishing her son, in fact it had been Drina he was harming and she hadn't deserved it. He was so grateful now that Vicky had been caught and their bid for vengeance had been halted before it was too late and he'd ruined an innocent woman. As he rose from his chair, in a voice choked with emotion, he uttered, 'I'm sorry.'

Moments after Reg had left the office, Artie came charging in. 'Reg Brady has just left, taking his daughter with him, telling me that you aren't going to be bringing any charges. Are you thinking straight, dear? They were trying to ruin you.'

Drina wanted to tell him what had transpired but before she could get a word out the tears came, a great flood of them that washed down her face, and she jumped up from her chair, threw her arms around him and sobbed uncontrollably into his shoulder.

CHAPTER FORTY

Outwardly, Drina appeared her normal self after discovering the truth behind all the sabotage attacks on the camp, but inwardly a great sadness was filling her that even in death her son's selfish deeds were still affecting the living. She might not have liked her son as a person, but as his mother she'd loved Michael and her arms still longed to hold him, have him to care for, and she knew until her dying day that would never change. As terrible as she felt for thinking it, she was glad that she had Harold's problem now to give her something to focus on and help her return memories of Michael to the back of her mind, along with all the pain and hurt their resurfacing had brought with them.

Tuesday evening found her sitting in her car a little further down the road from Harold's house as she knew that since their engagement Marion had been travelling home with him after work each evening and eating a meal with him there before she returned to her own home. Once she saw Marion leave Harold's house Drina meant to follow her to her lodgings on foot, and after a suitable amount of time had passed surprise her with a visit on the pretext of having urgent wedding business to discuss with her. She could have telephoned the employment agency to ask for her address, which they would have on file, but she didn't want to risk the possibility of Marion being informed of her enquiry and then the plan to pay her a surprise visit would be scuppered.

Aware of her plan for tonight, both Jill and Eileen were at

Jill's house anxiously waiting for Drina to join them later, hopefully with the good news that she had managed to record on tape in Marion's own words enough for them to be able to confront her with the fact that they knew she was only marrying Harold for his money, and maybe even something to take to the police to have her charged for pushing Jill downstairs.

Finally at just after eight o'clock Drina saw Marion leaving Harold's house. Drina got out of her car and locked it up. Carrying the capacious handbag with the tape recorder secreted inside it, a hole cut in the side for the microphone head to poke through, a scarf draped over it to conceal it, she followed after Marion. Her target took her down several streets towards the centre of town then and on through it into an area full of slightly rundown Victorian palisade houses offering bed and breakfast, the odd cheap hotel slotted in between. Knowing Marion lived in lodgings, Drina assumed that this was where she must live. But it seemed she didn't as she kept on walking, making her way down street after street, the area growing more and more rundown.

They arrived at a crossroads, the houses in all directions dilapidated back-to-back terraces, where the occupants showed no sign of taking any pride in their properties. The front steps were dirty, paint peeling off doors, filthy curtains at grimy windows, weeds growing out of guttering, kerbs in the road and corners beside doorsteps filled with accumulated rubbish. The sort of place that only desperate people lived in, not the sort of street she'd imagined Marion would inhabit at all. Drina knew that the fee the agency was charging them weekly for secretarial services was considerable. Surely Marion's portion of it would have stretched to her living somewhere a little better.

There was a shop on a corner and Drina had to hide herself in a doorway as Marion entered it. A gang of dirty-looking youths were loitering outside, drinking from cans of Tennent's lager and smoking cigarettes. Automatically, Drina clutched her bag to her as they looked the sort who wouldn't think twice about relieving her of it. To her relief, though, the youths took their leave, heading off down the street in the opposite direction. Ten minutes or so later Marion came back out carrying a bag of shopping then continued on down the same street. Drina followed her.

Halfway down the street, Drina was able to see a scrapyard at the end of it. Marion kept going until she arrived at the yard, then started to negotiate her way down a rutted mud path to the side of it. Wondering where on earth she was heading, Drina discreetly followed her. At the end of the scrapyard was a large area of wasteland filled with rusting dilapidated-looking caravans. In surprise Drina saw Marion make her way over to the most dilapidated one of all, step up on to two breeze blocks before the door, open it and disappear inside.

Drina couldn't imagine how a woman like Marion could be acquainted with living in such dire conditions. Drina did not look down on people who were reduced in their circumstances, nor did she judge them. There were all manner of reasons that could have brought them to this place, and bad luck could strike anyone at any time. Besides, she herself had been born in a wagon at the side of the road in Romania and would still be living the life of a traveller had her father not been the kind of man who wanted better for his family and did something about it. After half an hour Marion still hadn't come out of the caravan to return to her lodgings, so Drina decided to give up for the night.

Jill and Eileen were disappointed by her news that she hadn't managed to execute any of their plan tonight, but also intrigued, just like Drina herself was, as to who Marion had been visiting in a decaying caravan on waste ground in an area of the town where only the most desperate people lived. None of them had a plausible answer to that question, though.

'So I'll just have to be waiting for her outside Harold's house tomorrow and hope when she leaves this time she goes straight to her lodgings and not to the caravan site again.'

They both vehemently agreed as time to save Harold from a miserable future was running out.

Well aware what his wife was up to, as there were no secrets between them, Artie was keen to hear how Drina had got on that evening. He was disappointed for her that she had no news to tell him other than Marion's seeming acquaintance with someone who lived a very poor existence. Artie always wanted to see the good in people and said that Marion could have met the person during the course of her everyday life, taken pity on them and was visiting them with some food . . . she had stopped off at a shop on her way there after all. Drina was not convinced. She might not know Marion that well but instinct told her the woman was not a benevolent sort of person. Artie was as worried as they were that time was running out to save Harold from a fate he was himself very familiar with: a woman marrying him for what he could give her. He liked Harold, had a lot of respect for the man, and didn't enjoy the thought that another man had been swept off his feet by an attractive woman and been so blinded by her charms that he didn't see her true intentions. Artie didn't care for the thought of another man suffering the disillusion he had.

As she lay in bed that night, trying to get to sleep, it did strike Drina that the person Marion had been visiting might just know a little more than they did about her. It could be worth paying them a visit, to try and learn a snippet or two towards their ultimate aim. Marion would be at work tomorrow so there was no risk of Drina bumping into her at the caravan. Having formulated her plan of attack, sleep then overtook Drina.

Ten thirty the next morning found Drina back at the caravan site, stepping over the rutted ground towards the vehicle she had seen Marion go into the evening before. She had a vague plan in her head for how to get herself inside and into conversation with the occupant, but that depended on them believing her tale of woe and taking pity on her plight enough to ask her in.

She knew someone was inside as she could hear them moving around. Whoever it was seemed heavy-footed as their thudding steps were making the caravan shake on its dubious-looking mooring. She knocked in a feeble manner on the caravan door, then holding her breath, stood back to wait for her summons to be answered.

The door open outwards, which Drina had forgotten that caravan doors did, and the edge of it just missed hitting her. A huge woman filled the doorway. She eyed her visitor with suspicion. 'What do you want?' she asked in a brusque, verging on rude, manner. Then before Drina could utter a word she snapped, 'If you've come to cadge anything you've wasted your time as what's ours stays that way. And, if you don't mind, I'd prefer you didn't call again as I'm particular who I entertain, and let me tell you, it's not the sort who live in this hellhole!'

But you do, thought Drina. This woman was not pleasant at all and Drina wondered what Marion was doing, befriending someone like her. Drina couldn't see anyone taking pity on someone with such an aggressive nature.

She smiled sweetly at Ida and said, 'I'm not here to borrow anything. I'm so sorry to bother you but I couldn't find anyone else at home on the site. You see . . .' Then she clasped her free hand to her head and swayed as though she was going to faint. She said in a feeble voice, 'Oh, dear, you don't think I could have a drink of water, do you, please? I don't feel too good.'

Ida stood weighing her up for a moment before obviously deciding that she looked respectable enough and telling her, 'You'd better come in and sit down.'

Drina said a silent thank you as she made it look like it was a great effort for her to climb up on to the breeze blocks then on inside.

Ida indicated she should take a seat on the threadbare bench sofa at the front of the caravan, while she heaved up a plastic water container and poured a measure into a cup.

The caravan inside was shabby to say the least, but it was clean and tidy. While her hostess's back was turned Drina quickly delved into her handbag to switch on the recorder, praying the huge woman did not hear the loud click it made, and then draped her scarf over the top of it to help muffle the whirring sound made by the spinning tape in the cassette inside. She shut the bag and positioned it by the side of her so that the head of the microphone faced where she hoped the woman would sit down near her. Drina just prayed that as the handbag was black and so was the microphone head the woman wouldn't notice it. She had just managed to put her hand back to her head in an effort still to look faint when Ida came over and handed her the cup of water, then lowered her heavy body down on the sofa a little away from Drina, looking at her hard.

'Feeling any better?' she asked.

'A little, thank you. I don't know what came over me. My name is Matilda Gillows and I'm very pleased to meet you. Have you lived here long?'

Ida's face filled with indignation. 'Oh, I don't live here! Well, I do, but it's only a temporary arrangement. Between houses at the moment. In fact . . . What is that noise?'

Drina's heart started thundering inside her chest. As casually as she could she said, 'Noise?'

'Yes, that sort of whirring sound.' Ida started looking around. 'It's coming from . . .'

Drina cut in, 'I can't hear a thing and my hearing is very good.'

'Must need my ears cleaning out then. So why are you here at the site? You were about to tell me when you felt faint.'

'Oh, well, you see, it's very embarrassing for me but I've fallen on hard times. My husband died recently and left me rather badly off. In fact, I'm about to be evicted from my home. I can't afford much so I'm here to enquire if any of the caravans are for rent.'

Ida puffed out her chest importantly. 'Well, this might be your lucky day as I'll be moving out of here on Saturday after the wedding. The man who owns the caravan lives in the big one further over the site. You can't mistake it, it's got a pile of empty beer bottles and cans at the side of it. I gave notice last week so unless he'd already got someone else lined up for it, you can have this one.'

Drina's heart leaped. Harold and Marion's wedding was Saturday. Was there any connection here or was this just a coincidence? 'I'll keep my fingers crossed that he hasn't. I'll go and see him as soon as I've finished my water,' she said, taking a little sip out of the cup. She wanted to get back on to the subject of the wedding, to see if there was any connection or not. 'Oh, I love weddings. What will you be wearing?'

Ida didn't answer her for a moment. Marion had warned her what would happen if she blabbed to anyone about her plan to lift them out of a life of poverty and ran the risk of ruining it. But then this woman was a stranger, what harm would it do to brag a little about her daughter's success?

She puffed out her chest and told Drina, 'I've a nice blue costume and a hat I wore for a do I went to a couple of years ago. The wedding is only in a register office but I still want to look the part of the mother of the bride.'

Drina nearly choked. Mother! This woman was Marion's mother? Did Harold know that Marion had one, a woman who it seemed was moving in with him along with his new bride after the wedding? 'Oh, so it's your daughter that's getting married?' she said.

'Yes, it's her second marriage.' Ida screwed up her mouth in disapproval. 'This wedding is hardly a patch on her first. That was in a church with a reception in a top hotel, sit-down meal and champagne for the toasts, dancing afterwards to a proper band, then a hot food buffet later in the evening. The reception for this one is being held in a holiday camp, can you believe? I can't imagine what it's going to be like. Cheap and nasty, I expect, like the food I've heard those camps serve up for the sort who holiday in those awful places. The man she is marrying works there, so I expect he feels obliged. He runs the place. He's well off so the life we'll be living after she's married him, although not as good as the one we led during her first marriage, will be a cut above this one, I can tell you. Like you, you see, we fell on hard times. Nothing to do with me, let me tell you. It was all Marion's fault we landed up as we did. She had everything she could ever have wanted with her first husband. Beautiful home, all mod cons, good allowance he gave her each month to spend on whatever she liked. They even had a tennis court in the garden. She gave all that up for a fling with a married man.'

Drina blurted out without thinking, 'Oh, it was Marion who had the affair not her husband then?' She then realised what she had said and hurriedly added, 'Well, what I mean is, it's usually the husband who strays, isn't it?'

'Yes, but unfortunately not in this case. When it came to light after Marion was caught in the office with this man, over the desk in the middle of . . . Well, Lionel was furious, couldn't forgive her, so she ended up being thrown out with only what was in her purse. Silly, stupid girl. I certainly let her know how I felt about her behaviour! I lived with them, moved in after my husband died and ran their home. I insisted on it. Mothers always know best, don't they? Children these days don't even know how to make a bed properly with neat hospital corners, they're always in too much of a rush to be bothered. I can't live like that so when I move into my new son-in-law's house I shall be taking over the running of that too. Anyway, when Lionel threw Marion out, he turned me out too. That's gratitude for you after all the years I looked after him and his home. And then we ended up here.'

'So how lucky for you both that Marion has met another man and you don't have to stay much longer.'

Ida snorted. 'Luck has nothing to do with it . . .'

From then on she needed no encouragement whatsoever to spill every single little detail. Ida herself had advised her daughter that the only way she could see a way out of this dreadful situation for them both was for Marion to find a well set-up man to provide for them. Her daughter had listened and so had come to be getting married on Saturday Drina felt sick as Ida boasted and gloated over her daughter's cunning and conniving to get what she wanted, not giving a thought to her prey. Drina now just wanted to get away from this odious woman before she risked telling her just what she thought of her and her despicable daughter. And that she could kiss goodbye to the new future she thought she would be starting as soon as the wedding was over this coming Saturday afternoon.

As soon as Ida had finished, Drina gathered her handbag to her and stood up, saying, 'Well, thank you so much for allowing me to rest a while. I feel so much better now. I'd best go and see the owner of the site, to ask him if I can have this caravan when you leave, before someone else beats me to it.'

Before she risked Ida encouraging her stay any longer, she hurried over to the door and let herself out, breathing fresh air deep into her lungs by way of trying to rid herself of the nasty taste in her mouth. One thing she did know was that Marion wasn't going to be very happy with her mother's need to brag of her daughter's prowess, and her failings too. Maybe this would teach Ida to check just who she was spilling all her secrets to in future before she opened her mouth.

Drina hadn't wanted to take the chance of leaving her car in the area Marion lived in so had parked it in a street about a quarter of a mile away. On her way to it, still reeling from what Ida had told her, she entered the first telephone box she came to and called Jill, telling her she was on her way over and asking her to put a telephone call through to Eileen at the camp, tell her to drop whatever she was doing on the boss's orders, order a taxi on the company and get herself to Jill's as soon as possible. What she had managed to get on tape was going to shock them both rigid.

A good while later the tape came to a stop and the on button clicked off. Jill and Eileen sat in stunned silence for a few moments before Jill declared, 'My God! Oh, my God. She drugged Harold . . . drugged him to fool him into thinking he'd slept with her and also proposed marriage, stealing his mother's engagement ring to prove to him he had. I can't take this in. How could someone be so wicked? But I *knew* she'd pushed me down the stairs, I just knew it had been her.'

Eileen was looking pale and worried. 'We need to get Harold

free from this . . . this . . . monster as soon as possible. It pains me so much to think how this is going to hurt him, finding out that the woman he thought loved him, and whom he loved, was just using him for what he could give her.'

'Yes, we must intervene,' Drina vehemently agreed. 'I'll go and fetch Marion now, bring her here. We'll play the tape to her and then get the police to arrest her for her attack on you. To get her to come with me, I'll tell her I have a surprise for her, something to do with the wedding. Then after that we'll go and see Harold.' Drina sighed. 'I wish there was some way we could spare him from finding out her true colours, but at least we've saved him from a miserable life with her and her awful mother.'

A short while later, despite feeling inwardly furious with Marion, Drina strolled into the general office in a casual manner, surprised to find only Sandra working away, typing envelopes for letters to future customers confirming their holidays.

'Marion popped out on an errand in the camp or visiting the ladies'?' Drina asked the young girl.

'She's out, but not just popped out, Mrs Jolly. I got the impression they might be a while. I shouldn't think they'd be back today, considering.'

'They?'

'Yes, her and Harold . . . er, Mr Rose, Mrs Jolly. They went out about ten minutes ago.'

'Did they say where they were going?'

'No, 'fraid not.'

Drina frowned thoughtfully. It wasn't at all like Harold to leave the office without a senior member of staff present to deputise. He might have tried to get hold of her to cover for him meantime but he wouldn't have been able to as she was out trying to save him from a fate worse than death. It must therefore be something very important that had made Harold act so out of character. And Marion had gone with him too . . . Drina sighed. It seemed she would have to come back later to bring the woman to task for her crimes. She made to go into Harold's office and telephone Jill to update her and Eileen on developments. But then something Sandra had said struck her. 'Did you say you shouldn't think they'd be back this afternoon *in the circumstances*? What circumstances?'

'Well, you wouldn't, would you, after . . .' Sandra then realised she was about to blurt out something she wasn't supposed to know, only guessed at through putting together several bits of information that had come to her accidentally.

Drina had a really bad feeling gnawing away in the pit of her stomach. 'After what, Sandra?'

The girl looked worried. 'Well . . . I . . . I . . . don't want to get into trouble with Marion for speaking out of turn. I'm only guessing where they've gone, from the telephone call.'

'Sandra, I am the boss here, and I will personally make sure Marion will not be cross with you for telling me where you think she and Mr Rose have gone. Who was the telephone call from?'

'The register office, Mrs Jolly. I think they were ringing to tell Marion they had a cancellation this afternoon because I saw her look at her watch and heard her say, "Three thirty, yes, we can be there." I have to say that when he left Mr Rose didn't look very happy considering he was off to get married. Ohhh, but you won't tell him I told you that, will you, Mrs Jolly? He could have just been nervous. Well, you would be, wouldn't you? It's a huge thing, getting married.'

By now Drina wasn't listening to Sandra rattling on as her thoughts were racing, heart pumping madly. It was twenty past two now and to get to the register office in Skegness, calling on the way to pick up Jill and Eileen from Jill's house, a distance of around twenty-five miles, it would be pure luck if they did manage to get there by three thirty, to stop Harold being saddled for life with that selfish woman. They must at least try, though, for Harold's sake.

She urgently ordered Sandra, 'Put a call through to Jill . . . Mrs Clayton. You'll . . .'

Sandra interrupted, 'Oh, the lady who had the accident who Marion . . .'

'Sandra, please shut up,' Drina ordered her. 'I've no time to waste. You'll find Jill's home number on the personnel telephone list kept in Mr Rose's top tray for emergency contact purposes. Tell her that I have asked you to call and warn her and Eileen to meet me in ten minutes' time, no later, outside her house. She is to bring the tape recorder with her and I'll explain everything on our way to Skegness. Do it now, please.'

Drina then shot out of the office.

As Sandra went to do her bidding she thought how nice it was that the boss was at such short notice doing her best to rally people together to support the bride and groom on their special day. Sandra was very happy about the wedding herself as once she married Harold Rose, Marion would more than likely not have to work any longer. Then hopefully Sandra would get someone much nicer to work for than Marion had been.

Drina screeched the car to a halt outside Jill's house just over ten minutes later. As asked, Eileen and Jill were waiting at the roadside. 'Quick, get in, we've no time to waste,' Drina shouted out of the window to them. As soon as they'd slammed the doors, she revved up the engine and, completely forgetting all she had learned in her driving lessons, immediately shot out into the road at speed. Thankfully it was a quiet street and nothing was coming either way at the time.

Drina drove like her own life depended on it, out of the town and on down the winding narrow country road towards Skegness, with the two women in the back clinging on for dear life to the edge of their seats. Eileen was in fact terrified as she had never been in a car before, let alone with a driver seemingly hell-bent on killing them, but then considering what was at stake in respect of the man she loved, she would be driving as fast and recklessly as Drina was if she was behind the wheel. But then Drina was forced to slow to a crawl as a tractor, travelling at a snail's pace, was blocking the road ahead.

It was very unusual for Drina to lose her temper, but now she banged her fist against the driving wheel and cried out,

'Bloody hell, this is all we need.' She then began continuously jabbing her fist against the horn by way of getting the farmer's attention. He took no notice so she honked it even harder. Next thing she knew a police car was behind her, flashing at her to pull over. Drina was tapping her fingers impatiently against the steering wheel as the policeman slowly got out of his car and walked to hers. She had the window down ready to address him. Before he could utter a word she blurted out: 'I'm sorry, officer, I know I shouldn't honk my horn like that . . . but we have to get to the register office in Skegness before three thirty, to stop a man having a life of hell once he's married a woman who wants him purely for his money.'

The policeman pursed his lips. 'Oh, same reason my wife married me . . . and torture it's been ever since. Well, I can't knowingly let another poor bugger suffer the same fate, can I? You leave it to me. I'll get you there as quick as I can.'

Drina wanted to kiss the middle-aged constable but he dashed back to his car, revved up his engine, put on his flashing light and warning siren, and as he drove past them indicated her to follow him. The farmer soon pulled his tractor over to the side when he heard the sound of the police siren as did all traffic on the way. There were no red traffic lights as they travelled through Skegness to waylay them either. Both cars pulled to a halt outside the register office at just after three thirty-six. While Eileen pulled Jill out of the car and steadied her on the pavement with her walking sticks, Drina shot over to the policeman, who had now got out of his car. She gave him a hug and a kiss on the cheek and said, 'Thank you so much. You're my hero, you really are.'

Heedless that she had made the man blush, she then dashed off into the register office, along with Eileen who was nursing the tape recorder like something infinitely precious, leaving Jill to struggle in on her own.

At the reception desk Drina demanded she be informed in which room the Rose wedding was being conducted. Thinking them to be late wedding guests, the woman hurriedly pointed them in the right direction, up the stairs on the first floor, room number three. As soon as they arrived at the door, Drina thrust it open and she and Eileen both burst inside.

There were only six people in the room. The registrar and his assistant stood behind the desk. Before it stood Marion and Harold along with two women they had obviously asked to be their witnesses. Both had obviously been shopping at the time as they had full shopping bags by their feet.

Harold was in the process of saying, 'I . . .' and about to say 'do', when he was stopped short by the noise of Drina's and Eileen's sudden arrival.

Knowing what he was about to say Drina shouted out, 'No, Harold, don't say it! Don't say another word until you've listened to what we have to tell you.'

It was Marion who regained her wits first. She angrily shot at Drina and Eileen, 'What on earth do you think you are doing, interrupting our wedding vows like this?'

Drina informed her, 'The game is up, Marion. We know all about your diabolical plan to marry Harold because you saw him as a meal ticket for you and your mother.'

'Yes, we do, and Jill will be along any minute now and she will confirm it too,' said Eileen. 'You are nothing but a nasty, horrible woman and Harold will be well shot of you.'

'Mother! You never told me you had a mother?' Harold said to Marion, bewildered.

Drina said, 'There's a lot Marion hasn't told you, Harold, and what she has said has all been lies. Jill didn't fall down the stairs, she was pushed by Marion who didn't care a jot that she was risking Jill's life. All she cared about was destroying Eileen's hope of ever having a relationship with you. Later she wickedly lied to her that you were seriously involved with another woman. She knew from what Jill had told her that Eileen was in love with you, and she knew you were with Eileen, so she wanted her out of the way. Marion set her sights on you because Jill had told her what a good catch you were.

'You see, Marion was desperate to find a man who could

provide a good living for her and her mother after they had both been left with nothing and homeless after Marion's husband threw them both out. She'd betrayed him by having an affair with another man simply because she was bored. Her meeting you apparently by accident at the theatre was no coincidence, Harold, Marion planned it. Originally, it was intended by Jill that you and Eileen should meet at the theatre by accident, and that hopefully by the end of the night you or Eileen or both of you would have found the courage to tell the other how you felt and finally get together. But Marion made sure that didn't happen when she pushed Jill down the stairs to stop Eileen from getting the theatre ticket Jill had actually bought herself, though she was going to pretend it was complimentary, along with one for you too, Harold.

'Marion never was attacked, it was all lies to make you feel sympathetic towards her. Later on she drugged you. She slipped something into your drink, knowing it would remove any memories you had of the night she came to cook for you at your house. Then the next morning she made you believe that you'd taken her to bed and proposed to her. She even stole your mother's engagement ring to corroborate her lies, making out you gave it to her. Of course she knew you would have no choice but to believe her as you wouldn't be able to remember a thing about the night after she'd drugged your beer.'

Marion had listened to all this feeling absolutely stunned, not able to work out just how Drina could possibly have found out every minute detail of her scheme to land Harold. But regardless, she was convinced not a word of it could be proved. Grabbing hold of his arm and shaking it frenziedly, she begged him, 'Don't listen, it's her who is lying. I don't know why she would try and blacken me this way. I don't understand what she could have against me. Please, Harold, don't listen to her.'

He was reeling from these revelations, so much so that he couldn't think straight. One thing he was positive of and he told Marion so. 'But Drina doesn't lie.'

'Well, she is now. Ask her to prove what she's saying about me then. She can't, because she's made it all up.'

'Oh, but I can, Marion,' Drina told her. 'Your plan to marry Harold was a very clever one but you made one big mistake. You see, you told your mother about it in great detail, and so proud was she of you for finding a saviour for you both, she just couldn't stop herself from boasting about it to me this morning when I visited her at the caravan you have both been living in . . . not lodgings as you told Harold. Of course, your mother didn't have a clue who I was, and so didn't think it would hurt to gloat to a stranger she believed had no connection to Harold in any way about her daughter's prowess in ensnaring Harold. And I recorded the whole conversation on a cassette tape. Have you heard of these new portable recording machines? In fact, I just happen to have it with me. Would you like to listen to your mother boasting about your achievements or are you going to take my word for it?'

By now Harold was sitting down on a chair with his head cradled in his hands.

The registrar and his assistant were both staring at the wedding party open-mouthed over what they had heard so far. They were eager to listen to what Drina had recorded on the tape she claimed to have, desperate to tell their colleagues and later their respective wives the whole sensational story.

Marion's face was contorted in fury. She was clenching and unclenching her fists. Knowing it was over for her, she screamed, 'My mother and her big mouth! I should never have trusted her . . . never, never, never, never. I told her what would happen if she broke her promise to me and did anything to wreck my plans for our future. I will kill her for this!'

With that she ran from the room.

Just then Jill struggled in. Leaning heavily on her sticks, she called out to Drina, 'Marion just missed knocking me over as she came hurtling out of here and down the stairs. Please tell me that means we managed to stop her making a fool of Harold? We did, didn't we? Please tell me we did?'

Before she responded, Drina helped a tired-looking Jill over to a seat, then sat down beside her. 'That's not all we achieved, Jill,' she told her, inclining her head in the direction of Harold and Eileen, who were sitting together, holding hands, deep in conversation, at the other end of the room. It wasn't hard to guess what they were talking about.

CHAPTER FORTY-ONE

'Well, that's it for another season,' Drina said to Artie as she turned the key in the huge padlock that secured the chains around the large iron entrance gates to Jolly's Holiday Camp. She then leaned back against them and peered into the camp that would resemble a ghost town for the next five months, until it became full of life again at the start of the next season.

'I can't believe how quickly this one has gone by. It seems only yesterday that we were opening the gates for the start of the season.'

Artie mused, 'Yes, it might have flashed by, but it didn't come without its ordeals once again, did it, love?'

Drina gave a wan smile. 'No, it certainly didn't. At the beginning of each season, I think to myself: this year at least, please can we have one season where we don't have to deal with any traumas or life-threatening situations or anyone trying to fleece us in any way . . . but that never seems to happen. Makes me wonder what we will have to deal with next year. Can't possibly be any worse than this one, can it?'

'You said the same this time last year, my love. But we've had so many good things happen this season too.'

Drina smiled. 'Yes, we have, haven't we? Rhonnie is well on the mend and enjoying life again. We've had our first baby delivered on the camp. Eric discovered he's a father, well, actually that his brother was, but good man that Eric is, he has decided to let the girl believe he is her father instead of the true one who didn't want anything to do with her. And what a terrific father Eric's making her, and such a lovely daughter Ginny is too. They're so close, you wouldn't believe they hadn't known each other all their lives.

'And we might be saying goodbye to our lovely Patsy after all the years she's worked for us, but I'm so pleased that the reason she's leaving is because she's found the love of her life in Jamie. I've no doubt they'll be together for the rest of their lives. And we can lay claim to the fact that Jolly's is responsible for making a star out of a certain talented employee, namely Trevor. Yes, I know that was purely down to Patsy using her initiative, but then she was working for us at the time. Patsy told me that Trevor has a spot on a variety show on the television next week so we mustn't miss it. I shall send him a good luck card from all of us here.

'Jill is back working for us with thankfully no after-effects from Marion's attack on her, and Sandra is proving a worthy assistant. The police finally caught up with Marion and she's being charged with grievous bodily harm for what she did to Jill and facing a jail sentence. I did hear that Ida was still living in that dreadful caravan I visited her in, so Marion must have been so angry with her for wrecking her plans that she went off and left her mother to fend for herself. To supplement her government pension, Ida's working for the council cleaning the public toilets in the town centre.'

She then clapped her hands together in delight. 'Oh, and I have another wedding to arrange for Harold too, but I couldn't be more pleased about it, unlike the last one. And now I've made all my decisions about what I'm going to do with the cleared land the farmhouse stood on, I can't wait to start bringing those to fruition. And I've so many ideas I want to pursue by way of improvements to the camp too.'

'I thought you were going to semi-retire and be taking things a lot easier in future?' Artie reminded her.

Drina grinned at him, eyes twinkling. 'I announced the same thing to you this time last year, didn't I?'

The Time of Our Lives

Lynda Page

When Rhonda Fleming runs away from home the last place she expects to end up getting a job is at a Jolly's holiday camp in Mablethorpe. Thrown in at the deep end, Rhonnie discovers there's never a dull moment – particularly with gorgeous staff like Dan around. From the beauty contest by the pool to jiving in the Paradise dance hall and from the rollercoaster at the fair to donkey rides on the beach, the holiday-makers are guaranteed to have the time of their lives. But it's not all fun and frolics and Rhonnie has to deal with situations she would never have imagined, particularly when the boss's son surfaces to claim what he believes in his . . .

Praise for Lynda Page's previous novels:

'All manner of page-turning twists and turns. Expect the unexpected' *Choice* magazine

'Filled with lively characters and compelling action' *Books*

'Inspirational and heart-warming' *Sun*

978 0 7553 9845 4

headline

Where Memories Are Made

Lynda Page

Jackie Sims aspires to be in charge of the general office but she never dreams that her lucky break will come about through such tragic circumstances. In order to come to terms with her grief, Drina Jolly asks Jackie to keep the camp running smoothly in her absence. It's a monumental task made even more challenging by the lack of support from the temporary camp manager, abrupt and humourless Harold Rose. But Jackie is determined to prove her worth and she can always count on fun-loving, red-headed receptionist Ginger Williams to pull her through the turmoil, chaos and heartbreak that's about to come her way . . .

Praise for Lynda Page's previous novels:

'All manner of page-turning twists and turns. Expect the unexpected' *Choice magazine*

'Filled with lively characters and compelling action' *Books*

'Inspirational and heart-warming' *Sun*

978 0 7553 9848 5

headline

For more heart-warming sagas from your favourite
authors purchase these from your bookshop
or direct from the publisher:

From Liverpool With Love by Lyn Andrews	£7.99
The House on Lonely Street by Lyn Andrews	£8.99
All The Dark Secrets: The Families Of Fairley Terrace 1 by Jennie Felton	£6.99
The Miner's Daughter: The Families Of Fairley Terrace 2 by Jennie Felton	£6.99
The Time Of Our Lives by Lynda Page	£5.99
Where Memories Are Made by Lynda Page	£5.99
A Liverpool Legacy by Anne Baker	£5.99
Wartime Girls by Anne Baker	£6.99
On Her Own Two Feet by Pam Evans	£5.99
The Apple of Her Eye by Pam Evans	£6.99

TO ORDER SIMPLY CALL THIS NUMBER

01235 827 702

or visit our website: www.headline.co.uk

Prices and availability subject to change without notice.